"You are...unexpected," the baron said.

"I don't know what that means."

His brows drew together, as if he was searching for words. "You make me feel things I don't..." He trailed off.

"Things you don't want to feel," Katherine finished for him. Because this Lord Doctor was unexpected too. And because no matter what she tried to tell herself, they were indeed the same. Different. Alone. Untouchable. Until the moments when they weren't. In a cottage. In a tunnel. In this room.

"Yes," he agreed on a whisper.

ACCLAIM FOR KELLY BOWEN

LAST NIGHT WITH THE EARL

"Bowen's ensemble offers a feminist character study in how to build a cast that is bursting with complex, nuanced women and men who are not only noble, but outright allies. *Last Night With the Earl* pulses with a lush romanticism, and its central characters' deep wounds give the text a palpable yearning that will sweep you up into Bowen's world of compassionate souls who drop lines from Shakespeare and lose their s— at the sight of a Titian painting."

—*Entertainment Weekly*

"Skillfully crafted with intriguing characters, this historical romance will appeal to fans of Mary Balogh."

—*Publishers Weekly*

A DUKE IN THE NIGHT

"If you read one historical romance this year, make sure it's this one. I cannot wait to see what comes next in this series. Final Grade—A."

—FictionVixen.com

"4½ Stars! Top Pick! What a way to start the Devils of Dover series! Bowen strikes all the right chords with readers: touching emotional highs with powerful storytelling. This is a book not only to savor, but a keeper that will stay in your heart."

—RTBookReviews.com

BETWEEN THE DEVIL AND THE DUKE

"[T]he fun, intrigue, and romance crescendo in a whopping plot twist. Bowen's Regency romances are always delightful, and this is one of her best yet."

—*Publishers Weekly* (starred review)

"Bowen again delivers the goods with this exquisitely written historical romance, whose richly nuanced characters, unexpected flashes of dry wit, and superbly sensual love story will have readers sighing happily in satisfaction."

—*Booklist* (starred review)

A DUKE TO REMEMBER

"This isn't a Regency comedy of manners. It's way better. This bright, surprising romance sets aside the intricate social rules and focuses on forging trust and love even when it seems like the whole world is against you."

—Best Romance of August selection,
The Amazon Book Review

"*A Duke to Remember* has everything you want in a romance…a truly satisfying happily ever after that will leave you misty-eyed."

—BookPage.com

DUKE OF MY HEART

"Bowen's irresistible Regency is like the most popular debutante at the ball: pretty, witty, mysterious, and full of coquettish allure. From the first line to the happy dénouement, Bowen builds enough romantic heat to melt midwinter snow."

—a *Publishers Weekly* Best Books of 2016 selection

"In her latest, Kelly Bowen offers up a vibrant, clever heroine in Ivory Moore—think Olivia Pope in a corset. The romance here is deeply satisfying, and Bowen excels in writing secondary characters and scenes. What's more, the nooks and crannies of this book are delightful, much like those in our real world, perfect to be discovered alongside true love."

—*Washington Post*

YOU'RE THE EARL THAT I WANT

"This story has it all: romance, suspense, wit, and Bowen's trademark smart and slightly quirky characters. Bowen's thrilling plot, spot-on pacing, and savvy characterization will delight her current fans and seduce new ones."

—*Publishers Weekly* (starred review)

"4 stars! Bowen is at the top of her game, and all readers could desire is more."

—*RT Book Reviews*

A GOOD ROGUE IS HARD TO FIND

"Where have you been all my life, Kelly Bowen? If Julia Quinn, Sarah MacLean, and Lisa Kleypas were to extract their writing DNA, mix it in a blender, and have a love child, Kelly Bowen would be it."

—HeroesandHeartbreakers.com

"Bowen's impish sense of humor is expressed by lively, entertaining characters in this wickedly witty Regency. This is pure romantic fun."

—*Publishers Weekly*

I'VE GOT MY DUKE TO KEEP ME WARM

"With this unforgettable debut, Bowen proves she is a writer to watch as she spins a multilayered plot skillfully seasoned with danger and deception and involving wonderfully complex protagonists and a memorable cast of supporting characters...a truly remarkable romance well worth savoring."

—*Booklist* (starred review)

"4 stars! In this delightful, poignant debut that sets Bowen on the path to become a beloved author, the innovative plotline and ending are only superseded by the likable, multidimensional characters: a strong-willed heroine and a heart-stealing hero. Get set to relish Bowen's foray into the genre."

—*RT Book Reviews*

A *ROGUE*
by *NIGHT*

KELLY BOWEN

FOREVER

New York Boston

Copyright © 2019 by Kelly Bowen
Excerpt of *Duke of My Heart* © 2016 by Kelly Bowen

Cover illustration by Kris Keller
Cover copyright © 2019 by Hachette Book Group, Inc.

Forever
Hachette Book Group
1290 Avenue of the Americas, New York, NY 10104
read-forever.com
twitter.com/readforeverpub

First Edition: May 2019

Forever is an imprint of Grand Central Publishing. The Forever name and logo are trademarks of Hachette Book Group, Inc.

The publisher is not responsible for websites (or their content) that are not owned by the publisher.

The Hachette Speakers Bureau provides a wide range of authors for speaking events. To find out more, go to www.hachettespeakersbureau.com or call (866) 376-6591.

ISBN: 978-1-4789-1862-2 (mass market), 978-1-4789-1863-9 (ebook)

Printed in the United States of America

OPM

10 9 8 7 6 5 4 3 2 1

For Jhet and Lincoln

Acknowledgments

Once again, a heartfelt thank-you to Stefanie Lieberman, my agent; Alex Logan, my editor; and everyone at Forever who works so hard on my behalf. Each book is a team effort and mine is second to none.

And a special thank-you to my readers and the entire romance community. You have made this journey one of joy.

Chapter 1

Dover, England, 1820

The bullet wound, as far as bullet wounds went, was not dreadful.

The bullet had caught her patient at the top of the shoulder, punching a messy hole in flesh and muscle, but not shattering bone. The icy cold of the sea had slowed the bleeding and the fact that he had been half-naked and shirtless at the time meant no remnants of fabric would be caught deep in the tissue. More concerning was the long gash that ran beneath the bullet hole, across the muscles of his upper back. The gaping, bloody edges would require a substantial number of stitches, and unlike the bullet wound, neither the cold nor the sea had slowed the bleeding much.

"Jesus, Kate, are you trying to kill me all over again?" The question was accompanied by a groan.

Katherine Wright increased the pressure she was applying to the wound, watching as the linen turned scarlet in the pool of lantern light. "Maybe I should." She kept her voice steady, though inside she was shaking with fury. "If only to keep the damn soldiers from having the satisfaction of doing so."

From the front corner of the cottage, her father wheezed, his laughter made ominous by the rattling in his lungs. "Stop your whining, lad, or your sister might just decide to get careless with her wee knives." The meager light from the hearth illuminated his wizened profile.

There were a couple of snickers from the rest of the men crowded in the tiny abode who had carried her brother in. Most of the men she recognized, a couple she had never seen. Katherine glared up at them, and the snickers faded. She wished she had drawn the heavy curtain she'd put up in the center of the cottage for those times when she and a patient needed privacy.

"Get out," she ordered the lot of them.

In response, they scuffed their feet and looked uncertainly between Katherine and her patient.

From where he lay facedown on the table, her brother lifted his head and tried to look back at her. "There's no call for—"

"Stop talking, Matthew, or I'll let one of these loggerheads sew you up. And then you'll have a scar of the likes you don't want to consider."

Matthew's forehead came to rest on the table again. His dark blond hair was still wet and twisted strands fell forward against the sides of his face. "I'm told women like their men with scars."

"Women like their men safe," she gritted out through clenched teeth, still glaring at the assembled crowd. "Not shot and at the wrong end of a blade."

Matthew grunted. "Kate—"

"Off with you then, lads," her father said, his voice like

gravel. "Let her do her work. Go home, keep your heads down, and let the soldiers chase their tails for the rest of the night. Matty will be right as rain by morning."

The men muttered but obeyed the order, and one by one they vanished soundlessly into the darkness. Katherine knew they would each go in a different direction, slipping through the blackness like wraiths in the night, evading the blockade men and patrols who hunted the coast for prey. Since she'd been a child, she had watched as smugglers deliberately scattered, men with generations of experience behind them. She had watched her father do it. Watched her brother do it. When she had gotten older, she had done it as well.

But occasionally, they weren't as invisible as they thought. And the proof of that was still bleeding all over her table.

"They didn't follow you here, did they?" Katherine asked her brother. "The soldiers?"

"Don't be daft."

"I'm not being daft. I'm being careful. Something you might want to do more of." She peeled back the linen and grimaced at the gaping wound, though the bleeding was starting to ebb. She despised deep cuts like this. Forget the deeper damage to the muscle tissue; wounds like this could fester.

"We lost them in the tunnels." Matthew's words were muffled against the table.

"You're sure? If you were bleeding, you'd have left a trail—"

"I'm sure, dammit."

"How did they know you'd be in that cove?"

"Someone must have tipped the patrols off," her father answered.

Katherine glanced up at her father. He had stood and pulled back the heavy fabric covering the small window at the front of the cottage, peering out into the darkness. Wrapped as he was in the bulky blanket, he almost looked like his brawny former self. Before he'd been shot. Before his lungs had weakened and deteriorated.

"What was it tonight?" she asked Matthew. "Silk? Tea?"

"Brandy. From Boulogne," he replied. "The patrols were hidden on the beach, waiting for us to retrieve it. Didn't see them until it was almost too late."

"Almost?" Katherine asked angrily. "Dammit, Matt, do you have any idea what your back looks like?"

"It was hard to run in the surf, at least until I got deep enough to swim. But I drew them out, and they couldn't run either. The other boys got away clean, and that's all that matters."

"You matter. Your life matters. And you almost lost it—"

"Those men, those boys, are my crew, Kate. My responsibility. What kind of leader am I if I don't lead?"

"You said that you would stop doing this, Matt." Katherine pulled a candelabra closer and reached for her suture kit. "You promised me."

Her brother mumbled something unintelligible into the table.

"What was that?"

"He asked how you think we're all to eat if he stops," her father said harshly from his post at the window. "How we're supposed to keep a roof over our heads and coal in the hearth in winter. How we're going to pay for the medicine you keep stuffing down my throat every time you get the chance. That all takes coin, lass."

Katherine set her kit aside. "I earn—"

"You earn the occasional chicken," her father said

wearily. "A handful of carrots, or a measure of dried her-
ring if you're lucky."

"I can't not help someone who needs me," she snapped.

"Aye, I know that. And you've a rare gift for healing,
and this parish and its people desperately need you, especially now. But they have nothing, and thus, neither do
you."

"You almost died at the hands of the king's men, Father.
Five inches is all that kept Matthew from dying tonight
from another soldier's bullet. You—" She stopped, trying
to keep her voice from rising. "You speak of having nothing. If the two of you die for the sake of a bale of smuggled
tobacco or a tub of brandy, then I'll truly have nothing."

"I'm not so easy to kill." Her father was still looking out
into the darkness.

"And neither am I," Matthew added irritably from the
table. "French artillery and guns couldn't do it. A handful
of leftover Englishmen with inferior weapons and high-
strung horses will not be able to do what the French could
not."

Katherine suppressed the urge to throw something. "Are
you not hearing what I'm trying to say? I—"

"Douse the light," her father said, his voice hard with
urgency. "We've company."

Katherine immediately blew out the candles surrounding the table. She reached for the lantern hanging above her
head on its hook and extinguished that, too, fear spiking
and making her pulse pound. "Soldiers?"

"Can't tell." Her father shuffled across the darkened
space, illuminated now only by the dim light struggling
from the hearth. He stopped beside the only other window
in the cottage, on the far side of the door, and eased back
its covering.

Katherine moved slowly around the table, reaching for the long curtain that hung from a rope across the center of the cottage and drew it closed. The heavy fabric concealed the rear of the cottage from the view of anyone at the door, but it would be a poor solution in the face of a regiment of soldiers hunting for a smuggler.

There was, however, a space beneath the floor, big enough for a man to crouch in, accessible from a trapdoor. She eyed the corner of the bed that her father and brother shared, just visible in the gloom. It would need to be pushed away from the wall, and the threadbare rug peeled back if she were to get her brother hidden.

She took a step closer to her brother. "You need to hide."

"There's not time. Get me the rifle." Matthew staggered to his feet, swaying slightly and reaching for the edge of the table to steady himself. His breathing was shallow and labored.

He kept a rifle near the cottage door, always loaded with fresh powder. Though Katherine doubted very much that Matthew would be able to manage the heavy weapon in his state. And she knew that her father couldn't.

Without considering what she was doing, she slipped past the curtain, stole across the dimly lit space, and snatched up the gun.

"Single horse and rider," her father warned from the window.

That was better than a posse of soldiers, but it still didn't bode well.

"Bring that damn gun back here," her brother whispered weakly. She saw the curtain twitch and knew he was watching her.

Outside, the sound of boots on the packed earth was faint but unmistakable.

Katherine swallowed hard, raising the gun to her shoulder and leveling the muzzle at the door.

"Jesus Christ, Kate, get away from that door and bring me the gun." Matthew's demand was both faint and desperate.

"Do what he says, lass," her father pleaded.

"Sit down before you fall down, Matthew," Katherine murmured in a voice that sounded surprisingly steady in her own ears. "You've lost a lot of blood. Keep the curtain closed. And you stay where you are, Father."

There was a soft tap on the door, and the latch creaked. The door opened a crack. Katherine felt her brows draw together, even as she adjusted her grasp on the stock. Soldiers would not have knocked first. At least not that quietly.

"Mr. Wright?" The voice was low and male. The door swung open a little farther, and a tall figure carrying a bulky bag of some sort ducked carefully into the cottage. "Mr. Wri—" He stopped abruptly, and Katherine guessed he had finally seen her silhouetted in the firelight. And the gun she was holding.

From the side of the room, her father muttered something under his breath and moved from the window. He ducked past the man and shoved the door closed, though not before he scanned the darkness beyond. "Dr. Hayward," he said by way of greeting. "Welcome."

"Mmm," the doctor replied drily, gazing at Katherine. "I'm not so sure I am."

Katherine lowered the gun and set it back against the wall. She put a hand out to anchor herself, the tension abruptly broken and leaving her a little more wobbly than she'd like. She tried to will her heart back into a normal rhythm.

Not a soldier, but a doctor. One who spent his summers

in Dover with his family and saw to a great deal of the county's medical needs while he was here. Katherine had never actually met him in the short time that she'd been back, but she'd seen him at a distance, usually accompanied by pretty young women who seemed to hang on his every word. Which wasn't surprising because Dr. Hayward was not only a doctor, but a baron as well. A wealthy, widowed baron. Which was surprising.

And made no sense to Katherine at all. Because rich, titled men did not labor in such professions. They did not lower themselves to toil in a field hallmarked by disease and blood and gore. They didn't spend time worrying about people who did not possess an address west of Haymarket, London. And they certainly didn't prowl the back roads of Dover on a night like this when the air was heavy with the promise of rain.

Which, altogether, made the baron's sudden presence here inordinately suspicious. She wasn't about to test the doctor's discretion recklessly. Who knew what Harland Hayward—Baron Strathmore—did or didn't know about what went on along the shores of Kent County? And where his allegiances might lie? To king and country or to the peasants who struggled to survive both? Baron Strathmore was a grand lord, after all.

He was certainly not one of them.

Katherine deliberately did not look back to where her brother remained concealed. "What do you want?" It was abrupt and rude, but with Matthew still bleeding behind her, she needed this baron-turned-doctor to leave.

"Miss Wright, I presume?" The baron hadn't moved from where he stood in the shadows. Nor did he sound the least bit offended by her utter lack of decorum. "Your father has told me a lot about you."

Katherine's eyes narrowed. Well, her father certainly hadn't returned the favor. She hadn't even realized that he was well acquainted with the baron. Everything she knew about Strathmore she had gleaned from gossip as she worked. Strathmore's youngest sister was the new Countess of Rivers. His oldest sister was a bloody duchess. They all stayed at Avondale House, the imposing manor outside of Dover, perched on the cliffs overlooking the sea. A nest teeming with grand titles and insufferable pomposity, no doubt.

She shot a glance in her father's direction, but he ignored her, concentrating on relighting the candles, though not fast enough for Katherine's liking. She wanted— needed—to see this Lord Doctor clearly, to see his face and read the nuances of his expression.

"Yes," she replied finally into the silence, acknowledging her identity but ignoring his suggestion that he was familiar with anything about her. "Again, I'd ask what you want—"

"He's come to help you, lass," her father grumbled as he bent to retrieve the lantern and set to lighting it again.

"If you need it, of course," Strathmore added, sounding merely pleasant and polite.

Katherine was not at all prepared with a story to explain Matthew's bullet wound to his lordship any more than she was prepared to trust Strathmore with the truth. "I have no idea what you're talking about—"

A crash reverberated through the room, and Katherine spun. The table behind the curtain had upended and torn the fabric from its moorings. On top of the heavy wool, caught in the table legs, Matthew was inelegantly sprawled.

"That," the baron said in that annoyingly calm way of his. "I was talking about that."

Katherine jerked into action, cursing under her breath and hurrying forward. She dropped to her knees beside Matthew. In the soft light, she could see that his eyes were closed, his face pale. A dark, rusty stain was smeared over the surface of the wool where it had come into contact with his wound as he fell. She cursed again and pushed the crumpled fabric away from where it had bunched across his hips.

On the other side of the overturned table, her father hovered above her with the lantern, a worried expression on his face. "Is he all right?"

"He's merely fainted because he came in here bleeding like a stuck pig." Katherine put her fingers beneath Matthew's chin, searching for his pulse, relieved to find that it still beat steadily beneath her touch. She withdrew her hand. "Which is why I told him to sit down before he fell down."

"Brothers," came a voice by her ear, "rarely do what they're told. At least that's what my sisters tell me."

Katherine started, not having heard Strathmore crouch beside her.

"Bullet or blade?" he asked almost conversationally.

"Both," she said with a frown, not taking her eyes off Matthew.

The baron leaned forward, his long, graceful fingers sliding over Matthew's scalp in sure movements, searching, Katherine surmised, for any lumps that he might have suffered in the fall.

The baron has incredible hands, she thought. They were not the hands of a soft, pampered peer, but the capable hands of a man used to working. Hands that were used to soothe and discover and communicate— She averted her eyes. She should not be noticing a baron's hands while her brother languished insentient and bleeding in a pile at her feet.

Those hands had stopped, and he pushed the wool farther away from Matthew's shoulder. "Ah. Yes, I see the exit wound now. He was lucky. Minimal damage, more bruising to the muscle than anything else, I think. This the only bullet wound?"

"Yes."

"Mmm. And the laceration? That is on his back, then?"

"Yes." She couldn't really see Strathmore's face, his thick, dark hair falling carelessly over his ears and concealing his features. She tried not to notice his nearness or the warmth she could feel from his body.

"Has it been sutured?"

"Not yet." Katherine studied the back of his head. The baron wasn't asking the obvious questions. Like how her brother had come to be shot and wounded. Or why Katherine had greeted him at the door with a leveled gun. He hadn't asked any question that wasn't clinical in nature. He hadn't even expressed surprise or dismay or disapproval. She really didn't understand this man at all.

And she didn't like what she didn't understand.

The baron rocked back on his heels and pushed himself to his feet. "Well, then, let's get him back up on the table so we can get his laceration sutured, shall we? I need to examine the severity of the wound."

Well. The baron might not be asking the expected questions, but he was certainly giving the expected orders.

"*You* don't have to do anything, my lord," Katherine said coolly. "I can assure you that my brother is in good hands under my care." She had lost count of the number of times that a physician or a surgeon—a male physician or surgeon—had inserted himself into a situation, dismissing her and her talents amid a fog of condescension. That was not about to happen here. Not when it came to her own brother.

She got to her feet and turned to face the baron in the light for the first time.

Her mouth went dry.

Viewed from a distance, he had struck her as attractive. Standing as close as he was in the soft light, Katherine realized he was not merely attractive—he was striking. He was long-limbed and lean, his simple clothes doing nothing to hide the strong lines of his body. His hair was a rich mahogany, pushed carelessly away from a face crafted of impeccable angles—sharp cheekbones, a straight nose, a strong jaw. His eyes were dark beneath his brow, and they were watching her without expression.

Her insides did a slow, horrifying somersault, and she could feel a flush start to creep into her cheeks. No wonder he had women hanging on his every word. At another time in her life, a time long past, perhaps she might have been one of them.

"Doctor is fine," the baron said.

"I'm sorry?" Katherine had lost her train of thought.

"My title, I find, is more of a hindrance than a help when I'm attending my patients."

"He's not your patient, my lord." Whatever unwanted and unwelcome reaction she had just suffered was instantly cured by a healthy dose of irritation. "He's mine."

Strathmore held her eyes for a moment longer before looking down at her brother. "Of course."

Katherine blinked. He wasn't going to argue?

"Though perhaps you might need help getting him up?"

She blinked again, wary of his motivations. The Lord Doctor was being far too reasonable and agreeable. But he was also right. Her father, still hovering with the lantern, didn't have the strength to lift such a deadweight. And alone, neither did she. Matthew was not a small man.

"Yes, thank you." She swallowed her pride with effort and tried to sound at least a little gracious. "I would appreciate it."

Strathmore nodded and bent, carefully pulling the table away. As he heaved it upright, Matthew groaned, and his eyes fluttered open. He stared up at the ceiling with an expression of dazed confusion before his eyes found Katherine.

"You fell over," she said before he could speak.

Matthew winced and raised his head.

"You really should have listened to your sister," Strathmore added as he settled the heavy, wide table back in place.

"Hayward," Matthew grunted, and let his head fall back. "You don't need to take her side. I've had a trying night. Have a little sympathy."

From the far side of the table, her father barked out a laugh, and the shadows from the lantern light danced off the walls.

Katherine scowled. She did not see the humor. And was everyone in her family on familiar terms with the Lord Doctor? Something that they'd failed entirely to mention?

The baron straightened from the table. "How are you feeling?"

"Like I've been bloody well shot." Matthew grimaced and struggled to push himself to his good side. "Help me up."

Strathmore glanced at Katherine. "You take a side, I'll take the other. We'll try not to do any more damage than what's already been done."

Katherine sighed and did as she was instructed because

to argue for the sake of argument was petty and ridiculous. Between them, they helped Matthew to his feet and eased him back onto the table so that he was once again lying facedown. A sheen of sweat had broken out on Matthew's forehead, and he hissed in pain as he moved.

"Well, that is a bit of a mess." Strathmore bent slightly to peer at her brother's upper back.

"I've been told." Matthew rested his forehead on the table.

"A jealous husband, was it?" The baron sounded amused now. "Didn't get out that window fast enough?"

"Something like that," Matthew mumbled.

Katherine eyed Strathmore. He seemed happy to accept Matthew's nonanswer answer.

"Well, are you going to fix him up, lass, or are you going to stare at the doctor all night?" Her father laughed again, though it quickly dissolved into another round of coughing.

Katherine would have been incensed had she not been so worried about the sound of his chest.

"Why don't you come sit back down by the hearth, Mr. Wright?" the baron asked easily. He glanced at Katherine in question, and she gave him a curt but grateful nod.

She busied herself retrieving the basin of water and the clean towels she had set aside earlier, though she watched Strathmore out of the corner of her eye the entire time. The Lord Doctor took the lantern from her father and hung it back up on its hook in the ceiling. He was now settling her father back in his chair, tucking his blanket around him with an endearing gentleness that made her heart turn over. She could hear the baron murmuring something to her father, and though she couldn't make out the words, she saw her father nod his head a few times.

Are you going to stare at the doctor all night?

Katherine snatched up her suture kit, turning away from Strathmore. She wasn't going to stare at him at all. Because the Lord Doctor was not endearing. He was unwanted.

She set to cleaning up the new blood that had leaked from Matthew's wound and fetched the bottle of brandy from the sideboard behind her. Smuggled French brandy. Ironic that she should be using it on wounds earned in acquisition of the damn stuff.

She returned to the table, stuffing towels along the edge of Matthew's torso before opening the bottle. "This might sting a bit," was all the warning she gave to her brother before she poured half the contents over his wounds.

Matthew jerked and choked, his hands gripping the edge of the table so hard his knuckles were white. A loud string of curses exploded.

"You could have given him more warning."

Katherine almost dropped the bottle. She hadn't heard Strathmore approach her side. Again.

"Better to just have done with it," she said as her brother cursed under her touch. "Better, too, if he never had cause for me to do it in the first place," she said more loudly.

Matthew groaned.

She poured a measure of liquor into a cup and dropped her needles in, wiping her hands on the brandy-soaked towels. "You don't have to stay," she said to the baron without looking at him.

"I've nowhere else to be." He reached for the brandy bottle. She could hear him inhale. "Good stuff, this," he said with a note of approval. "Cases of this sell for a bloody fortune in London."

That was exactly the problem. And that was also why Strathmore wasn't endearing. Because comments like

that encouraged her brother and, for that matter, her father. Convinced them that their fortunes could be found
in contraband.

The brandy wasn't good stuff at all, any more than the
tobacco or the tea or the silk was.

Because one day, they were going to get her family
killed.

Chapter 2

Harland Hayward leaned against the near wall, sipping brandy and watching Miss Katherine Wright bend to her task. Her every movement was sure and steady, each suture done with efficient precision. A healer was how her father had described her, but Harland had seen experienced surgeons who had far less skill than what he was observing now. He would have intervened if she hadn't been up to the task, but as it was, Miss Katherine Wright was impressing him.

And not just with her surgical prowess. She seemed damn well fearless. A modern-day Valkyrie, who looked just as capable of handling the rifle she'd leveled at him in defense of her family as she did with her sutures. A woman who, in the face of both threat and calamity, simply did what needed to be done. It seemed that it was not only the men in the Wright family who possessed nerves of steel, though he supposed that shouldn't be a surprise, given that she'd grown up the daughter of one of the most intrepid smugglers in Kent.

Harland shifted, and Miss Wright glanced up at him. There were shadows of worry and fatigue beneath her eyes, and her expression was suspicious and resentful. He met her gaze and took another sip of his brandy, offering neither comment nor reaction, even as he felt a peculiar sensation wind through his veins. Something deeper than mere awareness and attraction. Something that he hadn't felt in a very long time. Something that he had thought long extinguished.

Miss Wright returned her attention to her task, though Harland continued to study her. Her hair, pulled back in an untidy braid, was light like her brother's, but its hue put him more in mind of champagne than honey. She had a generous mouth that he suspected smiled often in better circumstances and a scattering of freckles over the bridge of a straight nose. Her eyes were remarkable and startling—the color of a tropical sea—with an undeniable intelligence that blazed from their depths.

Miss Wright would be classically beautiful in a ball gown, Harland reflected, her fair hair adorned with pearls, a smile pasted on her pretty face, a fan fluttering coyly in her hand. Society matrons who measured value by appearance would nod in approval. Men who did the same would do a whole lot more than merely nod.

But dressed as she was now in a nondescript gray dress and a bloodstained apron, her hair disheveled, her mouth set in a grim line, a suture needle balanced in her fingers, she certainly wasn't classically beautiful. Or even pretty.

She was stunning.

Another wave of anticipatory sensation gripped Harland, and he downed the rest of his brandy, welcoming the burn as the liquor slid down his throat. He had pursued these sorts of feelings before, when he was young and foolish, and it had led to nothing but silent heartbreak and vociferous humiliation. He was much older and wiser now. He could recognize the threat when it arose and smother it entirely.

He set his glass aside with more force than was necessary, earning him another suspicious, resentful glare from Katherine Wright. Harland wondered how much she had been told about what had happened tonight. Clearly, Matthew would have provided her at least a moderately accurate account, given his injuries. He had a bullet hole high in the muscle of his shoulder for God's sake, and it was not from climbing out a lover's window.

It was reassuring, however, that since he had arrived, both Matthew and Paul Wright had remained decisively silent about the actual events that resulted in Matthew's injury. It meant that they still believed Harland to be nothing but what he presented himself as—a doctor concerned for the well-being of his patient. A doctor who was often called to strange places at strange times and asked no questions. A doctor who could move easily and invisibly about the harbor and the coasts and the vessels that came into port because medical help was always a wanted commodity.

The perfect cloak to keep his role in the network of smugglers up and down this Kentish coastline concealed.

It wasn't that Harland doubted Matthew and Paul's discretion, but even under extreme duress, one could not tell what one did not know. He was counting on the fact that Katherine Wright was equally unaware of his involvement. She might have grown up among smugglers, but Harland knew she had been gone from Dover for a long time. Long enough that her allegiances might have changed. And while she would be loyal to her family, it would be folly to simply assume that loyalty would be extended beyond the familial boundaries should the worst happen and Harland be exposed for more than just a simple doctor.

He was relieved that it had only been brandy that was to have been moved tonight and not—

"I can't quite figure out how it was that you knew Matthew was injured, my lord." Miss Wright's words broke the silence with no warning. She didn't look up but her unabated suspicion hung heavy in the space between them.

"Ran into Hervey Baker on the road," Harland replied easily. He'd thought she'd have asked that question sooner. His answer was, in fact, not a lie. Hervey Baker had been one of the men who had helped carry Matthew here. And it was always better to tell a version of the truth whenever possible.

"On the road?" The words were skeptical. "Where you just happened to be riding? In the dead of night? When a storm is threatening?"

"Kate," Matthew admonished, sounding annoyed.

"It's all right. Your sister asks reasonable questions."

Matthew scoffed. "It's rude, not reasonable."

"And I don't really care, Matt." Miss Wright reached for her scissor. "Why were you really out tonight, my lord?"

"Croup," Harland said. It was his standard answer. A doctor, after all, got called out for all manners of ailments in all manners of weather. No one ever wanted further details about common croup or common children or a combination of those two things.

"Who?"

No one except Katherine Wright, it seemed. "Who what?" he stalled.

"Who had croup?" She snipped the end of her thread and put her needle aside.

"The tinker's daughter." There had, of course, been no tinker, but he needed a transient patient whose existence could not be proven or disproven. "They were camped on the side of town."

"I see." She bent over Matthew's back, critically examining her work.

Harland had no idea if she believed him or not.

"Are you done with your torture, Kate?" Matthew sounded exhausted.

"Yes. How does it feel?"

"Like my bloody back is on fire." He groaned and gingerly pushed himself up, swinging his legs over the side of the table. "Give me the damn brandy, Hayward." He held out his hand.

Miss Wright made a sound of disapproval.

Harland retrieved the bottle and passed it to Matthew.

"You need to rest," Harland told him as he watched Matthew take a healthy swig. "No riding, no swimming, no strenuous physical work for at least a week. Probably two." Outside, a distant thunder rumbled.

Matthew rolled his eyes, though the effect was marred by a grimace at the end. "I'm not an old woman."

"True. You are, however, a man in possession of a bullet wound and four dozen very expertly executed stitches. And if you want them to heal, you shall not undo all of your sister's hard work."

Harland glanced at Miss Wright to find her staring at him. She looked away almost immediately and started gathering the blood-soaked towels. A few drops of rain splattered against the cottage window, and the thunder outside increased in volume.

Harland retrieved the brandy bottle from the patient. "You should have that arm in a sling so long as it doesn't catch your stitches around back. Your shoulder—"

"Stop." Miss Wright's voice was sharp. "Listen."

Harland's blood ran cold. The thunder that had accompanied the rain was not thunder at all, but the sound of many hooves bearing down on the cottage.

"Goddammit," Matthew swore under his breath, looking around him frantically.

Harland followed his gaze, taking in the bowls of pink water, the stained towels, and bloodied curtain still lying forgotten on the floor. The sound of approaching hooves was now accompanied by a shout. Soldiers, no doubt, and Harland cursed himself for not being more vigilant.

From the sound that was steadily building and the vibrations now rumbling through the ground, he guessed they had less than a minute before someone barged through that door in the name of the king, wanting nothing more than to arrest and make an example of someone guilty of smuggling.

"We have to hide him," Miss Wright whispered urgently. "There's a trapdoor under the bed. Help me move it, my lord. Quick."

There wasn't time. "No." In a swift movement, Harland snatched up the heavy wool curtain. "Get off the table," he ordered Matthew. The man obeyed, staggering slightly as his feet hit the ground. "Lie down underneath," he instructed him. "And for God's sake, no matter what happens, no matter what you hear, don't move a muscle."

Matthew stared at him for a moment before Harland helped him lower himself to the ground, sliding awkwardly under the table on his stomach.

"Good." Harland took the curtain by two corners and

threw it over the table, letting it settle as the edges pooled on the ground on all sides, concealing Matthew. "Get on the table, Miss Wright," he snapped.

"What?" She was pale.

"I need to explain all this blood when neither of us requires stitches. I need a patient. Get on the damn table."

Comprehension dawned, and she hitched up her skirts and clambered onto the wide surface. The unseen riders were upon them, light from their torches now flickering ominously past the edges of the curtains.

"Lie back."

She searched his eyes for a brief second before she obeyed, lowering herself so that she was staring up at the ceiling. Harland reached into one of the bowls, cupping a handful of water and letting it dribble across her forehead. He smoothed the moisture into her hairline to make her look fevered, trying to ignore the softness of her skin and her hair.

He glanced up to find the elder Wright staring at him from where he still sat opposite near the hearth. His faded eyes darted to the door, the sound of men's voices clear, and he gave Harland an almost imperceptible nod. Harland nodded back. Paul Wright had not survived as long as he had by being dull-witted.

The horses were being reined to a stop, their blowing and stomping audible. Boots were on the ground, the sound of steel being drawn.

Harland grabbed a handful of the bloodiest towels, shoving Miss Wright's skirts just above her knees and then covering them with crimson-stained linen. She made a small sound of distress but didn't move.

"I'm so sorry," Harland murmured, meaning it. But they were left with few options.

"It's fine," Miss Wright said tightly.

He nudged her knees apart gently with his hands, set a few more of the bloodstained towels under her legs, and swallowed hard. Streaks of blood marred the pale skin on her legs where the soaked towels had brushed against them. Jesus, it really looked like she was bleeding to death. He only hoped that—

The door reverberated on its hinges as someone pounded on it. Which was all the warning they got before it flew open, crashing against the wall. He saw Miss Wright jerk and put a reassuring hand on her leg, willing her to remain as she was. And then he went on the offensive.

"What the hell do you think you're doing?" he barked, none of his outrage feigned.

There was an officer standing just inside the door, his sword drawn, squinting into the light. Harland should have known. Captain Buhler. A bulldog of a man who had made it his singular mission to bring to justice by any means necessary every man, woman, and child who survived just outside the edges of the law. A man enamored with power and who was becoming more and more ruthless wielding it in the name of the crown. Harland had no respect for him.

Two more soldiers crowded into the cottage behind their leader, trying to get a better view of the interior.

"I said, what the hell do you think you're doing, Captain?" Harland repeated.

The captain's eyes were glued on Miss Wright's blood-streaked legs. "Jesus wept."

The men standing behind him were staring now, too, fixated on the sight of Miss Wright's exposed, bloody calves and the stained towels covering her knees.

Jesus wept, indeed.

"What's wrong with her?" one of the men managed in a strangled voice.

"She's bleeding," Harland snarled. "Isn't that obvious?"

"From where?" The soldier was ashen.

"From her woman parts," Harland snapped. "Now get out and give us some privacy while I treat my patient."

Buhler's soldiers visibly blanched and took an involuntary step back. One disappeared completely back in the direction he had come from.

"Dr. Hayward." The captain seemed to recover and was trying for an authoritative, if somewhat conciliatory, tone. "I must ask you to leave. We must search this cottage."

"I beg your pardon?" Harland tightened his fingers on Miss Wright's leg. Beneath his palm, her muscles were stiff.

From his position near the hearth, Paul stirred. "What's going on? What do they want?" he asked in a wavering, feeble voice that made him sound three hundred years old.

"Captain Buhler was just saying that he was sorry he lacked the common decency to allow me to treat your daughter in privacy," Harland growled, not taking his eyes off Buhler. "And that they were leaving now."

Paul labored to his feet and shuffled toward the soldiers, coming to stop directly in front of the men. "My daughter, she's very ill," he bleated plaintively.

"We have information that says there is a dangerous criminal on the premises." The captain had dragged his eyes from the scene on the table and was addressing Harland.

"A dangerous criminal?" Harland laughed without humor and made a great show of looking around him. "Which one of us would you consider to be most dangerous?"

"Dr. Hayward, again, I must ask that you leave—"

"What the hell is wrong with you, Captain? You can see the interior of the entire damn cottage from where you stand. There is no dangerous criminal here."

"I have orders from the king himself."

"Orders? To watch a woman bleed to death?"

Paul made a wheezing noise followed by a spate of coughing. "She's dying? Don't let my daughter die," he gasped.

"She's not going to die." Harland reached for one of Miss Wright's knives she hadn't put away. He held it up to the light, examining the edge of the gleaming blade. "So long as I can excise the source of the inflammation and bleeding." He was making this up as he went along.

"I have orders," the captain repeated with impatience, "to eradicate the scourge of this county. Smugglers. The men who would cheat their king of his due."

Miss Wright moaned then, her head thrashing from side to side, her eyes tightly shut. She looked, Harland thought with some admiration, like a woman about to suffer a seizure.

Or perhaps an exorcism.

"Dammit," Harland swore loudly, and moved to press his hand against the flat of her stomach.

"What's happening?" Paul had never sounded more pitiful.

"I need to stop this bleeding now," Harland said. "Before it is too late."

Buhler's expression was one of profound distaste, but still he refused to budge. "Dr. Hayward—"

"Search the barns, search the grounds, do whatever you need to do, Captain. But unless you want the death of this young woman on your hands, I suggest you take your men and get out."

"Not yet. Where is your son right now, Mr. Wright?" Buhler, apparently unhappy and unsatisfied with Harland's lack of cooperation, was now directing his questions at Paul.

"My son?" The man pulled his blanket more tightly around himself and looked confused. "I don't...what... who—"

"Matthew Wright is your son?"

"Yes?" Paul's answer sounded more like a question.

"Where is he?"

"He went to war," Paul said faintly, looking confused.

"War?"

"To fight the little French madman. He's artillery," he said proudly. "My son, not Napoleon."

Buhler shook his head in impatience. "Where is he now?"

"I told you he's at war."

"The war is over, Mr. Wright. Has been for years."

Paul twisted the edges of the blanket around his thin shoulders. "That can't be right."

"What has your son been doing since he's returned?" the officer demanded.

Paul shook his head helplessly. "He's not back."

"I can assure you, he is."

Paul put a shaking hand out as if to steady himself on the captain's arm. Buhler moved away in distaste.

"He used to fish," Paul warbled with a faraway expression. "Yes, my Matty loved to fish." He paused, his eyes widening. "Is he drowned? Tell me he isn't drowned. He's drowned, isn't he?"

The captain frowned. "What? No, he—"

"The selkies come ashore on nights like this, you know." Paul peered around as though he expected to see such a mythological creature crouched in a dark corner. "Come from the black depths to claim their revenge on the men who have killed their selkie sons and husbands. I've seen them, you know. Luring men out into the dark sea or off the edges of cliffs. I've warned my Matthew against them."

Harland was barely following Paul's babble but the soldier remaining behind Buhler paled and shifted nervously. Experience had taught Harland that soldiers, like sailors, were a superstitious lot. Paul, it seemed, had also been taught the same.

The captain, however, was having none of it. "Get out of the way, old man," he sneered, pushing past Paul and into the cottage, approaching the table.

A bloodcurdling scream from Miss Wright split the air and made the hairs on Harland's arms stand up. "Make it stop," she shrieked, her head thrashing again.

The soldier remaining behind Buhler in the doorway lost whatever color he had remaining and fled back toward the safety of the night. The captain tightened his hand on the hilt of his sword.

"Make it stop." Miss Wright was now sobbing in a performance worthy of a London stage.

Paul started swaying and moaning loudly, punctuated by words that Harland could only guess were supposed to be interpreted as a prayer. "Save her," he cried every time he stopped long enough to take a breath.

Outside, distant thunder—real thunder this time—rolled through the air and shook the ground.

Good Lord, if Harland closed his eyes, he would have thought he was in the chaos of a field hospital again amid the screaming of the patients and the booming of the guns.

Buhler's eyes were fixed on the incoherent Miss Wright. "I have a duty to the king—"

"I, too, have served the king for years, Captain." Harland pointed the tip of the knife in Buhler's direction. "As a surgeon on the battlefields of France and Belgium. I've treated the king's men—your men—in your own damn barracks."

"I am aware—"

"Then I'll trouble you to recall that I am not just a doctor, but a peer of the realm, and I have a very vested interest in this country and the men who uphold its honor. If you think I am harboring an enemy of the king in my damn medical bag, you may arrest me once I'm done here," he continued icily, "but I would suggest that you have a care with your accusations."

Buhler took another step forward. His small eyes flickered from Harland to Miss Wright's bared legs as she writhed, the toe of the captain's boot an arm's length from where Matthew lay concealed.

"You are dismissed, Captain," Harland said in a voice that would have made his ducal brother-in-law proud.

Buhler finally sheathed his sword. "Check the barn!" he shouted in the direction of his men still waiting outside as Miss Wright continued to thrash and moan. "Every nook and cranny." The captain lifted his eyes to Harland's. "Then burn it."

Anger surged. "There is no call for that. These people have nothing."

"Then they have nothing to lose, do they?" Buhler sneered.

"Captain—"

"I act in the name of the king." He spun on his heel and stalked toward the door. "And you can tell Matthew Wright that if you see him, *my lord*."

Paul shoved the door closed behind him and retreated

back to the window, peering outside through a crack in the curtain. "Goddamn blighters."

Relief filtered through Harland's fury, though he made no move to step away from the table. The soldiers could barge back in again with no notice. Outside, there was a muffled thump as the doors of the barn were hauled open. Muted torchlight flickered, and the crashing sounds of crates and barrels being turned over followed. The barn would be a loss, but far better they ravage the barn than the cottage. Barns could be rebuilt. Lives could not.

Miss Wright had stopped moaning and was listening as well, her head cocked slightly, though she was watching him.

"What are they going to find in the barn, Father? Before they burn it, that is." Her voice was steady and direct, and if Harland hadn't been there to witness everything he had, he would think she was merely inquiring after a misplaced crate of turnips.

"Dust and mouse shit," Paul muttered. "Bloody bastards."

Harland knew Paul and Matthew too well to think that they would ever leave something incriminating in the barn to be found by soldiers.

Miss Wright lifted her head and glanced down, and with some discomfiture, Harland realized that he still had his fingers on her bare leg. He withdrew his hand, as nonchalantly as possible, suddenly feeling flustered. Which was ridiculous. He had touched hundreds and hundreds of legs before. Men, women, children. He'd stitched them, dressed them, set broken bones in them, crouched between them to deliver a baby on occasion. And like each of those occasions, this intimate contact was a product of necessity, not—

"I'm so sorry, Father." The muffled, miserable voice drifted out from the space beneath the table. "The barn—"

"Is half rotted anyway," Paul grumbled. "Not a great loss. Don't worry yourself."

"I'm glad you're still with us, Mr. Wright," Harland murmured, trying to refocus on what was important here.

"Is Kate still with us is the better question." Matthew's muted jest from his hiding place sounded weak. "I'm convinced the Inquisition would have nothing on you, Hayward."

"Everyone tells me I have a way with the ladies," Harland replied lightly to hide his concern. He needed to get the young man up and off the floor. Just not yet. "Your performance was indeed impressive, Miss Wright." The torchlight was still moving in the windows. Another roll of thunder echoed, momentarily eclipsing the sound of voices outside.

"I think you should have led with the lordship bit," she muttered. "Your title has some use after all."

"Perhaps."

A crash of thunder obliterated whatever she was about to say. In the next second, the sound of a torrential rain drumming into the thatch and against the windows filled the silence. The sky lit up with lightning, and another round of thunder shook the ground and the very air around them. Outside, horses thrashed and snorted, their panic met with exclamations and angry shouts. The rain intensified even more, and rivulets of water dripped through the thatch and into the cottage. The wavering torchlight was abruptly extinguished. Within minutes, the sound of men and milling hooves gave way to retreating hoofbeats that faded quickly in the downpour.

"Hard to burn a barn in a storm, isn't it, you scaly buggers," Paul crowed before a round of coughing stopped him. He recovered and pulled the curtains tightly across the windowpanes. "Good riddance."

"They're gone?"

"Every last one of them."

"You sure?" Harland wasn't taking any chances.

"I'm sure."

Harland looked back at Miss Wright, still sprawled out on the table before him, wearing bloody towels and a look of worry. A sudden image of her sprawled out before him wearing nothing but a look of invitation assaulted him, and he flinched, horrified. What the hell was wrong with him? He was better than this. Certainly not so predictable as to be titillated by a pair of legs.

With a deliberate flip of his wrist, he cast the towels to the floor and then drew her skirts gently back over her legs. As graciously and as matter-of-factly as he could, given the circumstances, he extended a hand toward her. "I'm sorry about your skirts and your shift. I think both have blood on them now."

"I'm not worried about my skirts or my shift, Lord Strathmore." He was aware Miss Wright still hadn't taken her eyes off him. She was regarding him warily, a crease between her brow, but she accepted his hand without hesitation.

Harland would not notice how perfectly her hand seemed to fit into his. He would not reflect on the capable strength he could feel as her fingers wrapped around his. He would not wonder at the urge to keep her hand in his indefinitely. He would not imagine pressing his lips to the inside of her wrist and—

"My apologies if I made you uncomfortable." At least his words were civil and courteous, even if his imagination wasn't. He needed to pull himself together.

"You didn't." She sat up, and he released her hand immediately.

"Good. Right." He cleared his throat. "Well, let's get your brother somewhere a little more comfortable?"

"Of course."

Harland lifted the heavy wool curtain from the table. With a considerable effort and Miss Wright's help, he got the woozy man into bed, careful of his stitches and shoulder. Paul left the window to join them, shooing both Harland and Miss Wright out of his way. "I can see him settled," he admonished.

I need to talk to Matthew in private, Harland translated. Because Paul and Matthew would need to make decisions tonight. Decisions that Harland suspected Paul did not want to involve his daughter in. Decisions he most certainly didn't want to involve an interloper in.

Harland refrained from telling Paul that he knew very well that there were still a dozen tubs of brandy sunk in the north side of the cove after the failed retrieval attempt tonight. Harland didn't mention that it was this load that was holding up the remainder of the shipment that was already prepared and concealed, awaiting transportation to London. That the financier would need the complete delivery before he issued payment.

One could not tell what one didn't know.

Harland retreated back to the table and busied himself tidying tools. Miss Wright's surgical kit was still laid out on the surface of the battered wooden sideboard that was shoved against the wall. He ran his finger over the long, flat leather case that could be rolled up and tied for quick storage. Along the top edge, the initials *KW* had been etched into the leather. Secured along the length was an impressive set of instruments. Bone saws, knives, forceps, scalpels, clamps, probes. Tools of the trade and all things that a surgeon wouldn't go anywhere without. His own field kit was almost identical, though Miss Wright's was more complete. He wondered if she was as capable with the bone saws as she was with her needles.

"Why did you do that?" Miss Wright had come up behind him.

"I beg your pardon?" He kept his eyes on her instruments, stalling. Pretending he wasn't sure what she was referring to.

"Why did you help hide Matthew?"

Because I know him to be a good man and a better smuggler. Because I rely on him, even if he doesn't know it.

He would say none of that.

"No one should be hanged for the crime of climbing out a lover's window." Harland withdrew his fingers from the leather case and turned to look at Miss Wright.

Her expression was hard. "Do you think I am a half-wit, my lord?"

"No."

"Then have the decency to answer my question with something better than that."

"Why does it matter?"

"You're a lord. Your loyalty should lie with the crown and its agents. And yet you protected my brother. Why?" Her distrust was blatant.

"Because your father needs him." Harland had to give her something believable.

Her expression didn't change.

"My job is to heal people, not judge them, Miss Wright." He crossed his arms. "I am a doctor before I am anything else."

The lines around her mouth tightened. "Of course."

It was clear she didn't believe his last statement. For some reason that bothered him more than it should.

She tilted her head slightly. "Woman parts."

"I beg your pardon?"

"I was recalling your doctorly use of medical terms."

Harland almost scowled but caught himself in time. "I wasn't speaking to medical students."

"Good thing. You would have been asked to leave the theater."

"I spoke a language soldiers could understand. Because in my experience, references to woman parts, coupled with copious amounts of blood, make most men falter."

"But not you."

"I am a doctor. It will take more than that to make me falter."

"Of course." Again, her skepticism was clear. He'd faced plenty of doubt before. Learned not to rise or react to it long ago. Why he found Miss Wright's lack of confidence in his abilities so vexing was vexing in itself.

"He can't stay here."

Harland realized that she was no longer looking at him and instead was gazing at her brother.

"No," he agreed. The subject of his medical aptitude had seemingly been set aside for more pressing matters.

"The soldiers will be back again. The storm will keep them under their toadstools for a little while and will make a barn burning difficult, but they'll come back looking for him."

"Yes."

"They knew who he was." She sounded troubled.

"He must have been recognized." *Or betrayed.* The latter made Harland's blood run cold. If someone had tipped the soldiers off about tonight, if someone had knowledge of Matthew Wright and the brandy he had sought to recover, then there was no telling what else they knew.

Miss Wright's suspicious gaze shifted back to him, and Harland could feel the weight of it. He couldn't shake the feeling that he was being studied and examined. Measured, somehow.

"Matthew can't ride," she said abruptly.

"I agree. I am hoping that your family owns a cart of some sort." Harland didn't need to hope. He knew very well Paul and Matthew owned a long cart. A cart with a false bottom, large enough to hide tubs of brandy or bolts of silk. Or an injured man. "I'd prefer not to move him, but I think it's best if I take him with me when I leave."

Miss Wright's brows shot nearly to her hairline. "Take him with *you*? Where?"

Even given everything that had just transpired, everything he had done, she didn't even try to temper her distrust.

"To Avondale."

"Avondale? The Earl of Rivers's estate?" she asked incredulously.

"Yes. It's where I'm staying." He had no idea if she would know that or not. "I'll be able to keep an eye on that wound, and he'll be safe there."

"Why?"

"The Earl of Rivers is, coincidentally, married to my youngest sister—"

"No, I mean why would you continue to hide my brother?" She took a step closer, so close that he could feel the warmth of her presence, smell the faint scent of her soap even under the sharper tones of blood and brandy. This close, in the soft light, he could see that her irises were edged in a darker blue, flecks of gold dancing in the turquoise sea. It was suddenly hard to draw a full breath, and he wondered how many men had drowned in the depths of her captivating eyes.

"Because I can." That explanation was all that came to him. He was having a hard time thinking. He was generally a very accomplished liar, but his usually nimble mind was strangely sluggish.

"I don't believe you." At least she was being honest now.

Harland looked down at the pile of bloody towels in his hands. He would not leave Matthew Wright here because the soldiers would be back. And if Matthew was here when they returned, they would clap him in irons and drag him away and leave him in a dank cell. They would torture and starve him until he either died or until he told them what they wanted to hear. Things that might expose others. Things that might ultimately expose himself.

Neither option was acceptable.

Harland chose his words carefully. "All I know," he started slowly, "is that your brother is a good man. A good man who doesn't deserve to be punished for doing what he needs to do to support his family." That was not a lie. That was the truth. Harland knew that better than anyone. Because he had lived that truth for far too many years.

He was still living it.

Chapter 3

Katherine's father had instantly agreed to the Lord Doctor's proposal to transport Matthew to Avondale. Offered Strathmore the use of the old wagon that still languished behind the barn and had escaped the soldiers' attention due to the timely rain. Led him outside and showed him the hidden compartment that existed beneath the boards. Helped line the space with blankets and settle her brother among them before replacing the wide planks above. Held the Lord Doctor's horse while the baron unsaddled it and then deftly harnessed the animal with only a single candle to combat the dark.

Katherine had no idea what to make of any of it. A peer of the realm should at the very least question the disclosure of hidden compartments in farm wagons. A London lord should not be able to harness and hitch a horse that smoothly, in the dark, no less. But then again, a baron should never be a doctor, and a doctor should never be a baron. This entire night had been turned on its head long before Harland Hayward heaved his medical bag up onto the rough seat of a country cart and prepared to climb up after it, for the sole purpose of transporting a wounded Dover smuggler to a fine country manor.

She didn't understand it, she didn't like it, and she certainly didn't trust anything about the entire situation. She didn't trust him. Hayward. Or Strathmore. Or whatever the hell he called himself.

The Lord Doctor took the lantern from her father and reached up, securing it on the hook mounted at the front of the wagon. Katherine saw him glance at the sky, and though it had stopped raining, the air was still heavy with the promise of more, the moon and stars still concealed by clouds.

"I'll go as quickly as I can," he said to her father. "And get him settled and resting properly. It's probably best if you don't come to Avondale in the coming days. I do not wish to lead the captain or any of his men to your son in the event that they are watching you."

"Aye," her father agreed.

The Lord Doctor sounded like a bloody spy.

"I'm going with you." She was not letting her brother leave here alone under the care of a baron with dubious medical experience. A baron she didn't trust, even if her father did.

The Lord Doctor paused, his hand on the edge of the wagon, his face obscured by shadows. "That is not necessary."

"No? And if you're stopped? If the soldiers who just retreated did not retreat as far as you'd like to think, how are you going to explain yourself? They would have seen your horse when they arrived. It was not attached to an empty cart then. You need a patient, remember?"

The Lord Doctor's hand dropped. "There is no need to put you in danger."

"But putting me on my back with your hand up my skirts for an armed audience was quite safe?" She stopped, recognizing that she was being unfair. And offensive. No matter how she felt about the baron, his actions, as inexplicable as they might be, had probably saved her brother's life.

Her father grumbled a sound of deserved displeasure. "We owe Dr. Hayward our gratitude, Kate, not—"

"It's all right." The baron didn't sound offended at all.

Idly, Katherine wondered what it would take to truly provoke this seemingly unprovokable man.

She stepped closer to the wagon, looking up at the Lord Doctor, and tried for a more conciliatory tone. "My presence will just ensure Matthew gets to Avondale safely if we're stopped and challenged. I can return here in the morning, after I've been miraculously cured, of course." And after she saw to the continued treatment of Matthew's wound. Because when it came to medical expertise, a title most certainly did not give the Lord Doctor any degree of competence.

Strathmore considered her before nodding. "Fine."

Katherine had expected more of an argument.

Her father unwrapped the woolen blanket that he still had around his shoulders and extended it to Katherine. "Take this for the ride. You'll need it."

Katherine hesitated. "Will you be all right here—"

"Stop fussing," her father said. "'Tis not I who was sewn back together tonight. I don't need you to hover over me like a helpless chick. I'll be fine. Go with Dr. Hayward."

She reached for the blanket, fumbling slightly in the darkness.

"Come, Miss Wright, before the skies open up again."
The baron was holding his hand out to her in the pool of
lantern light.

She nodded, and for the second time that night, moved
to put her hand in his.

~

Katherine studied the Lord Doctor out of the corner of her
eye, his handsome profile in stark relief from the lantern
light that bounced and swayed as they rolled over the
uneven roads. The skies had held their rain, though the
ground was pockmarked with puddles, pools of reflected
lantern light glittering against the velvet darkness as they
passed. To her right, the surf crashed against the base of the
cliffs far below, the stiff breeze carrying a briny tang along
with a decided chill.

She had offered to lie in the back, to make it more real-
istic if they were stopped, but the Lord Doctor had shaken
his head. "I have the utmost confidence in your acting
abilities, Miss Wright," he had said, again in that imperturbable manner. "I trust, should the need arise, that you
will channel your best insensible self, slumped against my
supportive side. In the meantime, I think you'll find the
bench warmer and more comfortable."

He wasn't wrong. But he wasn't right either. Sitting this
close to him, she was indeed warm. Very, very warm. But
very, very uncomfortable.

Because sitting next to him was making her breath catch
at odd moments. It was making her inhale the scent of
him—rain-dampened wool laced with brandy and something richer, sending her pulse into strange rhythms. It was
making her overly aware of the feel of his thighs and his

hip where they pressed against hers as the wagon swayed. And it was making her fixate on his hands again.

Gilded with golden lantern light, there was a quiet efficiency to the movements of those hands and fingers as he guided the gelding over the darkened roads. Soothing, encouraging, gentle. Corrective only when necessary, giving the horse the time and space to find its own way in the darkness.

She tried not to recall how those hands had felt on her skin. How those fingers had rested against the bare length of her leg, communicating with the same steady surety. They hadn't faltered as the captain had barged into the cottage, nor had they faltered when he'd stood between her and an army that would see her arrested if only for her familial connections.

"I'm sorry," she said into the night.

He glanced at her. "For what?"

"For the way I spoke to you when we left. It was ungrateful." She still didn't trust him, but that didn't mean she couldn't be gracious, at the very least. Until, that was, he gave her a reason not to be.

"Your apology is not necessary, Miss Wright."

"It is necessary. Your quick thinking is why my brother is safely hidden away and not dangling at the end of a rope or already rotting in a prison cell as we speak."

He turned his attention back to the road. "My quick thinking put you in a terrible position, and you handled it with a courage not often found, Miss Wright."

For some incomprehensible reason, Katherine's face heated. She did not want his compliments. Certainly not if they made her blush.

"How long have you been a doctor?" she asked, attempting to redirect the conversation.

"Ten years."

"You went to medical school?"

"Yes. In London." His answer was short.

"Hmph."

"You don't believe that either?"

"I didn't say that."

He kept his eyes on the road ahead.

"You told the captain that you were an army surgeon in France and Belgium. Were you really there, on those fields? Or were you making that up?" She winced at the slightly hostile manner in which that had come out, despite her intention to be civil. But service like that was not something that should ever be an empty boast. Service like that was built on suffering and horrors that few could imagine and even fewer had experienced firsthand.

He turned to look at her, his expression unreadable in the shadows. "Would it matter to you if I was making it up?" It sounded almost defensive, a departure from his usual inscrutable demeanor.

Katherine absorbed that. "Yes."

He exhaled as he faced forward again. "Why?"

She didn't need to pursue this. She probably shouldn't pursue this. There were plenty of other topics that could fill the minutes. Like the weather. Or the tides. Or just plain silence would be fine too. "I want to know the truth."

"Will you even believe me?"

"Whether I believe you or not matters?" This was a circular conversation.

"Yes."

A slow heat curled into Katherine's chest like smoke. It shouldn't matter that he cared what she thought. She would not allow it to matter. Because that sort of thing worked both ways. And she had no interest in caring about this

Lord Doctor. What he had done with his life up to this point should be irrelevant to her.

"Yes, I was there," he said quietly. "Until the very end."

She stared out in the direction of the sea, a yawning abyss of inky black. Irrelevant or not, caring or not, she did, however, acknowledge that she may have vastly misjudged this man. And vastly underestimated him. "Why did you serve with—"

"Why did you become a surgeon?" He didn't let her finish her question.

Katherine looked down at her hands and reminded herself that she didn't care why he'd left his pampered life to become a field surgeon. It didn't matter that he had evaded answering her question by asking one of his own.

Her head came up. He had asked why she had become a surgeon. Not a midwife or a healer. Specifically a surgeon. As if he already knew what she had done with her life up until this point. And found it relevant.

"I'm not a surgeon," she said with a shrug, aiming for carelessness. "Or a doctor, for that matter. I'm a midwife. Or maybe a healer who gets summoned when a real doctor is not available. Or affordable."

The baron made an unintelligible sound. "That was not a midwife I saw treating her brother in that cottage tonight."

Katherine wondered if he was mocking her with his comment. "I am not a surgeon. Can never be a surgeon. Because, as you so adroitly stated earlier, I have woman parts." There was certainly a mocking tone to her answer.

"Ah, yes. Your woman parts. The bits that make every female hysterical and unable to understand manly things like medicine."

Katherine picked up a loose piece of straw that lay beside her on the bench and curled it around her fingers. "It's not funny."

"No, it's not. My sisters will be the first to tell you the same."

"I don't think you really understand."

"I might understand more than you think."

"I doubt that." The withered stalk tore in two, and she tossed the pieces away into the darkness.

"Tell me, Miss Wright, when we first met, you doubted my medical capabilities. I suspect you still do." There was no accusation or belligerence in his tone, just a quiet resignation. He adjusted his grip on the reins. "Why?"

He was asking a rhetorical question that they both already knew the answer to.

A baron should never be a doctor, and a doctor should never be a baron.

"Your lack of confidence in my abilities is the reason you insisted on accompanying your brother to Avondale," he continued in the same quiet way.

Katherine didn't bother to deny it.

"While I cannot pretend to know exactly how it feels to be a woman battling the prejudices of society, I can tell you what it feels like to be a man born to a title who is not to be trusted with a vocation outside of cards and horses, mistresses and money. In some ways, Miss Wright, we are not so different."

Katherine turned toward the sea again. They were not the same. They could not be the same because she didn't want to have anything in common with this Lord Doctor. She didn't want to like him. Especially when her insides were twisting about and her heart was skipping simply because she was sitting near him.

She didn't delude herself into thinking she was special.

No doubt the Lord Doctor knew just what to say to every woman he spoke with, his silver tongue tricking them into feeling the way she was feeling right now. Like he understood her. Like she could trust him with her deepest secrets and truths.

She kept her gaze fixed firmly on the black nothingness of the ocean. These feelings were all a product of loneliness. A chronic loneliness heightened by the awful strain of this night. Who wouldn't be tempted into wanting to believe, if only for a moment, that someone understood? That someone cared?

"How much longer until we get to Avondale?" she asked.

Beside her, the baron shifted, and the wagon began to turn slowly. "We're here."

Chapter 4

She had a vague impression of a hulking mass of a manor house, a pale, ghostly facade layered against the night sky. Rows of empty ebony windows reflected the wagon's meager light as they passed the silent entrance. The Lord Doctor drove them around the back, and they disembarked, helping an exhausted Matthew from the concealed compartment. A stable boy appeared like a specter, leading away the horse and wagon without a word as though these sorts of unexpected arrivals happened on a regular basis.

They entered through the kitchens, Strathmore leading them up the rear stairs and into the servants' quarters with an unerring sureness that told Katherine this wasn't the first time he'd done just that. She tried not to jump to disparaging conclusions about why a titled man would be this familiar with the sleeping quarters of maids. Tried not to be judgmental, if only because the Lord Doctor was taking a considerable risk on Matthew's behalf. On her family's be-half, really, by hiding a smuggler in his grand house, with no compensation.

Why would you continue to hide my brother? she had asked.

Because I can, he had answered.

Which wasn't a real answer at all.

Too late, she realized that he simply hadn't named his price yet. Too late she understood that he would, eventu-ally. No one did things like this without expecting some-thing in return.

Strathmore showed them into an empty room that boasted a single bed and a tiny washstand. The ceiling was sloped, making it feel even more cramped than it already was, and Katherine had to duck as she helped her brother into the bed. The Lord Doctor vanished, only to return with a pitcher of water, a stack of clean towels, and an additional pillow that he situated deftly under Matthew's arm to take the strain from his damaged shoulder. Her brother was al-ready asleep, and he barely stirred.

Strathmore adjusted the coverlet and stepped away from the bed, gesturing to the door. "Follow me."

"I'll stay right where I am." She wasn't going anywhere with this Lord Doctor and leaving her brother here alone. There wasn't even so much as a chair in the space, and she would need to doze on the floor, but that was fine. She had slept in far worse places than this.

"There is no need. Your brother is resting comfortably." The baron was standing directly in front of her, the tiny room impossibly crowded.

"I'm not leaving him." She refused to budge.

He put a hand on her arm. "Let me take you to bed."

Ah. And there it was. The price of his assistance. She

should have known. The baron was the same as every other titled man.

"I generally expect more artful propositions from men with your means and position."

His hand dropped from her arm, though his face remained impassive. "That was not a proposition, Miss Wright."

Of course it wasn't. It was an expectation.

Katherine's nails bit into her palm. "I'll find you the money."

"Money for what?"

"For this." She jerked her chin in the direction of Matthew. "For this room. For your discretion."

"I don't think you understand, Miss Wright."

"No, you don't understand, my lord. This will not be an exchange of services rendered. Whatever it is you might think I am, I am not a whore."

A faint shadow of something finally rippled across his unreadable expression, though it was gone before she could identify it.

"I know. It was never my intention to suggest otherwise."

Katherine was brought up short. "What do you want from me?"

"At the moment, to see you to a room so I can retire to mine. It's been a long night."

She saw only truth in his dark gaze, and she dropped her eyes to the floor. Humiliation and shame started to burn their way up into her cheeks.

It would seem she had misjudged him. Again.

She had been unfair and offensive. Again.

"I'm sorry." She forced herself to look at him. This was the second time she had apologized to him.

"You're exhausted."

"That's not an excuse." The fact that he was making one up for her made her feel worse.

The Lord Doctor clasped his hands behind his back. "Will you allow me to see you to a proper room with a proper bed downstairs?"

"What if Matthew needs me?"

"If he does, I'll have someone fetch you. Matthew is not the only patient who has convalesced in these rooms. The Avondale staff are not only discreet, but they are also well accustomed to such things."

"How discreet?" Katherine wondered just how many eyes and ears there had to be in a house this size.

"Matthew is safe here. He will never be addressed by name, just like those family members of the staff here who have cause to seek medical care or…temporary accommodations. Everyone on Avondale's staff has a stake in total discretion because they, too, have relied upon it at one time or another."

"And the Earl of Rivers knows this? He won't report these…disturbances to the garrison?"

"He has no respect or admiration for the captain."

"Why?"

The Lord Doctor hesitated. "He has had occasion to see things in shades of gray as opposed to black and white."

That told Katherine nothing. Not that it should matter, she supposed. She wasn't entitled to an explanation. Especially given how horrid she had been.

"In the meantime, it will do your brother no good if you're too tired to stay on your feet tomorrow," the Lord Doctor suggested in his perfectly reasonable tone of voice.

Katherine wavered.

Matthew snored.

The baron extended his hand.

"Thank you," she said as she took it.

Again.

⁓

Katherine woke to sunshine, the scent of soap, and a faintly steamy room.

Perhaps she had been more tired than she had thought or perhaps it had been the proper bed with its proper mattress and proper sheets, or maybe a combination of those things, but Katherine had slept like the dead. She hadn't meant to—she had only thought to sleep for a few hours at most, but it had to be midmorning now. She shoved the covers back and stumbled out of the bed, frantically looking about for her discarded dress.

She should have been up ages ago. What if Matthew had developed a fever? What if—

She stopped and blinked. Her dress had been laid out on the back of a chair near the door of the small dressing room. Her apron was folded neatly beside it, both garments apparently washed and dried, given the conspicuous lack of blood on each. Beyond that, someone had filled the small hip tub in the dressing room. Wisps of steam still curled from the surface, making the air redolent with a rich warmth. And next to all of that sat a tray with a pot of tea, biscuits, and a small bowl of preserves.

And a note addressed to her.

Good God, she had *slept* through all this?

Katherine strode over to the tray and snatched the note from the surface, ignoring her rumbling stomach. It was written in an unfamiliar hand, strong and slanted, though as she turned it over, the name scrawled at the bottom was certainly recognizable. *Dr. Hayward.*

Her fingers tightened on the note.

Your brother tells me that strawberry preserves are your favorite.

As if she was going to indulge herself and linger over tea and preserves while her brother could be suffering from a—

No fever. Expected bruising and swelling, stiffness in the left shoulder and arm. Minimal drainage, no redness surrounding damaged tissue. Sutures remain clean and intact. Patient complains of boredom, and I have taken the liberty of prescribing a collection of reading material from our library downstairs. I do not anticipate any change in his condition for the rest of the morning.

As such, Miss Wright, you have no excuse not to enjoy both the bath and preserves prescribed to you. For the record, your brother agrees.

Katherine stared at the words that had somehow gone blurry. With horror, she scrubbed at her eyes with the back of her hand. She was not crying. She should be trying to find some irritation at the Lord Doctor's presumptions and high-handedness. She should be trying to be angry that he hadn't woken her, even when he'd known that she would be worried and that she would want to assess Matthew herself. She should be trying to figure out why, even after the way she had treated him, he was being so damn nice.

Katherine looked longingly at the bath. She set the note aside and approached the steaming water, dipping her hand into the warmth. Her fingers trailed over the copper rim of the tub and dropped, reaching out to touch the sliver of hard soap that had been left on top of a towel. The temptation was too much.

She yanked her shift over her head and let it fall to the floor, climbing into the tub. Taking extreme care not to slosh any water from the surface, she sank into the warmth. She wasn't sure if she wanted to weep or laugh like a madwoman. If she wasn't careful, she would start wishing she was a fancy lady, if only for the decadence of hot water.

And if she wasn't careful, she was going to start liking this charismatic, considerate Lord Doctor far more than was safe.

Dressed in her freshly laundered clothes, her hair in a damp braid down her back, her stomach pleasantly full of biscuits and strawberry preserves, Katherine ventured from her room to find herself in the middle of a grand hallway that had been concealed by darkness last night. It, like her room, was tastefully appointed. A carpet runner, woven in shades of green and blue, muffled her footsteps and stretched the considerable length of the hall. Framed portraits of people who she assumed were Rivers's relatives and ancestors were hung at regular intervals along the wood-paneled passage, polished frames gleaming in the bright light spilling through tall windows at either end of the hall. The scent of wax and baking bread drifted around her.

"Good morning."

Katherine whirled to find a woman exiting a room just behind her. She was shorter than Katherine by a good half head and had silver hair pulled back into a neat bun at the nape of her neck. Her lined cheeks were flushed with color that could only be attained by spending time out of doors, and her gray eyes sparkled with warmth and curiosity.

"Good morning," Katherine responded out of pure reflex. She glanced at the wide basket the woman held over the crook of her arm and the well-made, if somewhat faded, deep green shawl tucked over her shoulders.

"You must be Miss Wright." The woman beamed. "Welcome to Avondale. I'm Theo, the earl's aunt. Well, Lady Theodosia, if one is keeping track of such, but everyone just calls me Theo. And you'll meet my sister, Tabitha. We call her Tabby. You shall also do so while you stay with us. Did you have a good night's rest, dearie?"

Katherine was unsure how to respond to that introduction. "I slept well, thank you." At least that answer was easy.

"Were you looking for your brother? Harland told us he has him tucked away under the eaves upstairs. I can take you there if you like?"

"No, that's fine, thank you. I helped see him settled last night. I know the way." And clearly, the Lord Doctor had been telling the truth. Strange people being deposited in Avondale's beds in the dead of night was something that seemed to be a familiar occurrence.

"Excellent. Ah, here is Tabby now. Tabby, come meet Miss Wright."

Katherine turned to find a taller version of Lady Theodosia approaching. She had the same silver hair, same pinked cheeks, and same kind eyes. She also had the same sturdy basket over her arm along with a pink shawl over her shoulders.

"Miss Wright." Lady Tabitha—Katherine wasn't sure if she could get used to addressing two strangers, her superior in both age and rank, by nicknames—came to a stop beside her sister. "Lovely to meet a young woman of such skill," Lady Tabitha said. "I hope you were able to sleep."

"Skill?" Katherine repeated before she could catch herself.

"Harland tells us that you're quite a neat hand with sutures." Lady Tabitha shifted the basket on her arm and looked at her sister.

"Indeed," Lady Theodosia confirmed. "Quite impressed him. And he's not an easy man to impress."

"No, indeed," Tabitha continued. "Not when it comes to sutures. Or any medicine, really."

"He's quite particular."

"Ridiculously so."

"Which is what makes him so competent."

"And an excellent teacher."

"Agreed."

"Tell me, Miss Wright, where were you trained?"

Katherine was trying to follow the conversation, only to find two pairs of sharp eyes abruptly focused on her.

"Um. Here and there." This was not exactly something that she had prepared herself to discuss in a grand hallway with two women she had met only moments before.

Theodosia and Tabitha exchanged a glance and nodded, as if that pitiable answer fully explained everything that had happened to her in the last seven years of her life.

"Well, we shan't delay you further, dearie," Lady Theodosia said. "I'm sure you're anxious to see your brother."

"And we should be on our way so as not to miss the tide. We search the beaches and shores," Tabitha explained. "For fossils."

Theodosia lifted her basket slightly. "An excellent array

of bivalves yesterday," she said happily. "Who knows what we might discover today?"

"Indeed," Tabitha agreed with a cheerful smile. "Have a lovely day, Miss Wright. Please let our staff know if you require anything while you are our guest. It is wonderful to have you here with us."

"Thank you," Katherine murmured. "Good day." She wondered if perhaps she'd woken in an alternate reality where conversation required no participation on her part. And where she had seemingly impressed one Harland Hayward with her fine hand.

The sisters departed and disappeared down the wide, central staircase that split the long hall in two, and Katherine watched them go. She would not dwell on what the Lord Doctor thought of her or her skill with sutures. Because if she did, little butterflies rose to tickle the inside of her chest and fan an unacceptable amount of heat into her cheeks.

She wouldn't dwell on that, either. She wouldn't dwell on the oddness of this day. Instead, she would focus on the reason that this day had happened in the first place. And that reason was still convalescing upstairs.

With renewed purpose, Katherine retraced her steps to the servants' staircase, her senses alert for the sounds of anyone else, but there was only silence. A silence that followed her as she made her way back up to the servants' quarters and to Matthew's room. She stuck her head in to find her brother propped up on pillows, his hair ruffled, his torso bare, his arm in a sling, a book in his good hand, and a fierce frown on his face.

For an instant, Katherine was transported back in time, a nine-year-old Matthew wearing the same expression of concentration as he had sat beside her, hunched over a slate.

He looked up, and his frown cleared. "Kate!" He shifted, wincing slightly.

Katherine strode to his side and peered at the exposed bullet wound at the top of his shoulder. Minimal drainage, and no redness surrounding damaged tissue. Though there was some impressive bruising spreading over the top of his shoulder and across his skin. It would appear that the Lord Doctor had been quite accurate in his assessment.

"I wish Mother could see you now with a book in your hand," she commented.

"I wish she had used these books to teach me to read." Matthew gestured to the open pages in front of him. "Have you heard the story of the Trojan horse?"

"I have."

"Can you imagine anyone being too thickheaded to be suspicious of an elaborate gift in the middle of a damn war?" Matthew sounded incredulous.

"I was not aware you were interested in Greek mythology."

"Neither was I. But Dr. Hayward suggested I might find it of interest, and so I have." He paused, then grinned. "How did you like your bath?"

Katherine forced her expression to remain neutral. "It was lovely, thank you."

"Don't thank me. That was Dr. Hayward's idea too. Though he asked me what you might like to eat."

A slow heat started to burn in her cheeks again at the thought of the Lord Doctor considering her needs and wants. She cleared her throat and reminded herself that she would not dwell on that. "It was a very nice thing to do."

"You deserved it," Matthew said with satisfaction.

"How are you feeling?" She redirected the conversation back to safe ground.

"Bored." Matthew snapped his book shut. "Sore. Like a damned pincushion."

"I thought you were enjoying your bloodthirsty stories." She put a hand on his good shoulder. "Lean forward."

Her brother heaved a sigh but did as he was asked. "The stories are fine but I'd rather not be in bed. And Dr. Hayward was already here. Already did just this. Twice," he added. "Is this really necessary?"

"Humor me." Katherine peered at her stitches. They still looked neat and clean. The Lord Doctor had been right about that too.

"Believe it or not, Dr. Hayward is very good at what he does," Matthew said, settling back when Katherine removed her hand.

"Lord Strathmore, you mean."

"He prefers Dr. Hayward."

"Hmph."

"You still don't like him, do you?" Matthew was watching her. "Even after everything."

"I didn't say that. I don't know him."

"He took a great risk on our behalves."

"I am aware."

"And does that not count for something?"

"I am grateful for what he did for us last night. I am, truly. But he is still a grand lord. When things get difficult, he will put his own interests first."

"Difficult?" Matthew tossed his book to the side. "You don't consider what happened last night difficult?"

Katherine opened her mouth to argue and closed it again. She didn't have a good argument for that.

"Dr. Hayward is not stupid, Kate. He knows exactly how I got shot."

"Exactly?"

"Well, not exactly, but he sure as hell knows it wasn't climbing out a damn window. He's never asked questions, never wanted to know. Just treated any one of us when we've needed it and said not a word. To anyone. Ever."

"But, Matt, he's not one of us. Don't let him fool you into thinking otherwise. He's a lord—"

"Enough, Kate. You're letting what happened to you cloud your judgment. Dr. Hayward is different. He won't run. He won't betray—"

"We don't need to discuss the past," Katherine said succinctly. "The past has nothing to do with Lord Strathmore." She took a step back. She did not want to endure a discourse on lords and their promises and vows and how lightly they took all of them.

"That is exactly my point," Matthew said, his fingers tapping out an impatient rhythm on the sheets.

Katherine looked away, her jaw tight.

Matthew heaved a sigh. "Thank you, Kate."

She glanced back at him, acknowledging his peace offering. "For what?"

"For what you did for me last night."

"Don't be ridiculous. I would do anything for you."

He glanced past her. "Shut the door."

Katherine gave him a long look but did as she was asked.

"I need a favor," Matthew said as the latch clicked shut. "I need your help."

Trepidation settled low in her belly. "With what?"

"I need you . . . I need you to take my place."

"Take your place? Doing what, exactly?" She was afraid she already knew the answer.

"We need a diver. Nothing you haven't done before."

Katherine clamped her teeth together to prevent her

from shrieking something she would regret. "No." There, that sounded calm. Rational.

"You were one of the best, Kate. A better diver than I ever was. A better smuggler than the entire lot of us. No one knows the channel ports like you do."

"I'm not a smuggler anymore."

"It's in your blood, Kate. You'll always be a smuggler. We need you for this."

Katherine spun and stared at the door. Her father had always insisted that the glass floats tethered to the bundles of sunken contraband be secured just below the surface of the water. It had been a system that had worked for years. And worked outlandishly well. The floats were tricky to find if one did not know the exact location, and they were invisible to scouts and patrolman on the shore. Most could be pulled up with a grappling hook. Some, attached to more valuable cargo unloaded overboard by the smuggling vessels, were just beyond reach from the surface of the sea and required a diver to secure an additional length of rope.

A diver like Matthew. Or once, long ago, like Katherine.

"You don't need me." She braced her hands on the door frame. "What you need is to stop before you are killed. Dead for the sake of a tub of brandy."

"It's not that simple. We're..." He trailed off.

"You're what?" Katherine spun angrily. "Measuring how much your life is worth against material goods?"

Matthew scowled and kicked the covers from his legs and sat up. He reached awkwardly for his shirt that was draped over the end of the bed.

"What are you doing?"

"Going home."

"No, you're not."

"Someone has to. The shipment from last night still needs to be fetched. And fetched soon."

"Don't be an idiot, Matthew. There will be soldiers crawling all over the place looking for you right now."

"I'll take my chances. Better the devil you know than the devil you don't."

"What does that mean?"

"There is nothing left, Kate. We need money. Father can't work. And what do you think will happen to him if I can't pay the rent for a roof over our heads? How long do you think he will last with no food? No heat? No medicine? He's not well, even if he won't admit it."

"I know that," she snapped.

"But you won't help."

"I am trying to help. I'm doing everything I can."

"I know." Matthew sighed. "But it's not enough. It's like trying to squeeze blood from a stone. The only money to be had out here lies in smuggling. If you would just consider coming back to—"

"No." Katherine looked away again. It was the second time in as many days that she had been told that what she was doing was not enough. She closed her eyes and shook her head. "There has to be another way."

"I'm all ears. But since the day I came back from Belgium, I've been trying to find another way. There are too many of us. Too many men—soldiers—and not enough work. You know that. You see it every day in the patients you treat." He sounded as furious and as helpless as she felt.

Katherine's fingers curled into fists. She hated that he was right.

"Just until I'm well," Matthew said in a subdued voice. "It's all I'm asking. Because there are other families counting on me—on us. Families with children. Families who have helped us out in the past. Helped me take care of Father when you were away."

"Matthew—"

"That wasn't a criticism, Kate," he said. "Just fact. You weren't here. They were. Hervey Baker's wife, Frannie, helped nurse Father for six weeks after he got shot. And I won't let them down. I won't turn my back on them because things have gotten hard. I—*we*—owe them this."

Katherine swore again. When she had returned to Dover, it had been with the full intention of persuading her brother to stop smuggling. To change his lifestyle before it got him killed. Only to find out that he was right. It wasn't that simple, and in fact, circumstance was making it damned near impossible. And now here she was contemplating returning to it herself.

"Please, Kate. And then I'll not ask you ever again."

"You'll not ask me again because we'll find another way," she said.

Matthew gave her a hard look. "Does that mean you'll do it?"

"If you promise me that, after a fortnight, that will be the end of it. We will go north. Away from Dover. Find work—real work."

Her brother was shaking his head.

"Promise me that if I do this for you—for our family— that whatever it takes, wherever we have to go, whatever we have to do, it will be the end of smuggling."

"Kate—"

"Do we have a deal or not?"

His mouth was set in a thin line. "Yes," he said grudgingly.

"Good." What the hell was she doing? "Tell me how

this works now." No doubt there would have been some changes, aside from the fact that it was Matthew and not her father who now headed the crew.

"Most of the people are still the same. Jamie and Joseph Jonson and their boys look after anything going to London overland, Charlie Nelson and Landry Willis and their oyster crews look after what needs transporting around the coast and down the river. Hervey Baker and I are responsible for deep water retrievals."

"What's different, then?"

"How we do business. When you were last with us, we decided what to bring in and sold it ourselves. We no longer have to do that. Now all we have to do is retrieve and deliver prearranged goods to London, which we package and conceal appropriately, of course. We're handsomely compensated for the service."

"By whom?"

"I don't know."

Katherine stared at him. "You don't know? How do you not know who pays you?"

"You can't tell what you don't know, I suppose. Safer that way for everyone."

"You must have some idea." Katherine didn't like unknowns, and she didn't agree that it was safer. Information made one safer.

"Some of the boys have said they've seen a blond bloke about town from time to time," Matthew said. "Maybe it's him. Or maybe not. But what I do know is that payment is delivered without fail. On time, every time."

"Where?"

"Buried in a different spot every time. Places soldiers won't be looking. Each payment is accompanied by a new set of instructions for the next shipment."

"That's insane. What if someone intercepted—"

"A letter from Grandmother? It's coded, Kate. Whoever is on the London end, whoever makes the arrangements on the other side of the channel, is not a fool. I collect and distribute desperately needed payments to the men and collect the next set of instructions."

"I don't like it."

"Neither did I, at first. But, Kate, there is something to be said for cargoes that already have buyers and don't have to be hidden for long stretches of time. Having every payment made promptly and in full is invaluable. There are a half-dozen warehouses scattered throughout London that we deliver to. We're instructed which cargoes are to be taken to which warehouse. Then we simply unload and walk away."

Katherine paced the cramped room, almost turning in circles because of its tiny size. Appropriate, that she should be going in circles. Because she had now come full circle here.

"What are you bringing in?"

"Brandy, silk, tobacco, lace mostly. Sometimes art."

"Art? Like paintings?"

Matthew shrugged with his good shoulder. "Most often paintings. Old ones. Sometimes sculptures and statues and things. Lots of times they're crated up and I don't see them, but those obviously can't be left in the cove."

"Since when have you started smuggling art?"

"Last couple of years."

Katherine stopped her pacing and looked at the ceiling. "I can't believe I'm doing this," she muttered under her breath.

"Look, Kate, all you need to do is get the tubs, get them to shore. There will be a crew waiting to meet you to make those tubs disappear. Once your boat hits the shingle, you disappear as well."

"Provided I don't get shot."

"I know someone who's good with bullet wounds."

"That's not funny. I don't want the baron having any more to do with this."

"I was talking about you."

Katherine scowled. "That's not funny either. None of this is funny. It's bad enough you are stuck here in Lord Strathmore's fancy house and at the mercy of his charity. I have no intention of joining you."

Matthew made an irritable sound. "Dr. Hayward is not the enemy here. Did you know that, aside from being a doctor, he also oversees his family's shipping trade?"

"Trade." She repeated it dubiously. "Aristocrats don't sully themselves in trade."

"Neither do they become doctors. Look, all I'm saying, Kate, is that Dr. Hayward—"

"Lord Strathmore."

"—is different. You could at least be cordial toward him. I think he's more than earned it."

Katherine snorted. "Cordial? Like the women who follow him around town? Because they certainly look all sorts of cordial."

"That's not what I meant, and you know it." Matthew scowled. "Dr. Hayward is a widower, not a damn monk. Not that that is any of our business."

Katherine averted her eyes, something unacceptable leaving a foul taste in her mouth. It took her a moment to realize what it was.

Jealousy.

She cursed under her breath. What was wrong with her?

"You're right, of course," she said, because there was

nothing else to say that didn't suggest utter lunacy on her part. She smoothed her hands over her skirts. "And for now, I'll give him the benefit of the doubt, if that makes you happy. But I will do whatever I think is right and necessary for my family."

Matthew sighed. "Kate—"

"Get some rest, Matthew. And don't worry. I'll leave immediately."

Chapter 5

"Miss Wright is leaving, my lord."

Harland turned from where he had been hunched in front of a pile of correspondence and maps at the library table to find Avondale's butler standing stiffly at the door.

"Thank you for letting me know, Digby," Harland said. He pushed back his chair and got to his feet.

"Of course." The butler paused, looking faintly unimpressed. "I believe she means to . . . walk the distance."

Ah. Well, at least she wasn't crawling out a window to avoid him.

I generally expect more artful propositions from men with your means and position.

Harland wondered if Miss Wright had any idea how revealing that comment had been. How much it explained her constant suspicion and distrust that hadn't abated since she had leveled a rifle at him. It wasn't he who was the object of her bitter cynicism. It was his title that she found so abhorrent. It didn't offend him. It intrigued him.

She intrigued him.

More than was wise.

Harland realized that the butler was still looking at him expectantly. "Have the carriage brought around," he instructed. "And please detain Miss Wright. I'd like a word before she leaves."

"Very good, my lord. Consider it done." The butler nodded in approval and disappeared as silently as he had come.

"Detain her? Good God, Harland, that sounds ominous."

Harland looked over to find his sister watching him with an amused expression. He had given Clara a brief account of the events of last night, or at least a censored version that omitted his part in everything except his brief appearance at the Wrights'. As much as he despised keeping things from his sisters, it was safer for them, for the same reasons that it was safer for the men who worked under his umbrella of anonymity.

But both his sisters and the earl were aware of Matthew's presence at Avondale, and they were not fools. He hadn't been lying to Miss Wright when he had told her that her brother wasn't the first of his patients to be brought to Avondale to recover, and in each of those cases, no one had asked for an explanation. They, too, were well aware of what the end of the war had meant for the families struggling to survive in the parish. They had seen it with their own eyes.

He crossed his arms casually. "I thought to detain Miss Wright on your behalf, dear sister. Well, on behalf of the Haverhall School for Young Ladies."

A dark brow rose fractionally. "Indeed?" Clara glanced at the ledger she had been working through on the table next to Harland and set her quill aside. "You wish her to apply as a student?"

Harland shook his head. "No, not as a student. As an instructor."

Her brow rose a little higher. "An instructor?"

"Yes. You haven't found anyone to teach Mrs. Arpin's class since she retired to the Lake District, have you?"

"Someone besides you, you mean?" Clara was watching him with keen interest. "No. Good midwives with additional medical experience and open minds are harder to come by than you might think." Clara tucked an errant strand of mahogany hair back behind her ear. "Are you having second thoughts?"

"Not at all. But I do believe those young ladies might be more comfortable with a female instructor. Am I wrong?"

"No. You're not."

"Then you need to talk to Miss Wright before she goes. I believe that you will find her to be quite extraordinary."

Clara rested her chin on her hand and gazed at him with eyes so like his own. "Good Lord."

"What?"

"You're smitten with her."

"I am smitten with her medical professionalism." Harland willed his face to remain blank. "When you meet her, you will be too."

"She's a midwife?"

"And a surgeon."

"A surgeon? She told you she was a surgeon?"

"No. It's not at all what she told me."

"Then how—"

"It's what she didn't tell me." Harland stopped, his fingers playing with the edges of the maps that were laid out in front of him. "She has field experience."

Clara's eyes narrowed. "Field experience? As in battlefield experience?"

"Yes."

"And you know this how?"

"Watching her work. Her instruments." Her unflinching courage under fire. Her unwavering nerve when faced with a very real danger. She was a woman who had been tested. Tested by men and circumstance and had triumphed over both.

Harland's pulse accelerated. Dammit, Clara was right. Forget intrigued. Despite his best intentions, he might also be smitten.

Though smitten was manageable. Smitten merely acknowledged that Miss Wright was attractive and talented. Smitten was not the same as besotted, and for that he was thankful.

"I see." Clara stood and wandered to the tall library window and gazed out at the sunny gardens. "Are you hoping she will assist you with—"

"Your Grace, my lord." Digby was back in the doorway. "Miss Katherine Wright to see you."

Miss Wright stepped into the library as Digby departed, blinking a couple of times in the relative brightness of the room before her eyes fell on Harland.

An electrifying bolt of pleasure shot through him at the sight of her. With her cheeks flushed a pretty pink, her hair in a damp braid over her shoulder, she looked...beautiful. Perfect. Touchable. Kissable.

He kept his arms crossed so he wouldn't do just that and cast about for something to say. Hell, but he felt like he was an inexperienced youth who had found himself at his first country dance, desperately trying to work up the courage to ask a pretty girl for the favor of her company.

"Good morning, Miss Wright." He was relieved at his easy delivery. "I trust you slept well?"

"I did." Her cheeks flushed a little darker, and she looked like she was waging an inner battle. "Thank you," she said finally. "For your thoughtfulness. It was unnecessary." She played with the damp ends of her braid. "But it was...appreciated."

"Nothing any good host wouldn't have seen done." Which was true. But a good host wouldn't have let his imagination drift all morning, conjuring visions of what Katherine Wright looked like in that steaming tub. A good host wouldn't be imagining it still.

Harland cleared his throat. "Clara, may I present Miss Katherine Wright? Miss Wright was kind enough to allow me to assist with the care of her brother, Matthew, who is currently upstairs resting and working his way through our collection of Greek mythology. Miss Wright, this is my sister, Clara. The Duchess of Holloway now, as it happens, but more importantly, the headmistress of the Haverhall School for Young Ladies. I wanted you two to meet."

Miss Wright's eyes left Harland. "A pleasure, Your Grace," she said to his sister. "And I must extend my thanks for—"

"Clara," his sister interrupted.

"I'm sorry?"

"Please call me Clara. Titles, you will discover, have little use at Avondale." She moved away from the window. "As such, may I call you Katherine?"

Miss Wright only gazed at Clara, her face expressionless. "Of course."

Harland felt his fingers dig into his arm, unsure if he was happy with that. The use of Miss Wright's first name made him feel like a careful distance had been closed, an intimacy embraced. Which was absurd. He'd been on a first-name basis with many women, including every student of Clara's that he had ever worked with at Haverhall, and he had found it only expedient. Not erogenous.

Clara grinned. "Excellent." She returned to the table but merely leaned a hip against the edge of it. "Welcome to Avondale. My brother tells me you are a surgeon with considerable field experience."

He heard Katherine inhale sharply, and her eyes snapped back to his. Her face was no longer expressionless, but wary.

"I guessed," he felt compelled to say.

"I see." Katherine's words were clipped.

"Is he correct?" Clara asked.

"He is," she said after a moment.

"Where?"

Katherine traced a patterned whorl on the rug with the toe of her boot. "Spain. Prussia. France. Belgium."

It was Harland's turn to inhale. She had described the movements of Wellington's army as they chased the French madman across half the damn continent.

"And you have midwifery experience as well?" Clara continued, as if she found nothing remarkable about Katherine's surgical revelations.

Katherine looked up at her, her expression still guarded. "Yes. It's how I started. It is what I do a great deal of now that I'm back in Dover."

"Then you are knowledgeable about intercourse? Pregnancy? Methods in which the latter can be prevented while engaging in the former?" Clara pressed.

Harland resisted the urge to interrupt. He knew Clara was doing this on purpose. There was nothing like putting an individual off balance to get a genuine reaction that would indicate their intentions and beliefs.

"You're referring to sponges? Pessaries? Washes? French

letters? Coitus interruptus?" Katherine's eyes were fixed firmly on Clara, as if she were issuing her own challenge.

And Harland wondered why he had ever thought he might need to intervene.

"I am." Clara stepped out from behind the heavy library chair. "You seem well versed and comfortable with the subject."

"I might say the same."

The two women gazed at each other.

"I've watched too many women die in childbirth," Katherine said eventually, her voice hard. "Some surrounded by their families, but many others shunned, alone, and terrified. I've treated babies that have been left to perish by women unable or unwilling to care for them. Seen unwanted children consigned to charitable homes that are only a small step up from hell. Those things make me uncomfortable. Showing a woman how to properly soak a letter or pessary does not."

"Mmm."

"I'm sorry, but is there a point to this?" Shades of suspicion and distrust were back.

"Would you consider sharing your knowledge?" Harland asked, doing his best to keep his manner professional.

"With you?" she asked incredulously, turning to stare at him.

"With my students," Clara corrected.

Katherine's gaze snapped back to Clara. "What students?"

"Every summer I personally select a number of students to take part in the Haverhall School's summer term held here at Avondale. These young women are...very forward-thinking individuals, with aspirations that go beyond the expectations that society puts upon them. As part of their curriculum, I offer a class on feminine health and hygiene. Including a discourse on sexual relations and the consequences of those relations, be it pregnancy or disease."

Katherine frowned.

"I've finally shocked you."

"I'm not shocked. Just mystified." She paused. "I had assumed that your students were daughters of the aristocracy."

"Most are. Some aren't."

Katherine glanced at Harland circumspectly. "Is this a trick?" she asked. "Because what I know about the nobility would lead me to believe that most would just as soon see me strung up for sullying their daughter's virtue and purity with such…"

"Truth? Fact? Information?" Harland supplied.

"Yes." Katherine's jaw was set.

"I agree," Clara said. "And it is something that I am trying to rectify. Ignorance serves no purpose—it can be dangerous. But knowledge will empower these young ladies to make their own informed decisions when the time comes. Some of my students are lucky enough to have a servant or friend or family member willing to speak to them about such issues. Most are not. I've had more than one student confess to me she thought she was dying the first time she got her courses. Very few have been able to explain to me exactly how babies are made."

"I see."

"Yes, I suspect you've seen more than you care to," Clara replied.

"Look, Your— Clara, while I admire your objectives, I'm not at all sure that your highborn students will care to hear about any of it. Certainly not from me." Katherine's lips thinned briefly before she wrestled her expression back into one of polite concern. "I'm not exactly their contemporary."

Interesting, Harland mused. She was doing it again. Using titles as a way to distance herself from young women who were the daughters of the wealthiest and most powerful of the British elite.

"I think you'll find you have underestimated these young women," Clara said mildly.

Katherine looked doubtful. She glanced once more at Clara before her incredible eyes settled on Harland. "You're a real doctor. Why don't you teach this class?"

"I would. Had intended to, actually, until I met you. And my sister and I both agreed that the students might be far more comfortable asking questions of an intensely personal nature of a female. Their *contemporary*. Should you be amenable to the arrangement, of course."

"But I'm not a real—"

"It is not impossible to be real and female and a doctor all at once," Harland said.

Katherine stared at him, her expression softening into one he'd never seen before, devoid of her constant caution. It was a look as if he'd just unexpectedly gifted her with something priceless and she wasn't sure what to do or say. Thank the gods she hadn't looked at him like that last night when she stood a whisper away from him in a tiny room under the eaves. Or he might have given in to the urge to kiss her.

"You will, of course, be paid for your time," Clara said.

Harland saw Katherine straighten at the mention of money, and her attention once again went back to Clara. He knew very well just how desperate things were in the Wright household. He'd quietly helped Matthew and Paul out on occasion when presented with the opportunity to do so without injuring their pride.

"If you were agreeable to our proposal, I can give you a course outline that was used by your predecessor, who was also a midwife, or you can develop one of your own," Clara continued. "We had a class scheduled for tomorrow and a second a fortnight from now, but we can, of course, delay the first class if you require more preparation time. Additionally, given the nature of your work, we are certainly flexible should an emergency prevent you from attending."

A clock on the library mantel ticked loudly into the silence that fell.

"Very well," Katherine said finally. "I accept your offer. And I'll start tomorrow."

Harland tried to ignore the now-familiar thrill of anticipation and pleasure that winged through him at the thought of seeing Miss Wright on a more regular basis. At the knowledge that she would be at Avondale at least twice more.

"Excellent." Clara beamed and straightened from the edge of the table. "Welcome to the Haverhall School for Young Ladies, Katherine."

Chapter 6

Y ou ready?"

Katherine jerked from where she had been standing near the base of the cliffs, leaning against the cool stone. Dawn hovered on the horizon, the darkness just now giving way to a watery silver.

"Yes," she replied, wondering for the hundredth time if she had completely lost her mind.

"Appreciate you doing this," Hervey Baker said from somewhere beside her in the gloom where they waited. "The boys appreciate it too. Wasn't sure who was ever going to replace Matty."

"Not you?"

"Can't swim that good. None of us can. We owe you, Miss Kate."

"Mmm." Katherine had known Hervey since she was a child. Only a few years older than she and, like Matthew, had served in His Majesty's artillery corps. Unlike Matthew, however, he had a wife and five children waiting for him at home.

There are other families counting on me—on us. Families with children, she heard Matthew say in her head. *Families who have helped us out in the past.*

"Thank you," she said, guilt pushing deep in her belly. "For what you and Frannie did for my father. For taking care of him when I was away." She should never have left. Her father could have died.

"Well, of course." The man's voice floated back to her. "We're all in this together. Look out for one another, right?"

"Mmm." Katherine wallowed in her regrets and listened as the water thumped against the entrance to the cove.

Fog sat thick and heavy, obscuring their surroundings and beading moisture on her hair and skin. Once the sun vanquished the mists, one would be able to see the chalky white cliffs that towered above them, enclosing a cove that opened to the sea by only a narrow passage. A passage too small for large ships to pass through, but plenty big enough for fishing boats and smaller vessels to slip in and out.

The cove had been used for generations to import and export goods, though by no means in any official capacity. Her father had used this cove, as had her grandfather and his father before him. It was a place of great solitude and sanctuary and, more importantly, boasted a network of caves and fissures, concealed by tumbles of sloughed rock.

"No sign of patrolmen," Hervey said. "Had men watchin' all night to be sure, least until the fog rolled in. But if we can't see 'em, they can't see us either. 'Bout time our luck changed."

"Buhler and his men will not be happy they returned empty-handed last time," Katherine warned.

"Know the feelin'," Hervey grunted. "I would have said

we should probably wait a little longer before coming back here, but those tubs are still sittin' on the seafloor. Can't leave 'em too long. Chance they'll get ruined. Or the marker will pull loose, and we'll never find the damn things."

Katherine shivered in the cloying dampness. Not so long ago, she was sunk in a tub of steaming water. Now she was preparing to dive into the freezing embrace of the Atlantic. "Your men watching the water too? If he's smart, Captain Buhler will have learned from his mistakes and try to take the cargo out in the open."

"Then Captain Buhler better know his way around an oar. In this fog, he's as liable to get caught in a current and dash his boat into the rocks near the mouth as he is to find us. Their horses are no use out there."

Katherine shivered again, dressed as she was in light-weight cotton trousers and a tight-fitting shirt, both dyed a mottled black. She closed her eyes, still not quite believing she was back here again. She hadn't done this in a long time.

"The men are waitin' near the caves. Pete, Davy, and Jamie. You know all of 'em. Once we get the tubs to the beach, they'll get 'em away and hidden, and you and I will be long gone. Just like old times."

"Just like," Katherine muttered.

"You back for good?" Hervey asked.

"No plans to leave."

"That wasn't what I meant." He hesitated. "I meant are you back with us?"

Back into the web of smugglers.

"We miss you," Hervey rushed on into her silence. "Miss your mind and miss havin' you there to patch us up if we be needin' it."

"Dr. Hayward seems to be doing just fine looking after—"

"Aye, don't get me wrong, the doctor is a good sort. No questions, just sees to the fixing. But it's not the same. He's not one of us. Not like you."

"I'm not—"

"Your father always told us you were smarter than the lot of us. He was proud of you, you know. Still is, I reckon, even if you've only come back to dig bullets out of us from time to time now."

Katherine didn't answer, her emotions twisting themselves up into an impossible knot. These men had been part of her family too. And abandoning them, removing herself from the danger and the illicit trade that had once been her life, seemed like a betrayal. Even if it was the right thing to do.

Katherine pushed a strand of hair off her forehead. "Do you ever think about doing something else?" she asked. "Something other than smuggling?"

Hervey blew out a heavy breath. "Sometimes. But there isn't any other work for a smuggler whose only skills are the sea and service in the artillery corps. 'Specially now. Just ask Matty."

"If you struck out on your own—"

"Don't want to go anywhere on my own, Miss Kate. These men aren't blood, but they're family. Stuck with me through everything, including a bloody war. Matty'll tell you that too. Hard to turn your back on your brothers, you know?"

"I know." She closed her eyes and rested her head against the rock. This wasn't getting easier.

A long, keening whistle sounded that could have been the cry of a gull. Katherine knew better.

Hervey's boots crunched as he moved out onto the stony shingle. "Time to go."

Katherine double-checked the knife strapped to her thigh and slipped from her place against the base of the cliffs. She picked her way across the beach, following the just-visible bulk of Hervey. She walked gingerly, feeling her way across the uneven shingle with care. Somewhere up ahead came the unmistakable sound of a wooden hull being dragged into the water.

A breeze lifted a loose strand of her hair. "Better hurry," she said. A breeze like this would erode their cover more quickly than she would like.

"Aye." The shadow that was Hervey stepped to the side and another joined him. "Hop in, Miss Kate."

Katherine could make out the edge of the small fishing skiff, rising and falling as it was held against the surf. She clambered in, taking her place at the bow. It felt like a million years since she had done this and like she had just done this yesterday, all at the same time.

The small vessel was pushed farther into the water and then it tipped slightly as Hervey found his place at the oars. In minutes, they were surging silently forward into the cloud-like abyss.

The oars creaked, and the water slapped against the hull as the dampness swirled around them. On the port side, the fog was darker, grayer, and every once in a while, a shrouded mass of rock would appear and then fade. The thump of the surf against the base of the cliffs became louder. The vessel slowed.

"Here somewhere," Hervey said in a low voice.

Katherine turned, leaning far out over the bow, staring hard into the depths of the water. She had no idea how Hervey even knew where they were, but this wasn't the first time he'd oared for her. Experience had taught her that he was rarely wrong. He knew this shore better than the very sea did.

Her fingers tightened on the edge of the boat as the small vessel crept forward, gentle swells rocking it beneath her. The surface of the ocean was a dark canvas, the watery light glinting dully in the surface. The float would be a brilliant white and without the blinding glare of the sun, would be easier to see. Twilight or dawn, those were the two best times to—

"Stop." Katherine was already reaching for the length of rope coiled at her feet without taking her eyes from the water. "I see it."

The float was suspended eerily below the surface, like a bright moon rising from another world. She heard Hervey grunt slightly as he hauled on the oar to keep the vessel steady against the pull of the water.

"On with you, then, Miss Kate." Hervey secured the far end of the rope to the gunwales. "I've got you."

Katherine tied the rope around her waist in movements long remembered. She took a few deep breaths and stared at the surface rising and falling beneath her. Without giving herself time to reconsider, she dove.

She had, however, forgotten just how cold the water was. It stabbed at her everywhere, rendering her stultified and motionless for a fraction of a second. And then old instinct took over, and she pulled herself ever downward through the darkness, her eyes fixed on the brilliant sphere that hung before her eyes. It was always deeper than it looked, she remembered, and she forced herself to measure her motions.

In moments, she had reached the float. She slipped the rope from around her waist and looped it deftly over the glass sphere with old, practiced movements that hadn't faded with time. By feel, she knotted it neatly to its tether and gave the rope two hard tugs before kicking upward, her lungs beginning to protest.

Her head broke the surface, and she sucked in a deep breath. The small boat was just in front of her, and she could see Hervey already hauling up the heavy load, hand over hand. Katherine stroked over to the boat, her teeth beginning to chatter, feeling unaccountably weary as she treaded water, waiting with her knife. She heard Hervey curse softly as he strained against the weight, and then she heard the bump of the tubs as they hit the hull of the boat. Quickly, she swam over and cut through the portion of net weighted to secure them. The stone weights fell away, sinking immediately, and Hervey hauled the net and the tubs into the boat. He offered Katherine his hand, pulling her back into the vessel with the same quick efficiency.

"Got it on your first go, Miss Kate," Hervey said, sounding impressed. "Like ridin' a horse, isn't it?"

Katherine wrapped her arms around herself and hunched against the cool air. "Horses are warmer." Another breeze caressed her skin, and the air seemed to shimmer and brighten. "Better hurry," she said. "Wind's picking up, and the fog will clear. I'd prefer not to be caught sitting out in the middle of this cove with a fortune of French brandy at my feet."

"You and me both." Hervey resumed his position by the oars and hauled.

The little fishing vessel leaped forward, wind now chasing them. On the starboard side, the cliffs loomed above, the crevices and crags much clearer than they had been only minutes ago. Katherine shifted, feeling dangerously exposed, even though the fog on the surface of the sea was still thick.

"I'll take 'er as close to the caves as I can get," Hervey said. He looked worried.

She tipped her head and scanned the tops of the north cliffs. Patches of green were now visible, as the sky beyond lightened further, silver starting to give way to blue.

"Hurry," she urged. If there were soldiers up on the edges of those cliffs, if they had been detected, then they would be sitting ducks. Fish in a barrel.

"I'll get—"

"Shh." Katherine put her hand up, a sound that was out of place on the water reaching her ears. Bouncing across the surface, it was difficult to tell what it had been, where it had come from, or how far away it was.

"What do you hear?" Hervey whispered, going still.

Katherine shook her head. There. It came again. A dull grinding sound, followed by a muted splash. The sound of an oar rotating on its pin as the blade hit the water.

"We've got company," she murmured, moving sound-lessly to the port side, her eyes straining to see through the fog.

"Up top?" Hervey whispered.

Katherine shook her head. "On the water."

"Shit," Hervey swore.

Katherine knew as well as he did that there would only be one other person out on the water. No fisherman in his right mind would risk taking his boat out in fog like this.

Another gust of wind danced across the sea's surface, and the fog dispersed, just enough for Katherine to see the unmistakable shape of a boat nearly the same as theirs, drafting low in the water under the weight of a dozen soldiers bristling with guns held at the ready.

A shout went up as the fog closed back in, but it was too late. They had been seen. And with only a single man at the oars, they were at a distinct disadvantage. Katherine's heart lodged firmly in her throat. There came more shouts, and now the sounds of oars plunging into the water with hard frequency was audible.

A vision of Hervey Baker—a bullet hole in his barrel chest, his wife and children sobbing over his body—assaulted her.

Katherine whirled on Hervey. "Take the boat in. As quietly and as quickly as you can. Get it unloaded and get out of this cove."

"Wait, what—"

She didn't hear whatever he was going to say because she had jumped overboard and was underwater now, angling away from the boat and the beach. She surfaced, slapping her palms on the water and kicking furiously. Her efforts were rewarded with a frantic cacophony of shouts and orders and the sound of oars banging against the hull. They were reversing in her direction. Thank God.

Katherine treaded water, trying to control her breathing and trying to get her bearings. She looked up, focusing on the tops of the cliffs, just visible in the dissipating mist. She was much closer to the beach than she had thought, which was good news for Hervey and the rest of the men. Now she just needed to keep the attention on herself for a few moments more. And try not to drown or get caught in the process.

She started stroking toward the base of the cliff that jutted way out from the beach, her body rising and falling with the swells. The hissing of the surf as it broke and slid over the rocks became louder. Somewhere on this edge there was an indentation—an almost flat ledge of rock that she had swum to as a youth. Above that ledge, the sea had carved out a deep crevice. Almost impossible to see from the water, it was her only choice. Her only hope, really.

Even if she wasn't trying to draw the soldiers away from the beach, she could not possibly outpace a boat full of men. If she swam deeper, closer to the mouth of the cove, there was a very good chance that the ocean would save the soldiers the trouble of shooting her. She was a good swimmer, yes, but not invincible. The sea was king, its justice impartial and instant, and she had seen far better swimmers than she drown from arrogance and recklessness.

Something slapped at the water close to her, and a sharp crack echoed above her head. Another smack, another delayed report. They were shooting at her. Shooting blindly in the direction of the noise she had made.

Katherine swallowed her terror and focused her concentration on the dark shape of the rocks just in front of her. She let the swells push her closer, trying not to fight the sea, trying not to tax limbs that were already heavy and sluggish with cold and fatigue. She was looking for a point, a jutting formation of rock— There. It suddenly loomed out of the fog before her, and she kicked hard, reaching out a hand to keep herself from getting pushed into it.

Beneath her touch, the rock was rough and covered with slippery vegetation. The swell dipped, and she was sucked around the side. Another bullet cracked off the face of the cliff above her head and sent fragments of rock raining down above her. She gathered her strength and made one more effort, trying to reach the ledge before the ocean pulled her away and out of its reach. Her fingers touched rock and then slipped away. She was going to get pulled out toward the sea—

A hand clamped around her wrist in a merciless grasp. She was unceremoniously hauled up and over the ledge, the rock scraping painfully at her legs. Had she not been so shocked and exhausted, she might have fought. As it was, she simply allowed herself to be yanked from the sea like a half-drowned mermaid.

Katherine was deposited on her rear, and instantly her wrist was released and a strong pair of arms snaked under her arms and across her chest. She found herself pulled to her feet from behind.

"We have to hurry," a voice whispered in her ear.

A very familiar voice. Her head snapped around in shock and confusion.

"We're losing the fog," the Lord Doctor murmured against the side of her head.

His arms slipped from under her arms, apparently satisfied that she was steady enough on her feet. But then he grasped one of her hands with his and half pulled, half guided her across the ledge, farther up and away from the sea, the surf hissing around their ankles. He put his free hand over her head as they ducked beneath the overhang that Katherine remembered well. With an unerring sureness that no bloody Lord Doctor should have about coastal caves, the baron led the way deeper into the twisted shadows, not letting go of her hand as she stumbled on unfeeling legs.

The sound of her ragged, gasping breaths echoed off the surfaces around them, but she didn't stop. Nor did she yank her hand from the Lord Doctor's. There was a time for questions and a time for demands, and this was not it. Not until they were safe.

"Follow me." She felt, rather than saw, the Lord Doctor turn as he led her even deeper.

Katherine wondered where he thought he was going. The wide crevice wasn't that deep, and they were concealed as they were. Still, she allowed herself to be guided forward, her legs numb, the rock rough on the soles of her feet.

"Through here." The Lord Doctor had stopped, urging Katherine in front of him. She balked at the darkness that lay before her, the light filtering in from the entrance not enough to penetrate all the way back here.

"Through where?" she managed through chattering teeth.

The Lord Doctor took a firmer grip of her hand, stepping in front of her, and once again guided her behind him. She felt the air change, the coolness replaced with a damper, more stagnant air, and the darkness became absolute. The back of the crevice as she knew it wasn't a back at all, but a doorway to a deeper chamber.

Gently but relentlessly, he kept pulling her forward until they came to an abrupt stop. She stumbled into him, her muscles clumsy and tired, his arms steadying her.

She should move away, she knew. And she would. In a minute. But right now, the warmth of him after the freezing cold of the ocean was too great a temptation. Add to that the sudden weakness of her limbs as terror drained, leaving her shaking. For this moment, she would simply rest against him, regaining her breath, her wits, and her strength. Let his warmth soak through the pitifully thin cotton of her clothes. Which reminded her that she was dressed essentially in a shift. With legs and arms. She would worry about that too.

In a minute.

The Lord Doctor twisted and moved, and then something gloriously warm settled over her shoulders and against her back. His coat, she realized. His arms pulled her tightly against him once again. Only this time, only two thin layers of damp linen separated their bodies.

"What the hell were you doing out there?" he asked in a mild voice.

Dammit, he didn't get to ask questions. She didn't have appropriate answers prepared. Besides, she should be the one who got first stab at this line of inquiry.

"F-f-funny," she stuttered, her teeth chattering. "I w-was going to ask you the s-same."

"You first." He sounded angry now, though he was pushing her wet hair away from her face with the tenderness of a lover.

She should move away, she told herself again. Instead she closed her eyes and let her head rest against his chest, listening to the steady beat of his heart. "I c-crawled out my lover's w-window and fell into the s-sea."

"Try again."

"Th-that excuse worked for my brother."

"No lover worth his salt would ever let you crawl out his window."

Katherine would have blushed if she hadn't been so cold. "W-went for a m-morning swim."

"A morning swim?"

"I f-find it invigorating."

"Invigorating."

"Are you going to continue to r-repeat everything I say?"

"Just the parts that are preposterous."

"Well, then, you should know that I w-was having a lovely time until I came across a Lord Doctor hiding in a damn cave."

He exhaled. "A lovely time."

"Why is that part so preposterous?" Her shivers were abating.

"Because you were being *shot* at."

"Mmm. Yes, I suppose I could have done without that bit."

"Have you lost your mind?"

"Mmm." It was a possibility. She was, after all, being embraced by a baron-turned-doctor she shouldn't trust. She was half-naked and sopping wet, having narrowly survived a smuggling run. That she had lost her mind was more than a possibility, she reflected. It was quite probable. And that was one more thing she would care about. In a minute.

"What about you?" she asked in the interim.

"What about me?"

"Have you lost your mind? Or perhaps just your way? Awfully few patients in this neck of the woods, I should think."

"Jesus Christ, Katherine. We're not talking about me. We're talking about you and how you could have been killed."

Her fingers had curled against his shirt, where they were trapped between them at the sound of her name on his lips. It stole whatever breath she'd just regained. *Katherine* suggested an intimacy even greater than two bodies crammed into a cave.

"What were you *thinking*?" the baron muttered against the top of her head.

"I was thinking," she said into the front of his shirt, "that I could draw the soldiers away from the boat. I was thinking that a father of five should return to his family today. Hervey Baker is needed."

"So are you."

"That is kind," she said, her voice still muffled. "But

Matthew and my father have both managed to get along just fine without me. I'm not saying they wouldn't miss me, but they certainly don't need me. Not the way Hervey's family needs him."

The Lord Doctor was quiet, only the sounds of their breathing audible.

Katherine lifted her head, wishing she could see his face. "How are you even here?"

"I stopped at the Bakers'," he said, not loosening his arms. "Their youngest had an abscessed tooth last week. Frannie told me that Hervey was down at the cove. It didn't take much imagination to guess why. I thought I'd stay close, in case someone needed medical attention. Especially after what happened the other night."

Katherine frowned into the blackness. "But how were you on that ledge? And in this tunnel or whatever it is?"

"I was on the beach when I heard the shots out on the water. I came around to get as close as I could."

"You came around?"

"There really is an echo in here." It sounded like he was grinning.

Katherine ignored his humor. "So there is a back door."

"Yes. It's more of a crevice than a door. In the north corner of the cove, just above the high-water mark. If you know where to look."

"And you just happened to know where to look?"

"Yes. The Earl of Rivers has two aunts who are very fond of fossil hunting—"

"Yes, I've met them. They told me as much."

"And years ago they told me about this passage that they stumbled across. I explored out of curiosity."

Katherine could feel herself scowling at his neat, tidy answers.

"I'm not an idiot, Miss Wright," he said. "I know what Baker was doing out there. Or at least, I have a good idea—I don't want to know the specifics. But what I do want to know is what the hell you were doing with him?"

"I have retrieval skills," she muttered.

"Retrieval skills?"

"Did you hear that? Another echo."

"And you're making yourself sound like a bloody spaniel sent over the heath after a brace of dead pheasants."

Katherine pulled away from him a little more, and cool air snaked up to whisper unpleasantly against her damp skin. She tugged his coat more tightly around her.

"I swim," she allowed. "Which is occasionally required in the recovery of . . . certain lost items."

"I see."

"I doubt you do, but it is rather irrelevant at this juncture and of little concern to you." She took another step back for good measure, only to be brought up short by a wall of rock at her back. She frowned again. "As much as I've enjoyed this little parlay, do you think we might remove ourselves? I am, if you recall, due to be teaching a class this morning at Avondale, and while your sister seems like a remarkable woman who doesn't put a great deal of weight on appearance, I think that even she would have a problem with mine currently."

"You might be right." He sounded amused. "What is it that you call your current outfit?"

"Freezing," she gritted between clenched teeth.

"Ah. Well, we can't have that." In the darkness, he found her hand and tucked it into the warmth of his palm. Katherine knew she should remove it but couldn't bring herself to do so.

"And were you planning to wear this home?" he asked reasonably.

"No. There was—is—a dry shirt and trousers hidden on the beach."

"Ah. I can retrieve them for you if you like."

"Why would you do that?"

"Because I want my coat back. It's my favorite."

"Right." Katherine wasn't sure if she should believe him or not. "I'd appreciate it, thank you," she said gruffly. She owed him that at least. The alternative was to ... what? Wait until darkness fell and creep home? Shiver and shake until she dried in this damp cave or hope Hervey or one of the men came back looking for her and brought her clothes?

She almost snorted. None of the men were going to come anywhere near this cove for a good long while now. Another thought struck Katherine. "Will you tell her? Your sister? About me and this..." She trailed off, belatedly considering that she might have sunk her chances at a generous salary before she had even cast off. It was unlikely that a smuggler would be welcomed in the hallowed halls of the Haverhall School for Young Ladies.

"Tell her what? That you swim in the morning for the good of your constitution? I don't see why it would be important to her."

"Right." Instant relief trickled through her, followed quickly by suspicion. "You seem rather cavalier about this."

The Lord Doctor snorted. "Whose house is of glass must not throw stones at another."

"Did you just make that up?"

"George Herbert did."

"Who is George Herbert?"

"A poet, among other things, but we digress here. My

point is that you seem to be taking getting shot at with a peculiar amount of calm."

"It's not the first time I've been shot at, my lord."

"*What?*"

Katherine waved her hand in dismissive impatience, which was ridiculous because he couldn't see her anyway. "Forget I said that. I can assure you that it won't happen again." *Probably*, she added silently. "You have my word. Do I have yours that this...incident will be forgotten?"

The Lord Doctor was silent, his fingers still tight around hers. "Yes."

Oddly enough, Katherine believed him. "Thank you, my lord."

"Stop calling me *my lord*. Harland is fine."

Harland was most assuredly not fine. *Harland* suggested a closeness and affection and partnership that she didn't want to feel. Though given that she was standing nearly naked wrapped in his coat made that an absurd topic to argue at this point.

"We might have to wait a little longer before we can leave," he cautioned. "Make sure that the...cove is empty. I'll go first."

"And if it isn't empty and there is a boatful of His Majesty's finest waiting on the beach?" she demanded. "How are you going to explain yourself?"

"I simply followed the sounds of the shots. I'm a doctor. Someone might be hurt. And save for my coat, my clothing is currently dry, which is proof that it certainly wasn't I who threw himself overboard like a lunatic. In fact, I'd even offer to help search for such a lunatic who surely must be drowned by now."

"How magnanimous of you."

"Isn't it?"

"I still don't understand," she said abruptly. Dammit, but she wanted to see his face. Just like before, she didn't like having these conversations where she couldn't read his expression.

"What, precisely, is it that you don't understand?"

"You."

"You'll have to be a little more specific."

"Why you would take my side."

"I like you. I don't like the captain. I like the captain even less when he is shooting at you."

"Be serious. What I've done—what I'm doing—is wrong."

"Wrong for who?" he asked, and there was no amusement left in his voice.

That stopped her. "It's not just wrong. It's illegal."

"Well, there are many things that are legal that are wrong and many things that are illegal that aren't."

Peculiar words from a peer. "Like what?" she asked.

She felt his fingers tighten on her hand. "It doesn't matter."

"I rather think it does."

He was silent.

"I'm a criminal," she pressed recklessly.

"You're a woman who jumped into the water to save a family their husband and their father. A woman not only able and willing to save her brother in the physical sense, but also a woman who went to extreme measures to keep him hidden without hesitation." He stopped. "If you want to add criminal to that, I suppose that is your prerogative, but that's not what I see when I look at you."

Heat rushed to every inch of her skin. Her heart was hammering in her chest at an unnatural pace, and all she could concentrate on was the feel of his skin against hers where he still held her hand. She heard him move in the darkness, and then she felt the palm of his other hand graze her cheek. The air was sucked clean from her lungs, and her stomach somersaulted in a most delicious manner.

"I don't like labels," the Lord Doctor whispered in the darkness.

Katherine swallowed. This was dangerous, whatever was happening here. But then this entire morning had been dangerous, and perhaps it was remnants of what had happened in the cove—the thrill of survival, the rush of terror and triumph that gave a person inhuman power in the moment and then made them weak as a kitten in the aftermath. But standing in this cave, the recklessness still lingered. Still whispered in her ear and set her body on fire.

"I don't like to be told what I can and can't do. What is right and what is wrong based on nothing but preconceptions and ignorance." He stepped closer. "I don't think you do either."

Katherine might have shaken her head.

His hand that had grazed her cheek now traced the edge of her temple, where water still dripped from her hair. He shifted, and his lips brushed across the skin where his fingers had just been. She closed her eyes, a longing settling deep into her chest that was so acute it was almost unbearable.

He moved again, and now she could feel the warmth of his breath against her neck, and his lips grazed her cheek. Every nerve ending she possessed prickled with awareness. Her breasts grew heavy, and an ache lodged between her legs.

He was asking permission, she knew. All she had to do was turn her head. All she had to do was take what her body wanted so badly.

"We should go," she whispered instead.

The relief that she should have felt from that rally of strength was horrifyingly absent.

The Lord Doctor went very still. The air around her swirled as he pulled away, though he kept her hand in his. "You're right. We should."

Chapter 7

Harland should have known.

He should have known who would replace Matthew Wright at short notice. Paul had been one of the most prolific smugglers in the entire county of Kent until his wound had ended his participation. It had been natural that Matthew would step into his father's place, bringing with him his inherited knowledge of the coast, his clever attention to detail, and his absolute loyalty to his men.

It stood to reason that Paul's daughter would be just as adept. And just as selfless.

Harland, of all people, should have known just how thick blood ran in families. He should know just how far people would go to take care of those who they love. Because he had done things he'd never thought he'd do to save his own family.

Harland had been in that cave, concealed on that ledge long before the sun had struggled over the horizon, because time was of the essence and because he had a stake in the brandy that still sat at the bottom of the sea. What he hadn't realized at the time was how much of a stake he had in the woman he'd pulled from it.

Katherine Wright made him feel emotions he didn't want to feel, as evidenced by his all-consuming impulse to protect her at all costs. She made it hard for him to think, at least about anything that didn't involve the sensation of her body pressed up against his. She made it difficult for him to invent lies and excuses on the spot, and even worse, she made it hard for him to remember why he had to. Dammit, he wasn't smitten anymore.

He was besotted.

He had been besotted once before. Desperately, hopelessly besotted. It had blurred reality, bathing everything in a drunken glow of misplaced faith and imagined love. It had made him discard judgment for blind devotion, objectivity for overwhelming desire. When the beautiful Lady Patrice Neville had accepted his proposal, he'd genuinely believed it wasn't his family's fortune or the decadent lifestyle that she had loved. That it had been him.

He'd been a fool.

It hadn't taken long after their wedding for his vision to clear. And after the death of his wife and the storm of scandal that had followed, his few amorous relationships had been meaningless beyond the brief physical pleasure that both parties might find. Emotion and attachment had been deliberately absent, and subsequently, so were the preoccupations and distractions that accompanied such.

Distractions like Katherine Wright were downright dangerous.

It was bad enough that she was now involved in this smuggling network. It would be disastrous if he allowed himself to become involved with her on a far more personal level. Aside from muddling his focus and concentration at times when it mattered most, she made him want to believe in things he had long since stopped believing in. Made him want things he had promised himself he would never allow himself to want again.

He was smarter than he had been then. And he could prove that to himself by taking great pains to give Miss Wright a wide berth from here on in. Avoid her whenever and wherever possible—

"Lord Strathmore."

Harland started and then whirled to find a familiar man just inside his dressing room, examining the tip of a small knife and frowning fiercely.

"Dammit, Gibbs, someone is going to shoot first and ask questions later one of these days."

"You're without a firearm. I made sure. It wasn't hard given that you're also without half your clothes."

"As people found in dressing rooms are wont to be when the doors are locked."

"Your windows weren't locked." The short, blond man was still frowning at his knife. "Hmph. I damaged the tip on the frame."

"Serves you right." Harland reached for a fresh shirt. "You're lucky you didn't fall two stories to your death."

The man he knew as Patrick Gibbs made a face. Harland was quite sure it wasn't his real name. "You have trellises that run right up to the second-story windows. You might want to think about changing that."

"Housebreakers aren't so common in Dover as they are in London, Gibbs."

"I'm not a housebreaker. I'm a butler."

"I don't know how."

"I'm very good at opening doors."

"And windows."

"Exactly," Patrick agreed, eyeing Harland's discarded coat that bore faint but evident saltwater stains. "Were you swimming, my lord?"

"No." That was all he was going to say about that. Harland pulled the shirt over his head. "If you've come looking for the last shipment of Boulogne brandy, it is now on its way. There was a slight, unavoidable delay with its retrieval. It should arrive in London the day after tomorrow."

"I'm not here to inquire after brandy."

Harland already knew that. But one could hope. "Ah. Then what brings you all the way out to Kent?" He suspected that the answer to that question would be not so much a *what* as a *who*.

"I was hoping you'd ask." Gibbs slid his small knife back into its sheath and crossed his arms. He was around the same age at Harland, lithe and muscular, and looked more like a tumbler in a traveling circus than a butler in a fine London home. "Your London colleague has sent me to beg a favor on his behalf."

Harland retrieved a waistcoat and slipped it over his shoulders. "A favor?" Favor, his ass. This was an order.

"Nothing you haven't done before."

Harland worked the buttons unhurriedly. He had done a great many things for the man he knew only as King. A man who controlled the London underworld with a power that most monarchs could only dream of. A man who had offered Harland a lifeline to save his family's shipping company that had teetered on the edge of financial ruin after his parents' sudden death.

For a price, of course.

That price being Harland's loyal service along the Kentish coasts for twenty years. The voracious illicit markets in London demanded to be fed a never-ending supply of brandy, tobacco, lace, and silk, and all manner of specialty items, and in return, produced staggering profits for those who financed them. Men like King who sought out men like Harland to achieve their mutually beneficial ends.

Strathmore Shipping was no longer in danger of bankruptcy, his family no longer in danger of ruin. In fact, the ledgers of the now-thriving business showed a quiet accumulation of substantial wealth. Yet Harland's debt of service to King was far from recompensed.

"King wishes to double our shipments of silk and tobacco? More orders for lace?" As Harland spoke, he already knew that all of that was wishful thinking. The unexpected appearance of Patrick was telling. King wanted something far more complicated than that.

Patrick uncrossed his arms. "He's got other men and women along the coasts who can do that sort of menial math," he confirmed. "What he needs is someone with skills far greater than the mere transfer of imports. Skills like yours."

Harland blew out a breath. "How many this time?"

"Four."

"Four? That is going to make things difficult. Even with our connections at Newgate—"

Patrick shook his head. "They're not at Newgate Prison."

"Then where?"

"Woolwich."

Harland looked up at the ceiling as if he expected to find a different answer there. He found none save the obvious one. "Are they aboard one of the hulks?"

"At the moment, yes."

"And how am I supposed to get them off—"

"That is my job," Gibbs interrupted. "I've done it before. Your job is to keep them alive during transport."

"Transport to where?"

Patrick sniffed. "France, obviously. A specific port wasn't mentioned at the time of my departure." He crossed the short distance soundlessly, his movements fluid. The man was like a bloody panther. "They'll be moved up the river."

Harland grimaced. "The Thames and its estuaries are saturated with blockade men and spies. You can't move a damn muscle without someone noticing. King may want to consider moving them overland first, then use the oyster boats farther up the Kent coastline the way we've done with the other prisoners of war." Another commodity that had proven wildly profitable for King.

"I believe that was contemplated. However, the final consensus was that they are not healthy enough to survive such a journey. They might not even survive extraction."

"You've confirmed that they are actually alive?"

"For now. Though it was suggested that at least one will require a lower leg amputation to remain so. Hence the reason King asked for you specifically."

"Who are they?" Harland asked.

"I'm made to understand that all four are the youngest sons of French aristocrats who managed to maintain possession of both their heads and their fortunes after the revolution. They are willing to pay handsomely to get their progeny back."

"If they are aristocrats, surely there are alternate channels they can go through."

"The boys are all seamen. Valuable commodities. You know how tetchy the English are about giving back trained, experienced seamen to the French navy."

Harland did. Each prisoner had likely started their training at sea when they were seven or eight.

"Age?"

"The youngest of the boys was twelve when he was taken. Just before all the drama started at Quatre Bras."

Harland bit back a muffled curse. Good God. Training or not, the youngest had been a child when he was taken prisoner. He'd be seventeen now. Not yet a man. Yet still a prisoner of a war no longer being fought. He couldn't even begin to imagine how the child had managed to survive this long.

Harland had been on prison hulks. He'd seen the condition of the common prisoners of war who had fallen under his temporary care. Those vivid memories erased any twinges of guilt he might have felt at the idea that returning French prisoners to their country was a betrayal to his own. There was no excuse for the conditions that they had endured and somehow survived.

Harland tried to keep his expression neutral. "I suppose it's wishful thinking to believe that payment is in coin. Or liquor. Or—"

"Art," Patrick confirmed. "Your portion of payment and those to both my London crew and our French contacts will, of course, be made in coin for services rendered, but the clients will be paying King with something more… irreplaceable."

Harland scowled. Art was the most difficult of the contraband smuggled, but he was doing it more and more often as of late. It was often big and unwieldy and required a great deal of care. It couldn't be sunk, and it couldn't be hidden in false hulls or towed underwater. It couldn't be stashed in the damp of the caves and tunnels, and it wasn't easily disguised and concealed during transport.

Though he couldn't argue that it wasn't lucrative. The cut Harland received for successfully bringing in a contracted shipment of art was substantial. Which meant that the payments he anonymously distributed through Matthew Wright were also more sizeable than a typical run of lace or brandy.

"When?" Harland demanded.

"A sennight from now."

Harland laughed. "You're joking."

"I already have my men and contacts in place. King wants you in London yesterday. He sent me to make sure that happened. He also wants you to personally handle the artwork that you will collect upon delivery and bring to London. As such, he wishes to assure you that he will make this worth your while. Double your usual fee."

"Why does he need me to collect it?" Harland snapped, ignoring the mention of money for the time being. Money did a dead man no good. And Harland had developed careful measures over the years to minimize the chance of that sort of fate. For everyone involved. "There is an established network of men here who are quite capable of bringing in cargo," he continued. "The same network I use all the time."

Patrick shrugged. "Don't shoot the messenger."

"I can't leave on such short notice."

"The boy—the youngest—will be dead if we leave him any longer. And possibly his brother, who languishes in chains next to him."

"Says who?"

"Says the guards on the hulk who have demonstrated their happiness to pocket my coin in exchange for their... inattentiveness. We need to get these prisoners back to France alive."

Harland cursed.

"Two days to London. A day to extract the prisoners. Three, maybe four days up the river and across the channel. It shouldn't be a problem."

"It wouldn't if we were traveling with healthy men," Harland growled. "You said there are at least two of them languishing just this side of death. If their condition has deteriorated to the point that you say, and if I need to start amputating pieces to keep them alive, I can't treat them all myself. I'll need help. The medical kind."

"King won't like it."

"I don't see that he has a choice here."

"Then do what you need to do," Gibbs replied. "Because you're going to have to move fast whether you like it or not. This is a tight window of opportunity we're working with."

Harland cursed under his breath again.

"Don't you teach medical students here? Bring one of those with you," Patrick suggested.

Harland goggled at the man. "I'm not inviting the young daughter of a bloody earl to a Woolwich prison break if that is what you're suggesting. No matter how open-minded she might be. She won't yet have the skill to treat the sort of injuries and wounds that I suspect our prisoners have, and there are limits, Gibbs. I will not be responsible for turning a potential countess into a criminal. At least, not deliberately."

Patrick withdrew his little knife and examined the damaged tip again. "Surely you know another surgeon," he tried. "A chap you served with who is seasoned and can be counted on for his discretion?"

Harland shook his head. "It's been years since I last saw any of the men I—" He stopped.

And shook his head again. The idea flitted along the

edges of his mind, and he let it go because it was foolish. But it circled round and came back and lodged firmly front and center where he couldn't ignore it.

"Two days from now," Patrick said. "We need you in London in two days. Your patients will need you then too." The diminutive man moved out of the dressing room and back in the direction of the window. "I will tell King to expect you?" It wasn't really a question.

Harland heaved a sigh. There wasn't really a choice in answers either. "Yes, dammit."

Yes, he would travel to London to do whatever needed to be done. He could not refuse a request from King without reneging on their original agreement, and he could not refuse a request from a patient in need without reneging on his oaths as a doctor.

But he needed help.

Harland would not, under any circumstances, present the former of those two reasons to Katherine, but he could present the latter. He was certain that Katherine Wright would not turn her back on anyone in need, regardless of who they were or where they came from.

It was only a matter of convincing her to do so with him.

Chapter 8

Katherine had changed and braided her hair neatly, spending far more time on her appearance than she normally did. As she approached Avondale, she realized that she was nervous. She had never taught anyone anything before—had never been in a position where she would ever be paid for sharing her knowledge and skill. The idea was as thrilling as it was foreign.

Katherine circumvented the front door and went around back to the kitchen entrance she had used the last time she had arrived with her brother and the Lord Doctor. She wondered if he would be here. Part of her hoped that she wouldn't have to see him. The other part of her desperately hoped she would. Because he had been on her mind all morning, her imagination playing with what the outcome would have looked like if she had only turned her head in that cave, pressed up against him. If she had met him halfway.

What would have happened if she had not retreated?

She knocked on the kitchen door and waited. And waited. But no one answered. Hesitantly, she pushed the heavy door open. There wasn't a soul in sight. A fire was banked in a massive hearth to her left, and the air was thick with delicious smells. Pepper and bread and something savory. Katherine's stomach rumbled in response. There hadn't been much to eat at home. Perhaps if she was lucky, she'd get something here. Maybe even enough that she could take some home to her father.

The sound of feminine voices interrupted her thoughts, filtering from somewhere deeper in the house. Katherine went forward cautiously, half expecting someone to appear and demand to know why she was here. She passed the pantries and made her way along a narrow hallway, pushing open the door at the end to find herself in what was clearly the grand hall of Avondale. In the center stood a round wooden table, a massive vase of cut flowers lending the air a pleasant fragrance.

To the right, the wide, impressive staircase soared up to the next floor, the walls lined with gilt-framed portraits similar to those she had seen hanging upstairs. The windows set into the wall on either side of the main door let in a flood of late morning light, almost glaringly bright against the gleaming marble floor.

Laughter, clearly a woman's, drifted from a partially open door on the far side of the hall. It was immediately followed by a low baritone, smooth and sure, and Katherine recognized it instantly as the Lord Doctor's. A buzz of pleasure fluttered deep within her, igniting an instant heat. She remained motionless. If she was going to teach in this house, if she was going to earn her salary, she would need to better prepare herself to cross paths with the Lord Doctor on a regular basis. Yes, his actions had proven him to be a man of a peculiar honor, even if his motivations were murky. Yes, he had woken wants and needs and imaginings she had thought long dead. And yes, dammit, she liked him. But she would never pursue—

"Good morning."

Katherine started and spun. She found herself being examined by a man who was leaning against the wall and peeling an apple with a small knife. He was tall and golden blond, his complexion rich from hours spent outdoors and his rough clothes marking him as a groom, perhaps. Or maybe a gardener. Secondary to those first impressions, but no less plain, was the horrific scarring on the left side of his face. It had reduced his left eye to a twisted ridge of faded scar tissue and continued over his cheek and underneath the collar of his coat. A close-range artillery burn, Katherine guessed, one that very likely should have killed him. But it hadn't, and Katherine wondered at the treatment that had prevented—

"You're the surgeon," he continued, catching a piece of peel before it dropped.

"I'm sorry?"

"The surgeon hired to teach here. Am I right?"

Katherine nodded. She had thought to introduce herself here as a midwife but—

"I knew it." The man neatly sliced a piece of apple and impaled it with the tip of his knife. "You know how?" He didn't wait for her to respond. "Because you're looking at me the same way Strathmore does."

Katherine blinked. "Umm..."

"Like you're fascinated as opposed to horrified by my face. And wondering if I would sit down with you over tea and answer a dozen medical-type questions. Am I right?"

Katherine fought a smile that suddenly threatened, completely disarmed by this man's open, easy manner. "Not entirely."

"Oh?"

"I'm more inclined to whiskey than tea."

The man laughed. "I can see why Strathmore's enamored."

Katherine felt herself blush. Again. And she hated it. She did not want to think that she had been the topic of the Lord Doctor's discussions with Avondale's staff, even if his words had been complimentary. Especially if he was being complimentary. Because words like that stole her breath.

"Forgive me and my informality," the golden man continued, saving her from having to come up with a suitable response. "Eli Dawes, Earl of Rivers, at your service." He sketched a small bow. "Welcome to Avondale."

Katherine felt her jaw slacken. Surely he was jesting. Because otherwise he was another grand lord who was acting nothing like a grand lord. Who was acting nothing like she needed him to act, because she had already decided that she liked this man. She didn't want to like an earl. Just like she hadn't wanted to like the Lord Doctor.

"Katherine Wright," she managed. "Interim teacher. And . . . surgeon." There was clearly little point in introducing herself as anything else since the Lord Doctor had very obviously taken the liberty of doing so.

The earl pushed himself away from the wall. "Well, then, Miss Wright, please don't let me hold you up. But while you are here, you should know that my staff is at your disposal. Whatever you need." He made a face. "You won't be ordering bits from the butcher to pick apart, too, will you?"

Katherine had lost the thread of the conversation. "Um. No?"

"Thank God." Rivers popped the piece of apple into his mouth.

"Thank you for your hospitality," she tried, attempting to at least address his kind offer of assistance.

Rivers swallowed. "Of course. A pleasure to have you here," he said as he started in the direction of the kitchens. He paused briefly, turning back. "Strathmore is holding court in the drawing room if you were looking for him," he said as an afterthought. "Enjoy the rest of your day."

"You too," Katherine responded, though the earl was already disappearing.

She was left standing in the hall, alone again, feeling quite out of sorts. Another chorus of giggles drifted across the polished marble from the partially open drawing room door.

Hayward was holding court? What did that mean? Though by the sound of the feminine laughter, she had a pretty good idea. There was, without doubt, no shortage of callers who came to Avondale dressed in their finest hoping to ensnare a prospective bridegroom. Dover was a long way from London, and a sophisticated, wealthy, handsome, unmarried baron would be irresistible. The marriage-minded mamas here might not possess the glitter and the glamor of their London counterparts, but she was quite certain that they would possess the same ambition.

Not unreasonable at all. Expected even.

And not any of her business. Or her concern. What was her concern was the class she was scheduled to teach. She should, at this moment, be seeking out the duchess—Clara. She should be determining where, exactly, she would be teaching her class and show the headmistress of Haverhall School for Young Ladies what she planned to start with. The students must be sequestered somewhere. A watercolor class, perhaps outside in the gardens? Or perhaps a music lesson? That would most likely be on the second floor somewhere. Katherine started in the direction of the staircase, pausing as its base, her hand resting on the ornately carved bannister.

More laughter danced across the hall, followed by the Lord Doctor's voice.

And Katherine spun, heading for the drawing room.

She crossed the hall, slipping soundlessly through the partially opened door and stopping just inside the room. It was a bright, airy space, made so by the long windows that dominated the opposite wall and the pale, creamy color of the room. There was a minimum of decor, and Katherine frowned as she realized that the heavy rug had been rolled up and left on the far side near the empty hearth, the small tables and chairs that would have sat upon them set neatly aside.

In the center of the room, the Lord Doctor sat on a simple chair with his back to her. He'd discarded his coat, his shirtsleeves pushed informally up to his elbows. A dark-haired woman, her back mostly to Katherine, was standing next to him. She was young, no more than seventeen or eighteen. Dressed plainly, but the hallmarks of privilege were unmistakable. A pair of small sapphires dangled from her ears. A graceful, pale hand rested on the back of the Lord Doctor's chair.

"Feel it," the baron murmured to the woman, and she turned slightly and reached forward. The Lord Doctor caught one of her hands, guiding it down in front of him out of sight. Katherine heard him murmur something that she couldn't quite make out and saw the young woman nod before she closed her eyes, a look of fierce concentration on her face. The Lord Doctor made a sound of approval.

The ground seemed to drop out from beneath her, and Katherine struggled to take a full breath. No, no, no, no. She had wanted to believe better of him. So, so badly. And she hadn't realized how badly until this moment.

"Explore the firmness. Can you feel the difference?" the Lord Doctor asked.

The young woman nodded.

"Good," he continued. "Follow the length to the base."

There were words crowding into Katherine's mind in a disorganized cacophony, words that she needed to say, needed to shriek, but Katherine couldn't seem to speak, frozen in horror. She looked around frantically, waiting for someone to say something, only to realize that there was nobody else in the room. No maids, no chaperones, nobody. No one to stop this.

The Lord Doctor murmured something again, and the woman laughed again, that low, musical sound Katherine had already heard. The young woman turned to gaze at him, and the delight and rapture on her face was obvious from even where Katherine stood.

"That's incredible," the woman said.

"Isn't it?" he agreed.

Their heads were close, far closer than would ever be considered proper in a well-appointed drawing room. The woman closed her eyes again in concentration. Katherine wondered if the Lord Doctor would continue his seduction and reach up and run his fingers along her cheek the way he had done to her in a tunnel not so long ago. Press his lips to her temple and then claim her lips. Do what Katherine had wanted him to do before sanity had reasserted itself. The thought was excruciating. Mortifying. Infuriating. All of those things mixed together in a poisonous brew that made her feel almost ill. Enough was enough—

"Miss Wright, do come in."

Katherine jumped.

"I can see you in the mirror," the Lord Doctor continued without turning around, and Katherine's eyes flew to the far wall where a massive mirror hung over the hearth. She met his dark eyes, the top of his head just visible along the bottom of the gleaming mirror. "Your timing is impeccable."

"For what?" she croaked, trying to find her equilibrium. A furious burn of anger roared through her, and she embraced it. She stalked forward into the room. How dare he take advantage of a young, naive—

"The aorta."

Katherine stumbled to a stop, certain that she had heard him incorrectly. The woman at his side had turned fully and was regarding Clara with pretty gray eyes. But they held no apology and no shame. No embarrassment or unease. Just mild curiosity and welcoming interest.

"Suzette, may I introduce you to Miss Katherine Wright. Miss Wright is a midwife and, additionally, an accomplished surgeon in her own right. She will be teaching your women's class just after luncheon, but in the meantime, if I can trouble her to attend our lesson now, I suspect she would have a great deal to add to our current investigations." He hadn't looked away from her in the reflection of the mirror.

Katherine took a ragged breath and stepped closer. Now she could see a small table set up in front of the Lord Doctor, a tray balanced on the surface. The Lord Doctor had his hands on the edges of the tray to keep it steady.

Suzette's fingers rested on a heart.

A porcine heart, Katherine thought belatedly, the upper left and right atriums already dissected, the scalpel laid neatly next to the organ on a small towel.

"Suzette is my sole medical student this summer," the Lord Doctor continued on in that easy, imperturbable manner of his. "Law and architecture seem to be the more popular of the arts this year."

"They don't know what they're missing." Suzette grinned.

"Agreed," the Lord Doctor replied.

Katherine stared at Suzette and her bloody fingers and then at Harland Hayward. Medical student? That statement made no more sense than the scene before her. "What are you doing in here?"

"The light is best in Avondale's front rooms," Suzette explained. "The housekeeper doesn't mind if we use them for dissection so long as we move the rug first."

"What?" She still didn't understand what was going on.

"It's hard to get blood out of wool," the Lord Doctor murmured.

"Today we are examining the heart," Suzette continued brightly. "Specifically, the path and propulsion of blood through the arterial system. Tomorrow we will dissect both the kidney and the liver. Important organs, but not nearly so fascinating as the heart. Well, at least in my opinion."

Katherine closed the remaining distance, unable to resist, coming to stand just opposite Suzette. Most definitely a porcine heart; she recognized the shape.

"Do you have any experience with the heart, Miss Wright?"

The Lord Doctor's question was said with cool professionalism, but his eyes held hers with an intensity that sucked the air from her lungs. An intensity that suggested he was asking something far deeper, something far more personal than mere anatomy.

Yes, she had had experience with the heart. It was something that had almost destroyed her, and it was something she never wanted to repeat.

"I have," she replied, aiming for the same cool tone. She had no idea what the hell was going on here, but she would not allow this baron a window into the darkest parts of her past. "Forgive me," she said to the young lady called Suzette. "But I'm not entirely sure..." She trailed off, not entirely sure what it was she was not entirely sure about. She made a vague motion in the direction of the tray for lack of anything more intelligent.

"This is part of my anatomy prospectus," Suzette explained.

That didn't help.

"Ah." Katherine nodded anyway as if this made perfect sense. Because as an instructor at Haverhall School for Young Ladies, she should know things like this.

The tall clock out in the hall chimed the hour, and Suzette frowned. "It can't possibly be that late already, can it?"

The Lord Doctor dipped his hand into the pocket of his waistcoat and came up with a battered-looking pocket watch. He flipped it open with a deft flick of his wrist. "It is."

Suzette's frown deepened. "I had hoped to have both ventricles dissected before I diagramed."

"Diagram what you can. Focus on the arterial and the venous systems that are visible here. You can diagram the ventricles later. The organ is fresh, and it will keep awhile longer."

Suzette sighed and nodded, wiping her hands on the small towel. She carefully collected the tray and scalpel. "It was lovely to meet you, Miss Wright," she said earnestly. "Would there be any chance that I might observe your work sometime? Midwifery has always interested me."

Katherine blinked. "Um."

"At your convenience, of course, and so long as the patient has no objections."

Katherine nodded again because she had no idea what else she should do.

"Thank you, Miss Wright. And thank you again, Dr. Hayward," Suzette tossed over her shoulder as she made her way through the door, with a heart on a tray.

"Where is she going?" Katherine asked, and then cursed the inanity of that question. Of everything that she could ask, of everything that wasn't making sense right now, Suzette's destination was irrelevant.

"Art class," the baron said, as if that should be obvious. He rose from his chair and wandered over to the rolled rug near the hearth.

"Art class? With a pig heart?"

"She's working on anatomical diagrams."

"In art class?"

"That's what I just said." He nudged the rug with the toe of his boot, letting it unroll and flop back into place. "My other sister, Rose, is an artist and teaches here at Haverhall. Among other places," he added.

"And they draw pig hearts?"

"Suzette does. And only this week. The other students will be working on subject matter relevant to their own field of study or interests. Next week they will study the human form as it appears in the classics. Titian first, if I know Rose. Sometimes Botticelli."

"I didn't know," she mumbled.

"Clara doesn't advertise Haverhall's...unorthodox summer curriculum," the baron said as he replaced the set of embroidered chairs back on the rug. "It is taught in Dover and not London for that reason. The curriculum each student has goes far beyond the boundaries of acceptable learning for young women. I mentor the medical students. There is a barrister in town who does the same for the law students, an hotelier who looks after accounting and anything to do with hospitality, and an architect who has placed aspiring masons, artists, and draftsmen. Draftswomen, I suppose."

"Why didn't anyone mention this yesterday?"

"I think Clara wanted you to meet the students before you judged them." He stopped, and Katherine was aware he was studying her. "Both my sisters are well acquainted with the lack of tolerance for *different*."

Yet even as she had agreed to this position, Katherine had already been judging Haverhall's students. Judged them for nothing else than the sin of having the prefix of *lady* before their name. It was humiliating and humbling all at once.

The words Strathmore had spoken earlier, the words she had dismissed so scornfully came back to her now.

While I cannot pretend to know exactly how it feels to be a woman battling the prejudices of society, I can tell you what it feels like to be a man born to a title that is not to be trusted with a vocation outside of cards and horses, mistresses, and money.

"You too," she said.

The Lord Doctor leaned on the back of a chair. "Me too what?"

"You are also acquainted with different."

"Yes." He slid his hand over the rounded chair back. "But I am not forced to hide it the way women are. I am a man, with a title and a fortune and those three attributes combined eventually seem to eclipse and excuse almost anything. Peculiar ambitions, objectionable behavior—"

"Lack of character. Absence of honor." She looked down. She probably shouldn't have said that. But dammit, the Lord Doctor had a way of making her say things that shouldn't be said. Like Matthew said, what happened in the past had nothing to do with—

"Who was he?" Strathmore asked.

She froze. "I beg your pardon?"

"The man who made you so cynical. So...untrusting."

Katherine remained mute, her focus still on her hands.

"He was titled, wasn't he?"

She willed herself not to react. Hell would need to ice over before she would discuss her past relationship with the Lord Doctor.

"Did you love him?"

Enough was enough. "I have no idea what you're talking about. *You* have no idea what you're talking about." This conversation was over. He was poking at things that were not his business. Not only did it make her unbearably uncomfortable to remember just how foolish and gullible she had been, but it was also quite possible that the baron moved in the same social circles as her former lover. She realized with a sinking feeling that it was quite possible he might know him. That the baron might even know that she had once warmed the bed of—

"I have a proposition for you."

"I beg your pardon?"

"Not what you're thinking. I haven't come up with something nearly artful enough for that." The baron sounded like he was teasing her.

Katherine's cheeks burned.

"I need help with a patient. Four patients, to be precise."

"I see." She aimed for a distant, detached tone. The Lord Doctor was giving Katherine the perfect exit from a conversation about love and propositions and unspeakable regrets. She grasped it with vigor. "What's their diagnoses?"

"I'm not entirely sure. Malnutrition, certainly. Topical lesions and subsequent infections most likely. Broken bones are a definite possibility, some old, some more recent. I am told that amputation may be a distinct possibility."

Katherine frowned. "How do you not know? Haven't you seen them?"

"Not yet."

That made no sense. "Where are they?"

"London."

"What?"

"You heard me. They're in London. And I need you to come with me."

"No." It was instant. And harsh. It had to be, because there was a part of her that wanted to say yes. The same reckless, foolish part that had been drawn to this man from the moment she met him. But she had been down this road before. Had followed a man she wanted to be with so very badly across half a bloody continent. She'd let her feelings and longings blind her until the truth had shredded her heart and nearly broken her.

"You could at least consider it." He was studying her.

"Surely there are other doctors in London that you can ask."

Harland shook his head. "No. There aren't. Not for this."

"I can't leave my father. He isn't well. And I just put four dozen stitches in my brother. He's not back on his feet yet." Those were the easy excuses.

"I'll have Suzette look in on your father and brother while we're away. Your father's condition, while chronic, will not worsen measurably in the next sennight. And if

Matthew's wounds were going to fester, there would be
visible evidence by now. He'll be fine—"

"No."

The baron didn't move. His expression didn't change;
his voice didn't waver. "It's a paid position. A position that
will earn you far, far more than what you've been paid to
teach at Haverhall."

Katherine could feel her hands curl, her fingernails biting
into her palms. The Lord Doctor was good, she would give
him that. He drove straight for the soft, vulnerable spots.

"I've already committed to teaching classes here." It
lacked conviction.

"Yes. One today. You'd be back in time to teach the
second. You won't miss your teaching wages on my account. What I'm offering is a chance to augment them
significantly."

Back to twisting the knife in her most vulnerable place.
"Why me?"

"Because I need a competent field surgeon who understands the value of utter discretion."

A horrible notion struck her. "Are you blackmailing
me?"

"*What?*" The Lord Doctor straightened as if she'd
slapped him.

"My discretion in return for yours? I do this for you, and
you keep my secrets from the cove this morning?"

"Jesus." He shook his head. "No, Katherine, I'm not
blackmailing you. God. What sort of man do you think I
am? What do I have to do to prove to you that I am not—"
He stopped and visibly gathered himself.

She had finally provoked him. Only to discover that
there was no victory in that.

"I am asking for your help. Not because I wish to bed

you or blackmail you or anything else that that suspicious mind of yours has come up with. But because you are a competent surgeon. A competent surgeon who can be trusted." His words were hard.

Katherine looked away, feeling uncomfortable. "These London patients. Where are they? Specifically?"

"Woolwich Warren."

The military base just east of London proper. "They're soldiers?" At least that was familiar ground.

"Not exactly."

She frowned. It had been a long time since Katherine had been there, but she recalled barracks, a foundry, wood-yards, and thick-walled artillery repositories. A host of other buildings bunched along the banks of the Thames whose purpose she could only guess. And tethered to those banks and mudflats, great, hulking husks of ships long past their prime, crammed full of prisoners who—

"Prisoners." The description he'd given would be accurate. The predicted injuries and his lack of real assessment.

"Yes." He paused. "And no."

"I don't understand."

"When we treat them, they will no longer be prisoners."

"They're being released?"

"In a fashion."

Katherine's eyes snapped back to his, everything suddenly very clear. His request for utter discretion. Why he had asked her, of all people in the first place, medical competence notwithstanding. And why Harland Hayward had, at every step, demonstrated a complete indifference to the smuggling that surrounded him. Because it seemed that he dabbled on the other side of the law too. "They'll be fugitives."

"French fugitives," Harland said, a hint of challenge in

his voice. "Seamen. Captured during the war and held here for these last years. The youngest was twelve when he was taken."

Katherine's flinched. A *child*.

It made her want to weep. God, she hated war and all its aftermath. There was no glory or honor in it, no matter what the poets said. It was only a dark morass of death and cruelty and pain and hopelessness that swallowed everything in its path. The lucky merely survived. And never looked back if they wanted to keep surviving.

She hardened her heart, afraid if she didn't, whatever pieces the war hadn't broken would crumble further beyond repair. "I understand now. You need to hire a criminal to help criminals."

"If you insist on calling yourself such, then that would make us the same, wouldn't it?" he asked. "For this isn't the first time I've helped French prisoners of war get back to France."

"We are not the same." Maybe if she repeated that enough times, she would come to believe it.

"That's not how I see it."

It didn't matter what he saw or didn't see. If he chose to split hairs. This was a transaction, no different than any other she had executed along the shores of Kent, except there were far more unknowns in this scenario than she had ever had to face. Starting with Harland Hayward. The biggest unknown of all.

"What's in it for you?"

"I beg your pardon?" He gave her a wary look.

"You're taking a significant risk. And I assume that there are others involved as well. I'm not so naive to think that this is done purely out of gallantry. There has to be some reward."

"Their families will pay a fee to have them brought home."

"To you?"

"To a…colleague. He arranges the logistics. And will pay me—us—to treat them so that they arrive home alive."

Which proved that everything could be bought and sold. Everything had a price. Everyone had a price.

She hardened her heart further. She hadn't come back to England to live like that. It was bad enough she was helping her brother. But that would end. And she would not start down this slippery slope again. "I can't help you."

"Because you don't trust me."

"I do trust you." It sounded weak, given all her actions to the contrary.

"Do you really?" His hands tightened on the back of the chair. "You thought I was ravishing my student when you walked in here."

Katherine stared at the polished floor, wishing it would open up and swallow her whole. What made it worse was that it wasn't an accusation. It was a statement colored only by faint disappointment.

"You thought I was taking advantage of a young woman because I could. Because my title and position allowed me to feel I could do so without consequence."

"No," she lied. Badly. Her voice was shaking, for pity's sake.

"I saw your face in the mirror. You looked like you wanted to run me through."

She couldn't meet his eye.

"I don't have an agenda here, Katherine," the Lord Doctor said wearily. The chair creaked beneath his hands as he shifted his weight. "I'm not trying to trick you or use you, or otherwise mislead you. You won't trust me enough to tell me who is responsible for all that bitterness that you carry around, but take it from me, holding grudges is exhausting."

He wasn't wrong. But he wasn't right, either. "But sometimes, it's the only thing that gives you the strength to survive." She brought her eyes back to the baron's and found his hadn't wavered from her. "Sometimes a betrayal cuts so deep it makes you want to curl up and die." She knew she didn't need to say these things. Didn't need to explain herself. But dammit, the words kept coming and she couldn't stop them and Harland Hayward was there, just listening. "And if you don't embrace the hate that it left behind, then you have nothing."

"That's true," he agreed simply, and Katherine could feel the potency of his gaze crackle all the way through her.

He spoke the truth. Deep in her bones, she recognized that he knew. He knew what it felt like to have hope stripped away. He had known the same bleak despair.

She looked at him helplessly. She needed him to argue. Needed him to tell her that she was being unreasonable and vindictive because there were old emotions rising hard and fast and, if she sank any further into his steady understanding, she was going to drown. She hadn't ever talked about what had taken her from Dover and then brought her back. Her brother and father knew the bare minimum, just enough to understand why she did not ever wish to speak of it.

"But there comes a point when you have to let it go," he said. "The hate."

She swallowed with difficulty. He made it sound easy. Like taking off an apron or a pair of shoes and tossing them in a corner to be forgotten.

"Have you?" she asked suddenly. "Left your hate behind?"

He looked startled. Like he hadn't expected her to ask

that question. She saw his hands slide from the back of the chair and then he moved, coming to stand directly in front of her.

This close, she could see the faint lines around his dark eyes, the rich red hidden in his mahogany hair pulled back in its customary queue. Her fingers itched to pull it loose. Run her hands through the thickness of it. Draw his head down to hers to taste him. The way she should have done in that tunnel.

"Sometimes," he said.

"Sometimes?" She needed to step away from him. But she stayed right where she was.

"It's easier here."

"In Dover?"

"With you."

Katherine froze.

He was looking at her, a longing that she recognized all too well clear in his eyes. The same sort of longing that even now was surging through her and making her entire body heat and tingle in anticipation. He lifted his hand, carefully, cautiously, as if he expected her to bolt.

Katherine couldn't move. Couldn't breathe.

He traced the side of her face with his fingers, the way he had done that morning in the dark. Tracing the same path with the same reverent gentleness. Only this time, there was no darkness for her to hide behind. Nothing to conceal the desire that ignited the moment his skin had touched hers. She remembered the way he had felt beneath her hands this morning. Remembered the way his muscles had flexed and bunched as she had leaned into him, the way his arms had curled around her.

She remembered how much she had liked it. Wanted it. Wanted him.

At the time, she excused her reaction as a reckless response to the fact that she had narrowly avoided death. A temporary heightening of the senses, as it were. But here, in this room, with no smugglers, no soldiers, and no darkness to hide behind, the recklessness and the want hadn't subsided. They'd only intensified.

The baron took another half step closer, and Katherine's hand came up against his chest in the exact place it had been this morning. Over his heart. She could feel it banging beneath her palm.

"You are...unexpected," he said.

"I don't know what that means."

His brows drew together, as if he was searching for words. His fingers dropped to play with the end of her braid, the backs of his hands brushing the curve of her breast. "You make me feel things I don't..." He trailed off.

"Things you don't want to feel," she finished for him. Because this Lord Doctor was unexpected too. And because no matter what she tried to tell herself, they were indeed the same. Different. Alone. Untouchable. Until the moments when they weren't. In a cottage. In a tunnel. In this room.

And she was so damn tired of being untouchable.

"Yes," he agreed on a whisper.

She reached up and slid her hand around the back of his neck, her fingers finding the leather tie. She pulled it free, and his hair fell forward. She pushed her fingers deep into its thickness the way she had wanted to. She heard him catch his breath, his eyes hot.

Her hand against his chest slid up, his heart thundering at a pace that matched her own beneath her touch. The fingers of her other hand curled against his scalp.

"I shouldn't want this," she whispered. "I shouldn't want you."

"I know." It was barely audible.

"I'm not..." She wasn't what? Strong enough to walk away? Brave enough to risk taking what she wanted? Taking what she needed?

"I know." He dropped her braid and caught her hand with his, pressing it against the hard muscle of his chest. "Don't let go."

And then he kissed her.

It was a soft kiss, gentle and slow, giving her all the time and space that she would ever need to escape. Not that she had the power to do so. His kiss streaked through her like lightning, leaving her shaking. Her skin suddenly felt feverish, her clothing too restrictive. A restless ache settled low in her belly, an undeniable need pulsing in time to the pounding of her heart.

Everything around her faded, leaving only him. His touch, his scent, his strength. The can't and wouldn't and shouldn't that had shored up her defenses and defined the last few years of her life receded, leaving a broken landscape of need and want and hope.

It should have terrified her, this instant, uninhibited response to him. But then she felt his other hand slide up her back, pulling her closer to him, and she offered no resistance. This was as it should be. She was right where she should be. Her hand tightened in his, holding on for dear life.

Until a door slammed somewhere in the hall, and she was catapulted back into reality. She stumbled away from him, her hand slipping from his.

"My lord—"

"Harland," he growled. "You don't get to do this to me and then call me *my lord*." He was breathing hard, desire still blazing from his dark eyes.

"Do what?" she rasped.

"Make me want. Make me feel this much." He impaled her with a look so raw and so hot that she felt it sizzle through her chest and lodge between her legs.

She reached out with a hand to steady herself on one of the chair backs.

"Say my name, Katherine."

She was fighting for breath, fighting to find her balance against a riptide of confusion and need.

"I'm not him, dammit. Say my name."

"Harland," she whispered, unable to say anything else.

She saw him close his eyes briefly, his fingers flexing before they relaxed again.

The sound of footsteps rang across the marble, stopping as Lady Theodosia abruptly appeared in the doorway, looking piqued. She was dressed in her worn shawl, her familiar basket over her arm.

"Dr. Hayward," the woman said, her cheeks flushed from the outdoors or indignation or both. "Captain Buhler is here. He says it's urgent."

Chapter 9

Harland blinked at the woman who stood in the doorway, trying to get his bearings. Trying to fight through the fog of lust that had him completely disoriented and dazed. He should never have done that. Never in a million years should he ever have kissed Katherine Wright. It didn't matter how extraordinary she was. It didn't matter how much he wanted her. It didn't matter how violently he had despised the stark grief that he had seen on her face when he had gone prying into things that he should never have gone prying into.

He had wanted to make her forget. Forget whatever it was that had wounded her so deeply. Forget and heal. But he, more than anyone, should know that it was never that simple. Some things could never be healed. This urge to protect her had only gotten stronger.

But Harland was well aware that he couldn't protect her from her past. But he could do whatever was necessary to protect her from whatever danger Captain Buhler of the First Light Dragoons was bringing with him.

Apprehension crawled down his spine, but at least it cleared the fog around his senses. He couldn't protect Katherine from her past, but he could protect her from the immediate future.

"Are you available, my lord?" Theo inquired, smoothing her expression back into one of polite indifference, though Harland could still hear the distaste in her tone. Neither she nor her sister liked the captain and his unannounced visits to Avondale any more than Harland did.

"Yes, yes, he looks quite available." The captain strode into the drawing room. "And I trust I'll find him much more forthcoming with information than he was the last time we . . . visited."

Tabby was hot on the captain's heels, her own indignation visibly simmering at the intrusion. "I asked the captain to wait in the hall for you, my lord. He must not have heard me." She pinned him with a glare.

"Miss Wright." Buhler had stopped, ignoring Lady Tabitha, his eyes narrowing as he raked Katherine from head to toe with his gaze. "Good heavens. The other night I truly believed you hovered at death's door, yet here you stand, looking pretty as a rose. Your recovery is astounding. Miraculous, even."

Harland resisted the urge to fling himself in front of Katherine. Instead, he turned to the women who were still hovering near the door. "Thank you, Lady Tabitha, Lady Theodosia," he said coolly. "I'll take it from here." They didn't need to endure whatever grievance or accusations the captain had come to Avondale with this time. In fact, he didn't really want them hearing whatever the captain was going to say, especially if it involved what had happened out in that cove this morning.

Tabby sniffed. "I think we should stay."

"Indeed," agreed her sister. "Who knows what odious things a man with such odious manners might do."

"One would expect better from an officer."

"Everything has changed so much from when we were younger," Theo muttered. "Such behavior would never have been tolerated."

"'Tis a wonder he didn't tie his horse in the hall."

"Don't be giving him ideas." Theo made a face. "It would ruin the floors."

"And the furniture."

"'Tis a wonder anyone would tell anything of import to such an ill-mannered man. I certainly wouldn't."

The captain was staring now at the elderly sisters, pure contempt written across his face. "Consequences of treason or obstruction of justice are not limited to the common masses. You may wish to reconsider your tone."

Theo gasped. "Did he just call us traitors?"

"Surely not," Tabby replied, looking down her nose in clear outrage.

"I'm quite certain the captain would not be so uncouth as to imply anything of the kind," Harland said, an edge to his words. "Isn't that correct, Captain?"

Buhler inclined his head marginally.

"Very good. Now, please do not allow us to detain you any longer, Lady Tabitha, Lady Theodosia. I will give the captain the audience he seeks before he is back on his way."

"Very well. Just make sure he does not upset the students." Tabitha sniffed with disdain.

"I'll remind you, Captain, that the girls are the daughters of very powerful people who will not look kindly on an assault on their delicate sensibilities," Theo warned.

"Or a slur on their integrity," Tabby added.

The captain's lip curled unpleasantly.

Both sisters harrumphed and turned on their heels, departing the way they had come.

Harland faced the captain, moving slightly so he was partially blocking Katherine. "Miss Wright, may I present Captain Buhler of His Majesty's First Light Dragoons. You wouldn't have been aware, but he was...temporarily present during your infirmity."

"Ah. I see." Katherine's face was a convincing shade of red. "Well, I'm much improved, thank you for your concern," she said.

"Indeed." Buhler's eyes were now lingering on the end of her damp braid, and the tiny hairs at the back of Harland's neck stood up. Or maybe he was reading too much into that. Maybe the officer was just staring at her breasts. It was hard to tell.

"What a...coincidence that I should find you here with the doctor again," Buhler continued. "This morning of all mornings."

"Not so much a coincidence as a necessity," Harland said carelessly. "Miss Wright teaches here. Like Lady Tabitha reminded you, the Haverhall School for Young Ladies lets Avondale from the Earl of Rivers."

The captain's lips thinned. "I'm aware and in no need of reminders."

"Very good. So tell me, what brings you to Avondale today, Captain?" Harland continued in a bored voice. He moved to the side of the room to retrieve his discarded coat and shrugged it on. He returned to where Katherine stood, positioning his body so that he was fully between the captain and her. "I trust Private Melnick's wrist is mending to both your mutual satisfactions? Has a problem developed?"

The lines around the captain's mouth tightened in displeasure as he was forced to address Harland. "I did not come here to discuss Private Melnick," he said coldly.

Harland already knew that. But he didn't like the hostile way Buhler had planted himself in this drawing room. And he didn't like the way he had been looking at Katherine at all.

"Oh?" Harland feigned distant interest. "Then what can I help you with?"

Buhler shifted so that Katherine was once again in his line of sight. "Your brother, Miss Wright. Have you seen him recently?"

Harland's muscles tensed, and he wondered if the captain had brought soldiers with him. If they even now waited outside. Though the captain would search Avondale over his dead and bloodied body.

"My brother? No." Katherine's response was perfectly baffled. "He gets jobs on the oyster boats and is gone for days, sometimes weeks at a time." She paused. "Perhaps my father would know which vessel he's out on."

"Your father belongs in Bedlam," the captain snapped. "Like those two old biddies who were just here." He took a step forward. "May I remind you that liars are not treated kindly, Miss Wright?"

"I beg your pardon?" she gasped with just the right amount of affront.

Harland once again stepped in front of the captain, blocking his path. "Are you now accusing Miss Wright of something, Captain?"

Buhler didn't budge. "Not yet." His eyes swiveled away from Harland, trying to see Katherine again before they came back. "I don't suppose you've seen Matthew Wright since we last spoke, Lord Strathmore?"

"Regrettably, I have not. Is this why you are here? You could have saved yourself the trip and just sent a message."

"There were men in Avondale's cove again this morning, Lord Strathmore. Smugglers. Out on the water."

"This morning? In all that fog?" He tried to make it sound incredulous.

"Our riflemen flushed one into the sea." The captain's eyes drifted back to Katherine's damp braid, and an icy finger of trepidation slithered down Harland's spine.

"And this man requires medical attention?" Harland allowed impatience to drift into his tone.

"That was what I was hoping you could tell me, Lord Strathmore. He may have been shot."

"You think this man might have come here seeking help?"

The captain tapped his toe. "Did he?"

"Of course not." Harland scowled.

Buhler's lips twisted. "Someone knows where he went. Where he is." His eyes were still boring into Katherine.

"Have you considered the very real likelihood that a man out in that frigid water, in the fog, under a hail of your riflemen's bullets, is quite dead?" Harland said testily.

"There was no body."

"It would have sunk, Captain. If you like, I can give you a lesson on the variables that affect the decomposition required to make a drowned body float, but instead I suggest that you monitor the beaches over the next few days if you're hoping to find your dead man. You might get lucky, though any fisherman along these shores will tell you that the currents are unpredictable." Harland crossed his arms over his chest. "Many a man has been lost to the tides, never to be seen again."

"Perhaps." Buhler still hadn't taken his eyes off Katherine.

"Is there anything else, Captain?" Harland wanted this man gone. Away from Avondale, away from Katherine. Buhler wasn't clever, but he was cruel and ruthless, and he was becoming bolder and more brazen as time went on. Harland stalked to the door and pulled it open, his dismissal of the Captain unmistakable. "If I see or hear from Matthew Wright, you will be the first to know. But now Miss Wright has a class to teach, and I have a number of patients to see this morning. One of whom currently convalesces in your own barracks." His fingers drummed irritably on the edge of the wood.

Buhler's frown deepened at the dismissal, and an indignant flush stained his jowls. He set his hat back on his head and made his way to where Harland waited, pausing at the door. "I'll be watching your every move, Miss Wright," the captain said, and even a half-wit would have heard the threat in his voice. "Who you speak with, where you go, what you do. And if I find out that you are indeed lying about your brother and his role in the criminal activity that is a scourge on these shores, I will see you punished along with him and anyone who helped you along the way. Traitors to the crown die an unpleasant death, Miss Wright." He stroked the hilt of his sword. "Eventually you will make a mistake. And I'll be there to see it."

Chapter 10

I'll *be watching your every move, Miss Wright.*

The captain's words echoed in her mind over and over. If that threat had made her uncomfortable when it was uttered, by the time she had finished teaching her first class to the young ladies of Haverhall, she was feeling bloody well nauseous. And not on behalf of herself.

I will see you punished along with him and anyone who helped you along the way. Traitors to the crown die an unpleasant death.

She couldn't be here. She or Matthew. Matthew's presence here at Avondale might be a well-kept secret, but her overt role here only turned eyes in the very direction she wished to avoid. She could handle herself, but her presence here not only put Matthew at risk, it put everyone around her at risk, including the eight extraordinary young women she had just spent the last two hours with. Each one wealthy, most of them titled, and all of them, like everyone else in this damn place, nothing like she had once expected.

And dammit, she genuinely liked them all too.

None of this was ever supposed to have happened. This mess that she found herself embroiled in up to her neck had never been part of her plan.

Which is why she had to go. She just wasn't sure where.

There is an obvious solution, a small voice whispered in her mind.

An obvious solution, perhaps, until she had made the monumental mistake of kissing the Lord Doctor. No, not the Lord Doctor. Harland. Because now he wasn't a grand lord; he was a man. A man who made her body ache with his touch and his strength and made her heart ache with his kindness and compassion. Even though she'd been inexplicably drawn to him, she hadn't wanted to like him. And now she was so far past like that a retreat was damn well impossible.

I am asking for your help. Not because I wish to bed you or blackmail you or anything else that that suspicious mind of yours has come up with. But because you are a competent surgeon. A competent surgeon who can be trusted.

She believed him. And she believed that he believed in her. Which made the mess only that much more complicated.

She groaned and rested her forehead against the hard edge of a bookshelf.

"Was class that bad?"

Katherine spun to find the Duchess of Holloway leaning against the library door. Katherine straightened, smoothing her hair back from her face in an attempt to collect just a little bit of whatever composure she still had. "Quite the contrary. Class was that good." She meant it.

"I'm glad to hear it. Judging from their comments, the girls seem to really like you."

"I didn't do anything remarkable."

"You answered all of their questions with the unvarnished truth," Clara replied, wandering a little farther into the room. "You have no idea how remarkable that is for some of them."

"Why do you do this?" Katherine asked abruptly.

"Do what?"

Katherine tried to organize her words into a question that wasn't horribly rude. Or arrogant or ignorant. "Suzette is studying medicine while she is here. What happens when she goes back to the world she comes from? What good will it do her?"

Clara considered Katherine, her dark eyes so like her brother's. "How did you start? As a healer?"

Katherine shrugged. "My mother was a midwife and a healer. I assisted her from the time I was small. When she died, I took over her practice." That was the truth, if not the whole truth.

"And you were good at it?"

"Yes." Katherine wouldn't add that her mother had also been a smuggler alongside her father. Katherine had been well schooled in that trade, too, and pairs of hands that could deal with inevitable injuries that occurred was invaluable.

"Why did you choose to go to war?"

"I believed I could help." Again, another half-truth. That she had followed Jeffrey Walton to war, convinced that she was in love and loved in return, was not something she was about to admit to this woman either. It made her sound exactly like the gullible idiot she'd been.

"You were not turned away."

"I chose to ask forgiveness rather than permission. I watched and learned from some of the best field surgeons. When the fighting started, men fell in hordes. Gender gave way to necessity. Anyone who could suture and extract bullets and clamp vessels and work a bone saw was readily admitted in the fight to balance the scales of life and death."

"I see."

"And I see what you're doing here, Your— Clara. But my story is different from that of Suzette's."

"How so?"

"The circumstances of my journey were . . . extreme."

"Extreme?"

"We were in the middle of a war. And I had the advantage that most of my patients were insensible. Desperate. Uncaring who helped them so long as someone did. I couldn't treat the officers, of course, only the common soldiers. There were limits then as there are now."

"Of course. The limits society applies."

"They're certainly not mine," Katherine muttered.

"Exactly," Clara said.

Katherine stared at her.

"I don't know where life will take these young women," Clara said fiercely. "But wherever it takes them, I want them to believe in themselves. To leave here with the knowledge that they can and they have. And that they may and will one day do so again. The limits they face are not theirs."

Katherine wondered why that made her feel like crying.

"Did you know my brother before? When you both served as surgeons in the war?"

"No." Katherine welcomed the question because it had an easy answer. "The army was too vast."

"Mmm." Clara ran her fingers over the neat row of books lined up on the bookshelf. "He said it took you a long time to come home after the war." It was a statement and a question all at once, and Katherine was sure Clara was wondering if those limits they had spoken of had played a role.

But Clara wasn't the first person to ask why it had taken her so long to return. And she had practiced the answer to that. An answer devoid of the reason that she hadn't returned and made up solely of the reasons she'd stayed. Because those were two different things.

"The aftermath of war—of a battle like that—leaves a great need for medical care. For men who were too injured to be moved. Men who couldn't go home."

"You stayed to treat them?"

"That's generous. Mostly, I stayed to watch them die."

"I'm sorry."

Katherine shrugged sadly. There had been Englishmen and Prussians and Frenchmen, all reduced to mere souls, devoid of labels, struggling to survive another day so that maybe, just maybe, they could go home.

Not so different than the French fugitives Harland will treat.

That little voice was back. Reminding her that what Harland was doing was what she had already done. These men—boys—hadn't been the victims of artillery or steel blades but of circumstance and fate, but they were dying all the same. They were enduring each day in the hope that they could survive long enough to go home.

I can't help you, she had said.

Which was a lie. She could help him. She could help those young men.

Because not only was she a surgeon, but she was also a smuggler.

As much as she had tried to avoid it since she'd been back, as much as she'd tried to turn away from it, there was no denying that once upon a time, in a different life, she had been good at that too. She knew the coasts on both sides of the channel; she knew the rivers and waterways that led in and out of London. She knew how to hide and how to lie and how to make herself invisible by being obvious.

Yet she had chosen not to help Harland for reasons that were selfish and inadequate.

And that was unacceptable.

I'm not him, Harland had told her, and at the time, she hadn't recognized the truth in those words. Harland was not Jeffrey. And she was not the infatuated girl that she had once been, either. She was not following her heart this time, desperately clinging to illusion and false promises of a future. If she did this, if she went to London with Harland, she'd simply be following her conscience and a sense of basic human decency. Those young men needed her.

"I'm glad you took a chance on us, Katherine. I'm glad you're here." Clara's voice jolted her.

"Yet the chance that you've taken on me is not a safe one for you and your family," Katherine said. And that was unacceptable too. "My brother and I need to go."

Clara's expression didn't change. "I was under the impression that your brother should rest where he is for at least another sennight."

"His continued presence is not safe for anyone here—"

"As much as my title does not define who I am," Clara interrupted, "I have recently discovered that there are, in fact, a number of benefits to being a duchess. The chief one being that I, and my husband, outrank almost everyone." She paused. "Dragoon captains do not signify."

Katherine looked down at her hands. Cleary, Clara had been briefed on Buhler's visit.

"Harland told me about it just before he left," Clara said as if reading her mind.

"Left?" Her words sunk in.

"For London. Something about a medical case."

Katherine felt a horrible sinking sensation, as if something valuable had slipped away from her. Something she had let slip away from her. "He mentioned it," she murmured.

"Well, he also made sure to mention you and your brother before he went. Look, I don't need to know how your brother came to be injured or what that has to do with you. Harland gave the both of you his word that you would be safe at Avondale, and so you shall. You are both welcome to stay here as long as you like."

The urge to cry became more intense, and Katherine gritted her teeth against the feeling. This was ridiculous. "Why are doing this? For me? For my brother? You don't know us."

"Harland doesn't talk much about what he saw or what he did in his service on the continent. But I know it still wakes him sometimes at night even now. I know that you would have seen and done the same. And I know that you have sacrificed part of your life to help those in need and did so in bold defiance of those who didn't believe that you could. Or should." She shrugged. "I base my judgments on actions, not words. They tell me everything I need to know about a person."

Katherine thought she might have nodded.

"I'm glad your class went well," Clara said, seemingly sensing that Katherine was out of words. Out of excuses, out of hate.

This time she did manage to nod. "Yes."

Clara retreated to the library door and paused. "Whatever you need is yours," she said, echoing the offer that the Earl of Rivers had already extended.

Katherine blinked. *There is an obvious answer*, her mind whispered again. One that would safely distance herself from Dover, from her brother, from everyone at Avondale. One where she could set her own selfish fears aside and do the right thing.

"I think," she said slowly, "that I need a horse."

Chapter 11

Harland tossed and turned, finally sitting up to light the sputtering candle on the tiny table beside the bed. Darkness had fallen hours ago, and he should be tired from a long day of travel. He'd made good time, and he should have been pleased that he would reach London tomorrow.

Except the farther he'd traveled from Avondale, the more he'd regretted leaving. Regretted leaving without Katherine, he amended. Twice he had almost turned back, only to remind himself that Katherine Wright had looked after herself her entire life and to think that she now needed him as her personal knight in shining armor was both ridiculous and presumptuous. He had handled the entire proposition badly, he knew. And kissing her had been idiotic. Perhaps if he had kept things professional and distant, Katherine would be here now, safe from the reach of Captain Buhler.

She had fled that drawing room the second the captain had left. Buhler's threats had been poorly concealed, and

Harland had no idea what the captain would do. He had no idea the lengths that the captain might go to arrest a smuggler and make an example out of him. Or her.

Harland had talked with both Clara and Eli before he left, telling them in no uncertain terms exactly what had been said and exactly what had been threatened. Eli had given him his word that both Katherine and her brother would be looked after. But now Harland wondered if he had done enough. She might not—

A knock on the door interrupted his thoughts.

Not again. The buxom innkeeper had visited four times since his arrival to inquire if there was anything that Harland needed. A fifth time, at this late hour, was absurd. And unacceptable. And he would make that very clear. He strode over to the door and unlatched it, yanking it open.

"I do not wish to be bothered—" He stopped.

"I can come back at a better time." Katherine shifted a bulky canvas bag over her shoulder. "But I'd prefer not to. I'm rather tired."

She was wrapped in a plain gray cloak, her champagne hair loose around her shoulders and breathtakingly windblown. Her cheeks were pink, making her eyes seem even bluer. She was like an ethereal light in the dark, drab hall of the inn. Like an angel who had appeared at the most unexpected time in the most unexpected place. Harland wondered, for a fleeting moment, if she was a hallucination. A machination of his mind and his worry. "Katherine."

"Were you expecting someone else?" Her eyes dropped to his rumpled shirt, untucked above his breeches, and his bare feet.

"Um. No. But not…just…I mean…" He trailed off.

"May I come in? Or would you prefer I wait out here until morning?"

"Yes. God, yes. Come in." Harland jerked and pulled the door open wider, ushering her into the room and closing the door quickly behind them, latching it.

"Sorry I'm late. Class went longer than expected."

"What?" His sluggish mind wasn't keeping up. He had clearly missed something somewhere. "How did you get here?"

"I rode."

"By yourself?"

She might have smiled. "You forget, my lord, that I am but a mere mortal. A woman of unremarkable birth and thus trusted to get herself places without a phalanx of protectors to safeguard her virtue."

"That's not what I meant. There are highwaymen. Thieves. Cutthroats."

"Of which I came across none." It was dismissive.

He moved to face her. "What are you doing here?" he asked, still not sure what he was seeing.

"You asked me to come. We didn't really finish our conversation to my satisfaction. And then you left before we could."

"What?"

The coolness of the night still clung to her, bringing with it the scent of the outdoors and one that was uniquely Katherine. She glanced around the sparse space, her eyes flitting from the washstand to the single chair to the bed. He saw her worry her bottom lip with her teeth, and suddenly all he could remember was how it had felt to taste those very lips. And how very badly he wanted to do so again.

"I accept your proposition," she said, dragging her eyes from the bed to his face.

His mouth went dry.

"Not what you're thinking."

"I wasn't thinking…" He wasn't thinking anything at all because his brain had ceased to function. His libido, on the other hand, suffered no such difficulties. A buzz of anticipation crackled through him, making his pulse kick. She was standing not an arm's length away from him, in the middle of a tiny room of a tiny inn in a tiny hamlet, and right now, she was his. Only his.

"How did you find me?" He had finally managed to put a reasonable question together. Because he hadn't used his real name, and he had generally avoided as many public spaces as possible.

She shrugged and set her bag on the floor and slipped her cloak from her shoulders, draping it across the back of the chair. "Your horse," she said. "You're riding the same one you rode the night you came to our cottage. The one you drove home. And I didn't think you'd stay somewhere busy, given the whole discretion requirement." She met his eyes. "It didn't exactly require a Runner to find you, though it took me a few stable yards before I found the right one."

Harland wondered why he would be even remotely surprised, given he knew exactly how clever she was.

"The innkeeper caught me looking at the ledger. So I told her I was your wife," she said casually. "She seemed disappointed."

"My wife." His mind, just starting to work once again, slid back into a puddle of libidinous thoughts.

"It seemed expedient. *Mistress* seemed awkward."

He wasn't going to survive this conversation. Not without kissing her again.

Katherine bent and grasped the strap of her bag, pulling it to the side before straightening. "I'm sorry I didn't answer you properly this morning. I can offer no excuse other than I was thrown by Captain Buhler's visit and wasn't thinking clearly at the time." It sounded like she had rehearsed the words because they came out in a rush.

Clear thinking was still eluding him entirely. "Captain Buhler's visit?"

"Yes. Given some time to reflect on the captain's words, I realized that my continued presence at Avondale, in Dover really, puts not only my brother at risk but everyone else at risk too. Your sister, her students, the earl's elderly aunts—"

"I spoke to the earl before I left to—"

"You didn't let me finish."

Harland fell silent.

"My father is—was—a smuggler. My mother was a midwife but also a smuggler, and not above using her legitimate trade as the perfect cover for her illegal one. It was how Matthew and I grew up, how we lived, what we became. But then my mother passed away and my brother and I left for the war. And while we were there, my father almost died at the hands of soldiers for the sake of a dozen tubs of brandy. Matthew almost died for the same reason. And then it could have been me, trying to finish what he had started."

Harland remained mute in indecision. He could see what this confession was costing her. It made him want to repay her in kind. Which was dangerous.

"I don't want to live like that anymore. I've seen too much death. I can't live expecting everyone I love to be shot or hanged because they stopped looking over their shoulder for a second." Her eyes held his. "Do you understand?"

"Yes." Because for years, he had been looking over his

shoulder too. "But this job will require us to look over our shoulders to a significant degree—"

"I didn't say I wasn't good at smuggling and other… lawless endeavors. I said it wasn't how I wanted to live. But these men—these boys—deserve a chance to go home. I saw too many souls who never had that chance to go home. To say goodbye. And I couldn't live with myself if I let it happen all over again now. Not when I can change it this time."

Harland swallowed.

"This is the right thing to do. And this job, when it's done, will give me the means to start over. For my family to start over. Somewhere we don't have to look over our shoulders."

"I…" What was he supposed to say? That he was pleased? That he understood? "I'm glad that you have decided to accept my offer, then," he settled on, because at least that was the truth. "I didn't know who else I could ask for such a task." Also completely true. "I was worried that perhaps I had given you reason to doubt the motivations behind my proposition." He regretted that part the second it was out of his mouth. He had no idea why he'd said it. Other than it was a piece of unfinished business.

Her pink cheeks flushed darker, and Harland wondered if he had ever seen anyone so damn beautiful in his life. "When I kissed you, you mean," she said.

"I think I kissed you."

"I started it."

He shook his head. "I'm sorry. I shouldn't have brought that up—"

"No. You were right to do so. But it is I who should be apologizing to you."

"Whatever for?"

"Because I started something that I can't finish." She was staring at the toes of her boots now. "And I do not wish to give you reason to doubt the motivations behind my acceptance of your proposition or my presence here."

Harland took a step away from her to keep himself from touching her. The edge of the bed hit the backs of his calves, and he sank down on the mattress, the ropes creaking loudly in the silence. He tried to find words that would put her at ease. Words that would assure her that his offer had been genuine and well intentioned, free from intimate expectations. Words that would convince her that her confession had been heard and understood.

It didn't mean that, at this moment, he didn't still want her more than he had wanted anyone else.

"I can't be with you." Her eyes lifted from the floor and sought out his, her voice hoarse, her face a portrait of anguish. "I will help you and work with you, but I can't be your lover."

He knew that she was going to say that. Yet it stung far more than it should.

"Katherine—"

"There is nothing inside me left to give to you," she said quietly. "To anyone. Do you understand?" He saw that her fingers were wrapped around the strap of her bag so tightly that her knuckles were white.

Yes, he understood. He understood how utter emptiness felt. He understood that no matter how hard you worked, or how far you traveled, nothing was able to fill up the empty space that hate and betrayal left inside. And trying to fill that darkness up with brief, meaningless encounters only made it worse. He knew. He had tried. But he had stopped trying long ago, accepting that numbness was the better option.

But Katherine...she was different. She made him feel again. And it was glorious and painful in equal measures. And he wasn't ready to let her go just yet.

"Come here," he said, putting his hand on the mattress beside him.

Katherine hesitated.

"Please," he added.

She nodded, letting her bag fall to the floor. She stepped around it, lowering herself gingerly beside him, careful not to touch him.

"I want one thing from you," he said, which wasn't really the truth. Because he wanted everything from her. But to say that would send her running out that door and back to Dover faster than he could imagine.

She was looking down at her hands clasped tightly in her lap. He reached over and pulled one of her hands into his, resting them on the coverlet between them when she didn't yank it away.

"I need you to trust me," he said. "Trust that I will never betray you."

She stared at their intertwined hands before she looked up at him, and for the life of him he couldn't tell what she was thinking.

"I do," she whispered, and her forehead creased as if this was news to her too.

"Do you really?"

"I do," she repeated with more volume.

"When I said you were unexpected, I meant it," he continued, trying to pick his words carefully, measuring them against the need that still raged through him. "I have never met a woman quite like you. Talented. Intelligent. Brave and beautiful. And I will never regret kissing you." She needed to know that. "Or you kissing me, as it were."

Her fingers tightened in his, and a ghost of a smile touched her lips.

"I'd be lying if I said that I don't want you to do it again." She needed to know that too. "But I understand."

Katherine turned their joined hands over, the fingers of her free hand tracing the back of his. "What was her name?" she asked. "The woman who made you understand the hate and what it leaves behind."

Harland tensed.

"She was titled, wasn't she?"

He heard her repeat the same question he had once asked of her and knew she had done so deliberately.

"Did you love her?" Another matching, deliberate question.

"I thought I did. I wanted to."

Quiet descended once again.

Katherine withdrew her fingers but left her hand in his. "Jeffrey Walton. My...lover."

The name wasn't familiar. But the recognition of what she had given him was. Trust.

"Patrice Hayward," he replied. "My wife."

She looked up from their hands, her eyes wide and uncertain as they met his. "I'm sorry."

"Me too." This time it was he who tightened his fingers around hers.

She shifted and leaned her head against his shoulder, and he closed his eyes, breathing in the scent of her, feeling the softness of her hair where it fell across his arm. "You are a good man, Harland Hayward," she said simply.

He wasn't a good man. A good man would have told her about his own interests along that Dover coast. A good man would have told her what he had done and continued to do that risked her own family. A good man wouldn't desperately want to take her face in his hands and kiss her senseless. To yank on the ties of her dress and watch it fall to the floor and then push the rest of the layers she was wearing after it. To draw her down onto this bed, taste every part of her, and make her forget everything except him. And worry about the consequences of that later.

"You should get some sleep," he said roughly. "Tomorrow will be another long day of travel. You can have the bed. I'll take the floor." He made to rise but was brought up short by the feel of her hand on his arm.

"Stay," she said.

Harland closed his eyes. He wasn't sure if he had that kind of willpower.

"Please."

He nodded and leaned over, blowing out the candle and plunging the room into total darkness. He pushed himself back onto the bed, shifting his weight to the far side. He heard her pull off her boots before she lay down beside him, her back pressed against the length of him. His hand came to rest against her shoulder, and he cursed himself a thousand ways as a fool. *Trust me*, he had said. *I understand*, he had said.

Now, here, with her heat trapped against him, feeling the curves of her body where they rested against his own, he understood nothing except how very much he wanted her.

"Will you be here in the morning?" she asked suddenly.

Harland frowned. What kind of question was that? Where else was he going to go? "Of course," he murmured.

"Promise?"

"I promise."

He felt her nod and then her hand reached back to her

shoulder and found his, as if confirming he was still there. "Thank you," she whispered, which made no sense either.

Within minutes, her breathing changed, and her body relaxed fully against his.

And he closed his eyes, accepting that this was going to be the longest night of his life.

Chapter 12

She had forgotten what it was like to be in London in the summer.

The stench of the river and the stews that bordered it still made her recoil no matter how often she'd been. By the time they had made their way over Blackfriars Bridge, Katherine was missing the clean, fresh breezes that pushed along the Dover coast and the soothing, steady sound of distant surf. The sounds of the city were deafening and far from soothing. A cacophony of noise, human and animal both, all set against a background of wheels from a thousand carts and wagons and coaches that fought for space on the narrow streets.

But now they had left the bulk of London behind, and it was better here on the edges of the city. Katherine shaded her eyes against the glare of the setting sun, which danced across the slate of the massive house just coming into view. A stately manor, she thought, just another tribute to men with the money to build them. Except this one was different. This one had a fence that ran around the perimeter of its extensive grounds, putting Katherine in mind of a very pretty, pastoral prison. She wondered if the fence was supposed to keep people in or keep them out.

Beside her, Harland guided his horse up toward what looked like a gatehouse—something that would be more at home at the base of a castle as opposed to a manor. Katherine tried not to look at him. Just like she had tried not to look at him from the moment she had woken before dawn, his arm flung over her waist, his body hard against her side, her head tucked against his shoulder, and the steady cadence of his breathing against her ear.

It had been stupid to ask him to stay last night. A smart woman would have agreed to let him sleep on the floor while she took the bed. In the cool, predawn silence, when she had woken to find him exactly where he had promised to be, it had taken every ounce of her willpower not to turn into his strength and safety and heat and make a liar out of herself. Make him her lover and damn the consequences. The temptation was still there now. And it wasn't going away.

"When will we get a look at the prisoners?" she asked, running a hand along the neck of her tired horse in an effort to distract herself.

"I'm not entirely sure." His answer was subdued.

"Will they be brought here?"

"No. They won't leave the river."

"So we'll be taking them up the Thames. And then across the channel."

"Yes."

"In what sort of craft?"

"I'm not sure."

"Splendid," she muttered, thinking that these were questions she should have asked before today. And had her carefully rehearsed speech last night not crumbled into explanations and confessions, she might have. That baring of truths and secrets had left her feeling uncertain and adrift and…needy. Katherine flinched. She wasn't needy. She hadn't needed anyone for a very, very long time.

"You can still change your mind. Turn around now and go back to Dover."

Katherine scowled and didn't even bother to answer that. "What is this place?" she asked instead.

"Helmsdale House," Harland replied.

"I can see that," she said, gazing at the carved stone plaque just visible beneath an overhang of ivy near the squat gatehouse. "But what is it? A home? An asylum? A prison? An assembly hall?"

Harland made a strange noise that might have been a chuckle. "It's a little bit of all of that," he said.

"Helpful," she said sarcastically, turning toward him again. Which was a mistake, because now all she noticed was the way the setting sun was turning his hair a rich red, the way his simple coat was pulled tight across the breadth of his shoulders, and the way his breeches hugged his thighs.

She straightened in her saddle. She had to stop this. Get her mind back on the job she had promised herself she would do.

"Two men in the gatehouse," she said. "A dozen more that have been tracking our progress along this road, concealed behind that fence. Well, mostly concealed. What exactly do I need to know here?"

"The owner of this house is the colleague I spoke of earlier. He takes the safety of his home, his possessions, and himself very seriously."

"And is the fence made to keep people in or out?" she asked.

"Depends on the person."

Katherine cut a look sharply at Harland, unsure if he was joking. He didn't look like he was joking. He looked grim. She shifted her gaze and eyed the shadows that had stepped out of the structure to stand in front of the towering gate. They looked more like gorillas than men. Both had one hand on the swords at their sides. Both had a pistol in the other.

"Dr. Hayward," the one on the left said, though he was looking at Katherine. "We were expecting you. But we were not made aware that you would be traveling with a mistress."

Katherine's horse came to a stop, and she stared back without flinching. She knew this sort of man. Had worked with this sort of man on the coasts and had worked on this sort of man in the surgeons' tents. They weighed and measured demeanor and fortitude, daring and loyalty. But ultimately, they deferred the judgment of another. The leader of a crew. A commanding officer.

"A surgeon," Harland corrected.

"I beg your pardon?"

"Dr. Wright is not my mistress. She is a surgeon."

"That is impossible," the guard sneered.

"I can assure you it's quite possible," Harland said patiently.

The two men exchanged disbelieving glances. "Why is she here?"

"Ask your master." Harland rested the reins on his horse's neck.

Katherine watched as another look was exchanged. The weighing of whether their uncertainty and their questions warranted their superior's attention. She had seen that a thousand times before too. She stared back stonily, offering no indication that she found any of this less than expected.

"We've spent the last two days on the road because I was made to understand that time was of the essence," Harland said into the tense silence that fell. "But as that does not appear to be the case, we'll return on the morrow, after you've had time to verify that our services have been requested. Please give King our regards." He picked up the reins and started to turn his horse away.

"Wait." The taller of the two gorillas caught the reins in a meaty fist.

The other guard took his hand off the hilt of his sword and tucked his pistol into the waistband of his breeches. He moved, dragging the heavy wrought-iron gate open with his significant strength.

"If you're lying to us, Dr. Hayward—"

"You'll have me shot," Harland finished for him. "Yes, yes, I believe I am familiar with the procedure around here."

Katherine glanced at Harland out of the corner of her eye. His disregard for the covert, illegal activities in Dover was becoming more and more explicable given that he didn't seem to find anything about this current situation troublesome. She was beginning to realize that Harland Hayward was not at all who she thought he was. He twisted in the saddle as he guided his horse up the long drive.

"Come, Dr. Wright," he said. "Our answers await."

Chapter 13

Harland paced the study.

Aside from the entrance hall with its polished stone floors, gleaming paneled walls, and soaring ceilings from which glittering crystal dripped, this was the only room in Helmsdale House that he'd ever seen. He supposed that this room, like the hall, was meant to impress.

A massive mahogany desk, devoid of clutter, sat in the center of the room, a leather-bound chair behind it. An expensive rug with a subtle crimson hue woven through the wool was laid over the lustrous wood floor. Like the hall, crystal chandeliers and sconces lit the room, chasing away every suggestion of a shadow in the early evening. The walls were papered in a deep, rich red, something it had taken Harland at least a half-dozen visits to notice because it was the art that hung on their surface that commanded complete attention.

Though he barely noticed it now. With every passing

minute, he was starting to second-guess the wisdom of bringing Katherine here. Which was stupid, he knew. Katherine Wright had agreed to help him knowing exactly what sort of situation she was walking into, and it was important that she was here so that she could hear the same information he did. She was his equal, not a fragile flower that he had to protect.

He watched her circle the room, her hands clasped behind her back, studying the art intently. Portraits, portrayals of biblical scenes, and depictions of mythological beasts were all hung in gilded frames, age and history fairly dripping from each piece. She stopped in front of the painting that dominated the space behind the desk.

"This is rather...violent," she said without turning around. "I wonder what he did to deserve it."

"*Judith Beheading Holofernes*," Harland told her, coming to join her in front of the painting. Captured in vibrant color was a young woman wielding a wickedly curved sword that was buried in the neck of a man whose eyes bulged in terror. An old servant woman hovered over Judith's shoulder, her expression cruel and her eyes a little wild. "Holofernes was a general whose army was about to destroy Judith's home, the city of Bethulia. The night before, Judith was able to slip into his tent because everyone knew that the general was desperate to bed her. Most versions of the story say she waited until he was passed out from drink before relieving him of his head."

"Mmm." Katherine considered the painting. "That is certainly one way to deal with the problem. Though I'm not sure it was the best one."

"You have another solution, Dr. Wright?" The voice came from the doorway.

Harland spun to find King leaning casually on the

silver-tipped walking stick he was never without. He was impeccably groomed, as always, his shirt and cravat a blinding, snowy white, his coat and trousers an immaculate, midnight black. His red-gold hair was fashionably styled, and his boots were polished to a mirrorlike sheen. The man looked like a bloody prince. Though that flawless exterior hid a dangerous, ruthless, ambitious man. A man who could provide anything to anyone for the right price. A man one crossed only once and didn't survive to do it a second time.

Harland stepped forward. Clearly the guards had already advised King of Katherine's presence but he went ahead and offered a proper introduction anyway.

"Dr. Wright, may I present my colleague, King. King, this is Dr. Wright, the surgeon who will be assisting me in the coming days." He had chosen to address Katherine by her profession not only because it was the truth but also because it presented what he hoped was a clear portrayal of their relationship to this man. King had no tolerance for personal attachments when it came to business. Personal attachments meant emotion, and emotion made otherwise intelligent people make stupid decisions.

King's pale blue eyes flickered over Harland once before they returned to Katherine.

"A pleasure, Mr. King," Katherine said politely. It looked like she was bracing herself for the usual disbelieving comments.

"Just King," the man said. "And you have yet to tell me your solution to the dilemma Judith faced."

Katherine was considering King, as if measuring his sincerity.

"I'm waiting, Dr. Wright."

"Very well." She turned back to the painting. "Beheading is not only messy but also difficult, especially for a woman who may lack the strength to carry out such a feat. Aside from the muscles, ligaments, and tendons one finds in the neck, the spine can be difficult to sever, especially given that she is using a small sword and not something with more force like a guillotine. There would be arterial spray all over the body, the sheets, the tent, and Judith herself, which would have made it difficult for her to escape unnoticed. She might have killed the general, but she probably didn't survive her exit. Worse, she brought a witness, and the old lady offers no tactical advantage."

King moved forward so that he drew even with Katherine, and Harland shifted uneasily. The man's eyes were still fixed on her, and he hadn't looked back in Harland's direction once. "Go on, Dr. Wright."

"There is, I suppose, poison, but that has historically been a woman's weapon and suspicion again would lie squarely on her shoulders given her presence. And poison can be unpredictable and imprecise."

"You're saying she shouldn't have killed him?"

"Not at all. I'm saying, if it was my home I was trying to save, my city that was at stake, killing the general is not enough. I'd only be killing a man, not the cause. The general would simply be replaced by another officer, eager to carry out the commands of his dead and martyred commander. The city would fall even after he was dead, probably more swiftly and viciously in retribution."

Harland stared at the back of Katherine's head, a little unnerved by the serene manner in which she was imparting such opinions.

I didn't say I wasn't good at smuggling and other… lawless endeavors. I said that it wasn't how I wanted to live.

Harland clearly hadn't been listening very carefully when she had said that.

"Judith needs to give the general's officers reason to doubt him and the motivations behind his orders. Inject uncertainty and confusion," Katherine continued.

"And how would you achieve that, Dr. Wright?"

"If Holofernes desired Judith so desperately, she had the power to manipulate him. The power to lure him away from his officers and his camp. Make him simply... disappear before she killed him. Not only does it remove the issue of evidence, but also the body can be concealed somewhere it will never be found." Katherine shrugged. "Best case, the general dies, the cause dies with him, and the city is left alone, his officers believing their leader to have fled like a coward. Worst case, his officers delay the destruction, waiting for the general to return before making a decision, and the citizens of the city at least have time to flee."

King's fingers drummed along the head of his walking stick, a ruby glinting from his little finger in the light. "Tell me, Dr. Wright, do you have any experience in the business of contracted death?"

"I beg your pardon?"

Harland straightened. The man couldn't possibly be suggesting what—

"Assassinations," King clarified.

Katherine merely tipped her head. "No."

"Pity. You have the mind for it. And the vocation for it." He glanced back at Harland. "Why did you bring her here, Strathmore?" The interest was gone, replaced again with remote iciness.

It was clear Patrick Gibbs had not been back to speak to King since he had left Dover. Harland came to stand nearer

Katherine. "I'm going to need help over these next days. Medical help," he felt compelled to specify.

"I don't like surprises, Strathmore."

"Had I been given more warning, I would have sent a warning myself," Harland replied evenly.

"Mmm." King left the canvas and set his walking stick against the desk, lowering himself into the wide chair. "I suppose that is a fair point." He crossed his booted foot over his knee, his fingers drumming a rhythm at the top of the polished leather. "And you believe Dr. Wright to be a useful asset in that regard?"

"Don't ask me. Ask the men who returned from Nivelle, Toulouse, or Waterloo who are still breathing."

King's fingers ceased their movement. Silence fell thick and heavy across the room. Eventually, King's eyes drifted back to Katherine. "Tell me, Dr. Wright, what it is that you think you are doing here?"

"The situation has been explained to Dr. Wright," Harland interjected.

King waved a hand. "I want to hear what Dr. Wright has to say."

Harland saw Katherine's eyes dart to his before she faced King fully. "I am to assist Lord Strathmore in keeping at least four men of varying ages and varying health alive until such a time as they can be delivered to the coast of France."

King steepled his fingers. "You have a poetic way with words."

"What I have are questions." She didn't look at Harland.

Two red-gold brows lifted slightly. "By all means, ask away," King murmured. "I may choose to answer them. Or not."

"The captain of the ship that will transport us up the river and across the channel—"

"A very capable captain."

"Is he a capable liar?" Katherine asked.

"An odd question."

"An important question. Because your captain will be challenged at least twice on his way up the Thames in the eastern estuaries by patrols. Routine questions if the absence of your fugitives has gone unnoticed. Aggressive questions if not."

King's hands fell to his lap. "Like I said, Dr. Wright, he is quite capable. In all aspects. The fact that he's been working for me for years is a testament to that." His voice was cool.

"I'm glad to hear it. My life might just depend upon it." Katherine's was just as cool. "Where are our passengers to be delivered?"

"France."

"Calais? Dunkirk? Cherbourg?"

King tipped his head, considering. "Wissant," he finally said.

"The beaches or the town?"

King's booted foot slid from his knee to the floor, and he sat up. "What do you recommend, Dr. Wright?"

"The beaches are flat. Exposed. Easy landing, a large empty space, but not much cover. Best used on a new moon. On the other hand, the village is tiny. Count on being noticed, which can work to your favor if you're pre-pared to present something expected and mundane. In this case, I think we want to avoid notice. The port officials get uneasy and thus unpredictable if we are in a position where we need to carry men ashore on stretchers. The pox is still a concern." She lifted her chin. "Use the beaches."

King's eyes slid to Harland. "You introduced her as a surgeon, Strathmore."

"I did." Harland's reply was hard and unapologetic. God only knew what was going through this man's mind—

"Leave us, Strathmore."

Harland stiffened. "That's not necessary." All his previous oaths he'd made to himself to ignore his white knight tendencies fell away, and the urge to protect her from this man nearly overwhelmed him. Which was absurd because he had been the one who had brought her here.

Absurd because it was becoming very clear that what he thought he knew about Katherine Wright only scratched the surface.

King's face hardened. "And I can assure you, Lord Strathmore, it is. Like all individuals whom I depend upon to complete tasks I am ultimately responsible for, I will take the time to exercise due diligence and determine if she is both capable and trustworthy."

In other words, Harland thought, King had no leverage over Katherine. Not like the leverage he had over Harland. King would do his best to correct that.

Dammit, he shouldn't have brought Katherine here. This had been a mistake.

"This will take but a moment, Lord Strathmore," King said. He stood, turning away from Harland to study the painting of Judith again. "I can assure you that I hold nothing but respect for women who possess wit enough not to apologize for it. I will not ravish Dr. Wright nor kill her in the next ten minutes. Though," he added with what might have been faint humor, "if I suddenly disappear never to be seen again, you'll know who to ask should you ever wish to locate my body."

Katherine watched the man called King from the corner of her eye as a chill chased itself down her spine.

This was no soldier or gorilla-guard. This man was the general who would destroy Bethulia with no compunction if it served his interests and likely slit the throat of Judith afterward, but not before he'd made her watch the destruction. In Katherine's old life, she had met men like him, on deserted beaches and crowded taverns, on empty roads and in teeming ports, along coastlines from here to France. Violent, clever men who were driven by greed or control or fear.

Katherine wasn't entirely sure what drove this man. Greed to some degree, perhaps, given the fine things he had surrounded himself with. And there was certainly an element of control that he demanded. As for fear, whatever his personal demons might be, he covered them well.

"Tell me about Wissant," he said into the silence that Harland's departure had left.

Katherine clasped her hands behind her back and wandered over to another painting, this one depicting an armor-clad man slaying a writhing, scaly beast. She turned the query over in her mind but saw no reason not to answer.

"I used to work that section of coast," she said. "The beaches. When I was younger."

"Then you are familiar with Monsieur Mercier."

"Guillaume?" The unexpected name of her old friend caught her by surprise. "You are acquainted?"

King was now watching her with the intensity of a raptor. "Regrettably, we are not. It is something I wish to remedy. My current…associates along that stretch, while competent, operate on a small scale. Monsieur Mercier offers far greater potential and opportunities. However, he has proven to be…elusive as of late."

Old instincts rose fast and hard. Information was never volunteered. It was sold or used as a bargaining chip when one wanted or needed something. And Katherine had no idea what this man wanted or needed from Guillaume Mercier, though she had an idea.

"I haven't seen him in a long time. Years." She turned back to the painting. A vision of a blood-soaked French cavalry coat, torn open with her knife so that she could see the extent of the damage done to the side of his hip swam into her view. She had found him in the carnage that had followed that last battle, and he had lived, thanks to her. And a whole lot of luck. "Monsieur Mercier was one of the best smugglers France possessed when I knew him," she said carefully. "If he still operates along that coast, I can't imagine he has remained anything less than careful. The war is no longer a diversion for troops on either side of the channel looking to pick a fight."

"Indeed."

Katherine kept her eyes fixed on the dying beast.

"Lord Strathmore has never mentioned you."

"Oh?" Katherine left the painting and moved to examine another, this one a portrait of a young woman, her hair unbound, a sheet clutched to her naked bosom. "Until two days ago, he hadn't mentioned you either."

She heard King move from behind his desk, his footsteps just audible on the thick rug.

"What is he to you?" King asked. "The baron."

Katherine pivoted to face him. "I'm glad you asked. I was going to pose the same question to you."

King was standing directly in front of her, no emotion in his icy-pale eyes. "Are you fucking him?"

It was meant to shock, she knew, her response to be

evaluated and scored. There was more at stake here than a mere job interview. She just wasn't sure what.

She unclasped her hands. "Are you?" He was not the only one who had learned to read responses.

"No." He didn't seem offended. Or even mildly surprised. He seemed...contemplative.

"Then we have that in common."

"Mmm." King leaned on his walking stick. "For now."

Katherine resisted the urge to frown. Not for now. Forever.

"You are quite different than his late wife."

Katherine wasn't sure what she was supposed to say to that, so she said nothing.

"She demanded that he abandon his medical practice the day after they wed. He refused."

King was looking for a reaction, she knew. One she would not give him. "Good," she said simply.

"Did you ever meet her? His wife?"

"No." She wasn't sure where this conversation was going and even less sure that she wanted to find out.

"She was killed in a very public, very...lewd accident in Hyde Park," King went on. "Her lover was also killed in the same accident."

Katherine's stomach sank, even as an immediate, inexplicable anger kindled on Harland's behalf. There was the reaction King was looking for. She buried it, careful to keep her tone one of faint boredom. "And how could you possibly know she was with her lover?"

"Neither one was wearing any clothes at the time of their deaths." He ran his hand over the silver head of his walking stick. "I suppose there are other possibilities. But I've found that in most cases, especially when it comes to the ton and their predilection for selfish, destructive diversions, when one hears hooves, one does not look for zebras."

Revulsion joined her anger. Enough was enough. "I'm not sure why you think I'd be interested in this sort of gossip."

King smiled, though it didn't reach his eyes. "There are many who will tell you that Strathmore killed his wife. Drove her away and ultimately to her death with his... selfishness to chase his own ambitions and his defiance of expectations and responsibilities."

"And you think that that is what he's doing here? Choosing to chase his own selfish ambitions and defy expectations at my expense?"

"Is he?"

Katherine met his icy gaze. "You tell me."

"No," he said finally. "I don't suppose he is."

"Then I'm glad we are in accord. My choices are my choices. For better or for worse." She paused. "And perhaps Dr. Hayward's late wife should have been held accountable for hers."

"Perhaps, indeed." King wandered back to the portrait of Judith. "Does the baron know what it is you do?" he asked without looking at her. "Amputations and such notwithstanding?"

"What I did," Katherine corrected. "And yes, he is aware. The baron is not a fool. Nor does he have a loose tongue. Those two things, along with his medical practice, make him privy to all sorts of secrets along the Dover coasts."

"Yes," King agreed, turning slightly, a pensive look on his face. "And you're right. He's not a fool. And he is very adept at keeping secrets."

Katherine shifted, disquiet filtering through her. She had the distinct impression that she had missed something.

"You no longer work in the…import business?" King sounded almost disappointed.

"No."

"Also a pity." He gazed at her. "Your aptitudes and your mind are utterly wasted. I can rectify that at any time should you wish, with great reward. I always have need of individuals with rare skill sets." He smiled another one of his empty smiles. "Like those of Lord Strathmore. Or Dr. Hayward, depending on the day."

"The days you need a discreet doctor."

"Yes," King said slowly. "The days I need a discreet doctor." He paused. "Tell me, Dr. Wright, why did you agree to do this?"

She was not, under any circumstances, going to repeat her confession of last night to this man. A man like this wouldn't understand any of it. "Lord Strathmore asked for my assistance. I was in a position to offer it."

"Come, Dr. Wright. No one does anything out of the goodness of their heart. Everyone has an agenda, hidden or otherwise." His tone was disapproving. "You speak of choices. I wish to know what drives yours."

She shrugged. "Lord Strathmore offered to handsomely recompense me for my time and my abilities." She gave him a reason he would understand. Everyone understood money. "The same reason the baron is doing this for you."

He held her eyes for a fraction too long. "Indeed," he finally murmured. "Indeed."

Dammit, she didn't like this. There was something deeper going on here, something under the surface that she couldn't see.

King moved unhurriedly back to his desk. "There are numerous details to discuss before we proceed tomorrow now that you're part of the plan." He lowered himself back into his chair and looked at her. "Call Lord Strathmore back in here, if you would, Dr. Wright, before he wears a hole in the rug outside. It was imported from Constantinople, and I am quite fond of it."

Chapter 14

Harland stared up at the darkened ceiling, unable to sleep despite his exhaustion, his mind refusing to quiet.

The plan that would unfold over the next days was not his, and perhaps that was what bothered him. Though he could find little to criticize. The right people had been bribed, diversions had been planned, and quick, reliable transportation had been secured. The pieces and players were in place and Patrick Gibbs had been right. The approach to this assignment was not so different than any other. Except for the fact that they were extracting the prisoners from a veritable fortress and not the familiar labyrinth of Newgate and the surrounding areas of London. And save for the very real possibility that the prisoners might perish before they reached their destination.

Katherine had made it clear that she would prefer to be with Harland when he and Gibbs went into the Warren to fetch the prisoners, yet she admitted that her presence might attract unwanted attention. However, she listened carefully to the rest of the plan and then proceeded to ask probing questions that exposed potential weaknesses. Harland found himself on more than one occasion wondering how great an underground empire she would have built along that Dover coast and beyond had she not gone to war and instead continued in her father's footsteps. How great an empire she might build now, should she choose to do so.

What hadn't been discussed on the ride back from Helmsdale House was the private conversation between Katherine and King. She had made no references to it, and Harland had hesitated in asking. Because to ask would imply that he did not trust her, and their newly forged bond of friendship and trust was still fragile.

Harland groaned and rolled over in his bed. Thinking more about Katherine was not going to help him fall asleep. He'd chosen to bring them to Haverhall as opposed to the modest townhome he kept in a modest square in a modest section of London. The school sat on an expanse of sprawling grounds, with gardens and lawns and even a substantial pond surrounding the converted manor house. He kept rooms here, as did his sisters, but at this time of year, the school was vacant, save for a handful of staff who maintained the house and property. The fewer people who were aware of his presence in London, the better.

Though he was plenty aware of Katherine's presence. It was a peculiar sort of torture to have her so close and yet so far. He tried not to think about how it had felt to spend the night next to her, her body pressed against his, her hair soft against his cheek, her skin even softer. He knew exactly what she looked like. Knew exactly how she sighed in her sleep, exactly how she moved, how she smelled.

What he didn't know was how her skin tasted. Or the

sounds she might make if he was deep inside her, pushing her to the edge of ecstasy and then carrying them both over—

A thud from the other side of the wall had him sitting straight up. Another low thud, and a sound as if a chair or piece of furniture had been dragged across the floor. Without considering what he was doing, he dressed in his shirt and breeches, opened the door to his room, and hurried into the hall. He came to a stop in front of Katherine's door. From underneath, he could see an uneven glow of candlelight. He listened, straining to hear a sound from the other side of the door. Within seconds, he heard a rhythmic scraping that sounded a great deal like steel on stone.

She wasn't sleeping either.

He knocked, and the sound stopped.

A moment later, her door opened hesitantly, as though she was afraid of what was on the other side.

"I'm sorry," she said, looking up at him, her eyes a deep blue-green in the shadows. "Did I wake you?"

Harland opened his mouth to answer and found that he had no words. She was standing there in the soft light, dressed in what looked like her shift covered by a thick robe she must have found in the wardrobe. Her bare toes stuck out from under the hem, and her hair was loose down her back in a cloud of champagne-colored silk, putting him in mind of a fairy princess. He had never seen a woman so breathtakingly beautiful in his life. He might never again.

This had been a bad idea. He should have just put a pillow over his head.

"Harland?" Her brows were drawn together. "Are you all right?"

"No," he managed.

"What's wrong?" She opened the door wider, concern stamped across her beautiful features and tension emanating from her body.

What was wrong? He was standing outside the bedroom door of a woman who stole his breath and his wits and his words. A woman he wanted to hold close and protect. A woman he wanted and needed like the very air that surrounded him.

A woman who did not need him.

"I can't sleep either," he finally croaked, because at least that was the truth. She could draw whatever damn conclusions she wanted from that.

She held his eyes for a moment before stepping aside. "Come in, then," she said, holding the door wide.

Harland stepped forward, his bare feet carrying him into her room while, somewhere in his mind, a little voice screamed at him to go back. That he would not survive another night like the one prior without his instinct to protect her yielding to his instinct to have her. He got about four steps into the room before his traitorous feet stopped abruptly.

"What are you doing?" he asked, surveying the scene in front of him.

The bulky canvas bag that she had traveled with lay empty in a corner. Her leather sleeve of surgical tools was rolled out on the bed, the blades removed and lined up on a small, decorative table that she had pulled into the center of the room next to a wooden chair. A square stone, a leather strop, and a linen rag lay beside them. On a washstand just off to the side, the basin had been emptied, and a collection of small leather packets, each tied with string, were set in its bottom. Small glass vials were lined up neatly across the surface next to it.

"Double-checking what I have. Making sure my blades are sharp."

Harland turned to look at her. "You'll have time to do this tomorrow."

Katherine shook her head. "I need to do it now. I need to give these men—boys—a chance to get home. They need to get home."

"They will."

"You don't know that." She reached for the stone, her movements stiff.

Harland felt his forehead crease. Something was clearly bothering her. Perhaps she was second-guessing her agreement to help him. Perhaps this had something to do with whatever it was that King had said to her in that room.

He moved to stand in front of her, though he wasn't sure what he wanted to say. Wasn't sure of the right question to ask. "You don't have to come with me," he tried.

"Yes, I do." Her fingers worried the edge of the stone.

"No one will think poorly of you if you change your mind."

"I will think poorly of me. And if you're going to continue along this line of questioning, it would be best if you leave. My answer is not going to change no matter how many times you ask the question."

"Katherine." Harland put his hands over hers, stilling her fingers.

"We don't need to discuss this further—"

"I think we do—"

"King told me about your wife." She set the stone aside on the table with exaggerated care.

Harland recoiled, pulling away. "I see." If her aim had been to deflect the conversation from herself, she had certainly succeeded. Though there was nothing King could have told her that she couldn't have read in any one of the newspapers that had gleefully devoured every sordid detail and then shouted them out to the world for public consumption. "Why?" King never did anything that wasn't coldly calculated.

"He wanted to know if my choices were my own. Or if I was a victim of your ambitions."

Fury coursed through him. At King for telling her something that was not his to tell. At himself for not being more honest with Katherine when he'd had the chance. "A victim of my ambitions? Then he would have told you what was written in the papers. That I drove my wife away by refusing to relinquish my intolerable, *ambitious* practice of medicine." Remnants of the old, familiar hatred rose despite his best efforts. "My wife reminded me at every turn that my persistent pursuit of a common profession reflected poorly on her. That I was an embarrassment. That even my fortune was not worth the indignity she suffered. And when I wouldn't give up my practice, when I wouldn't become the man she thought I should be, she punished me. Over and over."

Katherine said nothing, only looked at him with steady eyes.

"I suppose he told you how she died?" His words were bitter.

"He said it was an accident."

"An accident? Well, I suppose you could call it that. Are you familiar with Thomas Rowlandson? No? He wrote a poem titled 'New Feats of Horsemanship.' It chronicles a man fucking his lover on horseback while they gallop—"

"Harland—"

"Which was just another one of her public stunts with

just another one of her lovers, except the horse stepped in a hole and—"

"Stop."

"I tried to change at the beginning, to be the man she wanted—"

She pressed her fingers to his lips, silencing him. "Don't you dare. Don't you dare change."

The hatred and fury that had risen suddenly drained with a swiftness that Harland wasn't prepared for. Those words—her words—were everything that he had needed to hear years ago. Perhaps they were still what he needed to hear. The chronic emptiness that had numbed the anger and the hate, the resentment and the regret over the years had been replaced with something new. Something that tightened his chest and felt an awful lot like hope.

"I only mentioned the conversation I had with King because your sister, Clara, asked me about my choices. Why I chose to go to war," Katherine said, her hand sliding to his collar. "I lied to her. Told her that I went because I thought I could help."

"You could. You did."

"The truth is that I went to war because I thought I was in love," she said. "The most foolish, selfish reason one could imagine."

Harland frowned. "You're neither foolish nor—"

"I met Jeffrey Walton in Dover, as his regiment was making preparations to cross to France." She interrupted him before Harland could finish his protest. "He was charming and witty and made me feel special. He made an effort to make time for me even though I knew he was busy. And he didn't laugh at me when I suggested that I could go with him. So I went, smug and secure in the knowledge that I was more than merely his mistress. I got on that ship sure that I had nothing in common with so many of the women who followed the army and provided the distraction of a warm bed on a cold night for a price."

"You don't have to tell me, Katherine." The bitter end to Harland's marriage might have played out on a public stage, picked apart and judged by all and sundry, but Katherine did not need to share something so intensely private.

"I do. So that you can understand why I'm here. Why I can't *not* do this."

He reached up and covered her hand with his, holding it against his chest.

"Jeffrey was an officer in Kempt's Eighth Brigade. They took heavy losses at Quatre Bras and Waterloo, and on that last day, before the French broke, a band of French skirmishers slipped past the far flank of our lines and caught him and his guard in a wooded copse near Mont St. Jean. Cut him off and trapped him and six of his men in an abandoned farmhouse. I was only told what had happened and that he was missing at dusk. Once darkness fell, and in the confusion of the retreat, I slipped through the lines. I thought I could help Jeffrey and his men escape if they were still pinned."

"Are you insane?" Harland demanded.

"No," she said a little sadly. "Just very experienced at evading men with guns in the dark." She had yet to look at him. "But by the time I got to them, two of his men were dead, the other four badly wounded defending their position. Defending their commanding officer, the way they had been trained, with loyalty and courage. Jeffrey was unhurt."

"Of course he was," Harland muttered under his breath.

"They were still there, the French. They hadn't yet

retreated with the bulk of their army, either because they were stubborn or confused or just plain angry. We had enough ammunition to keep them at bay. The skirmishers disappeared sometime before dawn. I managed to keep the remaining four of Jeffrey's men alive until then. And Jeffrey promised them that he would get them help and see them home once we were reunited with the bulk of the army. That they would be rewarded for their bravery." Her hand dropped from his collar. "But at daybreak, Jeffrey was gone."

"Gone?"

"I fell asleep," Katherine said flatly. "I didn't mean to but I hadn't slept in a day and a half. Jeffrey slipped away sometime before I woke. I was made to understand much later that he was on one of the first ships back to England with a number of other officers." Her lip curled. "Heroes, each and every one of them, to be feted and welcomed back to the bosom of England after a great victory."

Harland's teeth were grinding, and he forced his jaw to relax. He had never met Jeffrey Walton, but he had met others just like him. Men who couldn't begin to understand what true courage looked like. What loyalty looked like. Walton hadn't been the only one who had fled, quick to quit the battlefield and the horror that was left behind. Harland had watched them go.

"They all died, his men," Katherine continued. "I couldn't save them. The youngest was fifteen. He had lied about his age when he joined. It took him two months to succumb to his injuries, and he died crying for his mother. The other three lasted less than a fortnight, but they, too, died wanting what I couldn't give them."

"I'm sorry."

"Did you know that I believed Jeffrey would come

back? I honestly believed that he had left to arrange help. I wrote to him for a long time, believing he would keep his promises to his men. To me." She pulled her hands from Harland's. "Because he had promised that he would marry me when the war was over. That he would give me the children I always dreamed of and a place to call home with a garden in the back and a dog in the front. A life free from desperation and crime and full of happiness and security instead." She rubbed her forehead with her fingertips. "Jesus, but I was gullible."

"You're not."

"You're right. I'm not anymore." Her hands dropped. "I never saw or heard from him again. Though I did hear rumors not long after he'd left that he became a full colonel and was given an important position at Dartmoor Prison."

"Katherine—"

"The longer I stayed in Belgium, the harder it was to leave." She continued as if she hadn't heard him. "Because it wasn't only Jeffrey's men who struggled to live long enough to return home. There were so many. And not just Englishmen, but Frenchmen and Prussians too."

"I know," he said quietly, though he wasn't sure she heard that either.

"All of them used up and discarded without a backward glance because their lives were judged to be less valuable."

She was referring to the soldiers, Harland knew, but in truth, she was speaking of herself too. A soul used and discarded when she was no longer useful or convenient. The hate and rage were back. But this time, they were not on his behalf. The urge to gather her to him, as if that could keep her from all the hurt that she had suffered at another's hand, was overwhelming. Again, he couldn't protect her from the past, any more than she could protect him from his.

"They needed care," Katherine whispered. "But more importantly, they needed someone to sit beside them so that they didn't die alone when the time came. Someone who could pretend to be a mother or a sister or a wife to the men and the boys who would never see their own again. Who would never get home to say goodbye." Her fingers played with the handle of one of the knives resting on the small table beside her. "I know that you understand what it feels like to be powerless to do anything except watch a man die. I know that you saw the same things that I did."

He nodded.

"I stayed in Belgium for over four years. Even when the soldiers were all gone, I couldn't bring myself to come back to England. I couldn't bring myself to come back and face him. Still haven't faced him. It makes me a coward, I know, but you were right. Before, I mean, when you said that I haven't let go of the hate—"

"You're not a coward. Jesus, Katherine, what you did, what you continue to do, are not the acts of a coward."

Katherine shrugged. "It doesn't matter, really. But I wanted you to understand why I'm here, doing this. Because right now, I'm not powerless. I'm not a victim of anyone's ambitions. Not yours, not Jeffrey's, not anyone's. I am making my own choices. I couldn't get those four soldiers who were left behind back home, but I have a chance with these. If only to say goodbye to a family who clearly loves them enough to go to extreme measures to get them back. I can't just watch it all happen again. Do you understand?"

"Yes," he said hoarsely.

"And I know you can't make promises—"

"You're wrong."

"I didn't finish what I was going to say—"

"You don't have to. I need you to listen to me, Katherine, and I need you to listen well. I cannot promise you that these men will live until they get to France, this is true. But I can promise that I will do everything in my power to help them get there. I can't promise you that there won't be danger in what we're doing, but I can promise you that I will never leave you to face it on your own." He stopped, trying to regain some control over the torrent of words that were escaping from him.

She was looking at him, her face pale. "Harland—"

"I promise, Katherine, that I will not leave you. Ever." His fingers caressed the side of her cheek.

She closed her eyes, pressing her cheek into his palm. "I told you I can't do this. We…us…I—"

"I don't need you to do anything." He leaned forward, lifting her hand away from the table and tucking it in his.

Her eyes opened, turquoise-silver in the candlelight.

"I'm not him." It was the second time he had said that to her.

"I know." Her voice hitched. "But I'm still me. And I still can't…I don't…I can't give you what you need." It was the second time she had said that to him.

"You're wrong." His other hand slid down her cheek to her neck, his fingers curling around her nape. "You've already given me everything. Your acceptance. Your trust. Your faith. Your confidences. I don't need you to give me more, Katherine." What she had given him was priceless. Humbling.

"Harland—"

He lifted her hand to his lips and pressed a soft kiss to the inside of her wrist. "But I want you to take what you need."

Her lips parted, and a soft breath escaped.

This was madness, he knew. A reckless, glorious madness that he had probably been destined for since the moment he had walked into a cottage and Katherine Wright had leveled a rifle at him.

"Take it," he whispered. "Or don't. But I—"

Her fingers came up to still his lips again. Very slowly, she traced the outline of his mouth.

Harland forgot to breathe.

Her eyes followed the path of her fingertips, and it took every ounce of willpower he had to remain still. He'd had women touch him many times and in much more overtly sexual manners, but this, this gentle exploration of his lips, nearly undid him where he stood.

Her hand dropped to his chest, and she gently pushed him back. His legs hit the chair, and he lowered himself to its seat, his hand slipping from around her neck.

She caught it in her own hand, reaching for the other and bringing both up in front of her where she stood, studying them.

"You have incredible hands," she said, her fingers twining through his, turning them over. "I thought that the very first time I met you."

He swallowed, arousal crackling through him like an oncoming storm.

She stepped closer so that her legs bumped his knees. He didn't move. Didn't give in to the wild urge to yank his fingers from hers and haul her onto his lap where he would show her exactly what his hands could do.

She held his fingers a moment longer before she released them. Harland held his breath, terrified that she would turn around and walk away. Terrified that she wouldn't.

Very slowly, she reached down, yanking her robe and

her chemise up around her knees, and in a fluid motion, she slid onto his lap, her legs straddling him. The arousal that had been building flared to life, every part of his body straining toward hers.

She lifted the bottom of his shirt and pulled it up and over his head, letting it drop carelessly to the side. Harland remained motionless, his fingers gripping the sides of the chair, waiting for her to move. Waiting for Katherine to take what she needed.

Her hands came up between them, and with infinite care, she rested her palms on the planes of his bare chest, her fingers grazing the hollow of his throat. He wondered if she could feel the way his heart was thundering against his ribs or the way his breath came and went far too quickly. She shifted against him, her hands slipping down over the ridges of muscle in his abdomen, settling herself against his erection that was pushing at the fall of his breeches.

Harland sucked in a breath, and her fingers paused, trapped between their bodies. She leaned forward, her lips brushing the underside of his jaw and trailing fire down the side of his neck in an unhurried exploration. He closed his eyes, trying not to thrust against her glorious heat. Her hands slid back up his chest and snaked around his neck, and now her mouth found his, her tongue tracing the same path of his lips that her fingers had.

He allowed her to set the pace of the kiss, allowed her to taste and tease. She went slowly at first, need warring with what felt like caution. Or maybe control. It was hard to tell when his own control was in danger of slipping. But then maybe so was hers, because she made a small, desperate sound as her hands tightened around his neck and her hips rocked. Pleasure sizzled through him at the friction, and he groaned.

"Tell me what you want, Katherine," he rasped.

Her head dropped, her mouth grazing the lobe of his ear. "I want you to touch me," she whispered.

~

I want you to touch me.

Katherine had no idea what sort of madness had given her the courage to wield honesty with such raw brutality, or what sort of insanity had made her accept what Harland Hayward had offered. But at this moment, she couldn't bring herself to care.

I want you to touch me.

He moved beneath her, raising his hands to pull away the robe that had slipped from her shoulders. It joined his shirt somewhere on the floor, leaving Katherine in nothing but her chemise, the impossibly thin fabric caressing her impossibly sensitive skin. She'd expected him to remove her chemise as well, but he only ran his fingers up the sides of her thighs, delving beneath the sheer layer bunched where she rested on his lap. His hands slid to her backside, urging her more firmly against the bulge of his erection.

A new frisson of needy want twisted and coiled deep within her, and her back arched.

"How do you want me to touch you?" he whispered against her ear.

Katherine's head dropped to his shoulder, sparks of pleasure burning across every nerve. She had started this. She should be able to finish it. But right now, lucid words seemed beyond her.

"Like this?" he asked, his hands sliding up her back and then around her ribs, the backs of his knuckles grazing the underside of her breasts. The fabric of her chemise dragged against her nipples, the delicate friction sending showers of need straight to her groin.

She might have nodded.

"Like this?" His fingers continued moving upward underneath her chemise, tracing first the ridges of her collarbone, then the slopes of her breasts, and finally circling her nipples.

"Yes," she managed to gasp.

His thumbs flicked over each nipple, his palms supporting the achy weight of her breasts. Her head tipped, and her back arched farther, pushing more of herself into his touch. One of his hands slipped around her back, supporting her as she strained, the other trailing down the center of her chest.

His lips grazed her throat as he stroked lower, his fingers dipping over her navel and then stopping at the top of her pubic bone. Her arms tightened around his neck in anticipation, her breathing coming far too fast. She was wet, she knew, the throb at the juncture of her legs consuming her.

His fingers slipped lower, teasing the curls. "Like this?" he whispered again.

"Yes." Her legs tightened around him, and she lifted her body just enough for him to slide his fingers where she wanted them most.

The first stroke of his fingers through the folds of her sex elicited a sound from her that she didn't recognize and was powerless to prevent. The muscles of his thighs were like steel beneath her, the hand at her back rigid. He stroked through her wet heat again, this time applying a subtle, pulsing pressure to the nub at her apex. Her fingers curled into his hair as if that could keep her grounded, pleasure igniting a kaleidoscope of light behind her closed lids and setting her body on fire.

His hands really were incredible, she thought drunkenly, and what he could do with them even better.

"Tell me what you need," Harland demanded. His breath was hot against her neck, the scrape of the stubble on his jaw an erotic torment.

"You. More." The words were jumbled fragments, her body poised on the edge of the precipice, ready to fly apart.

Harland groaned, and then his mouth was on hers, hard and demanding. The unhurried exploration of earlier had given way to something much more primal, much more visceral. She met him with the same urgency, bearing down on the agonizingly perfect pressure of his hand as his fingers slipped deep inside her.

Exactly what she needed.

It was her last coherent thought before her body bowed and spasms of pleasure tore through her, every muscle contracting in blinding ecstasy. His name was wrung from her lips, but he caught the sound with his own mouth as he kissed her over and over. He kept her with him, his arms steady and strong, his clever, perfect fingers prolonging the eddies and aftershocks of her orgasm.

He was whispering her name as she finally came back to herself, and his hands were sliding up her back, along the valley of her spine, keeping her pressed close against him. She kissed him languidly, untangling her fingers from his hair, letting the glow suffuse her now-boneless limbs. He smoothed the hair back away from her face, and she rested her head against his chest.

"You really do have incredible hands," she murmured.

Harland chuckled, a low rumble that vibrated against her ear, before he shifted under her. Belatedly, Katherine realized that he was still rock hard beneath the fall of his breeches.

She straightened, her hand dropping to his waistband.

Harland caught it before she could go any further. "Don't. This was about you. What you needed."

"But—"

He kissed her hard, preventing her from finishing.

"I could watch you come apart beneath my touch forever," he whispered.

Katherine blushed to the roots of her hair. Absurd, given what had just transpired. Ridiculous, given what she had demanded of him. Idiotic, given that she wanted to ask him to do it again.

Without warning, Harland dropped his arms, scooping her up as he stood. He blew out the candle on the small table and carried her to the bed in the dark, placing her gently in the middle. He crawled in after her, the bed tipping with his weight as he lay down beside her, pulling her up against him.

His hand slipped over her hip. "Go to sleep," he said. "I'll be here when you wake up."

Katherine reached for his hand, entwining their fingers, emotion crowding up into her throat and making the backs of her eyes sting. Why couldn't she find the words she wanted? Words that went deeper than gratitude that this man had taken her vulnerability and somehow turned it into courage.

And made her believe, for the first time in years, that she was no longer alone.

Chapter 15

We have a problem."

The unfamiliar voice froze Katherine in her tracks, stopping her from pushing the door to Harland's rooms all the way open.

She heard a clatter and then a curse. "What did I tell you about knocking, Gibbs?" Harland growled from within.

"And what did I tell you about locking your windows, Lord Strathmore?"

Katherine's hand rested on the cool surface of the latch in indecision. Harland had risen from her bed not long ago, returning to his own rooms to dress and prepare for the day ahead. Through the partially open door, she could see him at his washstand, the glow from a lantern putting his features in profile against the deep shadows of predawn. The man he had called Gibbs could only be Patrick Gibbs, the other piece of this plan, but he remained beyond her view.

"I nearly severed my jugular with my razor just now

thanks to your entrance," Harland grumbled, wiping the remaining soap from his face with a towel.

"This can't wait." The words were grim.

Harland frowned. "You couldn't get your hands on enough explosives?"

"You're joking, right?" From out of the darkness somewhere, Gibbs sounded affronted. "There is ordnance literally everywhere I turn in the Warren, and it is stored behind doors with locks from the last century. Appropriating a little on our behalf is something I could have done when I was five years old."

"Then what's the problem?"

"The commanding officer overseeing the Warren, the officer I paid to be very busy this morning with unspecified duties and to mismanage any unexpected…chaos…died in a tavern brawl two nights ago. Hit his head on the side of a table, started shaking like a Bedlamite, and promptly expired. Or at least that was how I heard it told."

"Shit," Harland muttered, tossing the towel somewhere out of sight. "Does he have a replacement?"

"He does. Arrived at the Warren late last night. A colonel, no less. Some sort of war hero, but as far as I can tell, a pompous ass. This isn't the first prison he's been posted to, and rumor says he likes the taste of power. Takes his position very seriously."

Katherine's fingers tightened on the latch as her stomach lurched and her breath caught. A peculiar, icy dread wound its way through her veins.

"Heard he's a younger son who found himself the heir apparent four months ago," Gibbs continued. "The older brother was shooting strays in the Dials for sport when his horse spooked and left him in a puddle of filth with a broken neck, making the colonel next in line for an earldom.

Which is all irrelevant to the here and now save for the fact that he's not the sort of chap in need of my money. And now there's no time for me to find any alternative leverage."

"What's his name? As a member of the aristocracy, perhaps I can discover something about him that we could use," Harland said.

"Colonel Jeffrey Walton, now the viscount of something or other and the next Earl of Wheldham."

Katherine shoved the door open. "Hanveck," she said. "The courtesy title that now belongs to him is Viscount Hanveck."

She ignored Harland, directing her comment to the man called Gibbs. The short, compact man darted a look at Harland before his eyes returned to her.

"Dr. Wright, I presume?" Gibbs asked.

"Yes."

"And you are an acquaintance of this colonel?"

"Something like that." Katherine advanced into the room and put a hand on the back of a chair to steady herself. Somewhere the gods and goddesses who manipulated the strings of retribution and revenge, vengeance and justice, were laughing. And watching to see what Katherine would do.

"How well do you know him?" Gibbs sounded hopeful. "Enough to use to our advantage?"

Katherine felt oddly numb, but from somewhere deep, old bitterness and hate were beginning to stir. "Yes, Mr. Gibbs, well enough to use to our advantage."

"Absolutely not." Harland stepped toward Katherine. "Whatever you're thinking, don't. I'll take care of him. Stall him. Distract him. Trade a war story. Drown him in the Thames if need be."

Katherine shook her head. She could succumb to the hate and bitterness that was now starting to gather speed, thundering through her limbs like a herd of wild horses loosed in a storm, and finally take this opportunity to confront Jeffrey. She could publicly demand all the answers that she was entitled to. She could rail and rage and extract the apology owed not to her, but to the men who had risked their lives for his and had been abandoned and left behind to die for their efforts. She could address him as the disloyal, cowardly liar he was. All of which would change nothing.

Or she could make a very different choice.

"No," Katherine said, pleased with how steady that answer had come out. "You will not drown anyone. I will take care of Colonel Walton and make sure that he is nowhere near where he should be when it matters. You will take care of the patients. Nothing will change in that regard."

Harland was frowning fiercely. "We don't know if Walton will even be out in the yards that early—"

"Yes, we do," Gibbs interrupted unhappily. "A captain told me that he's planning to order the guards and their convict crews to assemble for inspection first thing, and when he does, he, or someone else, will notice that there are at least two particular convicts who should never have been rowed to shore this morning as part of the work gangs. They'll be ordered back to the hulk, the guard reprimanded and removed, and getting the prisoners out a second time will be damned near impossible—"

"Like I said, I will take care of the colonel," Katherine repeated.

Harland closed the distance between them, grasping her cold fingers in his warm ones. "You don't have to do this—"

"Yes, I do. I am done dodging. I will not hide at the expense of these patients' lives." She took a deep, deliberate breath. "I know I told you last night that you couldn't make promises, but I need you to tell me that we'll get these boys home. No matter what happens."

"That's the idea."

"Promise me, Harland."

"Katherine—"

"I know this is selfish. I know I'm being unreasonable. But I need this. I need to know that I will help make a difference. That here, I will succeed where I failed before. Promise me this."

"You didn't fail."

"Tell that to those who died hundreds of miles from those they loved. Promise me that these boys won't be one of them."

"I promise."

"Thank you."

Patrick Gibbs's head was swiveling back and forth between them. "Is there something I need to know here?"

"No," replied Katherine. "There is nothing you need to know other than that the plan has changed slightly. Though there is something that I need to know."

"What?" the blond man asked suspiciously.

"How fast can you find me a gown?"

Chapter 16

The morning skies were leaden, making the Thames a river of dull slate.

In truth, the dim skies cast a pallor over the entire Warren and dockyards. The buildings seemed colorless, as gray as the mud that surrounded them, and a smoky haze from the foundries' fires hung over the yards.

Just downriver from the Warren, the decrepit hulks chained to the shores and the bottom of the Thames were a sharp contrast to the sleek vessels that were anchored in front of the neatly ordered dockyards. The hulks were just jumbled shells of their former selves—their masts stripped, decking removed, ramshackle sheds sprouting up on the remaining deck like barnacles. Makeshift laundry lines were tied across the bow and stern, ghostly gray linen hanging limp and lifeless.

Not so different than the jumbled maze that was the Warren itself. Workshops, timber yards, and warehouses sprawled along the banks. Piles of ballast stone and earth sat in unordered hills close to the water. Farther back, barracks squatted, dwarfed by the chaos in front of them.

When it came to lawless endeavors, Katherine liked chaos.

Around her, the early morning air was stagnant and warm. Along the edges of the river, gangs of men were beginning their daily toil, unloading ballast from ships and lighters. Other teams of men were digging pile holes along the riverbanks and carting barrows full of stone to reinforce the edges of the bank eroding away into the river. Farther inland, crews of men were starting to spread across the timber yards, stacking and cutting and hauling. About a third were civilian day laborers, easy to pick out by their casual clothes. The other two-thirds were dressed in a standard uniform of a brown jacket, rough shirt, and breeches. And chains.

Some were chained in pairs, by the waist or the ankle. Others had heavy fetters on each leg, some with irons secured around their necks. Most were gaunt with fatigue or hunger or both. Many had open wounds or ominous coughs. And all were overseen by loud guards strutting about, their purpose presumably to enforce the work and prevent escape.

Katherine breathed shallowly, the stink of the mudflats combining with the chronic smoke and the horrific stench of the hulks themselves—too many bodies crammed into too small a space for too long. But the hazy, greasy air that hung still as death pleased her immeasurably. There was no brisk breeze that was clearing the noxious smoke from the foundry. Visibility would be further reduced when—

"Have you ever been in a prison?"

Katherine didn't turn from her position up on the road that ran above the Warren. It was the first question Harland had asked her since they had left Haverhall in a hired hackney to come here. After breakfast, after Patrick Gibbs had departed, Harland had kissed her, long and hard, and said nothing until now. For that, Katherine was grateful.

"As a prisoner or a visitor?" she asked.

"Either one."

"No," she answered. "Have you?"

"Too many times. Marshalsea most often, Newgate occasionally, one of these hulks sporadically. They are places of..."

"Misery?" Katherine asked.

"Worse. They are places where hope goes to die. And once hope dies, the soul dies with it."

Katherine kept her eyes on the men unloading ballast.

"We can still do this part without you," Harland said quietly. "You could still wait for us on the ship and we could find some other way to divert—"

"Shall we go?" Katherine asked. She tried to draw a deep breath, but the unfamiliar stays chafed mercilessly at her ribs beneath her unfamiliar dress. The discomfort was almost welcome, keeping her from dwelling on the pain buried far deeper.

"I won't be far."

"You'll do what you need to do. You made a promise to me. And more importantly, I made a promise to myself to do the same." She finally looked at him.

Harland was watching her, his eyes intense.

She forced a smile. "Besides, the sooner I can get out of this dress, the happier we'll all be."

"Speak for yourself. It's a nice dress."

Katherine glanced down at her breasts straining at the upper edge of her bodice. "You would say that."

Harland reached for her hand and pressed a kiss to the

backs of her knuckles, allowing a roguish grin to creep over his face. "Yes," he agreed. "Yes, I would." His grin faded as the teasing slipped. "I don't think you understand just how breathtaking you are right now."

"Why, thank you, Doctor. But it's just a few yards of silk." She was still struggling to keep her tone light because being called breathtaking by this man made her breathless. And she could not afford breathless. She had a job to do.

"It's not the dress, Katherine. It's you."

She released a shaky breath and forced a laugh. "Let's see how you feel once you critique my technique with a tourniquet. You may reconsider."

"I don't think so." He held her eyes. "Be my partner."

"I beg your pardon?"

"When we finish this. Join my practice. Be my partner."

Partner implied more than a friend. More than a lover. An ally. An equal. Harland was all of those things to her. And more. She just didn't know how to say that.

"I don't need an answer right now," he said, mistaking her hesitation for doubt. "But know that I believe that we could do great things together."

"I think we could too," she said. Impulsively, she went up on her tiptoes and brushed her lips across his. "Now, let's go get our patients."

———

There was a crowd at the gates, women milling about with baskets of produce or bread on their arms, hoping to make a few sales to those officers and laborers on their way into the Warren. A collection of small, ramshackle buildings had sprouted up, offering all sorts of services, from tailoring to shoe repairs to smith work, convenient services that officers and guards did not need to travel to London proper for.

Katherine and Harland wound their way through the crowd, Katherine very aware of the stares that were leveled in her direction. Or at least at the finery of the gown Gibbs and Harland had produced. It would have been deceptively expensive, she supposed. The unadorned sky-blue fabric was silk, the subtle lace trimmings imported. Not at all the sort of dress or the sort of woman who normally appeared at the gates of the Warren. The combination certainly made the two bored-looking guards who had been leaning against the stone wall stumble to attention.

"Miss Wright to see Colonel Walton," Harland intoned. He presented a sheaf of official-looking documents and launched into his rehearsed speech.

One of the guards took the documents from Harland's hand and pretended to scan them, but his eyes, like his partner's, never strayed very far from Katherine's décolletage. She stood ramrod stiff, allowing them to look their fill, and when Harland had finished speaking, she would have bet everything she owned that they had heard nothing Harland had even said.

"The colonel is a busy man," one of the guards said. "'Specially today."

"Indeed. He indicated as much when I made my appointment with him." She pinned the guard with a glare. "But he made time for me."

The guard holding the papers passed them back to Harland and exchanged a look with his partner. He shrugged and led them into a tiny room that housed nothing more than a sturdy table, a ledger, and a handful of chairs.

"Sign here," the guard intoned, stabbing the ledger with a thick finger. "Name and purpose."

Harland set his bulky doctor's bag aside and bent to the task while Katherine pretended to examine her surroundings.

"This ain't no place for a lady, you know." The guard was chewing on the end of a wooden toothpick, and his jaw moved in a bovine pattern as he continued to ogle her. "I could wait with you here. Or I could take you someplace nicer."

Katherine sniffed. "I can assure you, it is very much my place. I am the head of London Ladies' Goodwill Society for the Care, Education, and Rehabilitation of Convicts. The good doctor here has agreed to escort me so that I might tour the worksites and see for myself the work that remains to be done. Colonel Walton will be accompanying us."

The guard's toothpick fell out of his mouth. "The rebil... the rehebe... What?"

"The London Ladies' Goodwill Society for—"

"My lady has a very pious soul." Harland straightened from the ledger, patted her on the arm, and shot the guard an apologetic glance. "She believes that everyone should have a second chance. That earthly servitude can lead to a life of virtuous servitude to a higher power." He paused. "And she's willing to donate a significant amount of her fortune to such ends. Colonel Walton is most amenable to any proposal involving an influx of much-needed means. You understand."

The guard closed his mouth. He looked like he was going to say something but thought better of it.

Harland checked his pocket watch before he tucked her arm over his and retrieved his doctor's bag. "We must go if we are to keep our appointment with the colonel. Stewardship of time is such an important virtue, don't you agree?"

The guard was shaking his head. He waved them away, contempt pulling at the corner of his mouth.

"Stewardship of time is a very attractive virtue," Katherine murmured as they made their way out of the tiny room and down a crude wooden walkway toward the Thames.

"Isn't it?" Harland didn't break stride. "Twenty-two minutes."

Twenty-two minutes until they would execute a prison break.

They continued walking deeper into the Warren, getting closer to the riverbank. Here, the stench was more overwhelming, the never-ending clanking of the chains and the shouts of men louder. The smoke clung like a live, breathing miasma, though it was easier to see the prisoners as they labored along the shore than it had been from up on the road.

"Ah. Right on time."

Katherine looked away from the shore to find an officer approaching them. He was short yet powerful for his compact stature, his blond hair clipped neatly close to his head, a mustache of the same color hiding his upper lip, spectacles reflecting the light and making it hard to see his eyes. One hand rested casually on the saber sheathed at his waist; the other held a simple clay pipe.

"Gibbs," Harland said quietly.

Katherine studied the officer, a little shocked at the transformation of the man who had stood in the shadows of Haverhall's room only hours before. She might have passed him on the street and not recognized him. The captain who wasn't a captain offered her a bow before straightening.

"The colonel is on his way out now to muster his troops," Gibbs said.

Katherine smoothed a hand over the bodice of her gown as if doing so would smooth away her building apprehension. "Understood."

Gibbs raised his eyes over Katherine's shoulder. "Here he comes." He checked his own pocket watch. "Ten minutes," he said before he spun, heading toward the bank.

Katherine didn't look behind her. "Whatever happens, Harland, get the patients on the ship and get them away from here. Away from England. If you're able, wait for me. If not, go."

"Katherine, I'm not leaving you behind."

"You promised that you would get these boys home, no matter what. This is the *no matter what* part." She pasted on a prim smile and squared her shoulders. And turned.

Jeffrey Walton looked the same. Same blue eyes, same broad shoulders, same confident bearing. Things she had once found so attractive. A little heavier, perhaps, more gray in the sandy brown at his temples, but other than that, he looked to be a picture of health. A man who had been lucky enough to escape the punishment of war and had fled the aftermath, returning to a safe, secure life.

For a terrifying moment, the anger and bitterness she'd thought she'd defeated threatened to overwhelm her, surging through her veins and sending a red haze dancing around the edges of her vision. Beside her, Harland put a hand at the small of her back. She leaned into his touch, drawing strength from that small gesture and reminding herself why she was really here.

Jeffrey was almost in front of them now, surrounded by a phalanx of junior officers, all clutching papers and ledgers and looking harried. His brow creased as he studied a paper one of the officers had pushed into his hands. He looked up, his eyes skimming over Katherine and Harland before he jerked to a stop, his gaze snapping back to her as he blanched in recognition.

For a moment, it looked as if he were contemplating turning away, maybe bolting across the yards so that he would not have to acknowledge her. She almost wished he would do it. Run the way he had once. Run like the coward he was for everyone to see.

"Oh, good morning, Colonel Walton," Katherine called loudly.

Jeffrey's eyes darted to the sides as if he was looking for rescue, but there was none coming. Not this time. Not with the officers surrounding him gaping openly at Katherine.

"Good morning," he replied stiffly. "This is a... surprise. It's been a long time."

"Indeed. Why, the last time I saw you was at the fracas at Waterloo." She bestowed a blinding smile to the gaggle of underlings. "In fact—"

"You may wait for me at the barracks," Jeffrey barked at his officers, interrupting her. "I'll be but a moment."

"My condolences on your brother's passing." Katherine watched as his men drifted away. "I understand it was quite tragic."

Jeffrey folded the paper in his hand and straightened his back in an apparent effort to marshal his composure. "Thank you."

"That would make you a viscount now, wouldn't it?"

He nodded.

"In that case, my lord, may I present Baron Strathmore, also formerly of Wellington's army. Lord Strathmore, this is Colonel Jeffrey Walton, Viscount Hanveck, and of course, heir now to the Wheldham earldom." Katherine willed her voice to remain steady.

"Strathmore?" Walton repeated, seemingly noticing

Harland for the first time. "Yes, of course. You're a physician, are you not?"

"Today I am. I was asked here for a consult."

The viscount's eyes lingered on Harland's sleeve where Katherine's hand rested. "I heard you joined the medical corps after that nasty bit of business with your wife. Though I confess, I didn't expect a man who's come into his title to still be mucking about with such a hobby."

Harland smiled an empty, cold smile. "A man needs a purpose, don't you think, Colonel? After all, you still hold your commission."

"Indeed. And I will until my father dies. At the risk of sounding immodest, my military service has made me a hero. An inspiration for others. That is not something that I can simply walk away from, no matter how illustrious my family's title may be."

"Indeed." Harland's other hand, where it still rested against her back, was like steel.

Behind Jeffrey, Katherine could just see Gibbs where he had stopped near a pile of fresh earth that had been deposited on the far side of the ballast yards. He had lit his pipe, smoke wreathing his head in small, blue clouds. He dropped something and bent to retrieve it before he straightened and walked away.

It was time for Harland to go.

"Thank you, Lord Strathmore, for your kind escort, but I believe I've taken up too much of your time," Katherine said smoothly. "Colonel Walton will be able to escort me out of the Warren from here. It will give us a chance to catch up."

"Actually, Ka—Miss Wright, I am fully responsible for what happens in these yards under my watch, and I am late for my inspections. Perhaps I'll get another officer to see you to—"

"Oh, come now, Colonel. I think an escort to the Warren gates is the least you owe me. Don't you agree?" Even a fool would have heard the icy edge to her voice.

"I—" He stopped, his gaze flickering to Harland and then back. "Yes, of course."

Over Jeffrey's shoulder, Katherine could see Gibbs making his way along the edge of the timber yards, the smoke from his pipe trailing behind him. Again, he seemed to fumble with something in his hand, bending to retrieve what he'd dropped.

"You're sure, Miss Wright?" Harland's hand pressed against her back.

"Very sure," Katherine said. "Thank you, Lord Strathmore, and good day." She slipped her hand from Harland's arm and stepped closer to Jeffrey.

For a moment, Katherine was afraid Harland wasn't going to leave. He hesitated, adjusting his bulky doctor's bag in his grip.

"Good day," he finally said before turning away in the direction of the banks.

Katherine guessed they had less than three minutes before chaos reigned. She started walking toward the gates, forcing Jeffrey to follow.

"What are you doing here, Kate?" Jeffrey was frowning fiercely.

"I am the founding member of the London Ladies' Goodwill Society for the Care, Education, and Rehabilitation of Convicts. Lord Strathmore was kind enough to offer me a firsthand view of the work our society must face in our undertaking." The lies rolled off her tongue with more ease than she believed possible.

Jeffrey looked at her blankly. "You didn't come here looking for me?"

Katherine closed her eyes briefly. Of course he would have assumed that her appearance was about him. That she had come here looking for him. She kept walking. "To be honest, I didn't think that I would ever see you again." Amid all the lies, that was the truth. "When a man vanishes in the middle of the night, one makes certain assumptions."

"Good Lord, after all this time, you can't possibly still be angry that I left when I had to."

"When you had to?" She stopped, bile rising in the back of her throat, fury rising with it. "You left your men behind."

You left me behind.

"Look, Kate, you were a great comfort and diversion to me during a very trying time. And I don't dispute that you were very helpful to the surgeons and the physicians, but you are a woman. You can't possibly understand the political importance of a peer and an officer presenting our victory to king and country in a timely fashion. Men such as myself must be highly visible to the masses. Wounded soldiers would have slowed me down."

"You left your men behind," she repeated, unable to help herself.

"They were going to die anyway."

Katherine felt like she'd been punched. The hate she tried so hard to control slithered out, squeezing her lungs, constricting her throat. "They were your men, under your orders. They died protecting you."

"They knew they were fighting a war when they signed up," Jeffrey said impatiently.

"They didn't sign up to die."

Jeffrey rolled his eyes. "I can't help what happened to

them any more than I can help what happened to every other soldier. They were men of little consequence who did their duty protecting their better. I don't owe them anything for that."

A wave of nausea washed through her, most of it stemming from self-loathing. How had she ever believed herself to be in love with this man?

"You promised them you would see them home. That they would see their families again."

"Their families, I'm sure, got over it. Just like everyone else's." Jeffrey brushed at his coat.

"And me?"

"What about you?"

"Was it just as easy to leave me behind?"

"Kate, I didn't have time to deal with the inevitable hysterics."

"Inevitable hysterics? I—" Katherine snapped her mouth closed before she said something that she would regret. She scanned the banks of the Thames. On the deserted side of the ballast yards, near a pile of fresh earth, a new curl of smoke that wasn't from the foundries or anyone's pipe crept into the air.

Jeffrey was tapping the paper he held against his palm. "Look, it's unfortunate that I hurt your feelings, but there were more important matters that needed my attention. I do hope that you can understand that." He hesitated, his eyes slipping from her face to her bodice. "Perhaps I might make it up to you. If you would allow me."

Katherine stared at him, not sure she had heard him correctly.

"We were good together once, Kate." Jeffrey reached out and put a hand on her shoulder. "Perhaps we might be again."

"Are you offering to marry me again?"

Jeffrey heaved a sigh. "I should never have asked you that in the first place, and for that, I am sorry. But honestly, Kate, a man cannot be held accountable for what he says in the heat of battle. In a time of war. Besides, I am to be an earl now. You know as well as I that I will need a suitable bride. But there is no reason why we couldn't enjoy the relations we once did. I have the capital to keep you in comfort. Gowns, jewels, your own cottage—"

"No." She stepped away from him and started walking toward the gates with determined strides.

"I'll allow you some time to think about it."

"No."

"Then at the very least, you should have a care who you choose to spend your time with." He was following her, irritation clear in his voice. "I don't think it is wise to allow Lord Strathmore to become too familiar."

Katherine kept walking. "He's an excellent physician."

"He's a windy-fellow. Whole family is infamous for being peculiar. You don't want to be associated with that sort of madness. Strathmore couldn't even keep his own wife in his bed for that reason."

Katherine had reached the gates, and she whirled. "You—" She stopped and gathered herself. There was no need to reply to a statement like that. Because Katherine already knew exactly what sort of man Harland Hayward was.

And she knew exactly what sort of man Jeffrey Walton was.

"Was it dogs?" she asked.

"I beg your pardon?"

"Your brother. When he died, were you two shooting stray dogs in the Dials?"

Jeffrey's lips worked but no sound came out. A dull flush started creeping up his neck.

"Left him behind, too, when things went wrong, didn't you?"

The paper Jeffrey held in his hands tore in two, and the dull flush turned into a crimson stain across his face. "Watch yourself, Katherine. You can't possibly know any such thing. You would do well to remember who you are speaking to."

The curl of new smoke from the far side of the ballast yards had thickened into a column. It would be noticed within seconds. But it was already too late.

"I can know because I remember exactly who I am speaking to, Jeffrey."

The ragged pieces of paper crumpled in his fists.

"I'll see myself the rest of the way out." Something that had ached inside her for too long snapped and broke free, old hurts floating away like ash in the wind.

"You can't just walk away from me like this," Jeffrey seethed. He started to lunge toward her, brought up short by a panicked shout, the smoke finally catching someone's attention.

"Goodbye, Jeffrey," Katherine said softly just as all hell broke loose.

Chapter 17

The first explosion compressed the air with a dull thump, clods of earth erupting into the air to rain down around Harland. He ducked instinctively, though he knew very well that there was no real chance of injury. Nothing was burning save for mounds of tar-soaked, powder-laced straw that had been dumped beside all the other piles of refuse and earth from the banks. Flames erupted, thick black smoke billowing across the Warren. Shouts of fire rang out, and men started running, abandoning their tasks.

A second thump reverberated as a new explosion rocked the Warren, another mound of rotten earth and straw erupting into flames by the timber yards and instigating a new round of panic as men reacted.

In the stagnant air, the smoke quickly became difficult to see through. It swirled around the yards and buildings, spreading out across the surface of the Thames in greasy clouds. A blond officer appeared in the melee, shrieking contradictory orders at panicking men and adding to the general confusion. Harland was already moving toward the banks when that officer caught up to him.

"That was fun," Patrick said, wiping his hands with a kerchief. "We should do this again."

"Perhaps not." Harland didn't slow.

"Your Miss Wright is a woman of her word. She led the colonel right out of the Warren like the Pied Piper."

"She did." Harland had barely been able to put one foot in front of the other when he had walked away from her and Walton. It had taken everything he had not to return to her.

"Bleedin' hell, Mr. Gibbs." The guard who oversaw the ballast crew appeared in the smoke, rubbing irritated, watering eyes. "How many barrels of powder did ye use?"

"It's the oil and tar mixture one uses in the straw, not the amount of powder." Patrick passed him a leather pouch. "The balance of what's owed to you."

The guard tucked the pouch in his coat and passed Harland a heavy key. "Pleasure doing business with ye. You'll find your four Frenchies waitin' in the lighter. Got to warn ye, not sure the little one ain't already dead."

Harland cursed softly.

The guard disappeared into the smoke.

Harland scrambled down the bank, coughing. The bow of a lighter that was haphazardly hauled up onshore materialized out of the gloom, the sounds of chains thudding against wood.

Patrick pushed past him and clambered aboard, and Harland followed. Four prisoners had been chained to heavy rings bolted to the gunwales of the small craft. Two were lying in the bottom, the other two desperately working at the chains with no success.

Their eyes went wide as they saw Patrick and Harland,

and they scrambled back, the chains around their ankles and waist clinking, their eyes on the knife in Harland's hand. One of them started to shout something but abruptly stopped as Patrick held up the key in his hand.

"If you want your brother to live, you'll be quiet," Harland said clearly in French. "Now hold still."

Patrick moved first, unlocking the fetters with brisk efficiency.

"Is he alive?" Harland asked, not liking the stillness of the two forms in the bottom of the boat.

Patrick moved, freeing limbs with care. "They're both breathing," he reported. "For now."

Harland set his heavy bag in the bow with a thud and yanked it open.

"Who are you?" asked the nearest prisoner, who had been yanking at the chains. He was gaunt, his eyes too big for his face, his hair shorn almost to the scalp, making him look eerily skeletal. A wide scar ran over his left brow, adding to the macabre image.

"A doctor. Here to help you away from here." Harland kept his answers vague. If this all went wrong, there could be no names left behind. "Take off your coats."

"Why?"

"Because right now you look like prisoners." Harland withdrew a worn bundle of clothing and tossed it in the prisoners' direction. "Put these on. Yourselves and the other two."

Patrick undid the last fetter and dumped the chains overboard. "Time to go." He jumped from the boat and yanked the thick rope off its tethering post, tossing the end into the lighter.

Patrick put his shoulder against the bow as Harland took up a position at the oars, and the craft slid soundlessly back into the water. Deftly, Patrick vaulted back in as Harland hauled on the oars, and the small craft surged away from land and toward the open water of the Thames.

The two prisoners who were still upright had managed to shed their clothing and had donned the nondescript garb of common rivermen. They were struggling to do the same to the two lying still. The smallest of the patients moaned pitifully as his jacket was pulled away from his body.

"He's dying," the scarred prisoner said starkly, tossing the ragged jacket overboard.

"Not if I can help it," Harland muttered, maneuvering the lighter around so that the bow was pointing away from the Warren and in the direction of freedom.

"Where are you taking us?"

Harland was surprised that it had taken even this long to ask that question. He leaned into the oars, the lighter skimming over the water.

"Home."

Katherine was running, no easy task in a dress with stays that wrapped around her ribs like claws. She hurried along the edge of Plumstead Road, the din of the confusion and the chaos fading behind her. It was still easy to see the smoke billowing from the center of the Warren that had spread like a dark cloud, and the acrid scent of sulfur, pitch, and burning straw hung heavy in the air.

In her head, Katherine had already organized a list of excuses and explanations should she be stopped, most of them based on a solid foundation of inevitable hysterics, but so far, the road remained deserted. If everything had gone well, Harland and Patrick should be away, out onto the river with their own set of excuses and explanations should they be stopped. The ship waiting to transport them should be in place, ready to intercept and spirit them down the Thames toward freedom.

She hoped desperately that Harland had not tarried in the Warren. That he had not waited for her on those banks. She hoped even more desperately that they would wait for her ahead.

That she would not be left behind.

Her breath was coming in shallow gasps now as she veered off the muddy stretch and dropped down to the marsh, her feet sinking almost instantly in the soft, sucking ground, her skirts becoming soaked and heavy. She was never going to make it like this.

Without considering further, she yanked the pins and ties from the shoulders and front of her gown. The silk fell away, and Katherine stepped out of the dress, balling it up in her arms. She bent with some difficulty and rucked up her shift, reaching to yank free the dive knife strapped to the outside of her calf. With a single slice, the laces to her stays parted and she took a welcome, heaving breath. She jammed the stays under her arm with the dress and started running again, now clad only in her shift.

She revised her list of ready excuses to include only hysterical tendencies now.

There was a faint trail leading across the marsh and toward the river, created by men or animals or both. She followed it, the tall marsh grasses nearly closing over her head. The columns of smoke rising far away over her left shoulder kept her orientated in the absence of the sun.

Her destination had been her idea, an abandoned stone building on this side of the river, not more than two miles down from the Warren. It sat at the base of a massive, ancient oak tree that stood sentinel on the bank. Yet she'd only ever seen the decaying building from the water, and that had been years ago, on a smuggling run into London that she and her father had made.

She tried to ignore the doubts that were creeping into the back of her mind. Doubts like she wouldn't be able to locate the building from the marsh. Doubts like the building no longer existed, the tumbled stones long removed by people for their own use. Doubts like it was taking far too long for her to struggle through this marsh. Doubts like she would be left behind. Alone. Again.

She had to be close now. The ground became more saturated, and Katherine sank past her knees in some places. Still, she pressed on relentlessly. Startled birds shrieked and careened out of the marsh ahead of her, the only other sound that of her ragged breathing. She didn't allow herself to slow, panic that she would be too late driving her on. She stumbled, the ground abruptly rising, the footing becoming more secure. She staggered onward, following the trail, her feet now on relatively stable ground. And then, just ahead, the twisting branches of a towering oak came into view.

Katherine almost sobbed in relief. She wove her way through a maze of tangled bushes, almost tripping over a pile of abandoned stone. She'd made it.

The old building at the base of the tree was small, no bigger than Avondale's attic room where Matthew was recovering. It no longer had a roof, the wooden trusses that may have supported thatch long gone to either humans or the elements, and two walls had similarly surrendered. The remains of an old cooking fire were evident against one of the remaining walls, blackened streaks on the stone. Someone had recently used this structure as a respite. It was entirely possible someone might be using it still.

She dropped to a crouch behind the snarled mass of bushes, trying to recover her breath, trying to listen. But there was no movement, the grasses limp in the still air, and only the song of a thousand frogs and the lap of the water against the concealed bank reaching her ears. From here, she couldn't see the river. Form here, she couldn't see if there was a ship waiting for her. A ship that would see them all safely away from here.

She stumbled toward the sound of the water, stopping just behind the last curtain of rushes and foliage that lined the bank, closing her eyes. Afraid to look. Afraid not to look. And she cursed herself for being a coward. She opened her eyes and stepped out onto the bank.

The river was empty.

Katherine staggered slightly, hating the weakness and the emotion that rushed up to constrict her chest and her throat. Goddammit, this is what she had wanted. She gazed downriver, toward the Warren, but there was no ship. No masts, no craft at all, only a lonely stretch of open water. She tried to take a deep breath, but it came out only as a wheeze, sadness and loss crushing her like hundredweight. It had taken her too long to get here.

In her head, she knew that this had been a possibility—a likelihood, even. She was not on an abandoned battlefield in Belgium, left to care for dying men. She was not hundreds of miles from everyone and everything that was familiar. Circumstances now were different than they had been then. But the reality was just as devastating as it had been the first time.

She dropped to her knees, the blue dress falling from her grasp to slide to the muddy bank, and forced herself to think through the irrational pain that was coursing through her.

Harland had done what he'd had to do. He'd done what she'd told him to do.

And what she needed to do was pull herself together. Formulate a plan to get away from here and out of this marsh. Find a way to ensure that Harland had gotten away cleanly from the Warren—

"What the hell are you wearing?"

Katherine lurched to her feet and spun clumsily, her knife that was still clutched in her hand coming up in front of her.

"I didn't say I didn't like it," Harland said, holding up his hands. "I was only going to suggest that you are a bit underdressed."

Katherine dropped her knife and took a faltering step toward him and found herself wrapped in his arms. To her horror, the urge to cry crashed down on her like a wave, constricting her lungs and making her eyes burn. The impulse to cling to this man and sob and beg him to never leave her was suffocating.

Inevitable hysterics, indeed.

She took a shuddering breath and extracted herself from his embrace, wiping her face with the sleeve of her shift.

Harland was watching her, worry creasing his features. "Walking away from you in that yard almost killed me. I never should have left you with Walton—"

"I don't want to talk about Walton. Not now. Not ever again." It was the truth. She had faced the man who had cut her to her soul and survived. Not only survived but triumphed.

His eyes didn't leave her face. "Very well."

"The patients? Did you get them out—"

"The patients are safely on board." Harland shrugged out of his coat, draping the welcome warmth around

Katherine's shoulders. "We stopped just a little farther downstream. Captain's orders. He didn't like the exposure on the water at this bend. I have one of the landing boats here."

"You shouldn't have left the patients." She tried to make her words brisk. Detached.

"I shouldn't have left you."

She could feel the weight of his gaze. "I'm not at risk of dying any time soon." She retrieved her knife. "We should hurry—"

"Katherine—"

"We should hurry," she repeated. There was no room for emotion and no time for difficult conversations. Not now. Not when lives hung in the balance.

"I brought these." Harland fetched a canvas bag that she hadn't noticed behind him and withdrew her black shirt and trousers that she had once worn on a Dover beach.

"Thank you." Katherine slipped out of his coat and passed it back to him. Wordlessly, he took it and turned to face the opposite way. Which was as ridiculous as it was touching, given everything that had already transpired between them.

She dressed quickly, her sopping, stained shift joining the crumpled blue gown, both of which she gathered into a ball under her arm. "Let's go."

Harland reached for her hand, and Katherine allowed him to take it. Allowed him to lead her through the dense maze of wiry brush, past the abandoned building and down the bank. Half concealed by long grasses was the stern of a small landing boat, a man hunched over a set of oars.

"'Bout time," Patrick grumbled. He had lost his officer's clothing and now looked like a common fisherman. He eyed Katherine's appearance with barely a raised brow and gestured to the boat. "Get in. All this waiting makes me nervous."

Katherine stepped into the boat, Harland right behind her, and Patrick didn't even wait until they were sitting on the hard benches before he hauled on the oars, sending the boat out into the current.

Chapter 18

T he smallest of the boys would lose his lower leg.

Katherine hadn't needed to see the injury to determine the extent of the damage—the stench of the wound had suggested the only course of action long before she had seen the boy on the surgery's table and peeled back what was left of his trousers. His name was Bernard, she'd been told, and something, at some point in time, had carved a deep cut into the boy's calf. The wound had festered, the tissue dark and swollen and seeping. Bernard had been slipping in and out of consciousness, flushed with fever. For the moment, he had been given a preparation of Jesuit's bark, cold compresses applied, and made as comfortable as possible.

The next youngest, Rene, also drifted in and out of fevered consciousness and had received the same treatment. He would need to have at least three toes on his right foot removed. Katherine guessed that the bones had been crushed, infection setting in.

The other two patients, Luc and Claude, were in varying degrees of poor health. Luc had what she suspected was a broken arm, the break old and poorly healed. Claude, the oldest of the four, had escaped unscathed save for the malnourishment, dehydration, and weakness that afflicted all four. Those two had been escorted to the ship's galley where they were being fed. Away from the surgery and the task that lay before Katherine and Harland.

"Dr. Wright, I presume."

Katherine looked from where she was placing a thick towel under Bernard's leg to see the ship's captain standing at the threshold of the surgery. The address of *doctor* still caught her off guard when it was used by a man she had never met.

"You presume correctly, Captain Black."

With his long, dark hair and beard, Black looked like a dashing pirate out of a fanciful novel. Katherine had seen him briefly standing on the deck and barking orders at his men as Patrick had rowed their craft near the sleek cutter tugging at her moorings in the middle of the river. They'd been aboard only seconds before the ship once again started its journey down the river like a Thoroughbred released after being tied for too long.

"Welcome." Black bowed flamboyantly and straightened, twirling an antique tricorne in his hands. "It's not often we have the privilege of having a beautiful woman on board. A beautiful woman in trousers, no less. I confess I'm rather enamored of the fashion."

Katherine returned her attention to the instruments she was rolling out on the counter bolted to the surgery's bulkhead, watching the captain from the corner of her eye. "You have my gratitude for delaying our final departure. I'm not so sure I would have done the same."

The twirling tricorne stopped. "I beg your pardon?"

"The success of this venture depends largely on swift travel. Delays are not advantageous."

"Dr. Hayward seemed to think that you were necessary for the success of this venture, swift or not. He didn't give me a choice. Did he tell you he threatened to jump overboard to fetch you if I did not wait?"

Katherine's hands stilled over her instruments. "He did not."

"Which would have delayed us even more because I need at least one of you. I've seen Hayward swim, and there is a good chance that he would have sunk to the bottom of the Thames before he got halfway across the water." Black jabbed his tricorne in the direction of the boy on the table with a shudder. "And I certainly can't fix that unholy mess. Dead French prisoners do not make me money."

Katherine turned and leaned against the counter, studying Black. "I might suggest you return above decks, then, Captain. Because things are only going to get messier."

Black gave a sudden, roguish grin. "Good God. Are you concerned about my sensibilities?"

"I'm not concerned about your sensibilities, Captain. I am, however, concerned about those out on the river looking for missing prisoners or ships that haven't quite managed to be honest with their manifests. Should we be boarded, I would like fair warning."

His grin slipped, and a speculative gleam came into his eye. "You've done this before."

"Too many times. Amputations are often the only thing that might save—"

He stepped into the surgery. "I'm not talking about amputations. I'm talking about running a craft down this river that hasn't quite been . . . honest with its manifests."

Katherine regarded him steadily. "Yes."

Black crowed in delight. "Hayward's been holding out on me. I can see why your baron is besotted."

"He's not my baron." Katherine felt heat rise in her face. "And he's not besotted."

Black settled his tricorne back on his head. "In that case, I don't suppose you'd want a job when we're done with this one? I've need of a surgeon, one with smuggling experience all the better. Ever been to India?"

"She doesn't need a job with you, Black," Harland said, ducking into the surgery, two pails of steaming water in his hands. "She's not a smuggler."

Katherine returned her attention to the roll of instruments before her, assailed by longing and something that went even deeper than mere want. Something so acute that it made it hard to breathe and left her emotionally unsteady. Harland had led her to the surgery and then promptly disappeared to fetch buckets of water he'd ordered boiled, and she'd been glad for his absence. Because the part of her that had wanted to burst into irrational tears when he appeared on that bank still lurked, catching her at unsuspecting moments. Like this one.

The task at hand would require all her concentration. She needed to focus on the job, not the man who would be at her side.

"I would think the lady might like to speak for herself, Hayward. Gold and spices bring much greater rewards than brandy and lace." The captain sniffed. "I can offer you very attractive terms, Dr. Wright. Just ask your bar—"

"She's a surgeon, not a smuggler," Harland repeated, setting the buckets of water down with a thump.

"Thank you, Captain, but no," Katherine said.

Black stroked his beard, his eyes traveling from Harland

to Katherine and back. "Of course. Well, think about it, Dr. Wright. I might yet change your mind."

"You won't." Katherine left the counter and picked up the boy's left arm. As gently as possible, she buckled the padded cuffs that hung from the side of the table around his wrist. She was taking no chances that the boy might topple off the table once they began sawing. "Are you ready, Dr. Hayward?"

Harland was stoking a small brazier that glowed in the corner of the surgery, small cauterizing rods beginning to glow orange with heat. "I am."

"I think I shall take Dr. Wright's advice and return above decks," Black said with a grimace. He started backing out of the surgery. "I would wish you good luck, but I always find that sentiment redundant."

"Redundant?" Katherine asked.

"One must be very good to be lucky." He bowed again. "And you wouldn't be here, Dr. Wright, if you weren't very, very good."

⁓

Katherine hadn't been good. She'd been extraordinary.

Had Harland been able to work alongside another surgeon in the field with the competence and unwavering nerve that she possessed, he would have saved more men. But he, like Katherine, had been on his own, overwhelmed by death and pain and blood and desperation, stemming the deluge to the best of his ability with what had been at hand.

Harland leaned wearily against the bulkhead of the galley, the groans and creaks of the ship as it charged across the open channel a welcome respite from the sounds of the surgery. This day had not been a deluge, though it had still

possessed the same echoes of desperation and determination. Their saws had still made the same noises as they bit
into bone, the patients had still gasped and cried and suffered. Not once had Katherine flinched. Not once had she
been anything but steady and practical and deliberate as the
hours had dragged on. And as a result, Harland was cautiously optimistic all four patients would live to see their
families again.

Darkness had fallen long ago, the cutter picking up
speed as it reached the open sea unchallenged and uncon-
tested. Either Black was the luckiest captain Harland had
ever met or he was just as good as he professed he was.
Either way, it didn't matter. They were free of the Thames
and of England now with only the hurdles of a safe cross-
ing and a safe landing left.

A heavy thud brought Harland back to himself, another
pail of steaming water waiting at his feet, the impatient
cook already returning into the depths of the cramped galley. Harland bent and retrieved the pail, retracing his steps
back to the surgery where Katherine remained with the
four patients. When he had left for the galley, all four
patients had fallen into an exhausted sleep, and Harland
was quite sure that they would continue to sleep until they
reached the coast sometime tomorrow. There would be
dressings to be changed and stitches to be checked, herbal
preparations to be administered and cold compresses to be
switched out, but uninterrupted rest was the medicine that
their patients needed most right now.

Harland ducked into the surgery and set the bucket near
the counter. Overhead, the lantern swung, making the shadows dance drunkenly.

"Two of Black's men will keep an eye on our patients,"
he said, dipping a shallow tin into the water. "They're on

their way, and they've both assisted the ship's surgeon before. They know to fetch either one of us if something happens, but you need to get some rest. We both do."

He set the tin aside and reached for a sliver of hard soap, washing his hands and scrubbing at the remnants of blood that stained the creases of his fingers. "Black figures that we will make land early afternoon if the winds stay favorable. We'll wait for darkness to take them ashore." He rinsed his hands and reached for a towel. "The men who will meet us will send a signal. We'll take five of Black's crew when we go."

Katherine didn't answer.

Harland frowned and turned. She was leaning against the far bulkhead, but even from where he stood, Harland could see the tears tracking down her face. He dropped the towel.

"What's wrong? What happened?" He was at her side in a heartbeat. "Katherine?"

She still wasn't answering, only looking at him helplessly, tears falling unchecked from her reddened eyes. His own gaze flew to where the four patients lay motionless on their cots. "Did something happen? Did we lose—"

"They're fine. Just s-sleeping." Her voice was strangled, and the last word caught on a sob.

He put his hands on her shoulders, running his fingers down her arms and then back up to her face, as if searching for an injury. "Are you hurt? Sick?"

She shook her head.

"Then what's wrong?"

"I don't know." The tears fell faster. "I don't know. Nothing. I just..."

"Come here." He caught her hand and guided her from the surgery into the tiny surgeon's cabin attached. It wasn't much of a cabin—it consisted only of a berth and a table bolted in place—but it was private. He closed the door behind them.

"I'm sorry," she managed. "I don't know why I'm crying. This is em-embarrassing. You don't need t-to—"

"Shhh." Harland drew her into his arms.

Her breaths were coming in heaving, shuddering gasps, and she wrapped her arms around him like a drowning person. "This is s-stupid," she said into his chest. "I didn't cry when Jeffrey left. I didn't c-cry when his men died. Or any of the others. I didn't cry when the soldiers shot my brother and tried to shoot me."

Harland ran a hand over her back. "Maybe you should have."

"It achieves n-nothing. Fixes n-nothing."

"You've been strong for a lot of people for a long time. It's all right to be human for a while. It's all right to let someone be strong for you once in a while."

That seemed to make her cry harder. "You came back for me. I wasn't sure you would."

"I promised you I would."

She made a raw sound. "It was foolish. It could have gotten you caught. It could have gotten all of us caught."

"Are you trying to pick a fight?" he asked gently. "Because it's not going to work."

She made a sound that was almost a laugh but more of a sob. "You're not supposed to argue with someone picking a fight."

He drew back, searching her eyes with his. He wiped the tears from her cheeks with his thumb. "I wasn't supposed to do a lot of things in my life," he said.

"Like what?" she mumbled.

"I wasn't supposed to go to war. I certainly wasn't

supposed to become a doctor." *And I wasn't supposed to fall in love with one either.*

The last words slipped unbidden into his consciousness, the truth of them echoing like the report of a cannon. He froze, unsure what to do with them.

"That's all?" she sniffed.

I hadn't planned on falling in love with a woman who nearly shot me the first night we met. A woman who is smart and brave and talented and has lent her strength to so many for so long. A woman who once told me never to change. I wasn't ever leaving her behind, no matter what she said.

He couldn't blurt out something like that. Not when he couldn't give her what she so badly wanted. A family. A home with a garden in the back and a dog in the front. A life free from desperation and crime and full of happiness and security. A normal existence that didn't involve smuggling and soldiers, and underworld kingpins who had him at their mercy.

"I wasn't supposed to walk into a Dover cottage in the middle of the night and discover the bravest, most courageous woman I've ever met." It was what he could offer her.

"I was rather awful to you then." She ducked her head but the tears had stopped, and a glimmer of a smile touched her lips.

"You had good reason then."

She sniffed again, and the smile broke through, only to fade. "You are the best man I've ever met," she said quietly. She looked up at him, her eyes luminous pools of turquoise. Her gaze moved over his face to settle on his mouth.

Harland swallowed, afraid that if she kept looking at

him like that he wouldn't be able to step away when he needed to.

I wasn't supposed to fall in love.

He repeated it like a mantra in his head, but that changed nothing. It didn't change how he felt about this woman, and it didn't change how much he wanted her.

"Stay with me," she said.

Harland's heart banged painfully. She had no idea what she was asking. He should go. Before this got any more complicated than it already was. Before he fell any further in love with her. Because saying goodbye when this all ended would be agony.

But he couldn't step away. Perhaps he had witnessed too much death and suffering and understood that life was fleeting and that it was regret that was the enemy. Perhaps he recognized that the pain and hurt at the end would be worth whatever he might have with Katherine Wright for this window of time.

She went up on her toes and kissed him. It was feather-light but lacked any hesitation, as if she, too, recognized that this had always been inevitable.

He caught her with his hands, spinning her back against the cabin door. The time for uncertainty was gone. He kissed her, hot and hard, trying to put everything that he could not give her into something that he could.

His tongue swept into her mouth, exploring her heat, his body trapping hers against the unforgiving surface at her back. He yanked at the tie of her braid, pulling it from the plait. He held her head, still kissing her, and let her curtain of hair unwind and fall around her shoulders. He was hard and throbbing and knew damn well that she could feel every inch of him pressed against her belly through their clothes.

She made a soft noise, and her hands were at the hem of his shirt, pulling it up and over his head the way she had done that first night. He let his palm slide over the front of her faded black shirt, feeling her hard nipples beneath the fabric. He let his hands linger, caressing the sides of her breasts, loving the tiny, breathless sounds she made. And then that wasn't enough anymore, and his fingers dropped, finding the hem of her shirt and pulling it easily over her head so that she was finally bared before him.

"God, Katherine." He raised his hands, letting the backs of his fingers trail over the perfect, beautiful skin of her shoulders.

He set one hand at the center of her chest, feeling her pulse hammering beneath his touch. And then he bent his head, his mouth retracing the path his fingers had gone before.

Her head fell back against the cabin door as he explored the hollow of her throat and then each breast with his tongue, nipping and sucking as he went. He paid special attention to each of her nipples, listening as she gasped and writhed against him. Each small sound escalated his own arousal, and he rocked into her, the friction of that movement sending overwhelming desire pounding through his veins.

He should draw this out, he knew, prolong each moment for her, but he was no longer certain he possessed the control to do that. The need to be deep inside her, to be a part of her, was quickly eroding every good intention. He lifted his head and found her mouth again, his hands sliding over her backside, pulling her hard against him.

Katherine bit his lower lip. "Not enough," she whispered against his mouth, and Harland had barely processed that before he realized that her fingers were working the buttons at the fall of his trousers.

He stepped back slightly, feeling the cool air brush his skin as she shoved his clothing down his legs. He stepped out of his discarded trousers, intending to return the favor, but he gasped, the feel of her hands closing over the length of his erection making him see stars for a moment. He swayed, almost dizzy with want as she stroked him from the crown to the base and then back again.

"Yes." The syllable was hoarse and needy and made him sound like an adolescent again but he didn't care.

Katherine continued to stroke him, dragging the thumb of one hand over the tip while the other slid over his hip and across the contours of his buttocks. He groaned and thrust into her touch, more sparks of pleasure igniting a firestorm he was fast losing control of.

"Tell me what you want, Harland," she whispered.

He squeezed his eyes shut, remembering that he had once asked her the same thing. Except the wicked images that raced through his mind went way beyond what she had once asked of him.

"You," he managed.

"How do you want me, Harland?"

He dropped his head, breathing hard.

She shifted away from him. "Like this?"

Harland's eyes flew open as she took him in her mouth. Scorching heat sizzled through him, spreading from his groin up along his spine and through his limbs. He reached out and put one hand on the cabin door, trying to brace himself. Trying to keep himself from imploding right there.

Katherine had one hand at the base of his erection, caressing him in tandem with her tongue.

"Katherine." Her name was torn from somewhere in his throat, though he barely recognized his own voice.

She glanced up at him, her pale hair tumbling over her shoulders to brush his legs, her eyes hot and devoid of doubt. She lifted her head and pressed her mouth to his navel, her tongue swirling around the depression. One of her hands still stroked his erection, the other caressed his balls.

"Like this?" she asked, her teeth grazing the ridges of muscle across his abdomen.

"Katherine," he said again, unable to say anything else through his haze of arousal.

"I want you to take what you need," she said, and again he recognized his own words.

"You don't know what you're asking," he rasped.

"I know exactly what I'm asking."

Harland reached down and pulled her up, catching her at the nape of her neck and kissing her hard, a hot, licentious, and filthy kiss that offered no quarter and embodied exactly what he needed from her.

She met him halfway, her hands sliding down his back. "Take it," she whispered against his mouth. "Or don't."

It was the last of his own words that snapped his restraint. He spun her against the door so that her back was to him, pressing her hands against the smooth wood. "Don't move," he growled.

Harland pushed her hair to the side and ran his palms over the smooth skin of her back and down the hollow of her spine, the meager lantern light playing over the delicate ridges of muscle and bone. He grasped her hips, pulling them toward him. He let his fingers slide over the roundness of her backside and then around the front of her thighs, brushing the juncture where they met.

Against the door, her fingers curled.

He went to work on the buttons of her trousers, letting the fall drop open, working the waistband down over the swell of her arse and watching as they slid down her legs. He had never undressed a woman in trousers before, and it was excruciatingly erotic. He bent, working each leg over her calves and lifting each foot until she was as naked as he. He ran his hands up the insides of her legs, nudging them wide, and taking a fierce pleasure in the way they trembled.

He put his mouth where his fingers had been, branding the sensitive skin of her upper thighs.

Katherine whimpered and let her hips tilt further, and Harland needed no additional invitation. He slid a finger through her folds, her back arching as she moaned. She was hot and wet and perfect, and Harland withdrew his fingers and leaned between her legs, tasting her the way he had wanted to for too long.

Katherine moaned again, her forehead resting against the door, her hips flexing ever so slightly. He sucked and she jerked, her gasp catching on a more desperate sound. A sound that got louder as his tongue stroked and incited.

He finally straightened, the devastating need that had been building now roaring through every nerve ending. This time, when she went over the edge, he would be with her. He caged her hips with his hands and then moved to position himself at her entrance, nudging her folds. She pushed back toward him, and the head of his cock slipped into her heat. Harland hissed, fighting for control even as Katherine made a sound of frustration.

Harland released her hips and let his hands travel to her breasts, cupping their weight, toying with her nipples. His cock throbbed, but still he waited, kissing the side of her neck and shoulder. "Tell me what you want, Katherine," he said, turning the question back to her.

"You," she gasped, flexing her hips again.

"How do you want me?" He was sweating with the effort of restraint.

"Deep. Hard."

Those words were too much. Harland thrust, sheathing himself in her wet heat. He went still as his mind went blank, pleasure ripping through him like a lightning storm.

"Don't stop," Katherine gasped.

He withdrew and thrust again, a little deeper this time, letting her adjust to him. Her hips rocked, urging him on, and he thrust once more, seating himself fully.

"God, Katherine, you feel so good."

She flexed her hips, and he slid a little farther.

"I'll try to be careful," he said hoarsely.

"I already told you what I wanted," she panted. "And it wasn't careful."

Stars danced before his eyes as raw desire tore through him. He withdrew and slammed into her, and she made a sound of approval. He tried to slow his thrusts, but carnal need was overpowering reason. He ached with it, was consumed with it, and he needed this woman at this moment the way he needed air. This was a primitive sort of joining, each straining toward release, the only sounds in the room their harsh breathing mingled with that of skin on skin. Release was gathering deep within him, his muscles coiling, his nerves showering sparks of white-hot ecstasy.

"Come for me, Katherine," he growled in her ear, sliding one of his hands from her breasts, over her belly, and through her tight curls, finding the sensitive nub at the juncture of her legs.

Her head tipped back, and she was whimpering and

moaning now, her hands pressed against the door so hard her knuckles and fingers were white.

Harland ran his teeth along the back of her neck. "Come for me."

She cried out just before her inner walls spasmed around him, drawing him ever deeper and pulsing against his length. Harland grasped her hips, held his tempo, and let her ride the eddies of her climax as his own release roared down upon him.

He thrust once more before withdrawing, coming against the glorious roundness of her backside, waves of scalding pleasure drowning him in relentless succession. They went on and on, sizzling through his blood, obliterating his senses. He ground his cock against her, his hips still jerking, an incapacitating ecstasy like he had never known, making it impossible for him to catch his breath.

Slowly, the world came back into focus, and he realized that he still had Katherine against a cabin door, her body clutched hard against his, both of them slicked with sweat. He straightened, bending to retrieve his discarded shirt and gently wiping his seed from her skin. He dropped the shirt and pulled her up and away from the door, turning her so that she once again faced him. He bent his head and kissed her gently, resting his forehead against hers. He had no idea what to say.

"Let's do that again," Katherine said.

Harland laughed, happiness of the sort he hadn't felt in a long time catching him off guard. "That can be arranged."

"Good." She was smiling.

"I had intended to be gentle."

"Mmm." Her hands slid over his chest. "I'll tell you when I want gentle."

It was strange and liberating, Katherine's candid, casual

discussion of sexual intimacy. It suggested a bond of mutual trust, something he'd never had with his wife, and something he certainly hadn't had with any of the assignations he'd tried to distract himself with since her death.

"You'll also tell me when you like what I'm doing," he said. "And when you don't."

"Sounds intriguing."

"I have ideas where you're concerned."

Katherine looked up at him, her eyes hot. "I have a few of my own."

Harland shuddered. He wasn't going to survive this woman. But he couldn't think of a more delectable demise.

"I think that perhaps we could be lovers as well as friends." She was still watching him, her gaze unwavering.

It should have thrilled him, that statement. But it rang hollow because Harland realized that he wanted more. He wanted to be her lover and her friend, that was true. But more than that, he wanted to be her everything. Forever.

He kissed her softly again, because what he wanted was impossible. "Take whatever you need, Katherine."

"I think," she said, "that it is not so much about taking or giving. But about being made whole."

Harland drew her into his arms, closing his eyes against the tightness in his chest. "Yes." She was right. She made him whole.

He let his fingers tangle in the curtain of her hair. "You should get some sleep. Let me take you to bed."

She kissed his bare shoulder. "I'd expect a more artful proposition from a man with your means and position," she whispered.

Desire sparked and crackled through him all over again.

"That, Dr. Wright, can also be arranged."

Her lips found his. "Good."

Chapter 19

Under the inky sky, the beaches of Wissant were invisible.

The only thing that told Katherine that they were drawing nearer was the sound of the surf as the waves folded over on themselves and hissed up the flat expanse. Earlier, a lantern light had glowed once, twice, three times before it had been snuffed, a pattern repeated aboard the anchored cutter before the landing boats and their occupants had been lowered.

They were expected.

It had been a long time since Katherine had been to Wissant—the last time with her father and brother in a small oyster boat full of fine English wool to be traded for fine French brandy. She closed her eyes and breathed deeply. The earthy scent of the dunes and vegetation where sea met land was still the same, carried on the warm summer breeze. Though on this night, the faint scent of antiseptic, not lanolin, laced the air. She remembered being on edge back then, every sense tuned toward the beaches, tensed and ready for a discovery that never came.

She still used her senses now, but that unsettled edginess was absent, replaced only with a sense of determined certainty.

"Almost there." It was Harland who spoke.

Katherine opened her eyes. A suggestion of movement, of pale surf bubbling, was all the warning she had before the boat jerked slightly as the hull caught against the sand. Four sailors abandoned their oars and jumped overboard, splashing into the sea as they hauled the little craft up on the beach. Katherine didn't dare move from where she held Bernard securely in the bottom of the craft on a stretcher. Behind her, Harland did the same with Rene.

The boat came to rest up on the sand flat with a soft grating, the only other sound aside from the sea. There were no shouts, no telltale nickers or snorts from waiting horses. Even the seabirds remained silent and undisturbed. Claude and Luc were helped onto the beach by the sailors, whispered voices rising and then receding. Within minutes, the sailors were back, this time reaching for the rough ends of the stretchers on which the two youngest patients still lay.

"Careful," Harland cautioned as they were lifted away and into the darkness beyond. "Don't jar them."

Katherine stiffly pushed herself to her feet, feeling her way to the bow. She swung herself out, her booted feet sinking slightly in the wet sand. A hand came to rest at the small of her back.

"They're home," Harland whispered against her ear.

"Not quite yet." Their patients were on a beach but they were not yet home. Home was with their families.

She had barely finished that thought when a light flared briefly, up in the dunes that lay ahead.

"They know we're here." Katherine started forward, joining the knot of men who were waiting just above the line of the surf.

"*Il y a une lumière.*" It was Claude who spoke, his voice thin and hoarse with hope.

There is a light.

Harland pushed past Katherine in the dark toward the front of the group. "Follow me," he said in a low voice. "Careful of your footing." He disappeared up ahead as the group began to move forward slowly, Katherine bringing up the rear.

The sound of the surf grew muted as they traversed their way into the dunes. With each step, Katherine relaxed fractionally. Had there been soldiers or patrols, they would have taken them on the open beach where their horses and guns would have been used to their best advantage. No smuggler hunter in his right mind would have allowed their quarry to vanish into dunes or marshes.

"Stop." The order came as Harland lit a small lantern up ahead. The pool of light wavered against the scrubby vegetation, sending eerie fingerlike shadows crawling up the dunes.

"Now what?" one of the sailors asked.

"Now we wait." He gestured at the stretchers. "You can put them down. Gently."

The sailors obeyed and backed away, their hands resting on the hilts of their weapons as their eyes searched the darkness beyond the tiny pool of light.

"Bonjour, *Docteur.*" The address, when it came disembodied out of the night, made her jump.

Harland didn't flinch. "Bonjour, Martin," he said into the darkness. "*Une bonne nuit, non?*"

A movement in Katherine's peripheral vision made her

turn her head. Two men were emerging from the dunes, a pistol held loosely in each of their hands, wary eyes on the sailors who were regarding them with the same distrust. Both were tall and lean, their clothes constructed out of a rough homespun, battered hats jammed over fair hair. They stopped just before Harland.

"You look good, my friend," the first man said with a sudden grin, shoving his pistol into the leather holster across his chest.

"*Et toi*, Martin." Harland nodded first at Martin and then at the man behind him. "Bonjour, Leo. Your brother treating you all right?"

Leo gave Harland the same crooked grin his brother had just offered and tapped the barrel of his pistol against his thigh. "I tolerate him."

Martin snorted and jabbed his chin in the direction of the sailors behind Harland. "Nervous bunch this time, *non?*"

"Cautious," Harland corrected. "They've had to be as of late. We all have."

"Yes, yes. This, I understand." The man called Martin put his fingers to his lips and whistled a long, low note before turning his attention to the two exhausted patients standing with the soldiers. "They still stand. This is good." His eyes dropped to the stretchers laid out on the sand. "These two are alive, yes?"

"Yes. And with care, they should remain so."

Martin clasped his hands together. "Also good." His eyes came to rest on Katherine and immediately narrowed. "Who is this?"

"A surgeon," Harland answered before she could. "And part of the reason the men are all still alive."

"A surgeon?" Martin repeated dubiously.

"Forgive my brother." Leo pushed ahead of Martin. "*Bienvenue en* France." He sketched a bow. "I am Leo, and this cretin *est* Martin."

"Kate," Katherine replied. There were never full names given at times like this.

"Kate?" Leo repeated, exchanging a glance with his brother. "*Et vous êtes un docteur?*"

Katherine nodded, watching the brothers carefully. Martin gave Leo a quick shake of his head and whatever he might have said next was prevented.

Katherine might have asked but a new movement came from the dunes and two more men appeared. These men, while dressed simply, were not in rough homespun but in coats of fine quality.

"Jesus, Martin. You brought the clients?" Harland hissed. "Here?"

Martin shrugged. "They insist."

"And if things went badly?"

Marin shrugged again. "I tell them all the risks. These men, they don't care. Long time since they see their sons." He gave Harland another grin and patted his pocket. "These men pay extra not to wait. Pay to come tonight."

Katherine watched the two men, their steps slowing uncertainly as they neared the group, but only for a moment. Then they were rushing forward toward Luc and Claude, embracing the sons they hadn't seen in years. There was a flurry of strangled whispers, of emotional murmuring, before the two older men dropped to their knees beside the stretchers. Another round of murmurings reached her ears, these soothing but just as emotional.

One of the men looked up at Katherine from where he knelt beside Bernard, deep lines of worry carved into his face. "He will live?" he asked in accented English.

"Yes," Katherine replied. "We had to take his lower leg. I'm sorry—"

"I do not care about his leg," the man said. "I only care that he is home. You have given me my family back. Thank you."

A lump formed in Katherine's throat, and she was glad for the darkness. For the second time in as many days, the urge to weep was overwhelming. Only this time, it was tears of happiness that threatened.

"You have transportation for the stretchers?" Harland was asking Martin.

"But of course." Martin sounded mildly insulted. "Your English prisons are not kind. This I see too many times." He turned and murmured something to Leo, who promptly disappeared back into the darkness. "My men wait by road. Leo goes to tell them now to come fetch clients and bring paintings to the boat."

"Are the paintings crated?" Harland asked.

Martin made a rude noise in the back of his throat. "Of course." Martin motioned toward the direction of the beach. "We go now."

⁓

They left their patients with their family in the dunes as they followed the sounds of the surf and headed back to the wide beach. Up ahead, a small lantern bobbed, silhouetting the landing boat that waited for them. Harland could just make out the forms of Martin's men and Black's sailors as they worked to load the boat, an occasional thump reverberating as the crated paintings were handed in.

"These clients bring eleven paintings for our patron," Martin was saying as he walked briskly ahead of Harland.

"*Peu pratique à porter.*" He made another one of his rude sounds. "I do not understand art. So much trouble for old pictures, *non*? Me, I like the coin I get. Simple. Easy to spend on happy things. Good food, rich wine, warm women."

"Mmm." Harland responded noncommittally. He didn't profess to be an expert on art, but he knew enough to know that the value of the brandy and silk and tobacco he moved paled in comparison to the irreplaceable pieces he smuggled into England for King.

Harland slowed his pace, allowing Martin to draw ahead, and glanced at Katherine, who walked in silence beside him. In the dim glow of the small lantern he held, he could barely see her.

"Are you all right?" he asked her in a low voice.

"Yes."

Impulsively, he reached for her hand, finding it and tucking it in his. She had been quiet since they had left the dunes, and he had seen how moved she had been. How much reuniting those patients with their families had meant to her. She squeezed his hand as if she could hear what he was thinking.

"Thank you," she said.

"For what?"

"For this. For allowing me to see these boys home."

"I didn't allow you anything. You were my partner. I—we—all needed your help."

"I just feel..." She trailed off. "I just feel like what I did tonight helped balance the scales a little. I know that sounds silly and probably makes me seem a little self-seeking—"

"You are not self-seeking. My God, Katherine, you helped so many people. You still do. Your kindness and selflessness are something to be admired."

"I agree." It was a new voice that came out of the darkness, and Harland spun, stepping in front of Katherine as if he could protect her from the invisible threat.

"I see you, in the dunes, speaking with Martin and Leo," the voice continued. "And I think that perhaps I am imagining that the Kate I once met on these beaches, the Kate I once saw on a Belgian field might be a…How do you say? *Fruit de mon* imagination now."

He heard Katherine's sharp intake of breath. "Guillaume?"

A man stepped into the edges of the light, his gait hitching with a limp. He was dressed plainly, his carelessly cropped nut-brown hair the same color as his attire. He had the sort of open, guileless face that suggested benign benevolence and encouraged the unwary to confide their secrets. Harland knew better, if only by the way the man was watching him, the low light doing nothing to disguise the intelligence that lurked in his appraisal.

Those eyes finally left Harland and fixed on Katherine, still standing just behind him.

"It's good to see you again, Kate," the man said.

With a half laugh, Katherine brushed past Harland, and he watched as she was engulfed in an embrace. The man pulled back and touched her face with his free hand, kissing her gently on both cheeks.

Jealousy of the sort Harland had never experienced before streaked through him, robbing him of breath and making his hands curl into fists. It was a petty, immature response, he knew, but reason did not reduce the power of his reaction. He forced his hands to relax. The man was clearly friend not foe. Though who he was and what he was doing here on this beach at this moment was less than clear.

"What are you doing here?" Katherine breathed, asking the very question Harland wanted an answer to.

"I think the better question is what are you doing here?" Guillaume replied. "You say before I leave Belgium that you are done visiting my beaches. That you are never going back to your old life. To smuggling."

"I haven't gone back. Not exactly."

"Yet here you are."

"It's not what you think. They needed a surgeon. I could not say no."

"The French prisoners needed a surgeon?"

Katherine's eyes narrowed. "Yes. But you knew that. These being your beaches and all."

"I don't know this until now. Not for sure. Despite what you say, others use these beaches, and even I cannot know all. But I hear rumors that intrigue me. So I come to see for myself. I think maybe Martin and Leo Ducharme take too great a chance, smuggling prisoners of war, but now I think maybe this is not so. Maybe there is opportunity for me also." Guillaume shrugged with the same insouciance that Martin seemed to have perfected. "I will think on that."

"There are many French prisoners still on English soil," Katherine said.

"Ah. So is this to be a regular journey for you now?" Guillaume asked. He sounded hopeful. "You will be back again?"

"I don't think so."

"Ah. That is too bad. I did not expect to ever see you again, so I should be happy to have this moment, *non*?"

Katherine stepped back. "Guillaume—"

"Your father? How is he?"

"Not as he once was. He was shot by soldiers. His lungs did not heal properly."

"I'm sorry." Guillaume reached for Katherine's hand. "I did not know."

"It happened while I was away."

"What can I do? Your father was always good to me. He teaches me a great deal. I admire him very much."

"And he you." Katherine smiled wistfully. "But there is nothing to be done. Thank you for the thought."

Guillaume turned Katherine's hand over in his. "Mmm. What I think is that I owe you a debt I do not forget. I wish to repay it."

"You owe me nothing."

"I owe you my life."

Katherine shook her head. "Guillaume, I don't—"

"We will not argue this night. We will agree to disagree."

"Very well." She smiled up at him again and then turned toward Harland. "I want you to meet Guillaume Mercier. An old, dear friend."

A dear friend and a smuggler, Harland translated, based on everything the last minute of conversation had told him. A very handsome French smuggler whom she clearly had a great deal of history with. He smothered the jealousy that still refused to abate.

"Guillaume, this is Dr. Harland Hayward. A surgeon and my...partner."

Harland glanced at Katherine, his jealousy dissolving under emotions much more powerful. Love. Pride. Exhilaration.

"Ah." Guillaume inclined his head, and Harland was well aware that the man was still measuring him. "You have much in common." It wasn't so much a question as a statement. "I see why she chooses you—"

An urgent shout rose over the sound of the surf from the direction of the boat. Two more voices were raised, a dull thud reverberating as something struck the hull of the lighter.

"We need to go," Harland said. "We've already tarried too long."

Katherine hesitated.

"He is right, Kate." Guillaume nodded. "You should go. The beaches are empty this night, but dawn is not so far away."

"I know." Katherine touched the man's shoulder. "Stay well, Guillaume."

"And you, my Kate. You need anything, you know how to find me. Some things, they do not change."

Chapter 20

Dawn was still only a promise on the eastern horizon when Katherine extracted herself from the surgeon's berth, leaving Harland sleeping as she dressed in her shirt and trousers. She hadn't been able to fall asleep, the events of the night still chasing themselves around and around in her head and sending a restless energy through her veins.

She made her way above decks, finding a spot on the foredeck at the rail and lifting her head toward the wind that was snapping across the surface of the dark water below. Her hair whipped behind her, and her eyes watered as she took deep breaths, feeling more... whole than she had in a very long time.

There was a future that had opened up before her, dreams and possibilities unfurling like the canvas sails above her head, catching the wind and pushing her across choppy waters. When she had returned to England, she had believed herself broken. An empty shell of the ingenuous girl who, for all her cunning and ability to protect herself among thieves and smugglers, had not been able to protect her heart.

If you don't embrace the hate, then you have nothing.

It was what she had said to Harland, and at the time, she'd believed every syllable. She'd been wrong.

It was the hate that had left her with nothing.

A band of silver broke across the east, the clouds above tinged with a faint gray-pink. The cold bit through her clothes, but she made no effort to move, simply watching as the silver morphed into gold and the first rays of sunlight emerged over the sea. Letting hope and happiness fill the last empty spaces that she had carried for far too long.

"Good morning."

Katherine spun to find the captain standing just behind her, holding out a steaming mug in her direction.

Gingerly, Katherine accepted, wrapping her hands around the heated tin. "Thank you."

"It's chocolate, not tea," he said almost apologetically, gesturing to the mug he held in his own hand. "I prefer it, though I'll deny it to anyone who asks."

"Your secret is safe with me."

"I suspect it is." Black faced the sunrise. "You are an early riser."

"I find the dawn peaceful." She lifted the mug and inhaled the aromatic steam.

He turned to look at her, a devilish grin emerging under the shadows from his tricorne. "I was hoping that perhaps you had come to tell me that you have reconsidered my offer."

"Captain, I don't—"

"Whatever Hayward is paying you, I will double it. The last surgeon I had on my Indiaman, the *Azores*, eloped with a woman on the coast of Siam, and I have yet to be able to replace him. He was good. I think you're better."

Katherine raised her mug to her lips, letting the bitter chocolate slide down her throat and warm her insides. "And less likely to elope with a woman off the coast of Siam?"

Black barked out a laugh. "Something like that."

She grinned. "Again, thank you for the offer, but I must decline."

"Not everything I import is illicit," Black said with a sniff. "I submit manifests to the customhouses and pay taxes like everyone else."

"You submit a version of your manifests," Katherine said with a half-smile. "I know how the game is played, Captain."

"I know you do." He paused. "Triple what Hayward is paying you. Plus a cut of the manifest that doesn't make it to the customhouses."

"Generous."

"I prefer *prudent*. Money does me no good if I'm too dead to spend it because my surgeon was incompetent when I needed him."

"I'm flattered. But my answer remains the same."

Black heaved a dramatic sigh. "Probably just as well. Your besotted baron would hunt me to the ends of the earth if I stole you away. And I wouldn't blame him."

Chocolate sloshed over the rim of her cup. She could feel herself blushing, but this time, she couldn't bring herself to care.

"A smuggler and a surgeon with intelligence and beauty." He leaned against the rail and considered her with a grin. "Could there be a more perfect woman?"

Katherine wiped her fingers on her trousers. "I'm not perfect. And again, I'm not a smuggler. Merely a surgeon."

Black winked at her. "That's what the baron says about himself too. You are really perfect for each other. Hell, the two of you could build an empire that might rival King's should you take the notion. The brandy alone would be enough to get you started."

"I beg your pardon?" Katherine's fingers convulsed around her mug.

"I said, you two are perfect for each other."

"Because we're both smugglers. And surgeons." An awful, icy dread slithered through her.

Black looked at her askance. "Of course."

That icy dread crystallized in her veins, making her chest tighten. She struggled to draw a steady breath. Struggled to find words that wouldn't come, even as everything fell into place.

Harland had never needed to ask questions, because he already knew all the answers. The movements of men as they slipped through the night. The cause and effect of each and every injury suffered under the cover of darkness and brought to his door with feeble explanations. Harland was the puppet master that her brother had spoken of. The faceless, nameless entity that provided instruction and payment for cargoes of contraband that moved across the channel and across England.

Her instincts had tried to warn her. Dear God, her mother had used her own occupation in exactly the same way, a never-ending supply of justifiable medical excuses for being on roads and boats and shores and ports at otherwise suspicious times. Perhaps, somewhere deep down, the knowledge had been there all along but she had chosen to ignore it. Chosen to ignore the evidence, presented to her over and over, letting Harland Hayward's smooth excuses and magnetic touch distract her from the truth. Not because she was dull-witted, but because she had fallen completely under his spell.

And then she had fallen completely in love.

"Shit." Black was still staring at her. "Shit." He tossed the remnants of his chocolate overboard and braced both hands on the railing and dropped his head. "You didn't know."

"No." Harland's voice came from behind Katherine. "She didn't know."

Katherine didn't turn around.

The captain straightened, looking from Katherine to the man standing behind her. "I didn't mean... You didn't say... I'm going to go now. Give you two some privacy." Hastily, he departed.

Katherine kept her face to the rising sun, not moving even as Harland came to stand beside her at the rail.

"I should have told you," he said.

For the second time in her life, everything she thought she had known, everything she had believed in had been pulled out from under her. Lost as surely as a sunken cargo in the channel. "How long?" She hated how small her voice was. "How long have you been a smuggler?"

"Since my parents died at sea in an Atlantic storm and left our family in financial ruin."

"What?" He had never mentioned any of this to her. Never trusted her with any part of the truth. The chocolate churned in her belly.

"Will you at least let me explain?" he asked wearily.

Katherine looked at him then. He was leaning out over the railing, staring down at the sea churning below them as the ship charged across the gentle swells. She didn't answer him because she didn't know what to say. How to put into words how...deceived she felt at this moment. She wasn't even entirely sure how much of her nauseating horror was aimed at herself for allowing it to happen.

"I own ships like this," he said, apparently taking her silence for acquiescence. "Or rather, our family company, Strathmore Shipping, does. Ten packets, two sloops, four clippers. But I almost lost them all, along with Haverhall and our home. My father, before he died and unbeknownst to myself and my sisters, had invested heavily in Indiamen and high-value Eastern product. Diamonds, gold, spices, porcelain, expensive silks. Cargoes lost time and time again to incompetence, thievery, bad luck, or a combination of all three, leaving a hole of debt so deep, I'm not sure I ever did find the bottom. What I did find was an investor who offered a discreet...loan. A solution."

"King," she said dully.

"Yes. I made a deal with the devil to save my family from ruin." He looked at her then. "We do what we must to save the people we love. Your brother understands that. You understand that."

No matter how much Katherine hated his words, he was right. The moment she dove overboard into the sea from Hervey Baker's boat, she had done what she had sworn she would never do again. She had gone back to her old life, her old ways, because her brother had asked. Because her family needed her to do it.

The difference between them was that Katherine had offered Harland the truth. Had bared her soul, made herself vulnerable. Harland hadn't done the same.

"Do they know? Your sisters?"

"No." His response was instant. "And nor will they ever."

"You think to protect them from the truth?"

"I think to protect them from King."

"But surely that loan has been paid back—"

"It was never about the money for King."

"Then what? What did he want from you?"

"Twenty years of…service. Twenty years of being his operative on this coast, twenty years of expediting a business that becomes more and more lucrative."

Katherine recognized the brilliance of that, right along with the diabolical cruelness of the terms. In exchange for preserving his family, Harland had agreed to what amounted to a sentence. "End it."

"I can't."

"Why not?"

"Because it's not that simple." His fist came down on the railing with a furious thud. "My God, Katherine, do you think I like what it is I'm doing? Do you think I like risking my life and those of others for those greedy souls in London who have the wealth to indulge themselves? For men like King who are only interested in profits at any cost? Do you think I enjoy lying to my sisters?"

"You should have told me the truth."

"I thought I was doing the right thing. I'm still trying to do the right thing, but I don't know what that is anymore." He dropped his head. "All I know is that I made a deal, Katherine. A deal with a dangerous man who offered me a hand up when no one else would. I must uphold my end or risk losing everything, my family included. King is not a man to be crossed."

She knew this. Knew exactly what sort of man King was when she had met him.

"Katherine…" He stopped, as if searching for words. "I never thought that I would— I didn't expect this. You. Us."

The unfairness of it all was a blinding acute pain that was getting worse by the second. "There can't be an *us*, Harland. I've lived like that for too long, and I can't do it again." She shivered, not only from the cold, but also from the loss that was emptying her soul. "You know that. I told you that at the very beginning."

"Yes." He hadn't raised his head.

"You asked me to be your partner, Harland. How did you think that was going to work? Did you believe that you could keep me in the dark along with your sisters?"

Harland moved, and his coat came to rest across her shoulders, enveloping her in its warmth. She should shrug out of it, take it, give it back, but she couldn't move. It was like she was deadened, her thoughts and emotions sluggish against a rising tide of regret and sadness.

"I can't lose you." His words were raw.

Katherine gazed helplessly out over the rail.

"You're angry with me. I understand. I deserve it. I should have told you the truth—"

"I'm not angry." That wasn't a lie, really. Anger was a pale emotion in the face of utter heartbreak. "You have to do what you have to do, Harland. What is right for your family. And what is right for your family means keeping your word to King. I understand that. But I have to do what I need to do too. When I came back to England, it wasn't to go back to wondering if the people I love might die every night—"

"I'm not leaving you." It was vehement.

"I'm leaving you." Her fingers gripped the edges of his coat where it was draped over her shoulders, the buttons cutting deep into the flesh of her palm. "I'm taking my brother and my father away from this life. Up north to find work. The kind that won't get us all shot. Or hanged."

"Do they know that?"

"Yes. I made Matthew promise me after he was nearly killed."

"And what are you going to do up north?"

"I'm going to live. I'm going to practice medicine where I am able. I am not going to wonder if the next time someone comes to our door it will be to drag my brother or my father away to prison or the gallows." The back of her throat was thick. She was saying all the right things, she knew. The things that she had spent years of her life promising herself. Things that she was not going to walk away from now. She was not going to let that happen. She had come too far. "I can't watch someone die the next time Captain Buhler fires five inches lower and makes a hole I can't fix."

"I won't let that happen."

She dropped her head. "You don't have that kind of power. You can't make that kind of promise."

He stepped behind her, her body tucked securely between the rail and his warmth as the ship plunged across the sea. "I'll find a way."

Katherine swallowed against the thickness in her throat.

His hands slid around her waist, and he pulled her back against him, his head lowering so that his lips were at her ear. "Stay with me, Katherine."

She had made the mistake of following a man once. She would not make the same mistake again. She had come back from Belgium stronger and better and determined to make her own decisions. Determined to rescue her family from a life that had already cost them too much. That would eventually cost them even more. Of that she was certain.

"Please."

"Until Dover. I'll stay with you until Dover." She said it because she didn't have the strength to say anything else. Leaving this man would be the hardest thing she had ever done. But the die had been cast a long time ago. She needed to do what was right for her family. She couldn't let her own selfish wants and desires put her family at risk.

He was silent behind her. "I promised you that I would never leave you. And I meant it."

Katherine didn't answer, the fine mist of the spray beading on her skin.

Gently, Harland pulled her around and cupped her damp face with his palms and kissed her.

She kissed him back, feeling the quiet desperation of the gesture. The dreams that she had dared to dream about this man and the future that might have stretched out before them were slipping away, and there was nothing she could do to stop them. This wasn't a kiss of promise and possibility, a kiss of destiny and desire.

As a warm dampness joined the cool mist on her cheeks, she understood exactly what this kiss was.

Goodbye.

Chapter 21

The customs agent had boarded and given Black's cutter a perfunctory inspection, but the otherwise empty hold and whatever assortment of papers that Black held were enough to convince the agent that his time was better spent elsewhere. The paintings were loaded into the back of a long, nondescript wagon, looking inconspicuous among an assortment of empty barrels.

"Bon voyage, Captain," Harland said as he gathered his heavy doctor's bag.

The captain yanked his tricorne from his head and wiped his forehead with his sleeve against the warmth. "My apologies again, Hayward," he started, looking uncharacteristically troubled. "It was not my intention to—"

"I know." Harland shrugged heavily.

"I feel the need to offer recompense."

There was nothing a sea captain could do to fix this. There was nothing anyone could do to fix this. "Do not trouble yourself, Black." Harland looked to where Katherine was securing her own medical bag into the back of the wagon.

She had fallen silent as the chalky cliffs and then the port had come into view. Deep down, Harland knew she was already lost to him.

Black followed his gaze, and his eyes lingered on the crates. "You will go directly to London?"

"I will see Dr. Wright home and then I'll travel to London straightaway. King has asked me to deliver the paintings personally."

Black's brows crept up his forehead. "Mmm." He jammed his tricorne back on his head. "I travel to Scotland for a fortnight before I return here, to Dover. A small matter near Inverness that needs my attention. You will let me know if you change your mind."

"About what?"

"About requiring something."

Harland nodded, too weary to argue. It didn't matter that the captain had let the truth out. In hindsight, Harland had no idea what he'd been thinking. Had he truly believed that Katherine would simply accept the prison that he had found himself in? That she would wish to build a future with him knowing what he had become? What he did?

Katherine had never been anything less than clear about how much she wished to leave smuggling and the life that came with it behind. He couldn't blame her.

He wanted to as well.

～

"Stop." Katherine's sharp demand shattered the silence.

Harland reined the mare to a stop. The Wright cottage was somewhere up ahead, just beyond the ridge.

"Do you hear that?" she asked, her voice urgent and pitched low now.

Harland strained to hear whatever it was that had alarmed her, but he could detect nothing. "I don't hear anything."

"Exactly." Without warning, Katherine swung down from the wagon bench and started toward the cottage on foot.

"What the hell are you doing?" Harland demanded. He urged the mare back into a walk. "Get back in the wagon."

"Something's wrong."

Harland glanced around him. Brilliant sunlight beamed from the cloudless sky, and along the edge of the dirt track, the wildflowers bloomed with vibrant, cheerful color. But around them, an ominous silence seemed to have settled. No birds sang, no leaves rustled, no insects hummed.

He knew what was wrong before they crested the ridge.

The acrid scent of burnt timber and thatch reached him before he got his first look at what was left of the Wrights' home. The cottage had been razed to the ground, small tendrils of smoke still curling from places where the fire hadn't quite died yet. A few pieces of charred wreckage poked upward, gruesome black fingers against the idyllic sky. The garden and ground around the cottage had been churned by hoofprints, a sheet that had been hung out to dry trampled and twisted on the ground. Broken furniture and shattered crockery lay in the muddy mess, forlorn and abandoned. The barn behind the house had been similarly torched, save for the farthest wall, which was partially collapsed and stooped over the smoking remains of the other three.

There was no sign of Paul Wright.

Katherine was already running toward the wreckage.

Harland swore and clambered down from the wagon, pausing only to tie the mare and the wagon to the post at the front of the yard.

Katherine was circling the remains of the cottage, one hand pressed to her mouth as she skirted the blackened timbers. Harland followed her, heading toward the remnants of the barn. He stopped, but nothing stirred, that same unnatural stillness broken only by an occasional curl of smoke.

"What have they done?" Katherine whispered, her voice catching.

Harland didn't need to ask who she was referring to. This had Captain Buhler's signature all over it.

"Where is my father?"

He heard it the same time she did. A muffled thud on the far side of the barn, originating somewhere behind the partially collapsed wall. Katherine started toward the sound, but Harland caught her arm, dragging her back.

"It could be a trap," he said quietly. "Buhler or one of his men could still be here."

"It could be my father." She yanked her arm from his grasp, her face pale and her jaw set.

"I'm coming with you." Harland crept toward the charred wall, picking his way around the blackened remains of what looked like a barrel. Another muffled thud reverberated, and Harland stepped around the corner.

He had time to register movement and the glint of a rifle barrel before he flung himself to the ground, the sound of a gun being discharged nearly deafening him. He was on his feet in a second, a piece of broken timber clutched in his hand as a weapon.

And then he dropped it.

"Jesus, Matthew."

Harland sprang forward as the man staggered slightly,

his boot catching on an overturned chair that had somehow escaped the carnage. Harland caught him from the side, noting in a single glance the pallor of Matthew Wright's skin, the wildness in his eyes, the sweat that had plastered his hair to his forehead, and most concerning, the blood that was blooming across the back of his shirt.

Matthew dropped the rifle, the heavy gun thumping to the ground. "I'm sorry," he wheezed. "I didn't know it was you."

"Matt." Katherine was by his side now, horror and fear flickering across her features only to be replaced by the mask of steady calm that every good battlefield surgeon possessed. She righted the chair, helping to guide her brother into it as Harland glanced around him.

"I got here too late." Matthew sounded like he had run here from Avondale. Given his current appearance, Harland suspected that he had.

"What happened, Matt?" Katherine was speaking in careful, deliberate tones. She had her hand on her brother's shoulder, her fingers casually resting near his neck. Not to solely comfort, Harland knew, but to measure the speed of his pulse.

"They did this." Matthew had regained a little color, and his eyes had lost a little of their wildness, but his breath was still coming in harsh gasps. "And they've taken him. To get to me." He held a crumpled paper out toward his sister. "They left this for me nailed to the gatepost."

Harland saw Katherine falter slightly before she righted herself, taking the paper from Matthew's hand. As she read, her face leached of color to match that of her brother.

Harland stepped toward her, broken glass crunching beneath his boot. Carefully, he took the paper from Katherine's fingers. It was a reward notification, the sort that cropped up with regular frequency in Kent, offering money for information that led to the apprehension of any number of men suspected of smuggling. This one had Matthew Wright's name on the top, though it was the scrawled message in ink along the bottom margin that punched the air from Harland's lungs and made his skin crawl.

Present yourself to the garrison captain or the old man dies at sundown.

"When were they here?" Harland demanded.

"I don't know." Matthew looked up at his sister, flinching as he shifted. "Hervey Baker's youngest, Julien, showed up at Avondale an hour ago. Said he saw the soldiers here. Came to fetch me but it was too late." He closed his eyes, his fists balled on his knees. "Goddammit, I should have been here."

Harland crushed the paper in his hand. The blame for this landed directly on his shoulders. It had been Harland for whom Matthew had been unwittingly working these last years. It had been Harland who had controlled the strings that had put Matthew and his crew in that cove when they were ambushed by Buhler and his men. It had been Harland who had been responsible for drawing Katherine away from Dover and her father. And it had been Harland who had not adequately anticipated the dissolute depths to which Buhler would sink to get what he wanted.

"Where is the Baker boy now?" Harland asked.

Matthew opened his eyes. "I told him to go home. Told him to forget he saw anything. Hervey is out for oysters this week, and—"

"Good." At least Matthew Wright had had the presence of mind to send the boy to safety.

"I don't know where they've taken my father," Matthew continued.

"They'll have taken him to the castle," Harland said, reaching for Matthew's rifle that still lay where it had fallen. The old gaol in Dover had been destroyed by a mob last year, a new prison not yet reconstructed. "They'll have him locked up in the Canons Gate guardrooms."

"How do you know that?" Katherine asked, her forced calm slipping.

He didn't. He was hoping that that was where they would be holding Paul Wright. Hoping that they would keep him visible enough to flush out his son. "I've spent a fair bit of time at Dover castle," he said, trying to sound more confident than he felt. Because there were far worse places in the bowels of the castle where they could have stashed an ailing man.

"What about your sister?" Katherine was speaking to Harland. "She's a duchess. She can help, can't she? She outranks everyone—"

"She can't." Matthew stood, staggering slightly and leaning heavily on the back of the chair. "The duchess left for Canterbury with three of her students, the duke is still in London, Rivers and Lady Rose are up in Ramsgate for two days, and—"

"We can't wait."

"I'll get your father out and away," Harland said. He had little doubt that Captain Buhler had known that the residents of Avondale were away when he made his move. "Wherever Buhler has him, I'll see that he is released."

"They won't just release him."

"Not on purpose," Harland agreed.

"I'm coming with you." Matthew reached for the rifle in Harland's hand. "I'll do whatever it takes."

"No." Harland tightened his grip on the gun and si-dled away from Matthew, picking his way around the wreckage. "They will destroy you. Make an example out of you. A spectacle that will end on the gallows if you're still alive by then." And Harland would not al-low that to happen. He would not allow a father to lose a son and a sister to lose her brother, all because of his actions.

Matthew swayed. "I can't simply stand by—"

"You can barely stand at all," Harland snapped. "You were shot not so long ago, and right now, you're bleeding like a stuck pig. I don't need to be worried that you will faint dead away in front of an audience of soldiers."

Matthew looked like he was going to argue again. "Why would you do this?" he asked instead.

Because this is my fault. Because I am in love with your sister. There were many ways he could answer.

"Because I can." It was insufficient, but it was all he was going to offer. "I am expected at the castle," Harland forged on. "I am a doctor who is often there to treat a myriad of maladies. The captain may not like me, but I will not raise any alarms. I do not have a price on my head. I will not have every soldier with an itchy trigger finger aiming their weapon in my direction. By the time anyone realizes that we are away, they will never find us."

"You can't do that by yourself," Matthew protested.

"I'll be with him," Katherine said.

"You will not," Harland and Matthew said at the same time.

"You will need a second pair of hands if . . ." She stalled. *If my father is badly hurt* were the words that hung un-spoken in the air. "You might need help." Now her voice was unyielding. "This is my father. My family. And I have experience with this sort of thing, in case you might have forgotten."

Harland cursed silently. She wasn't wrong.

"What are you talking about, Kate?" Matthew asked. "This sort of thing? Hayward is speaking of executing a prison break. And while his title might keep him away from the noose, it will not protect you if you get caught. I won't let you do this. It's too dangerous."

"Dangerous? Yet you were fine asking me to dive in your place in that cove to recover tubs of smuggled brandy."

"That's not the same."

"It's exactly the same. You can't have it both ways, Matt."

Matthew brought a hand down on the back of the chair in frustration.

"You once told me I was one of the best. A better smuggler than the entire lot of you."

"This isn't a bloody brandy run, Kate! You're walking into their damn garrison." He was shouting. "You're on their ground, not ours."

"I'm going, Matthew. I have to."

"You can't let her do this, Hayward," Matthew barked.

"Dr. Hayward doesn't make choices for me," Katherine snapped back. "Any more than you do."

"Kate—"

"You want to stop me? Then you'd best chain me to something immovable."

Matthew stared at his sister before he hung his head in defeat. "Goddammit."

"I'll be fine, Matt."

Harland watched the exchange, feeling more wretched by the second. His actions, his agenda, may have already cost Paul Wright his life. His son had come within a breath of dying serving Harland's interests. And now the consequences of his actions would put Katherine Wright at risk too.

"Keep her safe, Hayward," Matthew said bleakly. "Please."

"With my life." He would offer no less.

Katherine looked away, her expression tight and miserable. "We need to go."

"Get your doctor's bag," Harland replied, already moving to the door. "And that blue silk dress."

Chapter 22

Katherine sat next to Harland on the seat of the wagon as they rolled ever closer to the looming castle. The impossibly stiff stays beneath the blue silk were doing nothing to help her breathing but at least they were preventing her from collapsing in a puddle of paralyzing guilt-ridden fear. She was terrified that they would be too late. That her father, in his already weakened condition, would have succumbed to whatever treatment Buhler and his men would have delivered to a suspected smuggler. In truth, the captain's aim was only to draw her brother from the shadows, and the welfare—the life—of her father was irrelevant. A man bent on rescue was just as exposed as a man bent on revenge.

Katherine gripped the edge of the wagon bench as the shadow of the outer castle walls loomed above them and fell across the narrow road. "What if we are too la—"

"We won't be." Harland cut her off before she could finish her sentence. "I promise."

Harland couldn't make any such promise, and they both knew it, but Katherine let it go because to argue was pointless. She tried to take a deep breath to quell the nausea that terror was stirring in her gut.

She glanced back at the wagon bed, empty now save for a stack of blankets. The paintings had been hidden safely away in Avondale's attics, a second horse collected and tied to the back of the wagon. Beside her, Harland drove in silence. Even the steady thump of hooves and the rattle of the wheels was swallowed by the sloping earth and the towering walls that sat above them. His face was drawn, the way it had been in the cottage, every muscle in his body rigid.

Shame joined the guilt and fear. Katherine had been so consumed with her own remorse that she hadn't given the enormity of what Harland was doing for her family—for her—a second thought.

"You don't have to do this. Take this risk. This is my fault. I should do this alone." That knowledge had festered since the second she'd seen the charred wreckage of her home. And it was something that needed to be said before the man sitting beside her did something he would regret.

Harland's fingers jerked on the reins, and the mare tossed her head in annoyance. "Your fault? This is not your fault, Katherine. The blame lies with me."

Her head snapped around to stare at his profile. "I beg your pardon?"

"Your brother was working for me when he got shot," he said. "Buhler took your father because he couldn't get to Matthew. They would never have been hunting your brother if he hadn't been serving my interests."

"Matthew was serving himself when he got shot," Katherine corrected. "Earning a living the same way he's done since he was a child."

"Yet if it hadn't been for me, and my deal with King—"

"Then it would have been someone else. Matthew would still be a smuggler with or without you."

"If I hadn't—"

"If?" Katherine felt a rush of anger, though she recognized that it was directed at herself and not at Harland. She welcomed it because it was a respite from the debilitating, nauseating fear and guilt. "Fine. Let's play the *if* game. We'll play because I will win. If I had stayed, I could have taken my father away from this place, this life, before any of this—"

"It was me who asked you to come to France. Again, to serve my interests."

"You never forced me to do anything. If I hadn't agreed—"

"This is foolish, Katherine."

"You started it. So I'll go back a little farther. If I hadn't abandoned my family and followed Jeffrey to war, then my father would never have been shot in the first place—"

"Stop." A muscle was working along his jaw.

"You've only done what you needed to do. No different than any of us."

Harland laughed, a sound devoid of humor. "Have I? Perhaps my wife was right. Perhaps I am simply an intolerably selfish bastard who puts my own needs and wants first no matter what—"

"Then you're going the wrong way."

"I beg your pardon?"

"You should be on your way to London, with a fortune in Renaissance art. Turn around."

"Katherine—"

"Turn around." Her anger was gathering force, like a bank of storm clouds roiling across the open sea, and she recognized that it wasn't wholly rational. That it was simply a release of emotion that she had, until now, hidden behind a facade of immovable calm.

"I don't—"

"Do it."

"No." He was looking at her, his brows drawn low. "What the hell is wrong with you?"

"Why are you here? With me? Now? Risking everything for a man who should mean nothing to you if you're as selfish as you say."

His fingers tightened on the reins, his knuckles white. "Jesus, Katherine. That's not—" He stopped. "I told you before, I'm not leaving you."

"Because you feel some misplaced sense of guilt that makes it too hard to walk away?"

"Because I love you," he snarled.

Katherine stared at him.

He kept his eyes on the road. "Because I'm in love with you," he repeated quietly.

I love you too. It was there, on the tip of her tongue. But she couldn't love him. Because love implied a future, and she didn't have one with this man.

"I don't want you to say anything." He spoke before she could. "Because I know how impossible this is. I know I can't give you the life you want. The life you deserve. You've made that clear."

Katherine stared over the ears of the mare, stands of trees on either side of the road hiding the walls of the castle and creating a darkened tunnel.

"I just . . . You needed to know that. I can't fix what I've done, and I can't fix what I will continue to do, but I can fix this. I can do this for you—"

Katherine twisted off the bench, her hand slipping

around Harland's jaw as she kissed him, hard. She tried to put the words that she could not say into that gesture because to tell him that she loved him, too, would make their goodbye infinitely more painful.

She sank back on the bench, her eyes fixed on her lap where her fingers twisted the pretty blue silk.

She felt Harland move, and out of the corner of her eye, she saw him transfer the reins to one hand and reach for her with the other. He caught her hand in his, threading his fingers through hers. She leaned her head against the solid strength of his shoulder and hung on tightly.

And neither spoke as the wagon turned up the narrow passage to Canons Gate.

~

"Private Melnick." Harland stepped into the cramped guardroom, stopping just inside the door.

"Dr. Hayward." The young private stood with a welcoming smile from where he had been sitting behind a desk shoved underneath a small side window, his lower left arm splinted and cradled in a sling.

The relief that Harland had felt when he had caught sight of the private in the Canons Gate guardroom was almost debilitating. He hadn't been sure who would be posted here, but the young private offered a glimmer of hope that this insane plan would actually work.

"How's the arm feeling?" Harland asked, gesturing to the injured limb.

"Still sore, but I'm not complaining. If it hadn't been for you, it wouldn't be sore; it would simply be gone. No one thought you could fix it."

"I beg to differ. I thought I could fix it."

"And I am in your debt. When do you think I can remove the splints? Being behind a desk all day is a decided bore."

"Give it another week," Harland replied. "And then only light exercises with it to start. Don't fire weapons, or anything else that might jar it."

"Understood." The private nodded. "You here to see the captain?" he asked.

"No. It was you I was hoping to see." It wasn't a lie, exactly. "I have a favor to ask of you."

"Anything," Melnick said with an eager smile.

Harland turned, holding out his hand to the woman who waited just outside the door. Katherine placed her gloved hand in his, allowing him to guide her into the tiny space.

The young man's eyes widened as he involuntarily straightened. Harland didn't blame him.

Katherine had pulled the hair away from her face, but left it cascading down her back like a curtain of pale gold. Her eyes reflected the brilliant blue of the dress, making them pools of ethereal luminosity. She looked like a princess from a book of tales. A delicate, fragile princess, who was clearly on the verge of tears.

Harland closed the door firmly behind her. "Miss Wright, may I introduce Private Melnick, of the First Light Dragoons. Private, this is Miss Katherine Wright."

Harland watched as Melnick's throat worked as he swallowed. "Miss Wright, did you say?"

"Yes." Harland took care to keep his tone steady. "Miss Wright is Paul Wright's daughter. The man you currently have in custody here."

Melnick's eyes swung wildly to Harland. "I'm sure I don't know what you mean—"

"Private," Harland chided gently. "This is a small town,

and even the garrison cannot guard all of its secrets. I know Mr. Wright is here, and I know he is to be hanged at sundown tonight."

The soldier shifted uncomfortably. "I don't know anything about a hanging—"

"The entire town of Dover knows about the hanging," Harland lied.

"H-he's a smuggler," Melnick stammered. "A criminal. A traitor to king and country." His gaze fell on Katherine and then skittered away.

"I'm not here to plead his innocence. It is not my place to interfere with the dispensing of justice. However, I am here to plead for just a small window of time in which his daughter might see him. That she should be allowed to say goodbye in private."

Melnick was shaking his head. "I don't have the authority to—"

"Please," Katherine broke in, her voice tremulous. She clasped her reticule against her bosom in a show of despair. "Please, Private. Just to say goodbye. Just for a minute."

Melnick wavered.

"I know you to be a decent and honorable man," Harland said quietly. "And this is the decent and honorable thing to do."

A tear slid down Katherine cheek, and she dashed it away.

"Very well." The soldier frowned. "But only a minute. And only her. Not you. The captain will have me lashed if he knows I did this."

"I understand."

"Thank you," Katherine whispered.

Chapter 23

Katherine followed the private who was barely old enough to shave.

The guardroom had been built when the castle's western curtain wall had been remodeled and Canons Gate constructed. It sat thick and squat, built into the massive structure next to the gate, the brick facade staring inwardly at the castle grounds. An immovable, impenetrable fortress that had swallowed her father deep within.

The private unlocked the thick door at the rear of the cramped office-like space, the hinges opening smoothly. Beyond the door, a narrow hallway stretched away, illuminated only by a lantern hanging on a hook embedded into the wall halfway down. Katherine followed the soldier into the hall, its brick walls punctuated by iron-bound doors at regular intervals. Storage rooms, in which supplies, weapons, or ammunition could be stored in the cool darkness. Or cells, in which prisoners could be kept in the same.

The private reached for the lantern hanging on the hook and passed it to Katherine.

"He's in here." His keys rattled again, and he opened the door.

The lantern light bounced off a set of bars that were set into the brick on the other side, a second barrier into the room, but she could see nothing but inky darkness beyond.

"Is he alive?" she asked, and the quaver in her voice wasn't entirely fabricated.

"He is."

"Will you unlock the bars?"

The soldier hesitated. "No. You will be able to see him and speak to him like this."

A weak cough rattled from the depths of the darkness.

"But—"

"This is the best I can do."

"Kate?" Her father's voice warbled from the shadows. "Is that you?"

"It's me." She pushed past the private.

"You have ten minutes. No more." The soldier spun on his heel and retraced his steps, the sounds of his boots on stone fading.

"Father." Katherine pressed the lantern against the bars, trying to see in. "Where are you?"

"Get that damned light away," her father mumbled from somewhere beyond. "I've been blind as a bat in this damn cave, and you're holding up the damn sun."

Katherine set the lantern behind her, reducing the glow, trying not to focus on the harsh sounds of his breathing.

She saw a movement in the cell, and her father shuffled toward the bars, blinking and shading his eyes with an unsteady hand. He reached the bars, and Katherine bit her lip to keep from cursing out loud.

The left side of her father's face was swollen, bruising already setting into the soft tissue around his eye. A rivulet of dried blood ran from the thinning hair at his temple down past his jaw.

"They beat you," Katherine croaked, fury coursing through her.

Her father laughed, though it was a horrible, pitiful sound that dissolved into a fit of coughing. "Couldn't make it too easy for the damn captain," he managed when the coughing had subsided. "Goddamn maggot-pated codshead."

"Father—"

"You need to go, Kate. You can't be here. You and Matty need to leave Dover."

"I'm not leaving without you."

"Don't be a fool, Kate. Raised you better than that," he wheezed.

"You'll die here."

"And you and Matty won't. I had a good go of it, Kate. No regrets. And I would give my life ten times over to protect yours—"

"Stop talking." She was already yanking her reticule from her wrist and pulling the strings open. "Here." With her gloved fingers, she extracted a handful of leaves.

"What are these?"

"You know exactly what they are." She reached through the bar and caught her father's hand, shoving the jagged leaves into his palm. "Rub them all over your exposed skin. Now."

"Kate—"

"Do it," she snapped. "Because I'm not going. And neither is Dr. Hayward. So unless you want the both of us to swing beside you—"

"What have you done, Kate?"

"Nothing you wouldn't have done for me. You raised me just right."

Her father glanced down at the leafy greenery she had shoved into his hand and then stared up at her, his face lined and pale, his body swaying. "You're going to be the death of me yet, daughter."

"That's the idea."

~

Harland leaned against the wall, looking out the window. It was an effort not to pace the small room, but that would look suspicious. So instead he crossed his arms, listening to Private Melnick rattle about his desk, and when the man stood up, Harland turned.

"Give her a little more time," he urged. "Please."

The private sat down for another few minutes before pushing himself to his feet again. "I can't." He was twisting the keys in his hand nervously. "I'm sorry. I've already given her—"

A bloodcurdling scream split the air.

Melnick jerked and dropped the keys on the surface of his desk, staring at the rear door that gaped open. "What—"

"Something's wrong," Harland snapped, snatching the ring of keys from the desk and hurrying toward the rear. He ducked under the low lintel and went directly toward the form that was crouched on her knees, silhouetted by the light from a lantern on the floor next to her.

"He's dying," Katherine gasped, and Harland came to a stop in front of a horrid scene.

Paul was lying motionless on the cold stone floor, as

though he had collapsed in an attempt to reach the bars that separated him from his daughter. He had clearly been beaten at one point, his face swollen and his head bloody, but most horrifying were the reddened blisters and pustules that had erupted all over his exposed skin.

"Get away from the bars, Miss Wright," Harland barked. "Now." He turned to the private, who had been hard on his heels. "And you. Stay where you are, Private."

Katherine struggled back while Melnick stood next to Harland, gazing in horror at the man on the other side of the bars lying just inside the pool of lantern light.

"What's wrong with him?" he choked, backing up a step.

"It looks like the pox." Harland whirled on Melnick. "How long has he been like this?"

"I...I don't know. I didn't see him when they brought him in. I didn't..."

Katherine had staggered to her feet and was cowering behind Melnick. "I couldn't see him," she babbled. "And then I heard a noise and he was there and then he fell and—" She wrung her hands. "Is he dead, Doctor?"

Harland was already opening the barred gate with Melnick's keys. "I can't tell."

"Should you go in there?"

"I've already been inoculated against the disease," Harland threw over his shoulder. "But there is a grave danger to anyone in the vicinity who isn't."

Melnick took another step back.

"I need to take him away from here, before your entire garrison falls ill," Harland said, crouching beside Paul. The man looked like he was barely breathing, but beneath Harland's fingers, he could feel the steady thump of his heart. "He needs to be quarantined."

"But..." Melnick was sweating, his forehead slick in the weak light. "You can't just take him out of here."

"The alternative will be calamitous," Harland snapped. "Your captain has unnecessarily put you and every one of his men in grave danger. No leader would do so if he was right in the head. In fact, I would be very concerned about your captain's sanity, and his ability to make lucid, rational decisions on your behalf, Private. Such irrational symptoms are the first signs of extreme illness."

Melnick sputtered. "I'm sure he didn't think—"

"I'm sure he didn't think at all," Harland agreed. "Has he been fanatical as of late? Unduly obsessive in his pursuit of what he believes to be justice?"

"Maybe? Yes?" The private sounded horrified.

"I fear he is no longer capable of recognizing the value of your life against whatever single-minded promotion and accolade he seeks by hanging an elderly man who may or may not have once been a smuggler. Dire illness can do that to a man."

"But—"

"Paul Wright will be dead before he is hanged. Your captain knew this, yet still chose to bring him here." Harland stood, his hands on his hips. "Unless Buhler is in the habit of hanging corpses?"

The private shifted nervously. "Perhaps I should get Captain Buhler to explain himself."

"If that is what you need to do, Private, then by all means. In the interim, I am going to do what I need to do to save this bloody garrison from an epidemic. I'm no longer trying to save your hand, Private. I'm trying to save your life."

The soldier opened and closed his mouth and then turned and bolted.

"Gravely concerned about Buhler's sanity?" Katherine murmured as the door banged shut behind Melnick. "Fanatical? Obsessive? Were you trying to—"

"Kill the cause. Give men a reason to doubt and question the motivations behind orders. Inject uncertainty and confusion. No one will follow a selfish lunatic into battle. I learned that from a smart woman once."

She bit her lip and put a hand on his arm.

"Time to go." Harland bent and hauled Paul to his feet, ducking under the smuggler's shoulder to carry him. "Let's hurry."

Paul lifted his head, peering at them through eyes that had swollen to slits. "Goddamn cock-bleeding nettles," he wheezed. "My skin is on fire. My bloody eyes are on fire."

"You're supposed to be mostly dead. As such, do stop talking," Katherine said as she snatched the lantern from the floor and led them back toward the entrance to the guardhouse.

"Your daughter told me that you reacted violently to nettles," Harland murmured, every movement as swift as was possible. "But I may have underestimated my expectations."

"Since I was a boy," Paul grunted as they carried him out into the sun. "Can't go near a damn nettle without this happening."

There was no one in sight, and the wagon was where they left it, the mare dozing in its traces, the gelding tied to the rear dancing impatiently.

"Get him up on the horse," Katherine said, untying the gelding.

"No." Harland shook his head. "The horse is for you."

Katherine stared at him, first in confusion and then in

anger. "No. My father is the one who needs to get to safety quickly—"

"Get on the damn horse, Kate," Paul rasped. "Get far away from here."

"I can't leave—"

"You can, and you will," Harland said grimly. "Buhler wants your brother, but don't for a second believe that he wouldn't just as happily hang you instead. I am but a doctor, a titled one at that, transporting a fatally diseased, contagious patient to quarantine. The captain does not have reasonable grounds to challenge me." Harland hoped he was right. But he wasn't sure that Buhler would be reasonable at all. He suspected he would be simply enraged. "You need to go, Katherine. Now. Or this is all for naught."

She was still staring at him. "You never intended to put my father on this horse."

"No."

"I wouldn't have allowed him to anyway," Paul mumbled, bent over double.

"Father—"

"Do as you're told for once, you hear me, Kate?" Paul peered up at his daughter through eyes swollen to slits. "You and your brother are everything to me."

Katherine cursed softly and then nodded. Harland held out his hands to give her a leg up. She swung onto the gelding's back, her skirts jammed up around her legs.

"Go straight to Avondale," he said as she gathered the reins. "Don't stop. Don't come back for anything."

She hesitated. "I don't—"

"Go, goddammit," Paul barked, and was instantly consumed by a fit of coughing.

Katherine watched her father, indecision and anguish written all over her face.

"I'll keep him safe," Harland said. "Trust me."

Katherine nodded once and then reluctantly turned the gelding's head in the direction of the thick-walled gate. With a sharp command, she and the eager gelding were galloping away, the sounds of hooves fading almost instantly.

Harland wasted no time levering Paul into the back of the wagon, trying to make him as comfortable as possible with the blankets that were in the wagon bed. "If anything happens, play dead," Harland warned.

"Shouldn't be too hard. Feel mostly dead," Paul grunted. "Where's Matty?"

"Safe. At Avondale. Told him to wait there." He glanced around him, but there were no men or soldiers rushing forward to block their exit. Harland wasn't sure how long he had.

"He listened?" Paul shifted, wincing.

"He was in no shape to help." He clambered up onto the wagon bench and seized the reins. "My apologies in advance, Mr. Wright," he said, turning the mare in the direction of the gate. "This isn't going to be a smooth ride."

"I'll live," Paul wheezed. "I'm hard to kill."

Harland kept his eyes on the road, asking the mare for more speed. The trees flashed by, the looming walls of the castle falling behind them. Harland steered the wagon around a sharp corner, the road climbing back up toward the top of the cliffs. The wagon groaned and rattled in protest as it banged and bumped over the rutted road.

The wind picked up as he crested the first rise, snatching at Harland's hair and whistling through the foliage of the thick bush that edged the road on his left. On his right and far below, the sea spilled away from the base of the cliffs, the crashing of the surf muted by the shriek of the wind.

Harland took a deep breath, daring to hope that he might make it to Avondale before he was caught. Daring to hope that he could get Paul hidden away before—

The report of gunfire split through the air, and the mare startled, skittering and making the wagon veer dangerously toward the edge of the cliff. Harland pulled hard on the reins, steadying the horse, and glanced behind him.

There were two men, mounted on fast horses, flying down the road toward them, their bright coats like brilliant spots of blood against the blue of the sky. Harland faced forward again, allowing the tired mare to slow, knowing that he would never outrun them. He forced himself to take deep, steady breaths, composing his expression. This would be the greatest performance of his life yet.

Paul Wright's life depended on it.

The mare dropped to a walk and then stopped, and Harland stayed where he was. Captain Buhler and one of the men Harland recognized from that very first stormy night at the cottage reined their horses to a halt just in front of the wagon.

"Just what the hell do you think you're doing, Dr. Hayward?" Buhler demanded. He was out of breath, his face an alarming shade of crimson.

Harland heaved an audible sigh. "Like I told Private Melnick, I am—"

"The private had no authority to allow you to leave," Buhler raged. "His disobedience and insubordination will be addressed and punished. As will yours—"

"Private Melnick's actions likely saved your damn life," Harland snarled. "And that of the man behind you. And that of the entire garrison."

Buhler extracted a pistol from the holster under his coat.

He pointed it at Harland. "You will surrender my prisoner to me. Now."

"You're not listening," Harland said evenly. "Paul Wright has the pox. Anyone who has come in contact with him risks suffering the same fate. And let me assure you, Captain, it is not a pleasant way to die." He paused. "In fact, Captain, you look a little flushed yourself. Are you not feeling well?"

The man behind Buhler shifted uneasily in his saddle, urging his horse back a few steps.

"I'm fine," Buhler shouted. "And so is my prisoner."

"Your prisoner is far from fine," Harland said loudly. "And now I fear for your health as well, given your sudden, uncharacteristic recklessness with the welfare of your own men."

The soldier backed up another couple of steps, looking uneasy, much in the same way Private Melnick had.

"In fact, Captain, I believe that it would be in your best interest if you ordered your man back to the garrison and let me examine you—"

"I don't need to be examined." Buhler was still shouting. "There is nothing wrong with me or my prisoner. Release him at once."

Harland threw up his hands. "Look for yourself, then, but keep your distance. I must quarantine the patient."

The captain dismounted and stomped toward the wagon. He let the rear baseboard fall with a crash and yanked the blanket away from a body that lay unmoving in the bed of the wagon. The blanket flapped wildly in the wind, its white and brown stripes undulating in waves before catching in the long grasses at the edge of the cliff.

The soldier still mounted made a sound of horror.

Harland glanced back. Paul's rash was even worse than

it had been when he had first got into the wagon, the tissue beneath the angry scarlet blisters swollen dramatically. The smuggler's head lolled to the side, the dried crust of blood over his temple and face adding to the macabre scene.

Buhler had stumbled back, far from the wagon.

"I don't expect him to live much longer," Harland continued in the same steady tone, devoid of inflection, that he had used on the battlefield to deliver the same news. "He'll be dead before the hour is out. I will see him buried safely and properly."

"No."

"No?" Harland asked.

"I don't care if he dies," Buhler said. "He is a smuggler and a traitor and does not deserve a Christian burial. I'll see his head on a pike, disease and all, on the castle gates as a lesson to those who would choose to betray their king. Including his son."

Harland jumped down from the wagon. "Don't be a fool. You can't risk the lives of your men like that. I am inoculated against such disease. Are they?" he finished, looking up at the soldier whose horse was edging ever farther away. He turned back to Buhler. "Are you?"

Buhler swallowed.

"I thought not. You can't touch him, Captain. Not without risking your men—"

"I have no intention of doing so." He pivoted toward the mounted soldier. "Seize this wagon, Ross, and drive it and the prisoner back to the castle. Lock him in one of the empty ordnance sheds, away from the barracks. And stay there. Guard the door."

The soldier didn't move.

"That is a direct order, Ross!" he bellowed.

A choking sound came from the bed of the wagon, and

Harland turned just in time to see Paul convulse with another fit of weak coughing, blood dribbling from his lips
and spattering over the front of his already bloodstained
shirt.

"Jesus," the soldier said, his face white. "I'm not touching him. I'm not going anywhere near him."

"I'll have you whipped to within an inch of your life,
Ross. Obey my order!"

"Melnick was right. You really have lost your mind."

"I'll have you whipped for insolence too, Ross. You
can't insult your superior like that and expect to get away
with it."

"I don't care. I don't want to die like that," the young
man croaked. He spun away, spurring his horse back in the
direction of the castle.

"Your soldier made the right—"

"You did this." Buhler was pointing the pistol at Harland
again.

"Did what?" He could feel a bead of icy sweat slide
down his spine. He recognized the look in Buhler's eyes—
he had seen it many times on the battlefield. The desperate
look of a man for whom control was slipping away and
who was willing to do anything to get it back. To prove to
himself that his efforts hadn't been for nothing.

"You did this," Buhler accused again. "Wright was fine
when we took him into custody."

"Mr. Wright simply didn't have symptoms at that time,"
Harland corrected, edging away from the wagon and the
limp form of Paul Wright. The last thing he needed was for
the captain to decide to shoot Paul anyway.

"Don't patronize me."

"I am doing no such thing, Captain. I am merely a doctor. I can only treat what I see—"

"A doctor who continuously consorts with traitors along this coast," Buhler ranted. "A doctor who treats them, even knowing what they've done to betray their king and country. You don't think I see what you do? Where your loyalties lie? I'm not stupid, Hayward. You are one of them."

Harland moved farther from the wagon. "It is my duty to treat—"

"Your duty is to your king!" Spittle flew from Buhler's lips. "A duty you have turned your back upon. If you had done your duty, you would have let them all die. You would turn them over to the men under my command who serve their country. Your title means nothing, and your actions make you a traitor, Hayward, no matter who your father was. No matter how much money your family has."

"Have a care with your accusations, Captain," Harland said, keeping his voice even as he evaluated his odds of wresting the pistol way from this bulldog of a man before he pulled the trigger. Pistols were notoriously inaccurate, but at point-blank range, it would be hard to miss.

"Or you'll what? Use your fancy title to see me discharged? To see me removed from my position? I'm done with empty threats, Hayward." Buhler raised his pistol. "I'm ready for justice. I may not have flushed Matthew Wright from whatever sewer he's skulking in, but two dead traitors are still a good day in my books."

"You don't want to do this." Harland tensed, ready to hurl himself at the captain. If he was going to die, then he would do so fighting.

"I should have done this a long time ago—"

"Put the pistol down, Captain." The voice came from behind Harland.

He forced himself not to turn around, even as Buhler's eyes flickered over his shoulder.

"Ah, Miss Wright. How nice of you to join us. I was wondering where you had hared off to after using your traitorous wiles to charm my gullible private."

"Miss Wright had nothing to do with my decision to remove her father. In fact, I told her to keep her distance so that she, too, does not risk exposure."

Out of the corner of his eye, Harland saw Katherine step through the bush, coming to stand beside him. She had the rifle she had once leveled at him pointed at the captain. She hadn't gone to Avondale at all but back to her ruined cottage. And then she had returned to intercept them on the road. He should have known that she had ridden away too easily.

"You should leave now, Miss Wright," Harland said, a little too loudly. God help him, she couldn't be here. She wasn't safe. He couldn't keep her safe like this.

"I'm afraid I can't do that. I'm not leaving you."

"Katherine." Those were Harland's words, not hers. They could not be hers. Not now.

"I'm happy to accept three dead traitors on this fine day," Buhler sneered.

"But the math is a problem, isn't it?" Katherine asked, sounding like she was merely entertaining polite conversation in a drawing room.

"The math?" Buhler scowled.

"My father will die soon. This is an unavoidable truth," she said grimly. "But that still leaves two of us and only one of you. Once you shoot one of us, how will you kill the other fast enough to prevent your own demise? Shoot Dr. Hayward, and I will shoot you. Shoot me and take your chances with Dr. Hayward."

Buhler's jaw was clenched.

"No one is shooting anyone," Harland said. "All you have to do is arrest me."

"Arrest you?"

"Arresting a mere woman will not earn you the same respect or acknowledgment as arresting a peer of the realm accused of treason. You'll be famous, Buhler."

"No." The captain was shaking his head. "I know how this works. I arrest you, and you simply wriggle off the hook. Titles make men like you slippery. The Earl of Rivers and the Duke of Holloway have ever been untouchable, and your association with them will inevitably make you the same. But you are far from untouchable here." With his free hand, he drew the officer's sword sheathed at his side. "You both deserve to die. I'll start with the woman and take my chances with you—"

A hair-raising wail rose from the back of the wagon, and Harland turned to see Paul Wright clambering from the back with stiff, jerky movements. His thin gray hair was tossed in the wind, blood still spattering down his chin, his eyes still swollen into slits. He staggered forward, his blistered hands waving before him, as if he were searching for something, looking like a walking dead man. "I see them coming," he keened. "The selkies. They're coming."

Buhler had turned to stare at Paul, transfixed in horror, and Harland sprang forward, reaching for the pistol. The captain jerked away, swinging wildly at Harland, and both men fell to the ground. The sword clattered away, steel ringing on rock, though Buhler did not relinquish his grip on the pistol. Too late, Harland saw the barrel of the pistol come up.

Not aimed at him but at the woman beyond him. Harland lunged.

And Buhler pulled the trigger.

There was no pain at first, just the sensation of being punched, the breath knocked clean out of him. The wind still tore at his clothes, but it had quieted somehow, the shriek replaced by a distant, muted ringing. He was faintly aware of being pushed to the side, a scarlet coat dancing up and away in front of his eyes and rising against the brilliant blue of the sky. A blue so deep that it almost hurt to look at it.

Or maybe he was getting the color of the sky confused, because the sky seemed to be moving beside him, that brilliant blue swirling in the wind. He frowned and tried to get to his feet but pain like he had never felt lanced through his chest like an inferno, wrapping around his ribs in a fiery vise. Every breath was an agonizing effort.

He fell back, but the pain seemed to have brought his surroundings back into focus. It was Katherine who was beside him, her blue skirts whipping in the wind, the rifle in her hands leveled at the captain in the scarlet coat.

Paul was there, too, beside her, and he was saying something in his rough voice, though it was hard to hear. The smuggler took a step forward, and the captain backed away, and voices gained in volume. Paul was weaving a little on his feet, though Harland couldn't seem to muster the strength to decide if he was doing that on purpose or because he was that weak.

Paul took another step forward, and Buhler backed up again. Only now, there seemed to be something rising from the grass. Something brown with white stripes, flapping in the wind like a great bird winding itself around the captain's feet. His scarlet-clad arms pinwheeled, and then he was gone. Vanished like he had never been there.

Harland blinked but Buhler didn't reappear. Thinking had become a chore. Perhaps it had all been a figment of his imagination, he thought sluggishly. A man couldn't disappear into thin air, could he? There was no such thing as magic, was there? But maybe there was because the blue sky descended, settling beside him like a glorious cloud and bringing with it a curious cold. Perhaps he had floated above everything. High up toward the clouds where the air was crisp and numbing. Someone might have called his name, but it seemed to come from a great distance. He tried to turn his head, but it had grown impossibly heavy. Impossibly tired.

He just needed to rest. Just for a moment.

He sighed and closed his eyes, welcoming the darkness.

Chapter 24

There was too much blood.

The wagon careened up the drive to Avondale, her father lying half across Harland in an effort to hold the remnants of his bloody shirt over the gaping wound across his ribs. There had been a blaze of an explosion when Buhler had fired the pistol, daring Katherine to believe that the captain had primed the pistol poorly. Making Katherine hope that the damage the ball had done, punching across the edge of Harland's lower ribs, was reduced and fixable. She refused to believe anything else. But whatever damage lay beneath the skin and bone, a vessel somewhere in that mess had been compromised. And it was slowly killing Harland Hayward.

The wagon swung precariously as Katherine hauled on the reins of the lathered mare, a shout from a keen servant summoning help before the dust had even settled. In moments, there was an army of hands helping pull Harland from the wagon and assisting her father into the house.

Harland was carried into the kitchens, the massive butcher block table swept free of clutter. Without being asked, someone had fetched both the doctor's bags from the wagon and set them on a sideboard. Katherine did her best not to look at the still, pale form of the man lying on the table, focusing every effort on preparing her instruments and preparing herself. The Avondale staff, to their credit, proved that such occurrences were indeed not irregular, as Harland had once told her. They moved quickly and efficiently, setting water to boil and placing stacks of clean linens next to her instruments.

"Jesus, Kate, what happened?" Matthew was standing just inside the door of the kitchens, dark bruises under his eyes and his arm back in a sling.

"Fetch the duchess's student named Suzette." She ignored his question, surprised that her voice sounded so calm. Because inside she was terrified. "And then I need you to find Father and make sure he's looked after and as comfortable as possible," she went on. "He's had a significant encounter with nettles."

"Nettles?"

"Yes, nettles. Now go, Matt. Hurry." She could only focus on what was ahead of her, not what had happened on the edge of that cliff. Not on Harland's sacrifice.

Matthew nodded and vanished. Katherine returned to Harland and peeled away his bloody shirt. Blood continued to spill from the ragged edges of the wound, and bits of white bone shone ghoulishly under the blood. The ball had punched into the front side of his lower ribs, breaking at least one, possibly two, before exiting. The wound was too low to have compromised his lungs, too close to the edge to have damaged a kidney, but it was possible that it might have nicked another organ. Or driven a bone shard farther into the tissue where it would become infected and fester—

She stopped herself. She could do this. She'd lost count long ago of how many times she had done this. But she was going to need another set of hands. Another set of competent hands. She needed Harland, but Harland was slowly bleeding to death on the table in front of her because the impossibly stupid man had done the impossibly stupid thing of throwing himself in front of a bullet meant for her.

"You fool." His skin had taken on a terrifying gray pallor, and he didn't so much as twitch as she probed the wound. She leaned forward, smoothing his hair back from his forehead. "You promised you wouldn't leave me," she whispered. "You promised."

Those last words caught on something that was suspiciously like a sob, and she swallowed it, bracing herself against the emotion. There was no room for emotion here. Emotion would paralyze her with fear and hinder her ability to do what needed to be done.

"Miss Wright?"

Katherine turned and found Suzette standing before her, her hands clasped tightly in front of her, her face ashen. But her eyes were as steady as her voice.

"What do you need me to do?"

Katherine straightened. "I need you to help me save him."

Chapter 25

H ow is he?"

Katherine started with a jerk, nearly tumbling off the chair before staggering to her feet. She rubbed at her gritty eyes, wondering how long ago she'd dozed off.

Her father hovered just inside the door, a steaming bowl of stew held in his hands.

"Resting."

It was all she could bring herself to say, the terror that had wrung her witless these last three days making it impossible for her to offer anything other than a simple word. Harland hadn't regained consciousness since he'd been shot, at the mercy of the fever that had wracked his body. He'd mumbled and thrashed in delirium as Katherine had covered his burning body in sheets soaked in icy water and forced broth between his lips and down his throat. He'd twitched and tossed, and mumbled and muttered, as she dressed and redressed the wound.

But this morning, Harland's skin had cooled, and he'd settled. And Katherine had cried, relief overwhelming her.

"Good." Paul shuffled into the room. "You need to do the same." He held out the bowl. "Eat something. Get some sleep."

Katherine took the proffered bowl and set it aside.

Paul looked on with a disapproving glare before sighing. "The duchess had word from the garrison," he said. "A note of thanks for Dr. Hayward's quarantine and care of Captain Buhler and acceptances of Avondale's condolences on the captain's death after a courageous, if short, battle with his grievous illness."

Katherine hadn't even considered how they would explain the sudden disappearance of Captain Buhler. "His body—"

"Was recovered by Baker. Buried as befitting His Majesty's officer."

"Good riddance." She rubbed her temples with her fingers.

"Agreed."

Katherine sighed. "You shouldn't be on your feet, Father."

Her father scowled. "I can't lie about anymore." The blisters had subsided, though remnants of the rash were still visible on his face and arms. The swelling on the side of his head had gone down, and Suzette had sutured the gash at his temple.

"You're not fine. You're—"

"Furious."

"I beg your pardon?"

"You've done a lot of dangerous things in your life, Katherine Wright, but coming for me—risking your life like that—was the most bird-witted thing you have ever done."

"I won't apologize for it," she said sharply.

"No, I didn't expect you to." He gestured to the man lying on the bed beside her. "People do idiotic things for those they love."

Katherine sat in the chair, her legs suddenly unable to support her weight.

"What are you going to do?" he asked her.

"What do you mean?" She was stalling, and they both knew it.

Paul wandered to where Harland lay. "You love him."

Katherine leaned forward and rested her forehead in her hands. "Yes."

"He's a good man," Paul said slowly. "But you never wanted to fall in love with a smuggler."

"No. I—" She stopped abruptly, the implication of her father's words sinking in. "What?"

"I know how you felt about wanting to escape this kind of life when you returned to Dover. In truth, I can't say I blame you. And I can't imagine those feelings have changed. But he makes this…complicated now, doesn't he, given what he does aside from his medical practice?"

"I…" Katherine trailed off, unsure what to say. "How did you know?"

"I'm old, not blind. You think that I believed for one second that the good doctor continuously happened to show up when he was needed most by coincidence these last years? That he protected our identities and our secrets because of some bizarre benevolence? He's a smuggler through and through. He was good, but he wasn't good enough to fool a man who had once been married to someone just like him." A ghost of a smile drifted across his lips. "Your mother would have adored him."

"Yes," Katherine whispered.

"He loves you," Paul said abruptly. "He didn't do everything he did for me. He did it for you."

Katherine didn't want to talk about this. Didn't want to discuss an impossible love. Not now. "No, he felt guilty about—"

"Guilt." Paul made a disgusted noise. "Guilt by itself does not drive a man to do what he did. To risk everything."

She tucked her hands in her skirts, worrying a thread that had come loose from a seam. "Agreed. It takes courage and honor. The baron possesses both. He would have done the same for anyone."

Paul snorted. "Courage and honor. Two more words that cannot exist by themselves. Courage and honor are born from things far more visceral."

"Like what?"

"Desperation, sometimes. Recklessness, occasionally." Paul paused. "Love, most often."

The thread snapped in her fingers. "It doesn't matter how he feels about me. He made a deal," she said, the words sticking in her throat. "A deal to smuggle in return for the preservation of his family. A deal with a man one does not cross and live to tell the tale."

Paul shrugged. "And?"

"And?" Katherine repeated incredulously. "He won't risk his family. As much as he hates it, he won't abandon the deal he—"

"Deals," Paul scoffed. "Come, Kate, I taught you better than that. All deals are negotiable. If you want Harland Hayward, then you just have to find something that this man wants more."

Katherine lifted her head and stared at her father.

Paul Wright stared back.

"I have to go," she said.

"Now?"

"Yes. I might be awhile."

"Hours? Days?"

"Weeks," Katherine told him.

"Ah." Her father nodded. "Well, in that case, eat that damn stew before you go. I've discovered that countesses and duchesses and their husbands are a tiresome, overbearing lot when it comes to their family and their well-being."

"But I'm not—"

"Family?" Paul scoffed. "Try to tell them that." He pulled up a chair next to Harland. "I'll stay with him. You do what you need to do for your baron."

Chapter 26

The gorilla soldiers extracted the paintings from their crates with far more care than Katherine had expected. It was clear that this was not the first time they had done this, settling each painting on a wooden easel, the colors of each work blazing to life under the study lights. There were eleven of them, all half-length portraits of ancient Roman men. Emperors or possibly generals, Katherine guessed, based on their attire and weapons. Whomever had painted them had had an eye for depth and detail and the ability to make Katherine believe that any one of these long-dead men might simply turn and speak to her.

Katherine watched as the last painting was uncrated and set next to the others. The gorilla-soldiers removed all traces of packing materials and vanished, leaving her alone with eleven silent generals. Katherine moved to the far side of the room, bypassing the men and regarding Judith, who was still beheading her would-be lover. She wondered at the courage it had taken for Judith to go through with his murder. Or perhaps she hadn't been afraid at all. Perhaps Judith's actions had been driven less by courage and more by her desperation and determination to protect the people she loved. To make sure that there was a future for them all.

"I was beginning to think that perhaps I had made a terrible error in judgment allowing your participation in this…undertaking, Dr. Wright."

Katherine turned to find King leaning on his walking stick, his pale eyes cold. She returned her attention to the painting of Judith, gazing at the woman and the expression of chilling determination on her face. "You made no error."

"It's been almost a month since you disembarked in Dover with my cargo. Captain Black sent word."

"There were complications."

"Complications are excuses."

Katherine shrugged and left the painting of Judith, wandering over to the easels. She stopped in front of the first of the paintings, examining the image of the powerful man who was glaring over his shoulder as though daring the world to take him on. He was dressed for battle, his head adorned by a crown of leaves, and he gripped a staff with formidable arms. "Striking," she said.

"Irreplaceable," King corrected sharply.

"Stolen?"

"I prefer *rescued*. The other works that these paintings once accompanied are nothing but ash in a Spanish wind." He paused. "Where's Hayward?"

"In Dover."

"Why?"

"He was shot."

King moved farther into the room. "By you?"

Katherine met his gaze. "Tsk. I believe we already covered what would happen to those I might kill."

"Will Hayward live?"

"Yes."

"His injury is unfortunate, but it doesn't explain why it took you this long to make a two-day journey."

Katherine turned from the glaring emperor. "I made a stop first."

King was leaning against his desk, his walking stick at his side, his arms crossed. "I do not like disobedience. And I do not tolerate duplicity."

"And I do not like assumptions."

King regarded her, his expression betraying none of his thoughts. "Assumptions?"

"I wasn't looking for a new buyer for your paintings. I do not know enough about art and the value of it to do so competently."

"I didn't suggest that you were."

"No? Then perhaps you assumed I was in Bath, taking the waters. Or Brighton, taking the air."

A faint shadow of annoyance flickered. "Why are you here, Miss Wright?"

"I came to deliver your paintings. And I came to negotiate."

"Negotiate?" King's long fingers were drumming impatiently on the sleeve of his midnight-black coat. "And what is it that you possess that I could ever want?"

"Wissant."

He straightened.

"Audresselles. Escalles. Sangatte. Calais."

"You found Monsieur Mercier."

"I did."

"You spoke to him."

Katherine shrugged. "At length. And like yourself, he is a reasonable man. A man willing to expand his own empire using partnerships with those who may share his interests."

King uncrossed his arms, retrieving his walking stick. He studied the silver scrollwork on the handle intently. "And what, exactly, do you want in exchange?"

"The baron."

The walking stick made a dull thud on the plush rug beneath their feet. "I beg your pardon?"

Katherine made her way back to the painting of Judith. "You will release the baron from the remainder of his service to you. In return, I will give you the keys to markets and opportunity that you have yet to explore. That you don't yet have access to."

King stared at her, his icy eyes sending shivers down her spine despite her best efforts. "The baron told you what it is he does in my . . . service." It wasn't really a question.

"Yes."

"He has no idea you're here, does he?"

"No." There was no point in lying.

"Why are you doing this?"

Katherine had anticipated this question, knowing what she knew of this man. "The bullet he took was meant for me."

"Guilt, then?"

"Yes." The response was easy to say because it wasn't necessarily a lie, just not the whole truth. Her father had been right. Guilt could not stand by itself.

A muscle flexed along his chiseled jaw. "Lord Strathmore will be difficult to replace."

"Guillaume Mercier even more so." Katherine smiled as her eyes drifted to follow the curve of Judith's blade. "And we both know that."

A heavy silence settled over the study, and Katherine had the peculiar sensation of being underwater, everything muffled and distant. The glass float that she had sought so many times under the surface bobbed just beyond her reach, not tethered to a tub of brandy but tethered today to freedom.

"Make your choice, King," Katherine said. "Decide who is worth more to you."

"You're rather bold, Dr. Wright. But then, I suppose I should expect no less from a smuggler."

She glanced up, the glass float so close she could almost feel it. "I prefer *surgeon*."

King's lips curled into what may have been a smile. "And if I were to agree to your proposition, Dr. Wright?"

Proposition. It had been propositions that had started this journey and a proposition that would end it.

Hope was beating in her chest like a thousand birds, drowning out the sound of her racing heart, and she took care to keep her expression blank. "If you were to agree, then I would write down the name of the inn and tavern in which Monsieur Mercier is currently staying. He seems to have, coincidentally, some business in London, and he has indicated that he will remain in town until the end of the day should anyone wish to speak to him about... opportunity. If not, he will simply return to France on the evening tide. He will be difficult to find again."

King's fingers were tapping a steady rhythm on the head of his walking stick, the ruby on his finger catching the light. "And if I were to need a discreet surgeon in the future, Dr. Wright?"

"I know a good one. Two good ones, in fact."

"I see." King set his walking stick against the desk once again and moved around it. He pulled on a handle, a drawer opening smoothly and silently. He extracted a heavy sheet of paper and set it beside an inkpot, straightening it carefully with his fingertips. "Not guilt."

"I beg your pardon?"

King picked up a white quill and a small knife, trimming the end with deft movements. "You're not doing any of this out of guilt."

Katherine remained silent.

"I thought so." He set the knife aside and held the quill out toward her.

And Katherine reached for freedom.

Chapter 27

Harland cursed and then cursed again.

Suzette scowled at him. "Does every physician make such a miserable patient?"

"They do when they are being cosseted like a child. I'm perfectly well—"

"You're not well." Suzette rolled her eyes as she tied off the stiff linen that she was using to bind his ribs, and Harland grimaced. "You were shot. You broke ribs. Badly. You could have died. You're better, but you're not well yet, believe me."

"Does every physician have such an infuriating sense of superiority?" Harland grumbled.

"They do when they're right. And when they've learned from the best." Suzette straightened and put her hands on her hips. "Can I get you anything?" she asked. "Tea? A pillow? A blanket—"

"I'm not a hundred years old," Harland nearly shouted, wincing at the stab of pain across his lower torso. "I don't need tea. Or a blanket or a pillow or a damn casket." He focused on moderating his voice. "I need to be left alone."

Suzette rolled her eyes again and collected the extra piles of bandages. "I'll be back to check on you later, Dr. Hayward. Don't do anything foolish in the meantime."

"Like what? Drown myself in the fountain? I've been, for all purposes, coerced outside into a rose garden by a domineering medical student and told to convalesce like a potted plant."

Suzette sniffed. "You are nothing like a potted plant. Potted plants are much more agreeable." She gave him a last look and then retreated back up the garden path in the direction of the house.

Harland cursed under his breath again and leaned back on the bench, trying to find a more comfortable position. He knew he was being irritable and petulant, but he chafed at the inactivity and inability to move freely yet without the constant shackles of pain. Pain that still occasionally stole his breath from time to time and left him sweating.

Suzette was right, he admitted with no little discontent. He was not fine but it had nothing to do with his injury. And he had lied about wanting to be left alone. What he wanted was to be searching for the woman who had stolen his heart, saved his life, and then vanished into thin air.

I have to go.

Those were the words she had said at some point in time, or at least those were the words he thought she might have said. The memories of what was real and what was imagined were fuzzy, reality blurred by pain and fever. He did know that the paintings that had been hidden at Avondale were gone. Delivered to King, presumably, given that the man hadn't sent one of his thugs to haul Harland into

London to demand their whereabouts. Harland was also quite sure who had delivered them.

What he didn't know was where Katherine had gone next. Her father didn't know where she had gone. Her brother, along with his entire crew, pled ignorance before they had been hired on by Black at Harland's request and left for distant, Far East shores on a ship named the *Azores*. No one seemed to know where Katherine had disappeared to. She had left no note, sent no correspondence.

I have to go. It was entirely possible that she was gone for good.

Harland shifted again on the bench, though it did not relieve the excruciating ache in his chest that wasn't the result of broken ribs. It didn't matter where she had gone or how far she had traveled. As soon as he was well enough, he would track her down. Track her to the ends of the earth if need be. He had ships. If it took him the rest of his life, he would find her. He didn't have the right to ask her to wait for him—

"My lord?"

Harland turned to find a footman hovering anxiously on the garden path, half hidden behind a leafy hedge. "What is it?" He tried not to snap at the hapless man.

"A message from London, my lord." The footman stepped forward and held out a sealed missive.

"Thank you." Harland accepted it and watched as the footman hastily fled back in the direction of the house. Even his sisters seemed to be giving him a wide berth as of late—

The tiny emblem of a crown froze all his thoughts.

King.

Harland broke the wax seal and unfolded the paper, his eyes scanning the brief note. He read it once, and then

again, and then wondered why he had to blink repeatedly
to read it a third time.

Strathmore,

> *In light of recent revelations, I consider the terms of our*
> *agreement completed in full. No further service on my be-*
> *half is required. I have been assured, however, that your*
> *medical services may be called upon if and when required.*

K

Harland let his hand drop to his lap, the paper crumpling
in his fist, his mind racing, his breath coming in shallow
gasps. No, no, no, no.

In light of recent revelations?

What had Katherine done? What had she agreed to do?

He staggered to his feet, a band of pain tightening
around his torso. He ignored it. King was not a man known
for his benevolence. He was not known for his charity or
his altruism. If he had released Harland from his service,
then it had come at a price. A steep price. Harland needed
to get to London. Now. He needed to know exactly what
Katherine Wright had—

"You should have listened to Suzette. A pillow at your
lower back would have made you more comfortable, you
know."

Harland froze.

"I can see why they stuck you out here," Katherine
continued, stepping out from behind a screen of crimson
blooms. "You're terrorizing the servants. Aggrieving your
sisters. Infuriating your physician. Patients like you are in-
herently tiresome."

She was dressed in the brilliant blue gown she had once worn to a prison break. Her hair had been caught up behind her head carelessly, strands of champagne silk drifting around her face. Her cheeks were flushed, her eyes just as captivating as they had been when she had leveled a rifle at him.

"Katherine," he managed to croak, twisting to face her. Another lance of pain streaked through him. It didn't matter. He would happily take another bullet if it meant that the woman standing before him was not a mirage.

She came to a stop in front of him, too far away to touch. Too far away for him to reach for her and drag her into his arms. He wondered, with a horrid, sinking feeling, if she had simply come back to check on her patient. If she had simply come back to say goodbye.

"Let me see," she said, gesturing to his side.

Harland pulled the hem of his shirt up and she gingerly unwrapped the bandages only recently applied. Katherine took a step closer and bent, examining the darker tissue of the healing wound easily visible against a canvas of skin that was still faintly discolored from bruising.

"You are an idiot, Lord Strathmore."

She was using his title again. "I don't—"

"I'm not done." She placed a hand against his skin, testing for tenderness. "Does it still hurt when you breathe?"

"Deep breaths, some."

"Mmm. No coughing?"

He flinched. "Not if I can help it."

"Pleurisy?"

"No."

"You're lucky."

"No, I had a gifted surgeon. Where have you been, Katherine?"

That wasn't the question he wanted to ask. Not really. What was wrong with him? Why couldn't he think?

She ignored him and, with brisk, efficient movements, rewrapped his ribs. He closed his eyes, her clinical touch a particular sort of torture he had not yet experienced.

"You're healing nicely." She tied off the bandage. "For a man who threw himself in front of a gun."

"It wasn't a big gun."

"It still shot a bullet that severed blood vessels and missed organs and your intestinal tract only because it broke your ribs." She stepped away from him again, as if establishing a barrier of space between them.

"Well, I suppose that is all a sight better than the pox. Which is what the entire garrison at Dover castle seems to believe I was afflicted with. They sent me a bloody note of thanks for my sacrifice and heroic efforts on their behalf. And for my care of the captain until he perished of the same."

"You don't say." Katherine didn't sound even remotely surprised. And that, in turn, didn't surprise him.

"Where have you been?" he repeated.

"Here and there." She sounded distant.

"You took the paintings. To King."

"Yes."

"What else?"

"What else?" Her beautiful eyes dropped.

Harland took a careful step toward her. "What have you done, Katherine?"

～

Harland had lost weight.

It was obvious in the sharp angles of his face and the

corded definition of his arms where his shirt had been pushed up past his elbows. But he had never looked so perfect. So alive. In her head, she had prepared herself for this moment. She'd had a carefully arranged speech, but now, standing in front of him, all of it seemed to have evaporated.

What have you done?

She raised her eyes to his. This was where a smuggler would speak of shrewd negotiations and good business. This was where a battlefield surgeon would keep her composure and speak of reasonable risk and expected reward. Except the words were all gone. Replaced by an emotion so strong and so overwhelming that it was rendering her mute.

"What you did...you could have died," she finally whispered.

"I didn't."

"You took that bullet for me. You should never have—"

"I'd do it again. I will do it a hundred more times if I need to." He took another step toward her and caught her hands in his. They were warm, his fingers curling around hers, keeping her from pulling away. "I would give my life for yours, Katherine, because I love you. Because I've loved you from the first time I saw you."

Emotion inundated her, swelling and expanding, filling her with hope and joy. Her throat thickened, and her eyes burned.

"I had a rifle pointed at you the first time you saw me," she said shakily.

"What can I say? It made an impression." He released one of her hands and touched her face, his finger tracing her cheekbone and then her lips.

And then his mouth found hers, and he kissed her with

a gentle desperation. She kissed him back, her fingers curling into the front of his shirt.

He stopped, his forehead resting against hers. "I want you in my tomorrow, Katherine. I want you in every day that I have left on this earth." He pulled away from her and slowly retrieved a crumpled paper from the garden bench, bits of red wax flaking away like dried blood. He returned to her and put it in her hands.

She smoothed out the paper and read the brief message.

"What have you done?" He asked that question again so quietly she almost didn't hear him.

"I fell in love with you," she whispered. It wasn't the answer he was looking for, but it was the answer that he needed to hear.

His eyes closed briefly before opening again to search hers, love shadowed by anguish clear in her gaze. "You are the strongest woman I have ever met, but I can't let you fight my battles. I can't let you give King—"

She kissed him again, a soft, unhurried brush of her lips over his. "I gave him France," she murmured, putting him out of his misery.

"What?"

"I traded France in exchange for you."

"I beg your pardon?"

"Well, only part of France. Wissant. Calais. The parts with beaches and towns and smuggling networks controlled by Guillaume Mercier. All of which, it seems, is worth more than a single surgeon on the Kentish coast."

Harland was staring at her, his jaw slack.

"Too much?" she asked with a small smile. "You'd prefer I renegotiate?"

He laughed. And then he groaned and bent double, holding his side. "Jesus, Katherine," he wheezed.

"Sit," she urged, a hand on his shoulder. "Before you crack another rib."

"No." He shook his head, reaching up with one hand to cover hers where it rested on his shoulder. Very gingerly, he lowered himself to one knee, her hand still tightly held in his. "I have a proposition for you."

Katherine caught her breath. She sank to her knees in front of him so that they were even. "Indeed?"

"I'm supposed to do this on one knee at your feet," Harland protested.

"I much prefer that we are equal."

Carefully, Harland leaned forward and kissed her, though the kiss he gave her was anything but careful. It was a searing kiss with the promise of forever. When he pulled back, she was breathless.

"Marry me, Dr. Wright. Be my partner. My friend. My lover. My wife."

She blinked furiously against the burning at the backs of her eyes. "I would very much like to be your partner and your friend and your lover and your wife." She leaned forward and kissed him. "I accept your proposition, Dr. Hayward."

Have you read Kelly Bowen's
Season for Scandal series?

Captain Maximus Harcourt, the
unconventional tenth Duke of Alderidge,
has returned home from his latest voyage
to find a naked earl—quite
inconveniently deceased—tied to his
missing sister's bed. And he has only one
place to turn, Miss Ivory Moore of
Chegarre & Associates, known
throughout London for smoothing over
the most dire of scandals.

Please turn the page for an excerpt from
Duke of My Heart.

Chapter One

London, February 1819

The silk was the color of sin.

It shimmered where the candlelight danced across its surface, its rich crimson and sumptuous garnet hues swirling in the cascading lengths. The silken ribbon was wide, its superior quality was evident, and it must have been expensive, a luxury only the very wealthy could afford. On the brim of a bonnet, it would have been impressive. On the bodice of a ball gown, it would have been spectacular.

Wrapped around the limbs of a dead earl, however, it was a problem.

Ivory Moore pressed her fingers over the pulse point at the man's neck, knowing she would find none, but needing to confirm. Beneath her touch the soft flesh was already cooling, and she let her fingers move to the bindings covering his wrists, tracing the silk to where it was knotted deftly around the bedpost.

"He's dead." It was a statement, not a question, from her pretty associate standing just behind her.

"He is indeed, Miss DeVries," Ivory murmured.

"That is the Earl of Debarry," Elise DeVries hissed urgently in her ear.

"I am aware." Ivory stepped back slightly to consider the tableau in front of her. The naked earl was spread out across the mattress like a marooned sea star, his wrists and ankles tied to the four corners of the bed. His barrel chest rose like an island amid a scattering of rose petals and decorative ostrich feathers and rumpled bedclothes. He was instantly recognizable, even stripped of the wildly expensive clothes he favored, whose absence exposed a body that was just beginning to lose its battle with fine wine and idle living.

The earl was still handsome despite the fifty-plus years of vice he'd enjoyed before this last unfortunate encounter. He was powerful, wealthy, and widowed—and everywhere he went in polite society, he was treated with the deference befitting his title. But privately, behind closed doors, he was known to all as the Earl of Debauchery, more famous for his love of women and his outrageous sexual exploits than anything else. Finding him tied to a bed wasn't a surprise.

Finding him tied to the bed of the demure Lady Beatrice Harcourt, the Duke of Alderidge's eighteen-year-old sister? Now that was more of a shock.

Ivory took another step back, pushing the hood of her cloak off her head, and placed her bag gently on the floor. There was little time to waste, but before she could analyze the potential damage and formulate a solution, there were preliminary matters to consider.

"The door is locked, Miss DeVries?" she asked briskly. Containment was critical.

"Of course."

"Good." Ivory turned to address the woman standing stiffly near the hearth. "Was it you, my lady, who summoned us?"

Lady Helen Harcourt was worrying an enameled pendant at her throat, but at Ivory's question she dropped it, clasping her hands in front of her hard enough to make her knuckles as white as her face. "Yes."

"A wise decision on your part, my lady." Ivory eyed the woman's greying hair, which had been pulled into a severe knot, softened only by a jeweled clip that matched her green ball gown. Deep grooves of distress were cut into Lady Helen's unyielding face, but despite her pallor, there were no signs of impending hysterics.

Ivory felt a small measure of relief. "May I ask who found the body?"

"Mary. Lady Beatrice's maid." Lady Helen unclasped her hands long enough to make a gesture in the direction of a red-eyed maid sitting in the corner, who, at the mention of the word *body*, had started to sob.

Ivory exchanged a look with Elise. The maid would need to go.

"And where is Lady Beatrice at the moment?" Ivory inquired.

"I can't find her. She's just... *gone*." It came out in a rush, the news delivered in a tone barely above a whisper.

Well, that wasn't surprising. Beatrice had very likely fled, and while the girl would need to be found, it wasn't the immediate priority.

Ivory eyed the crumpled bedclothes beneath the body, and the lavender counterpane that lay in a forgotten heap on the floor. She took in the size of the room, and the pretty dressing table with its collection of bottles and pots. A pale-pink ball gown, embroidered with tiny roses, had been tossed over the back of the chair, layers of costly fabric and lace abandoned with little care. Stockings and slippers, along with Debarry's evening clothes, had been discarded and had fallen in disarray on the floor. Two empty wine bottles rested on their sides at the edge of the rug.

Ivory frowned. If it had been Lady Helen's rooms, she would have had more options. An affair between an aging spinster aunt and a peer of the realm—no matter how unlikely—if properly presented, would cause gossip, but not ruination. A dead earl tied to the bed of a debutante in her first season posed a much greater challenge.

There was very little time to waste. Who knew how long they had before someone—

A sharp banging on the bedroom door snapped Ivory's head around and caused Lady Helen to emit a squeak of shock.

"Helen?" came a disembodied voice through the thick wood. "Are you in there?"

"Who is that?" hissed Ivory, her mind racing through the possible excuses Helen might offer for locking herself in her niece's room.

The older woman was staring at the door, her hand pressed to her mouth.

Another rap sounded, the urgent impatience of the blow making the wood shake. "What the hell is going on, Helen? Is Bea in there with you?"

"My lady!" Ivory snapped in low tones. Whoever was standing on the other side of that door was not going away. Worse, he would soon draw attention to this room with all his banging. Every servant in the house would descend on this scene, and even Ivory wouldn't be able to contain that.

"It's Alderidge," Lady Helen whispered faintly, as though she didn't quite believe it.

Ivory started. "The duke? I was given to understand he was currently in India."

"He was. Apparently he's decided to grace us with his presence." Lady Helen's words were tight with bitterness. "Too little, too late, as always."

Ivory fought the urge to groan aloud. It was clear there was no love lost between the duke and his aunt. Ivory only hoped the man held his sister in higher regard. She did not need family turmoil to complicate what was already a terribly complicated situation.

"Aunt Helen!" The knob rattled loudly. "I demand you let me into this room at once!"

"Can he be trusted?" Ivory asked, though she feared she had little choice in the matter. Someone was going to have to let him in or risk having the door knocked clean off its hinges.

Lady Helen's lips compressed into a thin line, but she gave a quick, jerky nod. That was all Ivory needed. She flew to the door, twisted the key in the lock, and wrenched the door open. She had the vague impression of a worn greatcoat, battered boots, and a hulking bearing.

"What the hell is going on?" the stranger bellowed. "And who the hell are you?"

"Welcome home, Your Grace," said Ivory, and grabbed the sleeve of his coat. She yanked him into the room. "Please do come in and cease making so much noise, if you would be so kind."

The man stumbled past her a couple of steps before coming to an abrupt halt, but not before Ivory had closed the door behind him and once again turned the key in the lock.

"Jesus Christ," Alderidge swore, getting his first look at the scene in front of him.

Ivory was standing just behind the duke, and she could feel the chill of the night still clinging to his coat. The only things she knew about Maximus Harcourt, Duke of Alderidge, were that he had inherited his title a decade ago and that he spent much of his time overseas captaining an impressive fleet of trade ships. But she knew nothing about his personality, his family relationships, or the motivations that had brought him home to London tonight.

She desperately hoped Alderidge was not going to be a problem. "Did anyone see you come up here?" Ivory asked.

"I beg your pardon?" The duke swung around to face her, and Ivory felt the impact of his icy grey eyes clear through to her toes.

"Is anyone else looking for your aunt? Or your sister, for that matter?" She refused to look away, dismayed to realize an involuntary flutter had started deep in her belly, radiating out to weaken the joints at her knees and send heat flooding through her body.

Good heavens. She hadn't had this sort of visceral reaction to a man in a very, very long time, and she wasn't pleased. Desire was a distraction, and distractions were perilous. Maybe it was because Alderidge was such a radical departure from the long line of polished, simpering aristocrats she'd been dealing with for years. Dressed completely in black, he looked a little like a pirate who had just stepped off the deck of a ship, what with his long, sun-bleached hair, his wind-roughened skin, and at least a week's worth of dark-blond stubble covering his strong jaw. A scar ran along the left side of his forehead, disappearing into his hairline. His clothes were plain, his salt-stained coat meant to be serviceable and warm. He looked dangerous and, at the moment, furious.

"No, no one saw me. I left my ship and crew at the damn docks after a long journey across uncooperative seas and came here, thinking to find some peace and quiet. Instead I find a swarm of gilded strangers packed into my ballroom, and more strangers locked in my sister's room with my aunt and a dead body. Someone damn well needs to tell me very quickly and very clearly just what the hell is going on here." The duke was making a visible effort to remain calm.

Lady Harcourt made little disapproving sounds with her tongue for every curse that erupted from the duke's mouth—and Alderidge flinched, as if on cue, after each of his aunt's tiny clicks and sighs. Ivory might have found this exchange funny in other circumstances. Right now, however, she needed to take control and make sure the duke and his aunt were aligned. Otherwise she hadn't a prayer of extracting the family from this mess unscathed.

"You may call me Miss Moore," Ivory said pleasantly, "and I am from Chegarre and Associates. This is my colleague, Miss DeVries." Out of the corner of her eye she saw Elise make a brief curtsy.

"And Chegarre and Associates is what?" Alderidge demanded. "A solicitor's firm?" He paused, a shadow of uncertainty flickering in his eyes as he regarded her. "I've been away from England for quite a long time, but I feel certain I would have heard the news if a group of women had set up shop at the Inns of Court."

"We are not lawyers exactly, Your Grace."

"Then what—"

"Your sister seems to have gotten herself in a spot of trouble," Ivory continued, nodding at the naked form sprawled across the sheets. "We've been summoned to get her out of it."

"That is not possible. My sister is the Lady Beatrice Harcourt."

"We're aware," Ivory agreed grimly, turning and marching over to the bed. "And the dead man currently tied to her bed is the Earl of Debarry."

The duke's jaw was clenched so hard that Ivory imagined his teeth were in danger of shattering. He turned to his aunt. "Where is Bea?"

"I don't know."

"What do you mean, you don't know?"

Angry color had flooded Helen's face. "I came looking for her when I couldn't find her downstairs in the ballroom, thinking maybe she was feeling poorly. The ball is in her honor. It took *months* to plan. Everyone who is *anyone* is downstairs." She stopped abruptly, as if suddenly realizing the awful import of that fact.

"She's missing?" Horror colored his words.

"The precise location of your sister is not known at this point, Your Grace," Ivory confirmed. "Though I have every confidence that we will locate her shortly."

The duke swung around to face her again, those ice-grey eyes impaling her as if she were somehow responsible for this debacle.

"We have a much more immediate problem that needs to be addressed, Your Grace, before we can focus our efforts on locating Lady Beatrice. And that is the body currently tied to her bed." Ivory jerked her chin in the direction of the maid still sniffling into her apron. "Your sister's maid, Mary, discovered this unfortunate scene, and most fortuitously, it was your aunt who intercepted her before anyone else could. It was also your aunt who did the sensible thing and hired us."

"Hired you? What the hell for?"

"We manage situations such as the one your sister has currently found herself in."

"And what sort of situation is that, exactly?" His tone was threatening, but Ivory didn't have time for niceties.

"You are a man of the world, Your Grace. I feel certain you are able to guess."

The duke's eyes darkened to the color of an approaching storm, and another unwanted thrill shot through Ivory. She curled her fingers into her palms, letting her nails bite into the skin.

"Have a care, Miss Moore," he snarled. "I assure you, you do not wish to insult my sister's—"

"I deal in facts, not in fairy tales." Ivory cut him off and was absurdly gratified to see shock wash across his face. "There are no signs of a violent struggle, nor are there any obvious wounds or marks on the body. It is likely that the earl died from natural causes induced from the exertions that usually follow being tied with red silk to the bed of a healthy young woman."

Helen Harcourt wheezed. "You can't possibly be suggesting that Lady Beatrice—"

"Further," Ivory continued, "it is also likely that Lady Beatrice panicked and fled the scene once she realized her companion had drawn his last debauched breath. It is a very common reaction, and in my experience, the young woman in question will return when she has had a moment to collect her wits and invent a suitable explanation for her absence. And if Lady Beatrice lacks the requisite powers of invention, Chegarre and Associates shall be happy to supply her with a credible lie that she may repeat to the ton." She paused. "Your loyalty is admirable, but I suggest you save the moral outrage for someone else. I care more about rescuing your sister's reputation than the truth of what happened here tonight. And frankly, so should you. We've got a great deal of work to do if your sister's future is to remain as bright as it was this morning."

The duke's expression was positively glacial. "I give the orders here, Miss Moore, not you. Don't presume that I will ever follow your lead."

Irritation surged. "Take a look around you, Your Grace. Do you see a crew of sailors anxiously awaiting your direction?" She put emphasis on the last two words. "This is not your world. This is mine."

"Get out of my house," the duke said, his voice as sharp as cut glass. "Now."

His aunt made a strangled sound of distress.

"If that is your wish, Your Grace, we will be happy to comply, of course. But I ask that you consider carefully. Our firm has been brought here by your aunt to preserve your good name and honor. Our objective is the same as yours: we want only to protect Lady Beatrice and the rest of your family. And what you must understand is that there is a window of opportunity here that is rapidly closing. Downstairs there is a ballroom filled with some of the most important and influential people in London. Soon those people will begin to wonder where the Earl of Debarry has gotten to. Soon people will start wondering where the comely Lady Beatrice—the guest of honor—is hiding. Soon people will come looking. And should they find a dead earl tied to Lady Beatrice's bed, I will no longer be able to help you. But it is your choice, of course, if I stay or if I go."

"I don't need you to fix my problems," the duke growled.

Ivory resisted the urge to roll her eyes. The duke was in so far over his head that he couldn't even begin to see the surface. Instead she adopted her most neutral tone. "I'm not here to fix your problems, Your Grace, I'm here to fix those of Lady Beatrice."

Lady Helen swayed slightly before straightening her shoulders with resolve. "Don't be a fool. We need help. Neither you nor I can make this all disappear."

The duke was shaking his head. "I can handle this."

"Can you really?" his aunt asked. "How?"

Alderidge blinked, and Ivory suspected the duke was finally getting over his initial shock and was now considering the magnitude of the problem before him.

Helen continued on, relentless. "How will you make certain the honor of the Alderidge family is preserved? How will you prevent this, this...scene from becoming known to everyone? Do you intend to let malicious gossip and baseless slander ruin poor Beatrice's life?"

Ivory rather suspected Lady Beatrice was doing a fine job of ruining things all on her own. But it was not for her to judge. Especially since a little ruin was always good for business.

"You're supposed to be her guardian," Lady Helen said bitterly. "A lady should have the protection of her brother. If you had ever once thought of anyone but yourself, we would not now find ourselves here, in this sordid and disgusting position."

"My lady," Ivory snapped, sensing that this conversation was in danger of veering badly off track. "Now is not the time to point fingers. If you must lay blame, I would suggest you conduct that useless exercise tomorrow over tea, when your guests are gone and there is no longer a body tied to your niece's bed."

Whatever color had been left in Lady Helen's stoic face fled, and her mouth gaped slightly. Ivory noticed Alderidge's was similarly hanging open.

She put her hands on her hips. "Now, what is it going to be? Do you require our services on behalf of Lady Beatrice or not? Make a decision. Time is running out."

The duke swore again, his expression black. "Very well. Consider yourself hired. My sister can't..." He trailed off, as if searching for words.

Ivory pounced. "You must agree to defer to my instruction and trust in my expertise, Your Grace."

Icy grey eyes snapped back to her. "I will agree to no such thing. I don't even know you."

"And I don't know you, which is irrelevant. But I will not be able to do my job if you get in my way. Dissent will cost your sister everything."

The duke muttered something vile under his breath. "Do what you must." It sounded strained.

"Do I have your word?"

"You heard me the first time, Miss Moore. I do not need to repeat myself."

"A wise choice then, Your Grace." She produced a small card from a pocket sewn into her cloak and handed it to the duke. "In the event you need to find me in the future."

Alderidge shoved the card in the pocket of his coat without even looking at it. "After tonight, Miss Moore, I hope to never see you again."

That stung a little, though Ivory had no idea why it should. No one in their right mind *wanted* to see her. Her presence in someone's home meant the parallel presence of some sort of acute social or family disaster.

She sniffed. "The feeling is quite mutual, Your Grace. The sooner we conclude this unfortunate bit of business, the better it will be for all involved. But I must warn you before I begin, if I may be so gauche, that the services provided by Chegarre and Associates are expensive."

"Are they worth it?" Alderidge asked in a harsh voice. Ivory held his gaze. "Always."

⁓

Maximus Harcourt, tenth Duke of Alderidge, couldn't remember ever having felt so helpless—or so furious. He had stepped into a nightmare that defied comprehension, and making it worse was the knowledge that he was not the person most qualified to handle it.

Unruly crews could be reformed. He could deal with tropical storms and raging seas. Pirates and smugglers could be summarily dispatched. Max had rarely met a problem he couldn't best. He'd rarely met a problem with the power to confuse him. But this? Well, this was an altogether different sort of beast.

Which meant he was now at the mercy of Miss Moore. A woman who treated the discovery of a dead, naked earl tied to a missing virgin's bed as though it were no more serious than a cup of spilled tea on an expensive rug. As though this sort of thing happened every day.

He'd never in all his life met a woman with such nerve. Or maybe it wasn't nerve at all but simply arrogance. It was difficult to tell how old she was, though certainly she wasn't any older than he. Even beneath her plain clothing and mundane cap, she was striking, in a most extraordinarily unconventional way. Her skin glowed like unblemished satin, framed by tendrils of hair the color of rich chestnut, shot through with mahogany. Her dark eyes were too wide, her mouth was too full, her cheekbones too sharp. Yet all of that together was somehow . . . flawless.

"Was that the ball gown your niece was wearing

tonight?" Miss Moore was asking his aunt, pointing at a pile of abandoned lace and rose silk draped over a chair.

Max wrenched his gaze away from her face and, with a jolt, recognized the embroidered silk that he'd shipped to Bea the last time he'd been in China. He'd been sure his sister would love the detail.

"Yes." Lady Helen pressed a hand to her lips, her face a peculiar ashen color.

"Then she'll not be downstairs," the dark-haired woman who had been introduced as Miss DeVries murmured. "Nor does she have any intention of returning to the ball." She plucked the gown from the chair and held it up to her body with consideration.

Miss Moore nodded. "Let's hope she has the good sense to stay away until we have a chance to speak with her." She paused, eyeing the gown critically. "Can you make it work?"

"Most certainly," said Miss DeVries, replacing the gown and then inexplicably loosening the ties on her own shapeless woolen dress. Max frowned, perplexed, then horrified, as the top half of her chemise was revealed. It slipped over a shoulder, revealing smooth skin puckered by scar tissue from what looked like an old bullet wound. He gaped before hastily averting his eyes. What kind of woman stripped in the middle of a room full of people? What kind of woman had cause to have been *shot*?

"Excellent." Miss Moore turned to his aunt. "If you wish to preserve your niece's reputation, and your own, you need to return downstairs. Your absence may have been noted by now, so I need you to circulate, smile pleasantly, and ensure everyone is having a marvelous time. If anyone comments on your absence, cite your nephew's unexpected, yet welcome, return. I can't stress enough the value of a good distraction, and the duke's arrival will be splendid."

"My sister is missing and you're telling my aunt she should go and dance a quadrille?" Max could feel a vein throbbing at his temple.

Miss Moore glared at him and then turned her attention back to his aunt. She didn't even give him the courtesy of a response. Bloody, bloody hell.

"Can you do that?" she was asking Helen.

Lady Helen nodded stiffly.

"If anyone asks about the whereabouts of Lady Beatrice, mention you just saw her at the refreshment table. Or near the ballroom doors. Somewhere that cannot be immediately verified." Miss Moore put a hand on the older woman's arm. "Your behavior is critical right now. No one must suspect you are anything but pleased with how successful the ball is. Do you understand?"

"Yes."

"In thirty minutes you will visibly exit the ballroom and make your way to the bottom of the main staircase."

"Why—"

"Thirty minutes. Can you do that?"

"Yes."

He'd never heard Helen so tractable in his life.

Despite himself, Max was grudgingly impressed that Miss Moore had managed to handle his battle-ax of an aunt with a deft touch. That was something he hadn't mastered, nor did he suspect he ever would. She was a good woman, but also a mighty annoyance. She delighted in repeating to him just how much she had sacrificed for *his* family, and it wore sorely on his nerves.

Miss Moore led her over to the door and cracked it open, peering out into the empty hallway. She turned back and softened her voice. "This will turn out all right, my lady. I suspect your niece is rather terrified right now. She'll need you, and your forgiveness, when she comes home."

Helen nodded and met Max's eyes, her expression stony. "Your parents would be turning in their graves," she said coldly. "If you have any regard for your sister, you will help Miss Moore do whatever it takes to find her and fix this."

Max fought the acerbic response that jumped into his throat. As if he were incapable of recognizing that Bea's future was hanging by a perilous thread. He became aware that Miss Moore was glaring at him again with those impenetrable dark eyes, and he swallowed his retort, nodding instead. Arguing with his aunt would get them nowhere.

"Arguing will get us nowhere." Miss Moore stole his thought as soon as his aunt had departed and she'd locked the door behind her. "She's upset, and I need everyone to keep a clear head."

Resentment rose hard and fast. How dare this chit lecture him on maintaining composure in difficult circumstances? He was a sea captain, for God's sake. Every day of his life brought difficult circumstances. The only difference being that he knew what to do with those.

Miss Moore had returned to the bed and was diligently working on the knots that bound the dead man's wrists. Max strode to the footboard and began working on the bindings at his ankles.

"I refuse to believe my sister had anything to do with this," Max said. He wondered for whose benefit he'd made that statement.

Miss Moore straightened slightly, brushing an errant strand of hair out of her eyes. "Your Grace, there is one thing you must understand. I do not get paid to form opinions or pass judgments." She bent to retrieve a cloth bag by her feet and began stuffing the silk ribbons into it. "Frankly, I don't really care if Debarry was your sister's lover or not. What I do care about is ensuring she is not ruined, or worse, because of it."

"Worse?"

"The earl is dead." She was now collecting feathers and rose petals, and they too disappeared into the bag. The wine bottles followed with a loud clink.

Max felt his skin prickle with unease. "You can't be serious. You think she *killed* him?"

"If she did, he went out a happy man," Miss Moore remarked.

Max recoiled. "Bea is barely eighteen. She is beautiful and innocent and—"

Miss Moore had stopped and now turned to meet his eyes. He hated the sympathy that was in them, yet somehow he couldn't bring himself to look away.

"My apologies. My comment was insensitive." She approached him, searching his face. "How long have you been away, Your Grace?"

"What?"

Miss Moore remained silent, simply waiting for his answer.

Despite himself, he couldn't think of a reason not to answer. "I own and captain Indiamen, Miss Moore. I am rarely in England. The last time was two years ago."

"Ah." She nodded, as if this bit of information somehow explained the situation in which they currently found themselves.

"I may not know my sister as well as you think I should, but I know she wouldn't have an earl tied to her bed,"

Maximus said, ignoring the tiny voice in the back of his head that was telling him he knew no such thing. "And I resent any implication otherwise."

Miss Moore was still studying him carefully, and for the life of him, he couldn't tell what she was thinking. Though he had the inexplicable feeling she was somehow seeing more than he cared for her to see.

"Is there a guest room on this floor?" she asked abruptly.

Max frowned, caught off guard. "There are two of them. At the end of the hall."

"I'll need your help to move his lordship." She left him at the bed, discarding her own cloak, and bent to collect the abandoned clothing strewn about the room. A pair of trousers, then a shirt and a waistcoat. "We'll need to re-dress him first to stage this properly."

Maximus stared at her. Bloody hell, but this woman was unnerving.

She returned, the clothes draped over an arm, a faint look of annoyance across her face. "Quickly. Time is of the essence, Your Grace." She plucked the ribbons from his unfeeling hands.

Max scowled. "If we're going to dress a corpse together, then at least give me Debarry's trousers."

Miss Moore gazed at him with shrewd speculation.

"I have my limits, Miss Moore."

"A gentleman," she murmured, and he wasn't sure at all that she wasn't laughing at him.

"A poor assumption on your part," Max muttered, but the woman's only response was to toss the trousers in his direction.

"Good" was all she said.

Ivory yanked the shirt over the corpse's head, careful not to touch the duke where he had the dead man braced. Alderidge had shed his greatcoat, and beneath the bulky winter garment lay a pair of broad shoulders and an impressive collection of muscles in all the right places. His own shirt and waistcoat hid some of them, but not enough to slow the pulse she could feel pounding at her throat.

It was ridiculous, but it was an effort not to simply stare at him.

He looked a bit untamed, Ivory thought, as she jammed a lifeless arm through the opening of Debarry's striped waistcoat. Like a lion that had suddenly appeared amid a clutter of domesticated house cats. She diligently attacked the row of waistcoat buttons, wrestling them into their buttonholes, considering further. It was obvious Alderidge was a man used to power and control, yet it would seem his sister's welfare trumped his disinclination to surrender either. That was certainly a relief—

"Miss Moore?"

Ivory blinked and looked up. "I'm sorry?"

"I asked you if you think I should retie his cravat."

Good God. This was no time for flights of fancy about untamed pirates. They were dealing with the Earl of Debarry here, and she could not afford any missteps. The man had too many powerful friends. The situation at hand required her undivided attention.

"No," she said, gathering her wits. "Leave off his cravat. And his evening coat and his shoes. But bring them with us." She pushed herself off the bed, where she had been kneeling. "Elise, stay here with Mary. Get her to stop sniveling and pick out the appropriate wig from the kit. She'll know what hairstyle Lady Beatrice was wearing tonight. I also need to know if there is anything missing of Lady Beatrice's. Clothing, shoes, jewelry."

Elise, now in nothing but her chemise, nodded, busy examining the rose ball gown. "Of course."

"There's water in the basin," Ivory said, pointing toward the washstand. "I'll need that. Please leave it just outside the door."

"Done. Anything else?" Elise asked.

"No, I think that will get us started. His Grace and I will take Debarry to a guest room." She gestured at the duke to get under one of the corpse's arms.

Alderidge frowned. "Why are we taking him to a guest room?"

"Because he's too big to stuff up a chimney." Ivory pulled a lifeless arm over her shoulder and together they hauled the man off the bed.

The duke's jaw clenched again. "I don't appreciate your humor."

Ivory sighed. "No, I don't suppose you do."

They made their way to the door, Ivory puffing under the dead weight. Thank God the duke and his muscles had shown up when they did. She and Elise would have managed it, but it would have been a struggle. She unlocked the door and cracked it open, peering into the hall. It was still deserted.

"Quickly now."

They made their way down the hall, the duke doing most of the work to support the body. Mercifully, the hallway remained empty, and they shoved their way into a guest room, Ivory pushing the door shut behind them with her foot. The room was dark, the only faint light coming through the window from streetlamps burning below.

She ducked out from under their lifeless load and pulled back the sheets. "Put him into bed," she whispered.

Alderidge dropped the bundle of clothing he had under his other arm and heaved the corpse onto the mattress. Together they arranged his limbs into a pose of peaceful slumber.

"Now what?" he asked in a clipped voice.

"Debarry was feeling poorly when you ran into him," Ivory said, pulling up the sheets and tucking them around the earl. "Though you had just returned home and hadn't even had a chance to change for the ball, you offered to have his carriage brought around. He refused, declaring that he was certain he would feel better with a brief rest. Being a gracious host, you offered him your guest room. You saw to his needs yourself, as the servants were all busy downstairs."

"Why don't we just take him back to his own house?" the duke hissed. "I don't particularly want him found dead in any of my rooms. People will talk."

"Probably. But Debarry shows no obvious symptoms of anything save a lifetime of overindulgence. His untimely death will be unfortunate but not shocking." She retrieved the earl's pumps and set them neatly by the bed. The forgotten evening coat and cravat she laid out over the end of the footboard, as if Debarry had been planning on redressing. "And the risk of taking him back to his own house is too great. Downstairs there's an army of guests and footmen and coachmen and grooms to get past, and then assuming we arrive safely at our destination, we'd have to navigate Debarry's own servants. It would be almost impossible."

"Almost?"

"I've done it once or twice when there has simply been no other option."

"What the hell does that mean?"

"It means I've helped others out of worse situations than this."

"Worse? How could it be worse? This man is dead, and my sister is missing!"

Ivory winced slightly. There was absolutely nothing she could say at this moment that the duke wanted to hear about Lady Beatrice. "I need you to dress for the ball now," she told him instead. "And you need to hurry."

"Have you lost your mind? I should be out looking for Bea, not prancing around a ballroom." His voice was absolute, and Ivory suspected that he was very good at commanding his crew.

Too bad for him she wasn't one of them.

"And you will look for her. But not right now." She was careful to keep her tone steady but firm.

"You think this is partly my fault, don't you?"

"As I said earlier, I am not here to form opinions, Your Grace. I'm here to make sure your sister returns safely to your protection. And to do that, I need you to trust me."

The duke raked his hands through his hair, creating an impenetrable shadow across his face. Ivory didn't need to see his features to know that furious indecision would be stamped there.

She took a step forward and placed her hand gently on his shoulder. The man might be a controlling ass, but he was clearly worried about his sister. And she needed his full cooperation if she was going to pull this off. "This is what will happen next. You will dress. Go downstairs. Welcome your guests, regale them with tales of your last voyage. Be visible. You are the perfect distraction, and your presence here will doubtless aid your sister tonight. Somewhere over a card game, mention to at least two people, but no more than four, your regret that Debarry is missing the hand because he was feeling poorly. In one hour you will instruct your butler to check on his lordship. Not a footman, but the butler. Butlers are far more discreet." Beneath her fingers his muscles were tight.

"What about Bea?"

"Leave her to me. Just for right now. Now let's get you dressed. Which one is your room?"

Alderidge opened his mouth twice before he managed a response. "You've done quite enough, Miss Moore."

"I will tell you when I've done enough," Ivory said. "You can either tell me which one is your room or I will simply find it myself. But I will remind you again that time is not our friend."

"I don't need—"

Ivory blew out a breath of exasperation and tiptoed to the door. She checked the hallway, but it remained empty, the only sound the muted noise of the music and the crowd below their feet. Silently she slipped from the room and started down the hall. She bent to retrieve the basin that Elise had left outside Beatrice's door, careful not to slop the water on the rug. "Which room, Your Grace? I will open every one of these doors, or you can just tell me."

"Jesus." Alderidge was on her heels, and not happy about it. "This one." He pushed by her and stalked to the end of the hall, opening the last door on the right.

The room was dark, yet the faint musty smell she had expected from a room left unused too long was absent. Though the room was chilled, it would seem the town house enjoyed the attentions of an exceedingly diligent staff. Ivory closed the door behind her and waited for her eyes to adjust, light suddenly flaring as the duke lit two lanterns.

The room was sparsely decorated with the basics, and there was not a personal touch in evidence anywhere. A bed with a Spartan headboard and footboard was covered in a plain white coverlet. A cumbersome wardrobe loomed against one of the walls, and there was a washstand with a porcelain bowl resting empty and cold in the center. A small cheval mirror stood near the washstand, and at the foot of the bed rested a battered trunk, the only indication that this space might belong to somebody.

"No dressing room, Your Grace?" Ivory asked, heading for the washstand. She dumped the water into the bowl and put Lady Beatrice's basin on the floor. Then she moved to the wardrobe.

"A waste of space." He was still standing near the cold hearth and the lanterns.

"Spoken like a man who chooses to live on a ship, I suppose," Ivory replied mildly. "I must assume you have a shaving kit in here somewhere?"

"Of course I do."

"Then I would advise you to get started."

"Are you ordering me to shave? Now?"

"Anything that deviates from an expected appearance will be remembered. Remarked upon. Speculated on. You cannot appear like a barbarous, disheveled pirate on the same night that your ball ends because there is a dead man in your guest room."

"What did you just call me?"

"I didn't call you anything. I simply commented upon your current appearance." Ivory had reached the wardrobe and stopped. "Do you need me to shave you?"

Alderidge's jaw dropped open. "*What?*"

Given his expression, she might as well have suggested she take him on a flying carpet to the moon. "Time, Your

Grace, is ticking. I don't know how many more times I need to stress this to you before you understand that we simply must find a way to get done what needs to be done. Either you shave, and make yourself look presentable to society, or I will do it for you."

"No, I don't need you holding a razor to my throat," Alderidge muttered, but at least he was moving now. He knelt before the battered trunk and released the buckles. He opened the lid and rummaged in its interior, then pulled out a leather case. He stalked over to the washstand and started extracting items.

Satisfied, Ivory turned back to the massive wardrobe, just as a terrible thought struck her. "Do you even have evening clothes?"

"Of course I have evening clothes." He stopped. "Somewhere. In there, maybe?"

Dear God. Ivory yanked open the two center doors and nearly swooned with relief when she wasn't met with a swarm of moths. The clothes, like the room, were neat and orderly, folded on shelves, as though the duke had just stepped out for two hours as opposed to two years. When it came to the domestic details, Lady Helen, it would seem, ran a tight ship.

Ivory ran her fingers over a collection of crisply folded linen shirts, waistcoats, breeches, and more formal pantaloons. The drawers below revealed an array of stockings, braces, and pressed cravats, each one separated from the next by a thin piece of tissue. Opening the long door at the side of the wardrobe, she discovered a collection of jackets sorted by function. It had been a very long time since she had had the pleasure of choosing evening wear. Of any sort.

The sharp scent of shaving soap had filled the room, and

Ivory could hear the faint swirl of water in the basin, followed by the scrape of a straight blade against stubble. A faint twinge of melancholy struck her, old memories surfacing of the pleasure she had derived from simply watching a man shave. In those memories she sat on the edge of the bed while her husband went about his ablutions, most often preferring to do it himself, as this duke did. In those memories those stolen moments of privacy were always filled with banter and conversation and laughter.

But they were just that. Memories. And they had no place in the present.

Pushing the melancholy and memories aside, Ivory carefully selected a shirt, waistcoat, and tailcoat, draping each over her arm. She stood on her tiptoes and pulled a pair of pantaloons from a shelf. The clothes were all of fine quality and understated in their color, making it easy to coordinate.

"I'll lay your clothes out on the bed," she started, turning around. She had the tailcoat and his shirt spread neatly on the coverlet when she made the mistake of looking up. And found herself staring.

The duke had stripped off his worn waistcoat and shirt, and had his back to her, peering into the cheval mirror as he ran the blade over his skin. He'd moved one of the lanterns to the washstand so that he might see better, and the light created an impressive silhouette, putting his torso in stark relief. The muscles in his arms and shoulders flexed each time he lifted the razor to his face—raw, male, physical power sculpted into beautiful lines. His spine created a valley of shadow that started beneath the ends of his long hair and traveled down through the ridges and planes of his back to dip into the waistband of his breeches.

She couldn't draw enough air into her lungs, and a peculiar light-headedness seemed to have impaired her ability to remember what she was supposed to be doing. He was stunning, and she couldn't even begin to imagine what that power and strength might feel like beneath her hands or between her—

"Am I not doing this fast enough for your liking?" the duke said irritably, and with some horror, Ivory realized he was watching her in the mirror.

"Are you almost done?" she said, and it was a monumental effort to keep her voice even.

"Yes." He picked up his discarded shirt and dried his face.

"Good." She placed the last items of clothing on the bed and turned back to the wardrobe, under the guise of fetching stockings. And while she was fetching him silk stockings, she would try to remember how to breathe normally.

Bloody hell. She needed to pull herself together.

"Get undressed," she ordered, not turning around. "I need you downstairs in ten minutes."

"And I don't need you in here at all."

Ivory jumped, not having heard the duke come up behind her. She turned and was presented with a view of his broad chest.

His broad, shirtless, beautiful chest.

She stumbled backward, only to be caught by a pair of strong hands. She could feel the warmth from his palms on her upper arms.

"I've been dressing myself since I was two, Miss Moore. I do not need further assistance."

"Congratulations, Your Grace." She was pleased that she seemed to have regained her sanity.

His icy eyes bored into her. "And the last woman who ordered me to undress was rather naked herself."

It was meant to shock her, she knew. He wasn't the first man to try to do so.

Ivory snorted. "Congratulations again, Your Grace."

The duke's jaw clenched again. Clearly not the response he'd been expecting.

"If I thought it would get you downstairs faster, you'd already have my gown at your feet," she said, silently cursing her traitorous body and the twist of lust that pooled deep within her at the very thought of her clothes on the floor at his feet. "But I trust that it won't come to that." She had to tip her head up to look at him.

It was he who now looked a little shocked.

Ivory ducked her head. Playing the flirt was entirely counterproductive and unwise, no matter that it felt deliciously wicked. She would leave him to his own devices. "Ten minutes, Your Grace." She turned, slipping from his touch. She had barely a second to miss it before one of his hands caught her own and forced her to turn back.

"I'm trusting you, Miss Moore." He dropped her hand. "Don't make me regret it."

About the Author

RITA–award winning author Kelly Bowen grew up in Manitoba, Canada. She attended the University of Manitoba and earned a master of science degree in veterinary physiology and endocrinology. But it was Kelly's infatuation with history and a weakness for a good love story that led her down the path of historical romance. When she is not writing, she seizes every opportunity to explore ruins and battlefields. Currently, Kelly lives in Winnipeg with her husband and two boys, all of whom are wonderfully patient with the writing process. Except, that is, when they need a goalie for street hockey.

Learn more:
   kellybowen.net
   Twitter @kellybowen09
   Facebook.com/AuthorKellyBowen

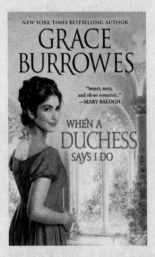

Discover exclusive content and more on
read-forever.com.

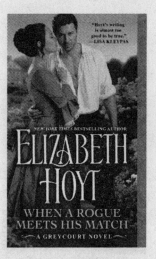

WHEN A ROGUE MEETS HIS MATCH
By Elizabeth Hoyt

After a decade of doing the Duke of Windemere's dirty work, Gideon Hawthorne is ready to be his own boss. But the duke isn't going to make leaving easy—he wants Gideon to complete one last task. And as payment, he offers the one thing that could seriously tempt Gideon: Messalina Greycourt's hand in marriage. Includes a bonus story by Kelly Bowen!

THE HIGHLAND EARL
By Amy Jarecki

Mr. & Mrs. Smith meets *Outlander* in this action-packed Scottish romance in which a marriage of convenience leads to secrets that could be deadly. Lady Evelyn has no desire to wed the rugged Scottish earl her father has chosen, but at least she'll be able to continue her work as a spy—as long as her husband never finds out. Yet the more time Evelyn spends with John and his boys, the fonder she grows of their little family, and the last thing she wants to do is put them in danger.

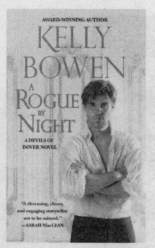